RICHARD D'AGOSTINO

RITE OF PASSAGE

Gold Imprint
Medallion Press, Inc.
Printed in USA

Published 2006 by Medallion Press, Inc.

The MEDALLION PRESS LOGO
is a registered tradmark of Medallion Press, Inc.

Printed in the United States of America

Library of Congress Cataloging-in-Publication Data

D'Agostino, Richard.
Rite of passage / Richard D'Agostino.
p. cm.
ISBN 1-932815-54-6 (pbk.)
1. Archaeologists--Fiction. 2. Egypt--Antiquities--Fiction. 3. Egypt--Fiction. I. Title.
PS3604.A334R58 2006
813'.6--dc22

2005037118

10 9 8 7 6 5 4 3 2 1
First Edition

ACKNOWLEDGEMENTS:

There are two important people in my life to whom I am grateful for their encouragement and persistence when the light was dim.

The first is Ron Walker who pushed, and cajoled, and preached, and supported, and inspired when those letters were not.

The second is Esther Gordon my dear editor who never lost hope, especially with my first rendering which, when returned to me, looked like a murder had taken place and someone bled all over my manuscript. You see she made her corrections, suggestions, neat little quips like "I don't think so" written with a large red pen. Needless to say, I thought the blood on my pages was surely a rejection. But . . . her first words were . . . "you are a writer." Those few words were the impetus, the influence that drove me to continue.

INTRODUCTION

His name means "Beloved of Thoth." In the annals of Egyptian history, Manetho, high priest, scholar, and historian, placed the enormous figure of 37,000 years to the entire duration of Egyptian civilization. In three volumes now lost, he recorded the grand adventure of the greatest civilization of all time. Four eras spanned the distance across the millennia: the time of the Gods, the Sages, the Followers of Horus, and the mortal Pharaohs. Curiously, only his dynastic lineage, beginning with "Scorpion" or Narmer circa 3200 BC, is considered to be realistic by most Egyptologists. The balance, the rest of the historical record written by Manetho in the Turin Papyrus and other supporting documents has been deemed apocryphal, myth, a tale wedged in fantasy.

HELIOPOLITAN THEOLOGY

In the beginning, God rode the sun, the solar bark, the boat of millions of years through the black firmament, sending its blinding, glorious rays upon the Earth where chaos reigned. Betaken by the turmoil, God raised His staff, staring into the eyes of chaos. With swiftness, chaos shrank beneath His feet, and the Earth ceased its ungainly wobble about the sun. The clouds parted for Him. The flood fled from Him. The earth warmed, and He stood upon the primeval Mound where one land stood out more than any other. He called it Msr, Khem, Egypt.

He is the Creator of all things. He is the face of the sun. He is the hidden One, the One One above all others, and He is called Ra. From his golden bark, He called forth His company: Shu, Geb, Tefnut, Nut, Osiris, Isis, Nepthys and Set, and they settled the land and begot Thoth, Anubis, and Horus.

Of men the Gods chose only the enlightened ones, the worthy, teaching them the ways, handing down the Ma'at, the laws of order and righteousness, as the

Holy ones traveled about the Earth and, when they had finished, they returned to the Mansion in the sky from whence they came.

CHAPTER 1

"Watch your step, Jack. Those ancient builders set traps all over the place."

"Frank, what do you think we'll really find?"

"I'm not sure."

"Sure you are. What does it say? Tell me what the crystal says."

"If you must know, it says treasure, treasure of Thoth."

"What does it mean?"

"You idiot! What do you think it means? Gold, lots of gold, mummies, statues, like that."

Sand crunched beneath their feet as they inched along a passage so black it ate the light, oblivious to the small mounds nesting here and there. Sweat beaded. Hearts pounded. It seemed the air was thin. Their flashlights lighted, in bouncing rings, a featureless corridor hammered out of stone thousands of years ago. A dank musty odor reached into their nostrils, signaling the absence of life for a very long time.

"Oh, Jesus, Frank!" Jack stumbled, dropping his light.

"God damn it, Jack, watch it."

Jack picked up his light and shined it. "What the hell is that?"

"A figure carved in the wall. Let's go."

"Well, shit. It scared the piss out of me. What is it for?"

"You wouldn't understand."

"You don't have to talk to me like that, Frank. I can understand if you give me a chance."

"I don't know why I brought you along."

"I know. Because you need me, Frank. You need me to help you, that's why." Jack's feelings were hurt. He was a slow person and knew little about archeology, but he would do anything for Frank, even when he talked bad to him.

"Jack, what is that?"

"What?"

"That!" Frank shot his light at chunks of broken pottery on the floor. "You broke it. Damn you, Jack, you broke it."

"I didn't. I stumbled right here. I didn't touch that."

"Who did?"

"I don't know, I . . ."

"There's just you and me in here, Jack."

"Yeah, but I thought I saw . . ."

"Don't give me any shit, Jack. I told you this place was booby trapped."

"Yeah, you told me. But, I didn't do it, honest."

"There! Shine your light over there."

"Frank, it's just some sand trickling . . ."

"SHUT UP, damn it! Do you hear that?"

"Yeah, I hear it. It's the dirt under your boots."

"I'm not moving, Jack."

"Frank? What is it?"

Stone ground against stone. The earth shook. Walls trembled. In a gush, sand poured from slots in the wall. Dust swallowed the air.

"I can't breathe." Jack fumbled his light. He clutched his nose, his mouth.

"Let's get the fuck out-a-here!" Frank screamed.

"What about the treasure?"

"We can always come back for the treasure. Now go, damn it!"

"I can't see, Frank!"

"God damn it, this way!"

Jack's arms flung in the darkness. He grabbed Frank's shirt.

"Let go! Follow the goddamn wall!"

"I don't wanna die, Frank. I can't see."

"Use your fuckin' light."

"It's dead, Frank. I dropped it."

In the thick dust-soup, Frank's light was less than a glow. Gasping, lurching forward, their fingers were torn ragged as they grasped and pawed the wall. With the next several steps, the quickened, tumultuous rasping of stone on stone drowned Frank's reply. Jack did not hear Frank say, "We've got to make the corner," as a huge granite plug smashed him to the wall.

Just making the elbow of the tunnel, Frank could not see what happened to Jack, but he smelled hot blood and felt the splatter of body fluids drench his head, his back.

In the sudden silence he whispered, "Jack?" He shouted, "Jack!" His voice slammed back, repeating in the dust filled passage.

Again, he heard the hiss of pouring sand and scrambled for the mouth of the opening as another monolith rumbled somewhere, shaking him to his knees.

Frantically, he crawled toward the mouth, trying to stand, sucking air, and reaching out in pitch darkness. His brain said twenty feet more, just twenty feet more. A breeze . . . Another thunderous clap.

Once more . . . absolute silence.

CHAPTER 2

Nearly five decades had seeped into the sand.

Dawn. The Giza Plateau, house of the dead, came alive. Some workers drove stakes and strung line. Others moved sand with shovel, trowel, and brush. Long shadows shifted with the rising sun, and huge monument lights had shut down. The Great Pyramid and its two enigmatic brothers stood yards away.

What drove this excavation was a quest for the truth. The team leader had become obsessed with pharaonic boats ever since a fleet of ocean-going vessels had been found fifteen miles from the Nile. The discovery happened at Abydos in 1991. Seventeen ships over seventy feet long and forty-five hundred years old were thought to belong to a Dynasty I Pharaoh. Egyptologists in general surmised that the vessels were purely symbolic.

The team leader, Doctor Karl Cassim, had disagreed. "Why seventeen ships?" he questioned. "Why such extraordinary workmanship and so many boats to carry one Pharaoh's soul into the afterlife?"

These unanswered questions lured him to the Great Pyramids not far from their own boats. Answers had to be here. Two boats larger and older than those at Abydos graced the eternal monuments. Tomb paintings and texts pointed to more boats buried here on this flat piece of land.

As Director-General of the Giza Plateau, Cassim had the choice to chase his convictions. This drive for solutions was suddenly realized when a large depression appeared near the Great Pyramids. Quickly a team was organized and put into action.

Doctor Cassim looked over the dig in the sharp air of a morning's breeze. It was early spring. The cool night had passed. The sun warmed, and the workers began chanting a psalm much like the cadence of oarsmen.

From a distance, Karl's assistant, Malak, waved. Then, excitedly, he called out. He had found . . . something.

Karl rushed over. He approached as Malak dusted off a long slab. Worn and unreadable markings appeared in the early light, and Karl knelt to study them. His dark eyes felt the stone as surely as his hand. He looked toward the Great Pyramid. His square jaw locked.

"What is it, Karl?" Malak asked.

"What made you come here so close to the Pyramid?"

"One of the men stumbled on it," Malak said. "As I

bandaged his knee, he pointed here. So, I came looking."

Hollows on Karl's tanned face seemed more prominent as he thought a moment. "Curious," he said, frowning. "Take two of the men and clear around it."

"Karl—"

"It would only be a guess."

Egyptian-born Malak called two workers he knew by name. He stood, brushing off his jeans. In striking contrast to the others, he was a mosaic of mixed cultures. His skimpy tilted turban, his plaid shirt, and his distinctly American vernacular were evidence that he had been educated in the US. When the twenty-nine-year-old returned to Egypt, he never wore native clothing again.

As the sun climbed the sky, tourists were everywhere. Camels, horses, buses, and taxis crowded the Giza Plateau. The world, it seemed, had come to wonder at the Great Pyramids.

Unknowingly, Karl had begun his career as a child. He had played in the ruins of Luxor. Obelisks and temples with their mysterious symbols became places for games, places to hide. Guessing what the striding figures were about, he invented scenarios. His uncle encouraged him to tell these stories to travelers in his shop. Orphaned early on, Karl's uncle Abedd was the only family he knew. Bright and eager, the boy's fascination for gods, pharaohs, and gigantic buildings grew to a full-fledged passion. Egyptology became his life.

Malak's small party worked around the stone, teasing away the sand. Slowly, it became clear. They would never see the underside. They had hit bedrock, bedrock that had been chiseled into a stairway, a stairway to . . .

On horseback, tourist police kept the curious away as excitement grew at the steps. Cassim pulled every man from the dig to clear the stairway. A brigade formed. Buckets of sand passed from one to another. Noon came and went.

Then, unexpectedly, the bottom was struck, unearthing a polished slab of limestone. It measured three paces long by two wide and led to an obstruction.

The work was stopped. Karl counted forty-five steps on his way down. All breathlessly watched as he examined the wall. He took a small tool and pecked at a maze of congealed rocks. Easily, they loosened. "Malak," he called.

Malak took the stairs two at a time. "Yes, Karl."

"Take a good look. Tell me what you see."

Malak touched the wall, pushing here, pulling there. Pieces of stone crumbled in his hand. "Back-fill," he said, "it's just back-fill."

"My thoughts exactly. We still have good light, Malak. Put the men on it and see what they can do before nightfall."

"Done," Malak said, and waved the men to the wall.

With picks and shovels, the fragmented stone toppled. Again, a line formed. Buckets of broken rock were lifted out. Hours passed. The sun began searching the horizon when four feet into the wall the back side suddenly fell through. A gaping black hole became clear as the dust settled.

The men backed away as Karl came down the steps. Malak followed. "Give me your flashlight," Karl said, cautiously leaning in, and switched on the light. "My lord," he breathed.

"What is it, Karl?"

"A tunnel, a passage, I don't know." Karl checked the ceiling, the walls, the floor. He stepped in. An odor unlike any he had ever smelled filled the space. He sent his light deep into the black.

Suddenly, Karl felt eyes, penetrating eyes that raised his flesh. He turned and gasped.

Piercing eyes stared at him. A life-size relief of Osiris peered through him. He took a breath and lit up the presence. The figure seemed as though it had been trapped in stone, half in, half out. The eyes were incredibly real, seemingly liquid. "Malak," he called, "bring in the lamps."

Malak too was taken back by the figure, by the eyes.

"Unnerving, isn't it?" Karl said.

"To say the least," Malak replied.

"Throw a cover over it, will you?"

"With pleasure," Malak whispered.

Malak set the lamps on the floor as he walked the length of the corridor. "It's sixty paces," he said, "from the mouth to the . . . the end?"

"Yes," Karl said. "It seems we have a . . . It's a granite plug!" He struck a match.

"What are you doing?"

"Seeing if I'm right." Karl held the match to the seam. He saw the flicker, the draw of the flame. "Air is being sucked to the other side. It is a plug. The passage goes on." He frowned.

"What . . ." Malak began.

"Give me your light." Karl shot the beam near the floor at a corner. Skeletal fingers curled out. Dried skin clung to the tips.

Malak said, "Poor bastard."

Karl closely examined the hand. "He did not die in antiquity. This is a recent intruder. I would guess forty, fifty years."

"Karl, on the floor."

"What is it?"

Malak picked it up. "I don't believe it. It's crystal."

"Is it a fetish or a seal?" Karl asked, turning from the skeletal hand.

"It looks like a cylinder seal of some sort, but I've never heard of one being so large."

"No doubt it belongs to this fellow," Karl said, his attention riveted to the granite block. "Can you read it?"

"I'll try."

"Try?" Karl looked over his shoulder. "What do you mean, try?"

"Well, Karl, it's . . . it's different." Malak moved closer to the lamp. "The hieroglyphs are . . . well, like those found near the ancient city of Abydos."

Karl felt along the edge of the plug. "Read," he said.

"I'll do my best." Slowly, he mumbled, *"Beware! The eyes . . . the eyes that fall upon . . . upon this . . . Providence must . . . must be pure. Beware! Death comes on... on wings to he who . . . who violates the word.* Karl . . . it's a curse."

"I wouldn't pay too much mind to curses. I think we can get through this rock. Malak, describe it to me."

"All right, but I'm not an expert. It's definitely crystal. It's heavy too, probably five, six pounds. The sentence structure is, well, archaic. But . . ."

"Here, let me see that."

Malak gave him the cylinder. "Is it getting warm in here or is it me?

"I hadn't noticed," Karl said. "Let's examine it in better light." He carried the cylinder to the bottom of the steps into the late afternoon sun. "There's the author's name," he muttered. "Kheph. I don't recognize that offhand. It's followed by Sabmer m A, Companion of Thoth. Malak, did you notice . . . Malak?" Cassim walked back into the passage. "Malak!"

Malak was on the floor slumped over a lamp. White gas crept out from under him, saturating him. Karl ran over and pulled him off as the fuel ignited. Flames shot to the ceiling. With bare hands, he banged away at Malak's shirt, frantically shouting for help. Men flew down the steps, ripped off the flaming clothing, and stomped it out.

Wide-eyed, they backed away. Karl stared as he knelt at Malak's side, swatting at the smoke to clear the air. A shriveled mass of burnt flesh shivered spastically on the floor. Without eyelids, his eyes bulged hideously while the rest of his body dehydrated, collapsing on itself in view of gaping workers. Like bees from a hive, the men fled the passage. Guards rushed in as Karl stroked Malak's totally white, singed hair.

"What happened to the old man?" a guard asked.

Karl stood. He rubbed his forehead. "That's not an old man; it's my young assistant, Malak." Dazedly, the fifty-five-year-old team leader walked to the steps.

A guard picked up the shiny cylinder and—

"Don't touch that," Karl shouted, grabbing it away.

"Are you all right, doctor?" another asked.

"I'm fine, I'm just fine."

"What happened here?"

Karl said, "Malak tripped on a gas lamp. I don't know."

"People don't age like that from a small fire," a guard said, as the body was put on a stretcher and carried out.

The police arrived with more questions while the huge lights of the pyramids went on. Karl told the story repeatedly, and finally the officer in charge said, "I suggest you close this dig. You are going to have trouble finding new laborers. As you know, they are a superstitious lot. Go home, Doctor Cassim."

"Officer, please don't let his mother see him like that."

"We'll do what we can. Can you drive, doctor?"

There was a nod.

𓅃 𓋹

At the Egyptian Museum in Cairo the next morning, Karl sat as his desk, reasoning against reason. "I don't believe in curses. It's nonsense. I read the crystal scroll the same as Malak," he mumbled. "What happened?"

He had exhausted half the night saying the same thing to himself, arriving at the same answer. He had checked the cylinder seal for poisons and fumes, but found none. Now it sat on his desk, on end, next to his calendar. It looked harmless enough. A guard had picked it up and nothing had happened to him. *But,* Karl thought, *the guard couldn't read it, could he? There has to be some other explanation, a real tangible reason.*

The cylinder seal measured twelve inches long and had a diameter of three. It weighed exactly seven pounds. The hieroglyphics were set in crystal, a clear, sparkling stone soft to the touch and as alluring as a diamond.

Karl took out his legal-size yellow pad and made a few notes. Then he read the seal in full.

Beware! The eyes that fall upon this Providence must be pure. Beware! Death comes on wings to he who violates these words. Beware! It is Amemait Eater of Souls who destroys the unworthy, the uninitiated. So commandeth Thoth whose word is truth, whose Words of Power enabled Isis to raise Osiris from the dead, a matter a million times true.

Hail to you of pure heart for what you seek is before you, the worthy. Of seven Sages there be seven mysteries written upon seven scrolls of thehen-t which must stand united. Of seven Sages, one imparts his mystery upon one of seven scrolls. Of seven scrolls, this shall be one.

Descend eighteen cubits to Osiris Lord of eternity. Enter skillfully for His eyes judge. To the worthy the signs are known. The treasure of Thoth awaits the pure of heart.

"Thehen-t," he thought. "Oh, yes, sparkling stone."

"So," he muttered, "they were looking for treasure."

Over the next few days, the cylinder seal was catalogued into the registry of the Egyptian museum. Because of its rarity, its incalculable age, it was put on display on the second floor in area 48 near predynastic artifacts. The daily Egyptian Gazette gave this find five lines on page nine.

CHAPTER 3

Darkness hid the shadows. High in the lofty corners, cobwebs gathered dust. The musty drape of ancient relics sweetened with varnished wood furled an educated nose. A pair of sneakers guided by nimble feet and legs, crept beneath an archway. A gloved hand silently squeezed a banister. A masked head with darting eyes tilted upward, commanding a body. One at a time, he quickly took the steps, his back groping the wall, heading for the second floor. A stair creaked just a little.

At the top in a hall, a feeble portrait-light became a universe, reflecting pinpoint stars from ancient Egyptian necklaces surrounded by glass.

In the distance, the faint knock of leather heels piqued the senses, and a circle of light found no rest as it jerked about in an uncertain hand, fleeting from door to statue, to case, to floor. A night watchman had heard the creak of a step. After sixteen years of guarding the museum, he knew every noise and where it lived. He was heading for the stairway.

As the knocks grew louder, the sneakers sprinted

to the landing and crouched. The light steadily became stronger, more determined. From the landing, he leaped up the remaining steps. A square pillar stood there four yards ahead; he dashed for it and glued himself to the back side, listening for the heels.

Suddenly, the pillar split the light in two like a wishbone and moved slowly as if the floor were turning. The security guard stopped, facing the stairway, searching the steps with his light, his back at arm's length from the pillar.

The shadow slid from the pillar as slime from a rock, reaching out, snapping his neck, and catching the flashlight before it hit the floor. For a moment, he held the body tight to his chest. Silence was everywhere.

Guards on the other floors were making their rounds at 2:17 a.m. deafened by ignorance.

Easily, the sneakers walked the body to the blackest corner, stuffed it in a sitting position, and tip-toed down the hall.

On holiday, one of Tutankhamen's treasure rooms had been emptied, having been packed for a visit to the USA. In its place was the museum's newest acquisition, set alone on a pedestal surrounded with glass under a beam of light, the only illumination in the room.

The sneakers examined the enclosure. An alarm was noted, would go berserk if tampered with. This was no surprise to him. Neither was the guard. A foregone conclusion realized that possibility. He listened intently with his eyes fixed on the ancient crystal seal.

There were four sets of stairs. There were four security guards, now minus one. He would have, under the best conditions, fifteen seconds if he gently lifted the glass, and forty-five seconds more before they would enter the room.

With a swipe of the arm, he smashed the case and grabbed the cylinder seal. To arouse more attention, he toppled the necklace case near the back stairway and ran to the front. Guards flew up the back stairs, bells ringing, horns blowing. With guns drawn, they ran into an empty room. In less than five minutes, the building was surrounded.

An hour later, a complete search of the building revealed nothing, no one.

CHAPTER 4

Spewing outrage, the Egyptian papers pointed blame. Their headlines accused the museum security force of incompetence, substantiating the charge with personnel histories obtained surreptitiously. Doting age combined with inadequate training topped the list. The Egyptian Gazette went so far as to call the intruder a tomb robber, an unlikely handle for a museum in the middle of Cairo.

Not sparing the ink, the world press echoed the Egyptian tabloids, while the London Times raised its head above the crowd. Rather than calling names, the Times chose a more subtle, in-depth approach. It described the cylinder seal and what made it so valuable, so priceless. Moreover, the Times took pains in its hypothetical assessment of who would profit by possessing it.

What gave this lengthy article considerable notoriety and credibility was not its author but the author's source. He was a world renowned British archeologist, historian, and Egyptologist who rarely gave interviews since leaving the academic stage mysteriously some years ago. However, the artifact was so unusual, and the reporter so persistent, that Sir E. Osborne Hunsdon finally gave in.

"In actuality," Hunsdon was quoted, "the artifact is not a cylinder seal in the truest sense, but a scroll in stone used like a seal. Because of its size and character, let alone its content, nothing like it had ever been discovered before. Therefore, by its very nature, its unfathomed antiquity, its value cannot be measured. As a result, the academic world may very well have to redefine the extent of Egyptian civilization."

In addition, global attention had been seized by the details surrounding the death of Doctor Cassim's colleague. Members of his team described Malak's departure as sinister, an evil curse handed down by the ancient gods themselves. When asked about the curse, its longevity, Sir Hunsdon abruptly ended his extraordinary interview.

Photographs of the skeletal hand, the tortured face of Malak and the security guard were headed by bold type. **"CURSE CLAIMS 3 VICTIMS"**

The details of Doctor Cassim's find at the foot of the Great Pyramid brought legions of tourists, reviving theorists' beliefs that miles of hidden chambers lay beneath the Giza Plateau. So intense was the scrutiny, the bald eye of public curiosity, that Doctor Cassim closed the dig.

While all points of the compass were trained on Egypt, Doctor Cassim, also Director-General of the Egyptian Museum, took advantage of the Pharaoh, Tutankhamen, and escorted him and his treasure to the United States, where an exhibition was scheduled in California.

CHAPTER 5

Damn it, Julian, where have you been?" Jennifer asked. She was on hands and knees, mopping water from the family room floor.

He wasn't about to answer that question, because she knew the answer.

"What are you doing?" he said, back pressed to the door.

"Someone left the damn patio door open and everything got soaked. Why are you late?"

"The weather," he said. "Traffic is backed up for miles. What's wrong?" he asked, knowing very well what was wrong. He was nearly three hours late, and Jennifer knew why.

"Nothing."

"Jen?"

Her hands moved quickly, squeezing a sponge into a pail. Her temper seethed.

"Jen, talk to me." He didn't know why he had said that, but he did. Their marriage had been on the rocks for a year, and the kids were holding together what was left. It wasn't much. She had drifted off, falling in love with her boss and her multi-million-dollar real estate sales business, which took all her time. He wondered how long it would be before one of them got the guts to really call it quits and say it out loud.

"All right. You've been seeing someone, haven't you?"

"No. I was at work. A simple telephone call would have settled that if it made any difference. I told you. Traffic is backed up for miles."

It was the truth.

She was angry because he hadn't been home before her, that he hadn't been where he was supposed to be when he was supposed to be there.

"What's really bothering you?" He didn't care, but asked anyway.

"The cleaners lost my new suit, dinner was ruined when the bags got wet, and the groceries fell into the street, and I haven't heard a word from the kids. I have a meeting—"

"Jennifer."

She gave him a look.

He walked over and pulled her up from the floor. "Sit down and take a breath, okay? Chrisy is taking her ballet lesson and Jimmy has basketball practice."

She plopped into a chair. Her blue eyes watered as she pushed back her hair. He didn't react. Jennifer could cry at the drop of a hat. She had used that one on him more than a few times. It was her way of trying to lay a guilt trip on him.

"Look at my hair. I just had it done."

"It looks fine," he said. "The color isn't bad either."

"I didn't do anything to the color. It's always been brown."

Well, I blew that one, he thought. He really didn't give a damn.

Tears ran as she looked outside. Rain was so thick she couldn't see across the yard even as lightning struck.

"This damn weather," she muttered, pouting. "It's bad for business."

"Better get used to it. They say this El Niño thing is going to be the worst in fifty years."

She moaned. "What am I going to do about dinner?"

"Order in. How about Chinese?"

"The kids don't like Chinese."

"I thought you forgot," he said. "What about pizza? I know they like pizza. Fix us a drink and I'll call." He got up out of a chair and threw his London Fog on the couch.

Jennifer blotted her running mascara as if nothing had happened and took the ice bucket into the kitchen. Julian checked the refrigerator door for the pizza delivery number.

"I almost forgot. There was a package left for you at the front door."

"That's funny. I didn't order anything."

"Well, I can't help that," she spat.

"Nasty, nasty," he said.

She made a face. "Right after I got home the doorbell rang and when I went to answer it no one was there. Just a package. I put it on your desk."

"What's the date today?"

"The seventh, August the seventh. Why?"

"No reason. I forgot," he said, heading for his desk in the den.

"Call for the pizzas first," she yelled after him.

"I was going to," he said, grinding his teeth.

Julian wandered into the den, loosened his tie and hung his jacket on the back of the chair. The burlap pouch sat on the desk. He telephoned the pizza place. When he hung up, he noticed the label. A white piece of cloth had been stitched to the burlap with only his name, Julian Rutledge. "No address," he mumbled. "Now that's strange."

Jennifer carried the drinks into the den. She set his on the desk.

"This thing is sewn shut. Where are the scissors?"

"Top left drawer," she said, as if he should have known.

"Weird, isn't it?"

She gave him an uninterested glance. "I haven't seen anything wrapped in burlap except potatoes."

Julian ignored her. He cut the bindings and raised the end, sliding out the contents. Five large sheets of papyrus were wrapped around a piece of glass that looked like a rolling pin without handles. "What the hell is this?"

Jennifer gave him a catty smile. "A large paper weight?"

"I don't think so."

"What do you think it is?"

"I haven't a clue. All I can say is that it looks like old glass. I'll be darned." He examined it closer. "I thought it was decoration, but it's hieroglyphics."

"Maybe somebody made a mistake?"

Julian turned the bag over. "There's no return address, just my name, nothing but my name."

"I wonder why?"

"I don't know. I teach astronomy not archeology," he said, and sipped his scotch.

"Isn't there a letter, a note, something?" she asked.

He shook his head. "Only papyrus and it's blank."

"I hear the kids. You did call for the pizzas, didn't you?" A glare.

"I did."

"I'll make a salad. The pizzas should be here any minute." She glanced back as she reached the door. "How bad do you want to know what that thing is?"

"Why?"

"I have an idea," she said. "But, after dinner."

"Figures," he muttered.

After dinner, Jimmy cleared the table and went to his room as usual. Chrisy did the dishes as she was told. They both were well aware of the situation between their parents, but didn't give it much thought. Most of their friends were from single parent families anyway.

Jennifer trailed Julian into the den where the rolling pin sat on the desk

"Isn't there someone at UCLA who could read it?" Jennifer asked.

"Not that I know of. Hieroglyphics isn't exactly a fashionable language these days. Now, what's your brilliant idea, dear?"

"I was thinking about what's-his-name across the street. He's the curator of a museum, or has something to do with a museum. He should be able to tell what it is, shouldn't he?"

Julian grinned. "Well, now, aren't you clever?"

"Yes, humm," she said, and threw her hips as she meandered out of the room.

Out of doors, the storm raged and Julian closed the shade on the large window of their Brentwood, upper-middle-class home. He gently rolled the glass stone across his blotter and sat at the desk. Thinking about this strange object, he opened the bottom drawer, finding the association booklet with all the residents of Brentwood listed. "Let's see," he murmured, flipping pages, "I think it starts with a G. Gobel, Goddard, God's house . . . What the hell is that? Goff, Goldstein . . . no . . . no. Gottlieb! That's it David Gottlieb."

Julian Rutledge was a physically adept, good-looking forty-six-year-old with light brown hair and eyes that kept his youth. With the jawbone of a brick, dimples and cheeks aglow with rouge-like pinkness, he had an allure that in the early years of their relationship had often caused jealousy in Jennifer. An astrophysicist, he taught astronomy at UCLA. He had studied the universe and what it was made of. He was a consulting astronomer for NASA and often used the facilities at the Mt. Wilson observatory. He thought about his background, his particular expertise, and saw no valid reason why he was made a gift of an unremarkable artifact, if that's what it was. He dialed David Gottlieb's number.

"Is this David Gottlieb?"

"It is."

"David, I'm Julian Rutledge, you know, the yellow house across the street?"

"Oh, yes. Funny how we never seem to meet and we've been neighbors for such a long time. What can I do for you, Julian?"

"Well, my wife tells me that you are the curator of

a museum."

"Not exactly, Julian. It's my wife. A lot of people seem to think it's me. Is there something I can help you with?"

"No, that's okay. It was just an idea."

"You might try her at the museum. She's working late these days."

"You don't think she'd mind?"

"I don't think so. If you like, I could call her."

"Only if it won't be a bother."

"Can I tell her what this is about?"

"Well, sure. The truth is, I'm not sure. You see someone left this . . . this round piece of glass at my door. It looks like a crystal rolling pin with hieroglyphics, and I'm just trying to figure out what it is and why it was left to me. It could also be a prank by one of my students."

"If anyone could tell you, it would be Nancy. Give me your number and I'll call you back."

Julian gave the number. "Thanks, David, I appreciate it." Hanging up, he smiled. "So, she's the curator. Huh, women's lib," he muttered.

Julian had barely settled in his thoughts about the sun-drenched blond who lived across the street when she called and invited him to the museum. He accepted.

CHAPTER 6

At a quarter of eight, Julian pushed through the heavy metal doors of the Los Angeles County Museum, shook out his drenched umbrella and was surprised to see a crowded hall. Many large posters announced "The Splendors of Ancient Egypt," and the gift shop was awash with interesting reproductions from the exhibit.

He approached a security guard near the entrance of the gallery. "I have an appointment with Mrs. Gottlieb," he said. "Could you point me in her direction?"

"Sure. She's usually in the New Kingdom Room. You can't miss it, just look for gold coffins right down that hall." He pointed the direction.

With the burlap bag under his arm and a few minutes to spare, Julian paused at one display after another. Never having been so close to such antiquity, he found it amazing that the ancient Egyptians were so sophisticated in so many fields.

Caught by penetrating eyes, Julian nearly forgot his purpose. Tutankhamen's solid gold funerary mask stared out at him from under glass. He was taken back by the boy's eternal gaze with eyes so real they seemed to tear. The rich blue lapis lazuli appeared liquid, puddling between fingers of gold on the royal nemes crown. Wading in a trance and lost in the epoch, Julian was startled by a tap on the shoulder and the sound of his own name.

"Julian?"

He turned. "Oh, Mrs. Gottlieb. My mind . . . I was . . . I was lost. Thank you for seeing me on such short notice."

"My pleasure, but first call me Nancy," she said, sparkling a smile. "After all, we are neighbors." She nodded to the death mask. "It's magnificent, isn't it?"

"Words fail me," he said, but he was not thinking about the mask. He fell into her aqua eyes like a schoolboy. Like hands, his eyes felt her sun-streaked hair falling to her shoulders, her high cheekbones bathed in tan, and lips so sensuous they needed to be kissed. Her figure . . .

"Julian? Is something wrong?"

"Oh, no, no."

"I was saying, would you like to look around?"

"I would like to very much, but I promised my wife I wouldn't be late."

"Maybe another time."

You can count on it, he thought. And since he was having this secret little confabulation in his own mind, it didn't matter that she was married. *That's what fantasy is all about, isn't it?* He smiled.

"I'd like that," he said.

"My office is this way."

As they walked from room to room, Julian explained the mysterious package. He couldn't take his eyes off her as she listened and nodded. It had been so long since he . . . another woman, especially one as appealing as Nancy. Not to mention the fact that it had been six weeks since he had had sex.

"Interesting," she said, closing the door, "and very unusual."

He handed her the burlap bag.

"May I open it?"

"Of course."

Gently, she emptied the contents on her desk. Her face sobered as she pushed back her golden hair. She reached into her top drawer and slipped on a pair of cotton gloves.

"What's wrong?"

"The gloves?"

"Yeah."

"It's customary. I wouldn't want to accidentally damage something."

"Well, if it's that fragile, I already have," he said.

"It seems quite substantial." She smiled, and took a serious look. "I've never seen anything like it."

"It's not a prank, then?"

"Oh, no. This is a cylinder seal, but the size . . . it feels like it weighs ten pounds."

"Is that good or bad?"

"Julian, let me tell you a little about what I think you have here. This is a cylinder seal. Normally in ancient times, a cylinder seal was worn about the neck or at the hip on a belt. They bore titles, words of power, pictures of gods, and sometimes phrases. Usually, they were no more than a few inches in length and were not completely round like this. Those that bore titles or names of officials were used in trade. Most of the time scarabs were used as religious symbols, sacred objects. But this is like an edict written on what appears to be either glass or crystal."

"Can you read it?"

"It isn't that simple."

"What do you mean?"

"This seal is surely predynastic. The hieroglyphics are primitive, yet they have a formality I do not recognize. If I had other objects, other writings to compare against it, I could probably make out some of it."

She took a magnifying glass as Julian looked on, watching her eye magnify twenty times larger than normal, while she turned the cylinder in her beautiful hands.

"The real question is," she said softly, "why was this

left on your doorstep? You're a professor of astronomy, chairman of the Planetary Sciences of the American Astronomical Society, are you not?" Nancy did not wait for an answer. "Perhaps you are not as well advertised as the late Doctor Sagan, but you do have an esteemed reputation."

"For a passing acquaintance, you know quite a lot about me, Mrs. Gottlieb."

"You're belittling your accomplishments, Doctor Rutledge." She smiled.

Quite a beautiful smile, he thought. Aloud he said, "That still does not explain why I was made a gift—I presume it is a gift—of some ancient Egyptian artifact."

"Would you mind if I show this to someone?"

"Not in the least."

Nancy picked up the telephone. "Would you find Doctor Cassim, please, and ask him to come to my office?"

As she set down the receiver, there was a knock on the door.

"Come in. Oh, Karl, I just asked someone to find you."

Doctor Cassim smiled. "Call it telepathy."

"Karl, I'd like you to meet Doctor Julian Rutledge, professor of astronomy at UCLA. Julian, this is Doctor Karl Cassim, Egyptologist, Director-General of the Egyptian Museum. He and King Tut are on loan to us for a little while."

Greetings were exchanged.

"Karl, Julian came into possession of something I think you should see." She pointed to the seal.

Karl lost his smile. A strange tightness seeped into his chest. His first thought was the stolen seal. "Do you have another pair of gloves?"

Nancy gave him a set.

"May I ask how you acquired the seal?" he said, as he pulled on the cottons and picked up the cylinder.

"It was left at my front door. That's all I can really tell you."

"Left at your door? How extraordinary."

"Is it valuable?"

"Indeed," he said, examining the stone. "Its size, age, and style make it one of the oldest surviving relics from an epoch that is much debated. I've only seen one other and it, too, was surrounded with mystery."

"How so, doctor?" Julian said.

"I was excavating what I thought to be a boat pit near the Great Pyramid, and to make a long story short, I found a seal identical to this in a passage completely unrelated to where my team was working. It was found several feet from a man's skeletal hand. He had been crushed by a large granite block. We have no idea how he came by it."

Nancy said, "What happened to it, Karl?"

"It was on exhibit in the Egyptian Museum, but it was stolen, unfortunately."

"You had a chance to read it then," Nancy said.

"Well, yes."

"You didn't have any difficulty?"

"I understand what you are saying, and, at first, yes, I did. It isn't written in the formal form of hieroglyphics such as, say, Middle Kingdom, but rather in a rudimentary style, yet still sophisticated. You see, we, at the museum in Cairo, have artifacts from Halfran sites in Upper Egypt where ostraka, pieces of pottery, were found with a similar style writing."

"Halfran, doctor?" Julian said.

"The name comes from Wadi Halfa in the Sudan and stretches north along the Nile from the Second Cataract to the Kom Ombo Plain in Egypt well over two hundred miles. What is remarkable is the date attributed to this site. Carbon dating places these few bits of pottery at around 24,000 BC at a time that most historians referred to Paleolithic Egyptians as hunter-gatherers. As you can see, they were much more than that."

"Karl, what can you tell us about this seal?"

Karl sat next to the desk across from Nancy. He folded his arms and brushed his chin while Julian listened.

"The most interesting thing is the signature on the seal. That's what I noticed first because there was a possibility that the one I found and this one could have been the same for some strange reason. But it isn't. Nonetheless, the name is that of a Sage."

"But I thought the Sages were mythical beings?" Nancy said.

Karl rubbed his eyes. He did not respond.

"Who were the Sages?" Julian asked.

"There is very little we know about them. Their only reference is written on the walls of the Temple of Edfu. They speak of the golden time of the Neteru, the Gods, who created the Earth, as we know it, a genesis written thousands of years before the bible. This genesis was not in some heavenly state in the clouds, but somewhere tangible in Egypt, when it was a lush garden paradise some thirty thousand years ago. The odd thing is, thirty thousand years ago Egypt did have a lush landscape and the Sahara was not a desert. Most importantly, the text speaks of the Seven Sages, the Lords of Light, the Divine Ones, who carried with them great wisdom. It is written that the Sages imparted this great wisdom to Thoth, the God of Wisdom, who understood all and wrote it down. The text also tells us that the Seven Sages were immortal beings, and bore witness to the chaos in the beginning of our time. It was by their instruction and through Thoth that the resurrection of Osiris was accomplished. And when they had finished their time on this earth, they returned to the Mansion in the sky on the banks of the Winding Waterway, the Milky Way, where Ra dwells."

"Karl, do you think that the seal belongs to one of them?" Julian asked.

"It is signed Sabmer m A, Bak, which means companion of Thoth and his name is Bak. He was one of the Seven."

"Could it be a fake?" Julian said.

"Absolutely not. Only a handful of people could duplicate this."

"But why was it given to me?"

Karl shook his head. "I cannot answer that."

Nancy asked, "Karl, would you read it for us?"

"Yes, please," Julian added.

"Very well, I'll try. It would be easier if . . . Nancy, do you happen to have some carbon paper?"

"Yes, I do," she said, opening a drawer.

"And maybe some shelf paper?"

"Maybe." She went to a closet on the far side of the room and rummaged around one shelf and then another. "Here we go. Karl, what are you going to do?"

"Transfer the seal to paper."

Nancy cleared off her desk. Karl unrolled the paper. On it he placed sheets of carbon paper end to end. Then, using two highlighter pens, he inserted them into the ends of the cylinder like handles of a rolling pin, pressing down and rolling at the same time. "There," he said, setting the seal aside. "Now let's see what we have."

He held it up to a lamp on the desk and looked at it from the back side.

Julian asked, "Why are you looking at the wrong side?"

"Because it transfers backward."

"I see you've done this before." Nancy smiled.

"I wish I had done it with the one I found. Now, bear with me as I struggle through it. It seems to begin much like the first one. And I must say that if I were a superstitious man, I wouldn't read it at all."

"Why," Julian asked warily.

"It begins with a curse."

Nancy said, "Are you sure you want to go ahead with this, Karl?"

"Nonsense, I've read curses before." He held it close to the light and read slowly, thoughtfully.

"Beware! The eyes that fall upon this Providence must be pure. Beware! Death comes on wings to he who violates the word. Beware! It is Amemait, Eater of Souls, who destroys the unworthy, the uninitiated. So commandeth Thoth whose words are true, whose Words of Power enabled Isis to raise Osiris from the dead. A matter a million times true."

"Excuse me, doctor, but do you think the ancient

Egyptians really believed that Osiris was brought back from the dead?" Julian asked skeptically.

Karl smiled and raised a brow. "I'll answer your question with a question. Do Christians really believe that Christ rose from the dead?"

"Well . . ."

"Let me point out that the first resurrection occurred thousands of years before the second."

"Yes, but—"

"And secondly, where do you think the Christians got their ideas?"

Nancy bit a lip, choosing not to participate in a futile disagreement.

"According to them, they were God inspired."

"Ah, yes, I know, voices from the clouds. Let me tamper with your memory and remind you that Palestine was under Egyptian rule for perhaps a thousand years or more. The influential truth is that Moses was an Egyptian prince, used Egyptian magic, and passed on Egyptian ideals to his people. And what persuasion are you, Mr. Rutledge?"

"I . . . I'm not much of anything."

"Well, then, let's not engage in religious warfare. I can only say that the similarities are much more than coincidental," Karl said, bordering on perturbation.

"Touché. I'm sorry. Please, go on."

"Yes, please do," Nancy said.

Regaining his composure, Karl said, "Very well." He raised the paper to the light once more. "Now there is a salutation to the worthy."

"One more question, if you don't mind?" Julian ventured.

A smile. "Certainly."

"What do they mean by 'the worthy'?"

"The words 'worthy' and 'initiated' refer to those selected by the Gods or the priests. The chosen ones, the smart ones, the talented ones, the ones who can recognize and appreciate knowledge and understand that with knowledge everything is knowable, possible. Ones who are learned in the ways and lead exemplary lives."

"Interesting concept. Please, go on," Julian prompted.

Karl's eyes returned to the page. He cleared his throat and spoke softly.

"Hail to you of pure heart for what you seek is before you, the worthy. Of Seven Sages there be seven mysteries written upon seven scrolls of thehen-t stone which must stand united".

"That's a curious choice of a word, thehen-t."

"Why?" Julian asked.

"Well, it means lightning stone. Very odd. Anyway, it goes on, *Of Seven Sages, one imparts his mystery upon one of seven scrolls. Of seven scrolls, this shall be one.*

"Be fleet of foot for time has spent and the heavens hold no mercy. Seek the Watcher of the Horizon for in his recline

lay the secrets of the universe. To know him look to the heavens. It is signed Sabmer m A, Bak."

"Riddles," Nancy said, "nothing but riddles."

Cassim smiled. "Not really. Remember the word 'worthy'. These clues are not meant for the uneducated in Egyptian history."

Julian asked, "Doctor Cassim, do you understand what it means?"

"I have some ideas. The reference to the Watcher of the Horizon can only mean the Great Sphinx."

"If that's true," Nancy thought aloud, "it casts some doubt on the age of the Sphinx, doesn't it? I mean, if the seal was authored by a Sage . . ."

"Yes, it would. Other than a supposed likeness of Khufu, Egyptologists are only guessing at the Sphinx's age."

"I still can't imagine why this cylinder was left to me."

"There may be some underlying implication. Perhaps because you are an astronomer. The references to the heavens and the universe clearly beg for answers."

"I hate to tell you, but I don't have them."

"Maybe in time."

"Was your seal similar to this one, Karl?"

"Well, yes, Nancy. The beginning was the same, the curse and all. However, the message was different. It was more instructive. Do you mind if I keep this carbon copy?"

Nancy looked at Julian and they both shrugged.

"I don't see why not," Julian said.

"Thank you." Karl rolled it up.

Julian noticed something in Karl's eyes. Nothing he could put a finger on, but it prompted a question he couldn't resist. "Is there something you're not telling us, doctor?"

He slid the carbon copy into his inside jacket pocket. "To be candid, Julian, this whole affair troubles me. The fact that the sister scroll was stolen means that someone seems to think these objects are very important."

"Isn't there any historical documentation that might hint at where these clues are headed?"

"I'm afraid not, Nancy. At least none that I know of."

"The curse doesn't bother you?"

"As I said, Julian, I'm not a superstitious man."

A few moments passed as Julian awkwardly found himself staring at Nancy. "I want to thank you both for your time and trouble," he said, standing. "My wife gets antsy—"

"Doctor Rutledge, may I offer a word of advice?"

"Certainly."

"I suggest that you deposit the cylinder seal in a safe place, for your own protection."

"For my protection?"

"I don't mean to alarm you, but there is one ingredient I haven't mentioned. When the seal was stolen from the museum, a guard was killed. This was not the deed of an amateur. The method of execution was that of an experienced killer who left no mark. He simply snapped the neck like a twig."

Stunned, Julian was speechless.

"If you like, Julian, I could put in the museum's vault."

"I would encourage you to do so," Karl said.

"Good idea. I'll leave it with you."

"I'll give you a receipt."

"That isn't necessary."

"I insist. It is the museum's policy."

Julian nodded. "All right."

"Next time bring your family," Nancy said. "I'm sure they'll enjoy the exhibit."

"How long will the exhibit be in town?"

"How long, Karl, two more weeks?"

"Yes."

"Then, you escort the exhibit back to Cairo?" Julian asked.

"That's right. And maybe when I get back there will be some news about the robbery."

Julian extended a hand. "Karl, it's been a pleasure."

"Someday, if more cylinder seals are found, perhaps I could call on you for your expertise as an astronomer, Julian?"

"I look forward to it, Karl. And by the way, I have a symposium coming up in the fall in Cairo. Maybe we can get together. Perhaps you would like to attend?"

"By all means."

"How does one get hold of you?" Julian asked.

"I have his address and phone number," Nancy said.

"Wonderful. Well, I have to go. Good night all."

After Julian left, Nancy locked the cylinder seal in the museum's vault.

As they headed back to the exhibit, Karl commented, "Someone went to a great deal of trouble to leave the seal at Julian's door at the same time that this exhibit is here. It seems too much of a coincidence to be one."

"I hadn't thought about that."

"When I get back to Cairo, I'm going to re-read the entire Edfu Texts. Just maybe there is some morsel I overlooked."

"Karl, do you think the cylinder seals are pointing to something tangible?"

"I can't be sure. It's possible the messages are a guide to a tomb, or a passage to the Hall of Records, or to nowhere. Of course, treasure is always a possibility. But what treasure is to one man could be something else entirely to another."

She nodded.

CHAPTER 7

On the following Wednesday, the Rutledge family attended "The Splendors of Ancient Egypt". Jimmy and Christine were fascinated with mummies from The Valley of the Kings and mummies of animals such as an ibis, a baboon, and a crocodile. While Jennifer and the kids were entertained with the bizarre, Nancy guided Julian to where she had found him the previous week, in the gallery of Tutankhamen.

Buried in the crowd surrounding the golden coffin, Nancy briefly traced the precarious lineage of the boy-king. Attracting attention with her gift of storytelling and her wonderful appearance, Julian watched and listened. Her animation teased his senses. Her voice was soft, smooth, and articulate. Her blues eyes flashed while her shapely form moved sensuously underneath a snow-white, calf-length dress. Julian's eyes fell into her cleavage as she looked away into her audience, which she held spellbound. Folding his arms, Julian dropped his gaze to the floor, working it up slowly, discovering long, wonderful legs with a birthmark on her left leg.

With a quality glint of the eye, a smile that lasted too long, an elbow to elbow nudge, he felt certain, he absolutely knew, the feeling was mutual. His mind fantasized as he tucked away his thoughts into his mental diary, promising to visit the pages at a more opportune time.

Snapping from behind him, Jennifer asked sternly, "Where have you been, Julian? The kids wanted to show you the mummies."

"Mrs. Gottlieb was showing me the solid gold coffin and telling me about the Pharaoh's family."

Nancy thanked them all for coming to visit the exhibit and everyone seemed content.

On Sunday the following week, the exhibit would move on. Julian thought about that, and the cylinder seal Nancy held in her vault. That would be a very good reason, a foolproof reason, to call on her again, alone.

CHAPTER 8

"Do you believe in God?"

"I beg your pardon?"

"Do you believe in God?"

Puckering with surprise laced with embarrassment, he replied, "Why would you ask me such a question?"

"It's a simple question. Do you or don't you?"

"Is my conviction a requirement for the position?"

"Mr. O'Donnell, please answer the question."

"I don't think it's any of your business."

"I'll take that as a yes, then?"

"I didn't say that."

"Look, Mr. O'Donnell, there are aspects of this position that require a certain set of mind. To determine that mindset I must ask revealing questions that, believe it or not, are relevant."

"Frankly, Dr. Cassim, I don't see what my beliefs or lack thereof have anything to do with the position I applied for."

"Your belief system is extremely important. If you choose not to answer I will terminate this interview immediately."

Shawn O'Donnell stared into Dr. Cassim's hardened eyes. The intense, penetrating glare that came back was uncompromising. Relenting finally in this visual tug-of-war, Shawn weakened, lowering his line of sight to his lap, his folded sweaty hands, weighing his earnest desire to work with one of the world's most esteemed archeo-Egyptologists. He said, "May I ask a question?" He glanced up. The afternoon sun flooding the room behind Doctor Cassim caused the likes of an aura about him.

There was a nod.

"Why is this important?"

"All right, Mr. O'Donnell." Cassim paused. His eyes dropped to a turquoise scarab on his desk. His fingers closed around it. He turned it over, and said, "I had hoped that you had no inclination whatsoever."

"Why?"

"Because someone whose mind floats in fantasy cannot make rational judgments based on facts." He looked up from the scarab.

"I'm confused. What kind of rational judgments are you expecting? About what?"

Cassim's face became hard and unreadable again. He said, "Usha, Hekau."

"Curses, magic, words of power? Do you believe in such things?"

"To turn the question, Mr. O'Donnell, do you?"

"I don't think so. But—"

"Mr. O'Donnell, my itinerary includes places regarded as sacred. Not only do Arabs believe this, but before them, the inhabitants of this land, the ancient Egyptians. There are places and things that have been consecrated and protected with Hekau, words of power spoken by the Kher Heb, the high priests, and before them, the Neteru, the Divine Ones."

"And you also believe that these places are cursed?"

"It is written," Cassim replied.

"Do you believe it, the curses I mean?"

"I am a devout skeptic, Mr. O'Donnell."

A moment passed.

"People say that Tut's tomb had a curse on it."

"Yes, and twenty-seven people died. How does that sit with you?" Cassim asked.

"Personally, I think the deaths were natural, coincidental."

Cassim nodded. His bronze face was molded in iron. He said, "Do you believe in God, Mr. O'Donnell?"

"Let me say this, Dr. Cassim. I was raised a Catholic. When I was in my third year of college, I began to research all the great religions of the world out of sheer curiosity. I wanted to know. I had to know.

"When I dug into their beginnings, into their foundations, I found very weak footings. I concluded that they were all man-made. And if there is a God, Doctor

Cassim, he has not shown himself on this earth."

"Very well, Mr. O'Donnell." There was a small smile. "I do hope you understand why I have to ask the question."

"I think I do, doctor. I've read the papers. I've seen the hysteria. I know what religious fanatics are capable of. And I know how it clouds the mind. To make a rational judgment based on fact, a mind must be clean, unencumbered with . . . what's the word . . . oh, yes, faith."

Cassim leaned forward and scribbled something on a pad. "Welcome aboard, Shawn O'Donnell."

"Thank you, sir. It will be a privilege to work with you, Doctor Cassim."

There was a nod. "Barring any unforeseen circumstances, I expect to be underway next week. Is that enough preparation time for you?"

"Yes, sir."

"Fine. Next week, then."

"A question?"

"Certainly."

"Are we going to re-open the passage at the Great Pyramid?"

"No. Not now. We are going to Abydos, the Seat of Osiris."

"I see. Has there been any word about the stolen seal?" Shawn asked.

"I'm afraid not. Is Tuesday morning at eight o'clock a good time for you?"

"Perfect," Shawn replied, "In the mean time if there is anything I can do around here?"

"Not at the moment, but I'll keep it in mind."

"Tuesday morning at eight, thanks." Shawn said.

Shawn was ecstatic. He had been looking for this position for months. He was willing to take most anything to get to Egypt.

After an accident that took his parents and brother, Shawn left his home and moved to France where he completed his PhD in Egyptology. While in France he learned of several excavations in Egypt that he tried to join, but there were no openings. While Shawn waited for other expeditions he monitored the activities of the famed Doctor Karl Cassim and the Egyptian museum in Cairo. He learned that Malak, the curator's assistant, had an unfortunate death. He felt sorry for what had happened to the young man, but he was pleased to get the opportunity.

CHAPTER 9

"Doctor Cassim, haven't we gone too far?" Shawn O'Donnell asked.

With a hand shading his eyes, Cassim looked to the west, into the sun. He did not reply.

O'Donnell persisted. "We're nearly forty miles from the Nile. To my knowledge no archeologist or Egyptologist has ever explored this far into the desert."

Cassim faced him squarely. "That's why we are here."

"Why, doctor? Why are we here?"

Cassim's westerly gaze was lost in the crimson ball as it touched the horizon; heat from the desert floor rose in wavy ripples, distorting the roundness of the setting sun. His lean frame stood on a mound of sand and rock. With his legs astride, he was determined to satisfy a nagging question. The nearly black eyes of a fifty-six-year-old glinted with savvy while he heard the question and hoped it would go away.

"Doctor?"

Cassim glanced at him with solemn eyes. Faultless sincerity creased the hollows of his tanned face.

Softly, he said, "Just a little further, a few more days."

O'Donnell threw a brow and bounced his eyes across the desert floor. "What do you hope to find?"

With a measure of confidence, he answered, "The beginning."

"The beginning of what?"

"Shawn . . . may I call you Shawn?"

"Sure."

"Shawn, I am looking for the beginning of civilization."

"But, Doctor Cassim—"

"Listen to me," he quoted parentally. "In the beginning God rode his golden bark, the sun, through the black firmament, his trailings creating the universe, the stars. He glared into the eyes of chaos and it withered beneath his feet. Standing upon the earth, upon the Primeval Mound, he raised his staff whereby the inundation fled from him and one land stood out more than any other. He named it Msr, Khem. And the earth warmed and all manner of things grew. He was called Ra."

"Doctor Cassim, with all due respect, I know the creation myth, but—"

"From His golden bark, Ra called forth his company: Shu, Geb, Tefnet, Nut, Osiris, Isis, Nepthys, and Set, whereby they settled the land in paradise."

"Have you really looked around, doctor? This is

not paradise. This is desert, cliffs."

"Now, yes. But after the Ice Age, this was a tropical paradise."

"Doctor?"

"Please call me Karl."

"Yes, sir."

"No, Karl."

A smile. A nod. "Karl, that epoch was ten, fifteen thousand years ago."

"Longer, much longer."

"You're taking the first time of the gods literally, aren't you?"

"Yes, Shawn, I am. I am proceeding just as if the myth were a historical fact."

"All right. But, I find this notion a little confusing. Common belief places the Primeval Mound in Innu, a suburb of modern Cairo. So, if you're searching for the beginning of civilization, aren't you looking in the wrong place?"

"Pardon me, Doctor Cassim?" his headman interrupted.

"Yes, Fattah, what is it?"

"Do you wish us to make camp?"

"Yes, this is as far as we can go today. Have your men set up camp between the trucks."

"Very good, doctor."

"Shawn, let's walk?"

As they headed for a small outcrop perhaps a hundred feet away, they were lost in their thoughts. Karl lit his pipe. As they approached a drift of rocks, he noticed a chair-like formation among the stones, and smiled. "Just what I was looking for," Karl whispered, and sat, puffing.

Shawn leaned against a man-sized boulder; behind him the scarlet sun fired the grains of sand clinging to his palomino streaked hair. His fair skin and lips, pummeled red by the dry desert wind, fiercely altered his blue eyes to green.

Cassim scooped up a handful of sand, letting it pour through his fingers. "You asked aren't we looking in the wrong place? Well, some will disagree with you. Some say the Primeval Mound is the Giza plateau, the place of beginning. But, for what I'm looking for, I don't think so, because the text also states that Osiris was the Great Civilizer and the fourth divine king of Egypt. Now, let me ask you a question. Why was Osiris called the Great Civilizer?"

Shawn sat cross-legged on the sand and drew a large circle between them. "Let's say this is the globe." He drew an irregular circle in the center and six others around it. "This is Egypt/Africa," he said, pointing to the center. "Osiris, the text says, having civilized Egypt traveled the world teaching mankind agriculture, writing, mathematics, astronomy, and the laws by which they must live to achieve harmony." Saying this, his finger had traveled the sandy globe.

"Good," Cassim said. "Now then, how do you suppose Osiris got around to do these things?"

"The text says that he traveled with a company of men on ships."

"All right. What did we pass back there fifteen miles from the Nile?"

His eyes grew round as he replied, "A fleet of ships moored and buried in the desert, ocean-going ships thousands of years old!"

"Yes, but not his ships. Those ships date to only about 5000 BC, hardly old enough to be from the golden age of the gods. Still, they are fifteen miles from the Nile. The important thing to remember is that the water level in that epoch was much higher than it is today. So, it stands to reason that if one seeks to find the remains of that epoch, he would have to look far beyond the Nile as it is today.

"The *Pyramid Text* gives further hints. In Faulkner's translation, the last sentence of utterance 437, which addresses Osiris' resurrection, says, 'You are pure for the New Moon, your appearing is for the monthly festival, the Great Mooring-post calls to you as to him who stands up and cannot tire, who dwells in Abydos.' That's why we are here."

"Doctor Cassim! Doctor Cassim!" Fattah shouted.

"Storm!"

Without warning, wind whipped the sand into funnels of frenzy. From the west, a thick wall of flying grit moved toward them. As high as the sky and as wide as the horizon, it slithered ominously, rapidly, carrying with it the blackness of night, drowning out the last rays of the sun.

Some tents had been put up. Some men made it to them. The rest of the party scurried to the trucks, rolling up windows, covering their faces with cloth. Cassim and O'Donnell made it to the lead truck just as the black wall pounded the vehicle, shaking it, pelting it with millions of tiny rocks. And all through the night, the storm raged as they nodded off.

The next morning brought no relief. Tan sheets of gritty rain swept around them. Like a fog with substance, it drowned the lead truck up to the hood. Howling at the day and moaning into the next night, it suddenly tired.

Calm came to the desert, and one by one lamps were lighted as the party dug their way out. Some of the trucks were buried up to the glass, while others had been spared. The amazingly clear sky was tinseled with billions of stars so bright, so close, they seemed reachable. And, despite the absence of the moon, the desert floor glowed as if neon were nestled in the sand.

Stoves were lit. Soon, the smell of food salivated

hungry mouths, while the aroma of brewing coffee lingered in the hands of a still night, and voices carried far into the darkness. Docile, with full bellies, and weary from the storm, one by one sleep overtook them in the wee hours of the morning.

Long after dawn, the party began to stir. Camp stoves were lit and again the flavors of food floated in an easy breeze.

After the late morning meal, Cassim studied his map, checking geological markers. Shawn leaned over his shoulder, following his finger across the route they had taken and where they were going.

From a dune in the distance, Fattah raced to the camp toward Cassim, calling out wheezing words of excitement. "Doctor Cassim, come, come!"

"What is it? What's wrong?"

Breathless, Fattah pulled at his sleeve. "Come, see!" he said, pointing over the sandy knoll.

Cassim, O'Donnell, and all the party of thirty-one men ran after Fattah. Reaching the top, Cassim gasped. He dropped to his knees. Shawn stood and stared. In Arabic, Fattah rattled on excitedly as his co-workers fell silent.

There, on the valley floor, stood a vast, desolate temple. All around the structure shafts of rock, mountains of sand, sheltered it from the harsh desert. In silence, they gawked, unbelieving what their eyes saw, what they thought to be impossible.

Unadorned, salmon-colored granite monoliths bore the weight of a portico that embraced the temple on all sides. Before it, an obelisk of monumental size pierced the sky. The roof was a pyramid. On either side of the steps, lion-headed sphinxes guarded the entrance and stared defiantly as the sun beat down, eating their shadows. So crisp, so fresh was the carving, the steps, the temple as a whole, one would expect life to stir at any moment.

Time passed quickly and yet stood still while their eyes embraced a spectacle, compelling admiration.

Cassim whispered, "Magnificent, absolutely magnificent."

"I'll get the camera," Shawn said, and ran back to camp.

Slowly Cassim rose to his feet and descended the dune into the gorge. Fattah tried to follow, but Karl fanned him back. He walked toward the towering obelisk. Judging from where he had come, he was certain the temple had been squarely aligned with the rising sun. With hands on his hips and chin to the air, he began to read the hieroglyphics on the obelisk.

On top of the dune, Shawn set up the tripod directing the first camera shot to the overall view.

Although the sun poured heat onto the valley floor, a chill inched up Cassim's spine as he read the inscription.

He knew it by heart. The words strummed through his brain. "Beware! Death comes on wings . . ." He turned away.

He faced the massive gold doors set deep within the portico. Draped in shadow, the doors had handles the size of a man.

Shawn snapped away, taking pictures until he ran out of film and sent Fattah back to the truck for more. While he waited, he went down into the gorge.

Suddenly, the floor became a sea of springs, spewing sand stories high into the air, blinding him, forbidding him.

"Stay back," Cassim shouted.

"What the hell's going on?"

"I don't know, but stay out."

Fattah and the men dropped to the east, calling upon Allah to protect them, while Shawn tripped up the dune and the sand settled.

"Don't anyone come down here," Cassim ordered.

He turned and faced the door. Placing one foot in front of the other, he began to see his image on the ground moving just ahead of him. He touched the lion's head and took the first step. He hesitated. The air was still, the sand quiet.

With the sun on his back, he took the twenty steps, visiting each quickly, hearing his leather soles whispering between the columns. He stood on the portico. The hairs on his neck iced. Fear became real. Curiosity drove him. Logic became a stupid word as he threw a look over his shoulder and walked the fifty paces to the giant door. With one hand, he clamped onto the handle. With the other, he dropped the latch below it and pushed. The energy he used had been wasted, for the hulking door swung open effortlessly. Its hinges were silent, while the very movement of its size sucked in a breeze.

Now clear of the door, of the sunlight, his eyes desperately adjusted to the dimness as they reached deeper and deeper between pillars, not finding an end. Dwarfed like a pebble, he gazed upward, estimating the ceiling height at nearly a hundred feet.

A thunderous bang shook him as the monstrous doors slammed shut. In that instant, light oozed from the pores of the granite walls, and he could see to the end of the hypostyle hall to another set of doors. Now he could see the black polished floor, doubling images of everything, shining like thirty coats of wax.

A feeling of presence . . . He spun around, throwing his eyes between columns ten times the thickness of a man. "Grab a hold," he muttered, and centered his attention on the door far in the distance.

He glided over the shine, trying to walk as quietly as he could, but the silence was so complete he heard his breath, his heart, and his steps as if someone were walking close alongside. He counted two hundred steps as he stood looking at the door, wondering who had walked this way before.

The austere design, he recalled, was symbolic of the earliest architecture of ancient Egypt. He realized at this moment that not a speck of dust, a cobweb, the smallest grain of sand had violated the cleanliness of this place. Cassim took hold of the handle while his heart thumped, and he pushed.

Galaxies in miniature filled the huge room. Three-dimensional worlds glowed, stretching out the zodiacal belt of planets in the heavens from the perspective of Earth. Floating freely, moons spun around planets, planets around suns, and comets flung through space. He stepped closer and found Earth orbiting the sun so tiny, so frail in the scheme of things. The universe was alive with all its celestial bodies dangling stringlessly.

Behind him, the doors closed. *Is someone here after all?* he wondered, slowly looking about. That sense of presence returned vigorously. He shivered, frozen in place, but what he saw was not menacing. His eyes followed the legs of a body up to the ceiling. On the wall, overlooking the universe, stood the God of Eternity. A gigantic statue of Osiris gazed down at him. Through the universe on the opposite wall stood the Weigher of Hearts, the black, jackal-headed

Anubis. And, to his right, the Master of Secrets, God of Wisdom, Thoth.

From beneath Cassim's feet, rising like a wisp of fog came the music of heaven scented with myrrh. In unrecognizable tones and language, the splendid sound gathered strength and filled the hall as the planets spun and the universe breathed. So overwhelmed was Cassim that he smiled as tears filled the wells of his eyes and flowed to his chin.

Suddenly . . . quiet. He blotted his face with a sleeve. He heard the door open. He turned. Beyond the threshold in the path he had taken stood a dais. On top lay a cylinder seal. Inch by inch the door began to close. He ran to the hall and grabbed the seal as the door forcefully closed tight. He tried to open it. It was locked, and turning away he saw the dais was gone. "I don't believe!" he whispered. "I don't believe!" he repeated, taking steps faster and faster, heading for the outer doors that swung open.

He ran as the sun fell through the doorway like a tongue. A breeze caressed his cheeks as though a soft hand had touched him. He fled through the opening, racing over the portico, down the steps, tripped and fell. He sat up hugging the seal to his chest, staring, gawking at the stern structure when the massive doors slammed shut, the sound thundering across the gorge.

Cassim stood and backed away. A heavy scent of

putrefied almonds came on a cold cloud that blocked the sun. His mind was blank except for a single word—RUN!

He sprinted to the dune rising taller than he remembered. Mounds of sand feverishly coiled like a serpent, spiraling high around the obelisk, the sphinxes, and the temple. He rushed up the dune, climbing, choking, while the earth boiled. Lurching from behind, the sandy floor rose as a mountainous wave of wheat lapping at his heels.

Anguished, he reached the top on all fours and smothered his face in an arm, expecting to be buried by the blizzard. He squeezed his eyes shut, took a breath and waited for the end. At any second, he expected the weight of the sand to crush him, to clog his lungs.

But suddenly, the sun was on his back! He could feel it. He rolled over to the blaze of a bright and still day. He looked for the gorge, the valley he had just climbed out of. What he saw was flat, endless desert with cliffs here and there.

Talking to himself, he strode back to the camp.

The trucks sat quiet. The tent flaps were tied. Everything seemed deserted. He ran to the tents, shaking them, throwing them open, calling for Shawn and Fattah. "Where in hell is anybody?" he screamed. "What are you doing? Why did you disappear? I was almost killed and you sleep! Get up! Get up!"

Shawn bolted from his tent. “What’s wrong, Karl?”

Cassim glared. “And you. Where the hell were you?”

“In my tent asleep. Where should I be?” Shawn glanced at his wrist. “Karl, it’s 6:30 in the morning.”

“You’re crazy!” He looked at his own watch and back to where the gorge had been.

“Karl? Are you okay?”

“What do you mean, am I okay? Of course I’m okay, no thanks to you. What did you do with the pictures?”

“What pictures?”

“The ones you were taking of the temple. What the hell is going on here?”

“Karl, let me take you to your tent.”

“Don’t patronize me. I’m fine. Leave me alone,” he said, and staggered back against the tent. Shawn and Fattah reached out, stopping his fall.

“Come on, Karl, let me help you to your tent.”

He did not argue. He knew what had happened, but for some reason they were trying to cover it up. Exhausted, he let them lead him to his tent. He sat on his cot and stared at his watch.

“Fattah,” Shawn said, “make breakfast. After he’s had something to eat he’ll feel better.” He squatted in front of Cassim and felt his forehead.

“What are you doing?”

“Just making sure you’re all right.”

“I’m fine, I tell you.”

"Really? How did you get those bruises? Look at your hands. They're all cut up. You look like you've been rolling in the sand."

"I have. Are you going to tell me that you didn't see anything, that they didn't see anything? Am I the only one around here who remembers what happened?"

"You had a nightmare, Karl, a terrible dream."

"It was no dream."

"I think you walked in your sleep, probably fell."

"You were there, taking pictures of the temple. You're telling me that was a dream? Look at me! Do I look like I've been sleeping? Listen to me. I saw a huge temple in a gorge. I went in, through massive doors. I saw the universe alive in a great hall surrounded with gigantic statues of Osiris, Anubis, and Thoth."

"Karl, calm down. There has to be some explanation."

Fattah opened the flap and handed them two large cups of steaming black coffee. Karl reached for the cup. The cylinder seal fell out of his shirt. The three men stared.

Karl posted a snide grin. "Now," he said, "tell me this is a dream. Take it. I don't want to look at it."

Shawn took the seal and wrapped it in a towel. For a long time the two men sat and sipped coffee. Shawn took a deep breath and said, "What do we do now?"

Fattah brought in plates of breakfast.

"Leave. Pack up and leave."

Shawn looked up at Fattah. "You heard the man. Break camp."

Fattah followed instructions. As the men broke camp, rumors flew. Rumors of spells and possession, rumors that Cassim had lost his mind, was out of control.

When Karl left his tent, the men politely kept busy, turning away. Shawn drove the lead truck. The others followed.

"You want to talk about it, Karl?"

The hot desert wind blew through the open window as Cassim stared. For a long while he did not answer. Then quietly, he began to speak. "It was real, Shawn. The obelisk, the stairs, the huge gold doors. I touched them. I read the obelisk. The curse was written on it as big as life."

Shawn glanced at him and back to the desert ahead.

Cassim's eyes were unfocused as he spoke, pleading with the windshield. "Try to remember, Shawn. You were there. You tried to follow me into the gorge. The sand went wild, don't you remember?"

"I'm sorry, Karl."

"How do you explain the seal?"

Shawn shook his head as the wheel twisted, fighting his grip against the sand. He could feel Cassim's eyes on his face. He shook his head.

Karl looked away.

CHAPTER 10

In a room contiguous to the large new-acquisition department of the Egyptian Museum, in a corner behind crates and boxes of items yet to be catalogued, Cassim cleared a desk.

He set the crystal cylinder on the desk, threw his thick yellow pad next to it, and made himself comfortable.

As he stared at the crystal he remembered the obelisk. Now he wished he had read it completely. But the fear that had swept over him also came back; it crept up his spine and reached into his chest in a shattering emotion of fright.

Anger quickly followed. He whipped the fearful thoughts from his mind, calling them cowardice.

Carefully, he examined every detail of the cylinder. Its weight was seven pounds exactly. The artistry was supreme. The crystal stone was in pristine condition as if it had just this moment been carved by the Sage whose name it bore.

Of the eight commonly accepted classifications, the closest Cassim could come to placing it was "columnar inscriptions". But this category didn't fit, because it would have dated it to a much later period. The style, by comparison, gave the only clue. It was a style typical of that found in and around predynastic Abydos.

Karl knew that the ancient Egyptians had placed great importance on words. No object or ceremony was complete or permissible without the words to make it reality. Repetition gave value to meaning and play on words incited a direction, an ending, and provoked magic.

In the writing style, Karl saw the roots of the formal systematized composition, which later dynasties followed, a style that was simple and yet dignified.

From a shelf behind, he pulled down a copy of *Scarabs and Cylinders* by Flanders Petrie. With a magnifying glass, he inspected the carving. Similarities were nonexistent. The graving was not hard point and scraping. It was not done with emery and copper saw, or pecked out with a tool. So perfect was the work, it appeared as if the symbols and pictures were pressed on the cylinder with some kind of stamp. *But that would have been impossible, wouldn't it?* he thought.

Defeated in the attempt, Karl put away the book and concentrated on the translation. The familiar curse cried out. *"Beware!"* He quickly passed over it and went on to the message.

"What is in the Duat? What is most sacred upon the earth? Seek the belt of Osiris and thou shall be equipped. For in the Age of Aquarius, the pitcher will once more tip."

Karl dropped his pencil and leaned back. He looked up to the ceiling where his eyes found a spot and rested. He muttered, "The constellation of Orion was to the Egyptians the standing Osiris. Three stars make up the belt of Osiris. Okay, that leaves me nowhere." He read the seal again. "Now, let's see," he mumbled. "The Duat is in both the underworld and in the sky. A duality where Osiris dwells, where he is Lord of Eternity."

Footsteps sounded outside the door.

"Doctor Cassim? Are you down here?" Shawn called out.

"In here, Shawn. You're just the person I'm looking for."

"Okay. But the people upstairs want to know if you're going to display the cylinder."

"Tell them, no. One has been stolen already; we're not going to lose another. What we can do is use photos, info cards, and surround them with other artifacts. Tell Sarah to handle it."

"I'll pass it on."

"Sit down a minute," he said, pointing to a crate. "I want to pick your brain. I've translated the seal. Listen to this." He read the copy. "What do you think?"

"Well, we are approaching the Age of Aquarius," Shawn said. "In the year 2000, we pass from Pisces to Aquarius."

"That's right. Every twenty-one hundred years the Earth passes from one zodiacal sign to the next. Very good. Now, what is most sacred upon the Earth?"

"I think the Primeval Mound where Ra stood at the time of the gods."

"I'll buy that. Now, where is it?"

"Some say Innu or On."

"And others say it's the Giza Plateau," Karl said.

"Okay, so what if it is?"

"I don't know, it's a jumble. The cylinder says they must stand united. Maybe, when and if we find all the cylinders we'll be able to make sense out of it."

Shawn looked at the seal. "Do you think we'll really find them all?"

A shrug.

"I'll tell them upstairs what you said about the display."

"Fine. I'll be in my office if they need me."

CHAPTER 11

A highly colored map of ancient Egypt hung on the wall behind the desk. A window was on the left. Beyond the glass, in the distance, minarets towered above mosques.

Two other walls separated by a door held bookcases that reached the ten-foot ceilings. The wooden floor was well worn from the door to the desk, which had not been moved in a quarter century.

Cassim was oblivious to all this as he read a copy of the Edfu text, laboring on the antediluvian flood imagery and those who survived. They were seven in number. They were divine beings with great wisdom. They were the Seven Sages whose great wisdom had influenced the gods. In particular, they supervised the building of the Great Temple, the Mansion of God where the treasure of Thoth lies. Further, Cassim read, the Mansion of God rests upon the Great Primeval Mound and in the sky. When completed, the Divine Ones stood hand in hand, whereby they cast their magical protection on this holy place.

Cassim's eyes drifted to a footnote on the page.

According to Professor I. S. Edwards, the Great Primeval Mound lies beneath the Great Pyramid of Giza.

Cassim rubbed his eyes. His mind swirled. He pushed back his chair and moved to the window. He focused on the very few clouds in a sky so blue.

A terse ringing pulled him from his thoughts. "This is Cassim," he answered.

"Long distance, doctor."

"Please, no more reporters," he said to Sarah.

"Doctor Cassim, it's from Germany, a Doctor Schweiger. He says it's urgent."

He considered this for a moment. "All right, put him through."

Doctor Schweiger was direct and to the point. He didn't understand why and didn't care, because he was honest and a very busy man. But someone had deposited a package at his door and he didn't want to be blamed for stealing it.

Cassim finally got a word in. "What is in the package?"

"The crystal cylinder seal," Schweiger shouted. "The one stolen from your museum. I wish to return it immediately," he insisted. "It's been many times in the papers here in Germany, and I want no part of it."

"Can you read it, Doctor Schweiger?"

"Of course not! I am a physicist. I deal with energy and matter, not hieroglyphics."

"Why are you so angry, doctor?"

"I am not a thief. I haven't been to Egypt in years, and I can prove it. I will not have my reputation ruined for a piece of old glass."

"I understand. No one will blame you, doctor, I promise."

Cassim gave him his address. He promised the good doctor he would not be blamed and he would not talk to the press. It would be their secret. He promised again, and hung up the phone. *Another anonymous delivery*, he thought.

Cassim dug through the books and papers on his desk searching for his yellow pad. He had written down everything he knew about the seals and where they came from. He turned the page. He made a new list. He wrote:

1. Thief . . . Passage . . . Directions.
2. Astronomer . . . Anonymous . . . Time, horizon, universe.
3. Egyptologist, self . . . Age of Aquarius . . . belt . . . Duat.
4. Physicist . . .

He left the space blank. He would wait and see. Maybe it was the stolen seal. Maybe it wasn't. He did not think it was.

CHAPTER 12

October 7

The package arrived.

A special courier sent by Doctor Schweiger had flown it from Germany aboard Lufthansa, first class, to Cairo. He would stay at the five-star Sonesta Hotel for one night and return to Germany the next day. He would deliver the package, in a briefcase shackled to his wrist, to Doctor Cassim at his office in the museum at 11:15 a.m. Cassim would sign for it, the shackles would be removed and Hans, the courier, would depart solemnly. He would go back to Germany, to his father, with the good news and with another promise of silence from Doctor Cassim.

Cassim opened the briefcase. The package was identical to the one delivered to Julian Rutledge, burlap, hand sewn and stuffed with Egyptian papyrus. The crystal scroll was the same in all qualities as the others.

The doctor rolled the seal on carbon paper, making an exact copy, and walked to the basement where he locked it in the safe with the other seal.

He was on his way back to his office when commotion swept through the museum, emptying everyone, including his personal staff, out onto the street.

Fingers pointed to the Nile. Horror registered on moaning faces as word spread that this ancient river, this vessel of the gods, had gone dry. A bad omen, someone said, and many superstitious Arabs fled to their homes and to their mosques.

"Nonsense," Cassim dismissed as he pushed through the door. *No doubt the empty river is the result of the Aswan dam,* he thought. Unconcerned, he returned to his office where the telephone was ringing.

"Karl, have you heard the news?"

"Yes, Shawn, I have. The Aswan—"

"I'm not talking about the Nile."

"What do you mean?"

"The Gulf of Suez . . . there's a path, a highway from the Egyptian mainland to the Sinai."

"Have you been drinking?"

"Karl, I saw pictures, walls of water holding back the sea, a dry road half a mile wide and twenty miles across. People are going crazy. They're calling it the beginning of the apocalypse, God showing his power and all that. Moses parting the waters."

"Shawn, don't believe everything you hear," answered Cassim.

"All right, Karl, I just thought I'd let you know. If you don't mind, I'm going to drive to Ayn Sukhnalt and see for myself."

"Shawn, you'll probably find it's an experiment gone wrong, a weather phenomenon, plates moving under the continental shelf. But if you want to go, go. Be careful."

"I will. Thanks, Karl."

He disconnected and returned to the copy of the seal. He took out his yellow pad. The window air-conditioner seemed unusually noisy and he went to check it. Outside, black clouds rolled across the heavens with flits of lightning bolting over the city in pockets of crackling light. At two-thirty in the afternoon, it was pitch as night.

He raced back to the telephone. "Sarah, have you seen the sky?"

"Yes, sir."

"Do you know what's causing it?"

"No, sir. Probably a storm. Or Saddam burning more oil wells."

"Sarah, if you hear anything let me know."

In all his years no storm, not even burning oil wells, had darkened Cairo to total blackness at 2:30 in the afternoon. He hung up the telephone.

While Karl's mind clicked from one thought to another like an endless computer file, his eyes fell on a book on his bookshelf. Entitled *Egyptian Magic*, the work had been translated in 1899 by Sir E. A. Wallis Budge from the Westcar Papyrus dating to the Old Kingdom. It seemed quite appropriate for the inexplicable happenings in the Gulf of Suez.

He pulled the copy from the shelf and thumbed the pages. Halfway down a certain page he read: "But the command of the waters of the sea was claimed by Egyptian priests many centuries before the time of Moses.

"The story is related to the father of Cheops and the powers possessed by the Kher Heb, the high priest whose name was Tchatcha-em-ankh.

"While voyaging on a great lake, maidens were rowing the king's boat and singing for His Majesty when one of them dropped a jewel in the water and it sank. The beautiful young woman ceased her rowing and began to cry, whereby the king promised to get back the ornament. By request of the king, Tchatcha-em-ankh was summoned. And lo, he raised his arms, uttering Words of Power, and parted the waters of the great lake. He retrieved the jewel and commanded the water to be as it was before. And, it was done."

Cassim closed the book. "Could it really be," he said wryly, "that someone knows these Words of Power, the incantation to part the Gulf of Suez?" He took a breath.

He hurriedly returned to his yellow pad on the

desk and switched on the lamp. From between the pages of the pad, he took the carbon copy he had made and began to translate the ancient message.

It started the same. *"Beware! The eyes that fall upon this Providence must be pure."* Quickly skimming it, he realized it was not the stolen seal, as Doctor Schweiger had thought.

Across the column of hieroglyphics, a new prediction startled him.

"Behold, it shall come to pass that on the cusp of Pisces, on the seventh day of the second division of the third season, the waters shall be parted. The winding waterway shall be made dry. The sky shall be blackened, hiding the imperishable stars. Behold His power for His deeds are pure. Do not guard against His magic."

His eyes shot to the window. His heart pounded. "What the hell is happening?" The script pulled him back.

"He is He who guides the Earth and judges the gods. He is the Keeper of the Way, Warden of the Great Portal to the sky. He is!"

Karl rubbed his aching temples. "A twenty-or-thirty-thousand-year-old prediction, a dream that produces a crystal seal, seas parting, a dry river . . . What the hell?" He picked up the phone. "Sarah, I have two appointments this afternoon. Cancel them."

He tucked the yellow pad under his arm and left

the building. He got into his jeep, a standard issue from the Supreme Council for Antiquities, and drove across the bridge over the dry riverbed to the West Bank. Noises came from his stomach, but the thought of food repulsed him.

Cars, carts, animals, people were all crowding the streets. Taxis and tour buses going to and coming from the bazaars, the hotels, the race track, the botanical gardens, all seemed indifferent to the black sky, the dry Nile. For twenty minutes he drove through the throngs.

A renewed sense of awe swept over him as floodlights in the distance flickered on, illuminating the magnificent monuments of the Giza Plateau. The Great Sphinx, shrouded in the backdrop of a black sky, staring eternally due east in its regal pose, defied wisdom for its very existence. Behind its recline, growing larger with each passing moment, the pyramids loomed, captivating the imagination with their extraordinary precision, their monolithic size, their inexplicable meaning on man's Earth.

Cassim slowed. Camel drivers tried to gather their disturbed animals as the tourists left the plateau. Taxis, horse-driven buggies and buses all scurried in the dark of the day's night.

He stopped at the Sphinx.

In the glare of artificial light, he sat atop the rock enclosure surrounding the lionine effigy. He checked his watch. "Nearly five o'clock," his lips mouthed.

His eyes explored the weathered form at his feet, resting as it was on the bedrock below, head and shoulders above the flat of the desert floor. He breathed deeply. Setting the yellow tablet on his knees, he skimmed his notes. He read his copies of the seals, ignoring the curse, and then looked again at the Sphinx. "You are the watcher of the horizon, aren't you?" he said aloud. "And to know you one must look to the heavens. What do you see?" he shouted.

He glanced over his left shoulder at the pyramids and back to his pad. He whispered, "What is the most sacred place upon the Earth?" Pointing to the Great Pyramid, he said, "You are." And he threw the pad on the ground. "So what? Bits and pieces," he mumbled. "I'm losing my mind. Here I am talking to a rock."

He picked up the pad and meandered back to his jeep. A slow, cool breeze softened the dry heat, and he put down the top and slid behind the wheel. A moment later he rested his forehead on the steering wheel, relieving some of the torment brewing within his skull. His eyes closed.

Faintly, he heard the moan of camels. The howl of desert dogs aroused him fully...in the light of day. "I must have dozed off," he breathed. His watch read seven o'clock . . . seven o'clock on the button.

The sky was completely clear. The reddened blush

of a huge sun sat on the horizon on the moment before dropping off. Behind him, the first stars of the night glimmered. "Seven hours exactly."

While Nut, goddess of the sky, swallowed the magenta sun, giving birth to the imperishable stars, Cassim watched and wondered. It was a beautiful way to explain to the masses the passing of day and the coming of night, even though the ancient Egyptian priest knew better.

"Steeped in mystery, laced with wizardry, imbued with astronomy, the ancient mythology carries a wisdom, a meaning meant only for the worthy. Am I the worthy? If I am considered so, a huge mistake has been made because I do not know the meaning. And, why now? Why this sudden appearance? What is so urgent?"

The windshield did not reply and the questions went unanswered as Karl left the Giza Plateau on the pyramid road, the Mena road, and over the bridge of the now flowing Nile to Zamalek on Gezira Island.

CHAPTER 13

On the northern end of Gezira Island, which lies in the Nile between Giza and Cairo, Cassim drove along a road on the edge of the riverbank. The waters had returned. The sky had cleared and everyone, it seemed, had returned to business as usual. The phenomenon was now left to gossip and speculation.

His second-story flat was several streets north of the Gezira Sporting Club. Parking on the street at the front of the building, he raised the top on his jeep.

Inside, he took the stairs to his comfortable apartment, a spacious nine-room flat with two bedrooms, two baths, a kitchen, a living room, a library, a den, and a master suite with its own bath. In a way, this was a time lock, a reflection of his life. An accumulation of nearly thirty years, his home held memories of hard times, sad times, but, most of all cherished moments with his wife Sinta, who had died giving birth to their daughter, Nanette. He loved the feel of his home where the essence of his wife and daughter lingered, where Nanette had been raised. Pieces of his life, his work, his family, were everywhere.

Murals were on at least one wall in all the rooms except the kitchen. His wife had selected full-scale reproductions of tomb paintings. They had been painted by artists employed by the J. Paul Getty Museum to restore damaged frescos, particularly those of Nefertari, Great Royal Wife of Rameses the Great.

In the kitchen, he threw his yellow tablet on the table and put a pot of water on the burner for tea. He opened a cupboard for a cup, promising himself he would not think about the happenings of the day, or the seals, or the Giza Plateau. He wanted to clear his mind. He wanted to sleep undisturbed, something that had not happened since Abydos. But he was going to try.

As the water began to boil, there was a knock on the door. Cassim turned off the burner.

"Doctor Cassim," accompanied the second round of knocks.

He recognized the voice. Opening the door he said, "Shawn, what's the matter?"

"I need to talk, Karl. I hope you don't mind."

"What is it? What's wrong?"

"May I come in?"

"I'm sorry, of course. You caught me by surprise."

"I know. I had trouble finding you. But after what I saw, I could only think of you."

"Come into the kitchen, I was fixing some tea.

Would you like some?"

"Karl, your home is beautiful."

"Thank you. My wife had a flair for such things," he said, walking through the hall outside the living room.

"Tea?" he asked again.

"No, thank you." Shawn took a deep breath and pulled out a chair.

Karl poured his tea and sat across the table from him. "You look drained, Shawn. Tell me what's wrong."

Shawn recoiled with his thoughts. "Karl, I saw hundreds of people die."

"How?"

"It was so strange. They went between the walls of water like kids playing in a fountain. Some even drove their cars in, trying to get to the other side, to the Sinai. I couldn't believe my eyes! I tried to warn them. I told them the walls could fall as quickly as they had gone up, but they wouldn't listen. When the police got there they tried too, but the people kept going. It was a sign from God, they said. A miracle, they chanted, and walked further and further down the road. I could do nothing but watch.

"Then, at seven o'clock sharp the walls of water collapsed. The roar drowned their screams. No one was spared. In seconds, the sky cleared like somebody had pushed a switch and the water was calm, barely a ripple. Jesus Christ, Karl, they all died!"

Many minutes went by without a word. Painfully, both men's eyes lay on the table, on the yellow pad. Shawn's vision blurred with the horror, with the tears that his manhood tried to restrain.

Cassim whispered, "What a terrible waste of life!" He went to the cupboard, took down a bottle of whiskey and poured Shawn a glass. He poured some in his tea. Putting a hand on Shawn's shoulder, he said softly, "Drink."

"Thanks," Shawn mouthed. He sipped. His eyes rose from the table, young blue American eyes unaccustomed to massacre, to death on a grand scale. He searched Cassim's face. "Why?" he asked, youth fading from his features.

Karl shook his head. "I don't know."

Time lapsed in silence.

Karl nursed his tea and cleared his throat. "Shawn, I got another seal today," he said, toying with the edge of his yellow pad.

"How?"

"It was delivered to me by courier from Germany. A Doctor Schweiger, a physicist, received it the same way Julian Rutledge did. He thought it was the same one stolen from the museum, and he was extremely upset about it."

"Karl, do you think those seals have anything to do with what happened today? I know it sounds silly, but—"

"Shawn, I translated the cylinder," Cassim said as he turned the pad and flipped pages. "It's not as silly as you may think."

Shawn's eyes came across the table suddenly curious and hard.

"Listen to this. *Behold! It shall come to pass that on the cusp of Pisces, on the seventh day of the second division of the third season, the waters shall be parted. The winding waterway shall be made dry. The sky shall be blackened, hiding the imperishable stars. Behold His power for His deeds are pure. Do not guard against His magic.*

"He is He who guides the Earth and judges the gods. He is the Keeper of the Way, Warden of the Great Portal to the sky. He is!"

Karl's eyes rose from the page.

"That's incredible!"

"It's more than that, considering the age of the seal."

"What does it mean?"

Karl leaned back in his chair and took a swallow of tea. "First of all, it predicts a date. Today. I know you're upset, but think for a moment. It says on the cusp of Pisces. Well, that's where we are . . . on the cusp of Pisces, on the seventh day. Today is the seventh. Then it says the second division of the third season."

"Ancient Egypt had three seasons," Shawn said. "Aakhet, the time of the inundation, the flooding of the Nile; Peret, the time of sowing; and Shemu, the time of harvest. All of which had four divisions or months of thirty days."

"You do remember. And the second division of the third season is October."

"All right, but who is 'He'?"

"According to the *Pyramid Text*, he is Osiris."

"But it says he is, present tense, which means . . . It can't be. It just can't be."

"Are you going to argue with what happened today?"

Shawn stared into Cassim's dark eyes. He did not answer.

"He is showing his power. He is showing us that he is not messing around and that we had better take this whole thing seriously."

"Do you think he's really alive . . . after all this time?"

"I don't know. All I do know is that today did happen. And this time, I'm not the only one who saw it."

Shawn emptied his glass and Karl filled it and added to his tea.

"Karl, can I translate the cylinders? Maybe—"

"No!"

"Why?"

"Because."

"That's not much of an answer."

"Look, Shawn, I'm the only one who has translated the seals, the cylinders, the scrolls, karkar, whatever you want to call them. I know you could do it."

"So? What's the problem?"

"The problem is . . . the problem is that I don't know . . . if it will affect you."

"The curse?" He snorted. "Are you kidding?"

Cassim's sharp look gave the answer. "All I can say is that I'm not taking any chances with your life. Especially after what I learned the other day."

"I don't know what you learned, but you're referring to Malak, aren't you?"

There was a nod.

"That doesn't mean it's going to happen to me."

"Do you really want to take that chance? I don't. You weren't there. You didn't see him shrivel like a prune. And if that isn't enough to convince you, I talked to Hassandi Talib, the Minister of Police."

Shawn's eyes were filled with questions.

"He found some interesting information. His records indicated that in the twenties, around the same time Howard Carter found Tut's tomb, two other tombs were found by an American archeologist. As you know, Tut's discovery attracted considerable attention. Anyway, this man's name was James Farley and the tombs were located in Abydos. One of the tombs was the alleged tomb of Osiris. In those days records were not very good, but we did find sketchy notes from Farley that said the tomb was empty and that he filled it in.

"After World War II, Farley returned to Egypt. He applied for and received permission to do some measuring of the Great Pyramid. He and an assistant disappeared. I'm convinced that it is his hand jutting out from the granite plug in the passage."

"You're crediting the seal for that?"

"I'm not sure. It could be his own stupidity that did him in. But whatever it was, there is where the cylinder was found." Cassim sipped his laced tea.

"What do you really think?"

"I think Farley found the seal in the false tomb of Osiris. Why or how it got there would only be a guess. It is obvious he couldn't read it, at least not at that time. I think that because of the Great Depression and the war, he couldn't come back to Egypt. In the late forties, Farley would have been middle to late fifties. That is the approximate age of the skeletal fist.

"Police records show that his family made inquiries as to Farley's whereabouts in the early fifties. He is the only person, outside of myself, who has read the seal."

"But, Karl, I handled the one from Abydos. I took it from you, wrapped it, and put it in the truck. Nothing happened to me."

"You're not listening. Yes, you did handle it and other people have handled the seals as well. But they could not read them. You didn't read the one I found, did you?"

"No."

"Julian Rutledge couldn't read his, and Doctor Schweiger couldn't read his. Malak did read it, and he's dead. Look, Shawn, maybe I'm wrong, but I don't think so. I don't have all the answers. However, one thing is for sure. After what happened today, I'm taking everything very seriously."

Shawn finished his drink.

"Want another?"

"Yeah, I think I do."

CHAPTER 14

Around the world, the Egyptian phenomenon pushed lead stories off the front page. In their place were photographs of water standing solid against itself, holding back the sea, while people acting like children poked fingers into it. In full color, the dramatization of blue water, black sky, automobile headlights, and people sauntering to their deaths captivated hearts and minds on all continents.

In Rome, the Pope pronounced it a miracle. In twenty-four languages, His Holiness predicted the Second Coming. Why the spectacle had taken place in Egypt instead of Israel, as foretold in the Bible, was not addressed.

In other capitals of the world, however, other lines of reasoning followed the graphic photos. El Niño, continental shelf displacement, earthquakes, and ozone holes all vied for prominence. The skeptical shouted "hoax," while creative minds weaved elaborate plots involving secret weapons. A few simply pointed fingers at witchcraft, black magic, sorcery, and voodoo.

Television captured the most vivid graphics while

splitting the screen between interviews with opinionated laureates and scenes of crushing water complete with bobbing corpses.

Day after day after day, the coverage went on. Scientists from every field, from every country descended on Egypt photographing, prodding, interviewing, dissecting. All for naught. The final analysis remained unresolved.

Amid all this, Karl Cassim did not step forward. Neither did Shawn O'Donnell. Who would believe an ancient Egyptian prediction? Both men were well aware of the scathing scrutiny that could follow them for the rest of their lives. Perhaps some day, when all the seals had surfaced and the riddle had been solved, they would consider that option.

By the end of October, the media had tired. Cassim was in his office sitting across from O'Donnell, discussing their plans, when the phone rang.

"Yes, Sarah."

"Doctor Cassim, there is a Julian Rutledge to see you."

"You're kidding? Send him in."

By the time Cassim got to the door, Julian was on the other side.

"Good to see you, Julian."

"I've been looking forward to this, Karl."

Karl made the introduction to Shawn. As they

shook hands, Shawn asked, "Are you on holiday?"

"Yes and no. I'm here for a symposium."

"I'd completely forgot, Julian. This month has been so chaotic," Karl said.

"Yes, I've heard all about it. The News in the states gave it quite a lot of play. Some evening I'd like to sit down with you and have a good chat about it."

"I'd like that. Maybe you can give me some ideas that make sense. I mean, after all, there has to be some logical explanation for what happened. Pardon my manners. Please, have a seat."

"Thank you. But I'm afraid I can't be of much help. I've thought about it quite a lot, Karl. You see, if the phenomenon hadn't been so isolated, happening only in Egypt, one could make argument. However, that was not the case. Nonetheless, there might be something the papers didn't reveal that you could. That's why I'd like to talk to you sometime."

"I look forward to it. Tell me, Julian, how long will you be in Cairo?"

Julian smiled. "The symposium lasts four days, but I've stretched my stay to two weeks."

"Did you bring your family?"

"No, I'm afraid not. It's the end of the semester with finals and parties. It just wasn't a good time."

"Ah, well, maybe next time."

"Karl, one of the reasons I stopped by was to invite

you to the symposium and to ask if you would be interested in being a guest speaker."

"Are you serious?"

"Oh, yes."

"Julian, what I know about astronomy only relates to Egyptian mythology."

"Exactly. I thought it would be marvelous weaving the two together. After all, the first calendar we have is from ancient Egypt. I took the liberty of speaking with the conference coordinator, and if you are willing . . ."

"What do you have in mind?"

"Well, I've been documenting a nebula surrounding Zeta, the first star in the belt of Orion. And as I remember, the standing Osiris was to the Egyptians what we call Orion. I thought it would be a nice twist if you could tell us something about Osiris and his relationship to his people. Maybe half an hour, forty-five minutes."

Cassim nodded.

"I'll follow you with my study and then open the session to questions. What do you say?"

"It sounds interesting. I'll do it."

"Great. I'll set it up. How is Saturday, November 1?"

"I'll mark my calendar. How about lunch?"

"I can't. I've got to get back. How about dinner tonight?"

"Wonderful."

"Shawn, will you join us?" Julian asked.

"I would like to very much."

"Eight o'clock, gentlemen?"

CHAPTER 15

After dinner, after a meeting of the minds, after eleven o'clock, Julian knocked on the door of Room 510 at the Cairo Mariott Hotel. In seconds, the door flew open.

"Oh, Julian!"

Frantically, he lunged into her arms, softly moaning, inhaling her face, while all his senses came to attention. "When did you get in?"

"Years ago. Seven-thirty," she gushed.

"I could hardly get through the day," he whispered.

"I counted the hours, the minutes," she breathed.

Feverishly, their mouths locked. He kicked the door closed and backed her to the bed. "I've been dreaming of this moment . . ." With tongues intertwined, and in rhythm with her sighs, he rapidly undressed her. She followed his lead, nearly ripping off his clothing. He pressed against her naked body, she wound her long, nimble legs around him. "Nancy, Nancy . . ." he moaned, delicately nibbling her breasts, tonguing her inner thighs.

"You're a monster," she teased.

Entering, he clenched his arms around her and . . .

Nearing twelve-thirty, he raked his fingers through her blond hair, moving it away from her face and those almond-shaped eyes. "Darling," he asked, his voice smooth, attentive, "would you care to walk with me under the full moon along the Nile?"

"I would like that very much," she answered, with a mischievous glint in her eye. She shoved him out of bed.

"You're a naughty, naughty girl." He flew from the floor and leaped on top of her. "Care for seconds?"

"You're a hungry soul, aren't you?"

"What's that supposed to mean?"

"Professor? Do you always answer a question with a question?" she said, locking her mouth on his.

In throes of passion, the idea of a walk under an Egyptian moon hung somewhere on a breeze from an open window.

In skivvies, Julian opened the door. Nancy groaned as room service rolled in breakfast. He tipped the waiter and followed him to the door.

She yawned and stretched, and said, "Aren't you an angel!"

"I like to think so. I'm working on my wings." He kissed her. "Hungry?"

"Starved." She ran to the bathroom. When she returned, Julian was standing on the balcony, orange juice in hand, taking in the view of Cairo. He said,

"Beautiful, isn't it?"

"In all the world, there is nothing like it."

"I had dinner with Karl Cassim last night."

"Is that where you were? How is Karl?"

"Karl is just fine. By the way, I asked him to be a guest speaker at the symposium, and he agreed."

"I have to get over there, let him know I'm here in Cairo."

"Yeah, and I'd do it soon. It would be a little awkward if he ran into you, especially if he saw you at the conference. He'd wonder why you didn't stop by to see him. And since he's giving a lecture, he'd wonder why I didn't tell him."

"I will. I really like Karl. We got along so well."

"What should I tell him about us?" Julian frowned.

"Tell him . . . tell him . . . I don't know."

"How about this? Tell him you wanted to surprise him with a visit, and my conference and your trip were just a coincidence. It's almost true."

"Sure it is. And we just happened to end up in bed."

"Well, you don't have to tell him that. Just make it sound convincing, and for God's sake remember what you tell him so you can tell me." Julian started to dress. "Sorry, Nance, I gotta go."

"See you tonight?"

"I'll call as soon as I can."

CHAPTER 16

With overwhelming attendance, the astronomical symposium was lauded a success. The gathering had become a historical event, attracting stargazers from virtually every country, including North Korea and China who had been absent for many years. Dealing with numerous astro-phenomena, leading scientists presented their theories. Some of the disciplines receiving special attention were astrobiology, astrophysics and astro-chemistry.

As president of the Astronomical and Astrophysical Society of America, Julian Rutledge had outlined his documentation on the nebula surrounding Zeta, the belt star of the Orion constellation. He then introduced Doctor Karl Cassim, the noted Egyptologist, for a historical and mythological perspective of this collection of stars.

Taking an easy thirty minutes, Cassim dramatized the importance of these stars to the ancient Egyptians, captivating his audience with gods, pharaohs, sphinxes, and priests. Stepping back to applause, he then yielded to questions from the floor.

With flair, Cassim entertained the rank and file with clear-cut answers that were laced with amusements. One of those questions, however, took him by surprise. It came from a tall, willowy gentleman in a white suit. With a slight impediment to a German tongue he asked, "Can you tell me the m-meaning of Tchaasu?" and he spelled the word correctly.

Trying to hide his amazement, Cassim said, "May I ask where you heard this word?"

Nonchalantly, the man replied, "Well, I read it in an old book and w-wondered what it meant. I knew it was an Egyptian w-word, but I could not find its m-meaning anywhere. Do you know this word?" he asked as his hand sliced the air.

Curious, Cassim looked at him for a long moment. The man stared back at him, challenging him.

Cassim began: "The word means the Seven Divine Masters of Wisdom, the Sages. The word is usually followed by the number seven. It is a word not often used and it surprises me that you came across it. May I ask how the word was used?"

Unresponsive, the man sat. He mouthed, "Thank you."

Cassim really wanted to pursue his question, even to ask it again, but other members of the audience flagged him with waving arms. He had little choice but to go on.

In the midst of questions, the lanky man in the white suit left with three other gentlemen.

Following Karl Cassim, Julian remarked about the eloquence with which Karl presented the ancients' scholarly fascination with the belt of Osiris. He publicly wished that his presentation would spark as much interest. However, after a very few minutes, it became clear that it did indeed.

By Julian's carefully outlined observation, the nebula, a mass of interstellar dust, gas, or both surrounding the star Zeta, had, in a short period of time, appeared rapidly. Too rapidly. The nebula, visible to the naked eye, was not immediately a cause for concern. Nonetheless, the mass of matter gathering at such an alarming rate without justification had triggered his investigation. Julian predicted that by the year 2002, with the nebula's present rate of growth, it would cloud over the entire constellation of Orion. What this meant, he declared, no one was prepared to predict. There were no imploding stars, smashing meteors, or other event to account for this unusual formation. Something from nothing wasn't viewed as an acceptable solution. When Julian had finished, the questions roared.

Soon after the question and answer session, the meeting was adjourned until Monday.

"Julian, can I drop you off at your hotel?" Cassim

asked.

"I'd appreciate that, Karl."

"Good, there are some questions I would like to ask."

Winding through the crowd, they left the auditorium. In the car Cassim said, "A very interesting subject, that nebula. Candidly Julian, what do you really think about it?"

Julian raked his hair, and said, "I don't honestly know, Karl. Whatever is causing it is very powerful and moving at a hellish pace."

"How long have you been tracking it?"

"For nearly a year."

"I have a wild thought."

"Let's hear it."

"Is it possible that this thing might have something to do with what happened in Egypt last month?"

"To be truthful, Karl, I don't know. To make something like that happen to such a relatively small area on this planet, is . . . is inconceivable. Think about it. Black skies, parting waters, a river dried up, all for exactly seven hours. Only if someone could micro-manage the machinery of heaven could he do such a powerful thing."

Their eyes saw the traffic in their path, but their minds were elsewhere, twisting with the possibilities.

As Cassim slowed near the hotel, Julian said, "Hear anything about the stolen seal?"

"Not a thing."

"Strange."

"Yeah."

CHAPTER 17

Maybe it was fatigue. Perhaps it was plain stress. Possibly, it was the excitement of the symposium. No matter the reason, Karl slept late into the morning and awoke groggy. A cold shower helped shake the dust from his mind, and strong coffee made him feel like himself again. In the light of the noon sun, he read the paper.

The telephone made its awful noise, and from the other end came Shawn's voice.

"Good morning, Karl, or should I say good noon?"

"I'm not sure myself, but I sense you have the devil on your tongue, Mr. O'Donnell."

"There's no fooling you, is there? Karl, there's someone here who wants to say hello."

A moment of whispers and giggles.

"Karl? Guess who?"

"Is that . . . No, it couldn't be. Nancy?"

"And all the while I thought I'd have you puzzled for at least a minute. How are you?"

"Wonderfully surprised. You have to be at the museum, am I right?"

"Right again."

"Have you had breakfast? Oh, my, I mean lunch?"

"Neither. I slept late."

"So did I. It must be in the air. Tell Shawn to entertain you. I'll be there in about twenty minutes."

When Karl got to the museum, Shawn and Nancy Gottlieb were in the main gallery. It was immediately clear; they were hitting it off.

Karl smiled. They could easily pass as brother and sister. Both were blond, pink-cheeked, blue-eyed, properly built, and attractive. Adding feather to the peacock, Nancy looked stunning in an orange sherbet dress that flattered, making the blond blonder, the blue bluer, and the pink cheeks pinker.

With a kiss on both cheeks, Cassim said, "Welcome to my home."

"Oh, Karl, this place is wonderful. I envy you."

"It is a joy. When did you get in?"

"Yesterday."

"Did you know that Julian was here for a convention?"

"Yes, isn't it a wonderful coincidence? I nearly ran into him in the hotel lobby right after you dropped him off last night."

"Dinner . . . we'll all have to have dinner together soon."

"I hope that includes me," Shawn said.

Smiling, Nancy said, "Of course, Julian would expect you. Oh, Karl, I've got to ask you a favor. Sometime before I leave Egypt, would you show me the pyramids?"

"I'll do better than that. How about after lunch?"

Her face glowed. Her liquid blue eyes danced with the prospect. "Oh, Karl, you're a darling." A peck on the cheek. A hug.

The attention caused Karl's face to redden.

"Why, Karl, you're blushing," Shawn whispered.

Nudging him kiddingly, Karl took Nancy's arm. "Have you seen the ostraka from Deir el-Medina?"

A blur pushed hard into them.

"My purse!" Nancy cried. "He took my purse!"

The man, woman, or boy streaked toward the front door. Shawn tore after him. An alert security guard stood astride in an archway with his arms extended to stop the thief. He was knocked down. Black garments flailed the air as the thief dodged statuary and ducked between cases. Visitors veered as if against a great current, and their garbled verbiage rose in moans of confusion and fright.

Shawn snagged his flowing wrap, spinning him to the floor near the entrance. But he was quickly on his feet, bolting for the door as security rushed after him. With force, the door slammed the wall as the thief jumped over the stairs, landing on the street. He raced through traffic into the enormous square. On the other side, a tan vehicle screeched to a stop. A door flung open. The thief dove into the back seat and the car peeled away, disappearing in traffic.

Shawn stood at the entrance, looking out. Breathless, Nancy and Karl came up behind him. Shawn turned, smiling. "Well," he said, "he didn't get your purse." He held it up.

"Thank God!" Nancy exclaimed. "My whole life is in that bag . . . and the seal."

Karl stared. "The seal?"

"I didn't have a chance . . . Julian didn't . . . Julian thought that you should have it, Karl. I was bringing it to you."

Shawn and Karl stared at each other.

"No, nay, nix," Shawn said. "I know what you're thinking. It's not possible. It was just a purse snatching, a blind act of attempted thievery."

Cassim said nothing. He lowered his lids to a squint.

"What's going on, you two?"

"It's a long story, Mrs. Gottlieb," Shawn said.

"Yes, it is. Now, if you are all right, I think we should go to lunch. I have a tour to give," Karl said.

"First," Nancy said, "put this in a safe place, please. It's beginning to give me the creeps."

"Good idea," Shawn said.

Nancy took out the package and handed it to Karl.

Chuckling lightly, he said, "I see it hasn't aged any. I'll be right back."

"All right," she said, after Karl left, "what's going on?"

Shawn said, "Lots of bizarre stuff."

"What do you mean?"

"Those seals . . . their predictions are just too damn close for comfort."

"I don't understand."

"A seal was delivered to a guy in Germany, a Doctor Schweiger, the same way Mr. Rutledge got his. It said stuff like the waters will part and the Nile will go dry. You did hear about that, didn't you?"

"My God!"

"Yeah, strange huh?"

"Why do you think this is happening?"

"I don't know. Change the subject. Here comes Karl."

Cassim put on his best smile. "How about the Mena House? They have a wonderful dining room, and it's right across from the pyramids."

"Wonderful, Karl," Nancy replied, taking his arm.

It was eleven miles from Cairo to Giza along the Pyramids Road once called Mena. As usual, the traffic was intense, but the light conversation made it pass unnoticed. Better than a tour guide, Cassim pointed out the famous mosques, the celebrated souks, and other points of interest.

The distraction for Cassim was a panacea after the weeks of inexplicable events. Nancy was all smiles and ears as Karl went on talking about his favorite subject.

"Egypt, above all others," he was saying, "draws on its history to attract the world to its aesthetic beauty."

They crossed the Kasr al Nil Bridge to Giza, passing Cairo University and the Botanical Gardens. Closer to the Mena House Hotel, Cassim pointed out the expanding net of sleazy nightclubs that was drawing so many Gulf Arabs. From rich to poor, the tapestry of Egypt was indeed colorful, with its limousines and carts, camels and taxis.

An attendant took their car.

"The Mena House was once a palace," Karl said, "built by Muhammad Ali's grandson, Ismail, around 1870. Ismail was also one of the people responsible for modernizing Cairo."

After a memorable lunch, Cassim took the blacktop to the Great Sphinx, pulling off the road near the front paws. Some twelve hundred feet in the distance, the awe-inspiring pyramids latched onto the mind. Rising nearly five hundred feet and covering thirteen acres, the enigmatic structure of the Great Pyramid demanded attention, analysis, and admiration. But most of all, it provoked a challenge.

"Pictures don't do them justice, do they?" Nancy said.

"I know what you mean," Shawn said quietly.

Cassim shielded his eyes from the blinding sun. "I've lived here all my life," he whispered, "and still the questions haunt me."

"What questions?" Nancy asked.

"Why were they built? Who built them? How did the ancients build them?"

"I take it you don't stand with conventional wisdom?"

Karl smiled. "That's not an appropriate word."

"What word?" Shawn said.

"Wisdom. And no, I don't stand there."

Shawn grinned. "A question, Karl."

"Be my guest."

"Who do you think the Sphinx really looks like?"

"I know what you're trying to do, young man, and I won't be led into a lengthy diatribe."

Shawn shrugged. He had failed.

"You don't think it's Khafre, his likeness?" Nancy asked.

"Absolutely not."

"Why?"

Karl tossed a look at Shawn. "All right. But I'll make it short. After all, Nancy, you are a guest in my country, and I am your host.

"You ask why not Khafre. In my mind's eye, it is very simple. The head is too small for the body.

Nowhere in Egyptian art or sculpture do you find intentionally skewed proportions. I believe that originally the Sphinx had the head of a lion. And that sometime in its very long history, someone re-carved it, claiming it as his own, as many pharaohs had done throughout their tenures.

"The Egyptians were fastidious in their re-creation of ideal life. Why then would they create such a magnificent sculpture with a head too small for its body?"

"I take it that you two have had some serious talks about this monument?"

"This and others," Shawn said.

"There is another reason," Karl ventured.

Nancy's eager eyes encouraged him.

"Look at the Sphinx closely. See how the head and face are much smoother than the rest of the body? How do you explain that?"

Nancy mused, "I see. It's a difference you wouldn't notice in a picture. But now standing here, it's very obvious, isn't it?"

Cassim went on. "As we know from the Dream Stela of Thutmose IV, the Sphinx was buried up to its neck in sand. The story goes that when Thutmose fell asleep in the shadow of the Sphinx, the Sphinx came to him in a dream. He was not yet pharaoh, but a young prince not in line for the throne. The Sphinx promised him that if he cleared away the sand, he would become pharaoh. The point is that for centuries sand covered the creature. Why then would the face not be weathered more severely than the rest of the body?"

Shawn asked, "Why haven't you published your ideas, Karl?"

"Maybe one day I will . . . to the consternation of my colleagues."

Lost in these thoughts, they gazed upon the Watcher of the Horizon in silence.

After a few minutes, Karl said, "Let me show you the first Wonder of the World."

As he drove closer, the pyramids grew grander, almost terrifying in their incredible largeness. The deep blue, cloudless sky stood in stark contrast to the beige of the stone.

"They give me chills just to see them in real life," Nancy remarked.

"I think that's exactly what they were intended to do." Shawn nodded.

Coming to the end of the parking area, Karl flagged a security guard and spoke to him in Arabic. He then parked very near the entrance of the Great Pyramid of Khufu/Cheops.

They climbed out. Nancy closed her door and gasped, "My God!"

"Impressive, aren't they?" Cassim whispered.

"Words fail me," she said softly.

With a sweeping gesture, Karl said, "This is another anomaly."

"How do you mean, Karl?" Shawn asked.

"There are too many things that don't add up. For example, here we have the architectural Wonder of the World, believed by most to be Khufu's tomb. Recently, some seventy tombs have been discovered there, to the west." He pointed.

"Among them, was found the resting place of Kay, a high priest who served under the first four pharaohs of the fourth dynasty. Three of these kings supposedly built the pyramids.

"Now, if you were pharaoh, a living god on Earth with all the power such a position entails, why would a priest, your priest, in your service, have a tomb with remarkable embellishments and tomb paintings, when none, none of these pharaonic monuments have a single decorative feature? Would it be too presumptuous to say that the king had no artistic taste? Or, that the priest jealously guarded his hidden passage to the next world? I don't think so."

"How do you explain it, Karl?" Nancy asked.

"Because I believe that the pyramids were built long before the fourth dynasty. And that they were never intended to be anyone's tomb."

"What then?" Shawn said.

"I think they were built to commemorate some fantastic historical event."

Absorbed in the moment, Karl's eyes mounted the steps, following the massive stones up to the pinnacle. "There was an interesting theory by an Australian fellow by the name of Robert Ballard. He believed that beneath the pyramids a vast series of tunnels, chambers, even a city existed for the holy ones, the priests and the Keepers."

Shawn said, "I read that Edgerton Sykes also believed this theory. He said there was a secret stone that swung to the touch and led to extensive underground passages."

"Strange," Nancy commented, "that no one ever found them."

"Not yet," Karl mumbled, "not yet."

"It's getting late. Maybe another day you'll show me the King's Chamber?"

"I'd be delighted, my dear."

CHAPTER 18

Even though they have stared, gawked, and gazed in wonder . . . even though His outer trappings have been brutally stripped away . . . even though His loins have been maliciously violated . . . even though the foul sons of man have trampled upon Him, in Him, around Him, pacing, prodding, probing, He stands.

"For thousands of years, He has defied reason. While civilizations have crawled, stood, fallen, and decayed, He stands. He stands first and foremost. He stands longer, larger, higher, thicker than any other. He is the first Wonder of the World and yet He stands. He is called the Great Pyramid of Khufu."

"Did you write that, Karl?" Nancy asked.

"No, a student of mine wrote it a few years ago. I thought it appropriate for our tour. A little something to get us in the mood."

Before the sun achieved its apex on Thursday, allowing shadows a rest, Cassim slowed to a stop.

Being a sensible woman, Nancy had left the pale orange sherbet designer dress she'd worn Sunday at the hotel. In its place, she wore sensible tan slacks and a loose white blouse. She was the first to get out of Karl's official vehicle and remarked that the breeze was rather indigent, a comment that drew narrowed brows.

The men wore varying shades of dull brown, except Shawn, who had poured himself into a pair of jeans. He followed Nancy, with Julian taking up the rear.

Karl had parked very near the entrance of the Great Pyramid, and from this vantage point they could see the hubbub of Giza. Tourists sprawled around the monuments with their guides: buggy rides, camel rides, and buses, a moving turmoil of people like ants upon a carcass.

"All right," Karl said to his friends, "this is our agenda. Shawn is going to be our official personal guide inside the Great Pyramid."

Shawn beamed. He stuck his hands in his pockets and shifted his weight. After all, it wasn't often that he was given this chance, especially as the three "tourists" included his boss, a curator of a museum, and a professor of astronomy. He felt rewarded and confident. He had been inside Cheops many times.

"He is going to begin with Al Mamun, who first broke into the pyramid, and who, after an earthquake, removed the outer casing stones from the pyramid to rebuild mosques and palaces."

Shawn's beam wasn't as bright.

Soberly, Karl went on, "He will then tell us the

importance of the Napoleonic Expedition, the Rosette Stone, Greaves, Lockyer and the Mameluke . . ."

Large eyes gazed upon Karl as if he were some rare jewel, as Shawn's memory scantly recognized these names in the confusion of history.

". . . Champollion, Petrie, Edwards, and their contributions."

All eyes settled on Shawn as his mouth dropped open in panic.

". . . and of course, the other notables I haven't mentioned which I'm certain he will remember."

Shawn's healthy tan reddened. His mind went blank. Deadpan faces waited. Karl's frown and nodding encouraged him to begin.

"Uh, hum . . . the, uh . . ."

Laughter echoed up the Grand Gallery as Karl's face cracked under the strain. "I had you going, didn't I?"

A sigh of relief. He mumbled, "You certainly did."

Nancy took his arm. "You thought he really meant it, didn't you?"

A weak smile. "Yeah."

The way was steep and narrow, and the lighting eerie. Suddenly, they entered the Grand Gallery.

"My God, the work in here. How long is this, Karl?"

"153 feet at a slope of 26 degrees, and the corbel vault rises 28 feet."

Nancy sneezed.

"Bless you," Julian said.

A few tourists were ahead of them, pointing, whispering among themselves. And, after an arduous climb, they entered the King's Chamber.

"Notice the blocks that surround us." Karl said, "They are estimated to weigh 70 tons each."

The tourists ahead of them left the chamber.

"Do you see the point I was making before?" Karl said, folding his arms. "The stark plainness of this the King's Chamber? If this were truly the Pharaoh's resting place for all eternity, one would think it should have the most splendid accoutrements."

"It is rather dull for a king, isn't it?" Julian commented.

"Was the coffer damaged by thieves?" Nancy asked.

"Tourists," Shawn said. "They chipped away pieces for souvenirs."

"What a shame!" she replied, running her fingers along the badly scarred pink granite. She sneezed, and then twice more. "Oh, my allergies!" she muttered. Another sneeze. As she caught herself with the tissue, her shoulder bag flung hard against the coffer.

Cassim quickly looked at her. "Do that again, would you, please?"

"Do what?"

"Hit the side of the coffer."

For a moment, she looked at him puzzled, but

unquestioning, then hurled her bag at the granite sarcophagus.

A low, muffled, bell-like sound escaped.

"That's amazing!" Karl said. "I wish I had something harder."

"How about a boot?" Shawn said, striking the coffer with his leather heel.

A resonating sound filled the chamber. With another strike, loose particles drifted from the ceiling; a deep, vibrating ring penetrated their bodies, and their eyes locked in wonder. A third strike brought a shattering rumble of stone grinding stone. Julian looked at Karl for explanation, but he saw only delight and followed Karl's eyes to the wall behind the coffer. On Shawn's fourth strike, a massive granite block was grudgingly swallowed by the hole it left.

Nervously, Nancy pressed against Julian.

"Incredible!" Shawn breathed as Karl examined the opening.

Inside the man-sized cavern, the eerie bell rang softly, repeating its toll endlessly, deep into the bowels of Cheops.

Shawn moved to Karl's side. "You're not going in there, are you?"

Cassim's eyes were lost far into the darkness. "I . . ."

"You don't have a light or even a string," Shawn persisted.

"I think I can find my way."

"Don't do it, Karl," Nancy begged.

"It looks like it ends about thirty feet in," Shawn whispered.

"It turns to the right," Karl was muttering. "Got a match?"

Shawn replied, "No."

"I've got some from the hotel," Julian said.

Again, Karl was muttering. "Just a little ways. I won't go far. I've just got to see."

He slowly stepped into the corridor and struck a match.

As if from the mouth of hell, a thunderous clapping of wings swelled, roaring into the King's Chamber. A huge, endless swarm of bats smothered the room in black, their horrendous screams adding to the horror. Nancy buried her head in Julian's chest and swatted her hair. Pushing her to the floor, Julian covered her with his body. Shawn leapt into the coffer.

For an unmeasured time, the symphony of sonar squeals bellowed in the chamber, magnified in the Grand Gallery and whimpered to death-like silence. Outside, a black cloud hovered, circling over the plateau and disappearing into the daylight.

Shawn's head peeked out of the coffer. "Is everyone all right? Karl?" He shot to the hole and called out, "Karl!" He blindly ran in. He had taken four paces when he met a force that blew him out of the corridor and against a wall. For a full minute he was stunned, then he shouted, "Karl!"

Nancy's and Julian's eyes were locked on the hole. It was so still, so quiet they could hear each other breathe.

Deep in the corridor, Karl came to his feet and lit another match. The foul smell of bat dung made him gag as he went a little way and turned a sharp corner. More steps and another turn.

Startled, he sucked air, backing into the wall. Unblinking eyes stared at him; outstretched arms reached for him. A life-sized woman body statue goddess stood beckoning him to a low altar. Her eyes seemed moist, seemed to tear as she gazed out from behind heavy black liner.

Karl's gaze dropped to her sandaled feet, rose to her multi-jeweled garment and settled on her horned crown which held the sun. She was beautiful, magnificent. He thought he saw her breast rise and fall. Suddenly, he noticed she was holding something in her outstretched hands.

"Damn it!" His fingers burned in the darkness. He struck another match in an explosion of light. "Isis," he breathed. His mind said, "Queen of gods, strong of tongue, mighty in words..." A sparkle emanated from what she held, a cylinder that seemed to snatch the light and send it back tenfold.

His heart pounded. His temples ached. Unthinking, he quickly grabbed the crystal cylinder, and the match flickered out.

He lit another. He looked, he stared into the darkness, into the empty darkness. Crazily, he ran further down the corridor, desperately trying to find her, turning one way and then another, coming to a blank wall. His last match burned out.

Karl could hear nothing, see nothing in the total blackness. In a panic, he shouted, "Shawn!" But the words failed somewhere in the maze.

Karl unbuttoned his shirt and locked away the cylinder seal close to his skin. If this was a trial of wits, he wasn't going to lose. He turned around. If he felt along the wall, he could go back the way he had come. Following his thoughts, he did. But he had run so quickly and turned so many corners, what seemed like a short distance stretched out in agony. Every time he turned right or left, he called out. Nothing came back but the vacant sound of his own voice.

Shawn leaned into the narrow corridor. He wasn't about to go any farther. "Karl?" he called.

The stillness was frightening. The smell of bat dung was stifling. Suddenly, scuffling noises came from everywhere. It sounded like many feet scampering in a basement. "Karl, can you hear me, Karl?"

"Keep talking, I ran out of matches." His voice seemed to came from a tube.

"Follow my voice, Karl."

"This way," Nancy said.

Footsteps on the stone floor echoed, making it hard to tell where they came from. Then they faded.

Karl called out again. It occurred to him that there might be more than one way back. It had been so dark and he had kept lighting matches . . . running . . . "Shawn! Say something!"

His voice was far away and weak, but they could hear it. "Here!" Shawn shouted, "Over here, Karl!"

More footsteps coming closer.

"I can see light!" Karl muttered, breathing fast and quickening his step. But the square hole of meager light didn't come closer. It was as if the floor stretched out, increasing the distance. He ran harder, faster, and abruptly stumbled into the chamber.

"Thank God!" Nancy exclaimed. "Are you okay?"

Karl had a grayish tinge to his otherwise tan face as he leaned against the coffer, trying to catch his breath. "I'm fine now," he gasped.

"What happened in there, Karl?" Julian asked.

"You're not going to believe me. I'm not sure if I believe me."

"I will." Shawn frowned. "I was blown out of that corridor like a paper wad out of a straw."

Karl looked at him. "You mean you tried to follow me?"

"Yeah, I tried."

"He's lucky he didn't get hurt," Nancy said.

"I wish you had."

Shawn cocked his head. "Why?"

"Because then I wouldn't . . ."

"What? What did you see?"

Karl cleared his throat. "It was there. And then it wasn't." He smiled miserably.

"You're not making any sense," Shawn said.

Hysterically, Karl laughed.

"Stop it, Karl, please."

"I'm sorry."

"Maybe we should take him to a doctor," Nancy said.

"*Him* doesn't need a doctor," Karl said.

"Karl, what happened in there?" Julian said with a smooth voice.

"All right, but you're not going to like it. I was lighting matches as I went along. Then I was out of matches and got lost. God, it was dark!" Karl looked back at the black square hole behind the coffer. "I saw something in there," he said, holding his chest.

Shawn asked, "What?"

"Isis."

"There is a statue of Isis in the corridor?" Shawn

shot back.

"No. I saw Isis in the corridor."

Nancy said softly, "Come on, Karl, it had to be a statue."

Julian smiled faintly. Shawn stared, expressionless.

"Her eyes teared. I saw her breast rise and fall. She breathed, damn it."

"Where is she now, Karl?" Julian said calmly.

"She's gone. I tried to follow her, but she disappeared."

Long moments passed.

"I know what you're thinking, but I am not crazy."

"Of course you're not," Nancy said. "You've just had a bad experience, Karl."

"Experience this," Karl said, as he pulled the cylinder from his shirt. "She handed it to me."

The crystal cylinder sparkled in the dim light.

"She handed this to me and disappeared. I tried to follow her, but she was gone . . . just gone."

"Oh, my God," Nancy cried, "another one!"

"Let's discuss this outside, okay?" Shawn said. "Can you walk, Karl?"

"I am having difficulty believing it myself," Karl said.

"Can you walk?"

"Yes, I am fine."

Julian and Nancy exchanged looks as they steered

Karl to the doorway, through the antechamber and into the Grand Gallery. Their steps echoed in the shadowy light, and before long the sun spilled into the entrance.

"It's just a little further," she said.

Julian looked at them strangely as they walked into the brightness ahead of him. "That's the damnedest thing I ever heard," he mumbled.

Overhearing him, Karl remarked, "It is, is it not? But now we know the truth. There are passages in the pyramid."

Seeing Cassim's party exit the Great Pyramid, several security guards rushed over with an explosion of questions about the black swarm that bothered the tourists.

Karl spoke ahead of his friends, saying that the bats had issued from the crawl space above the King's Chamber. Ordering the monument temporarily closed, he suggested that moisture carried in by the tourists had caused the bats' disturbance as well as salt deposits. Not challenging his professional opinion, the guards closed the pyramid.

The drive back to Cairo found them all speechless as each in his own mind thought about what had happened. They had stumbled, purely by happenstance, onto a secret passage that for centuries had been rumored to exist, had baffled the most brilliant minds on the planet, who had plotted and thumped and dug and measured and schemed.

CHAPTER 19

Night sweats . . . images of ancient gods . . . picture dreams of rituals . . . scents of heavy incense . . . embalmed corpses . . . Anubis applying unguents, reciting mysterious incantations, words of power above the dead . . .

As a member of the Supreme Council for Antiquities, Karl Cassim could not allow himself the luxury of unexplained, preternatural events to crowd his logical, skeptical mind. Nonetheless, the occurrences in question had, since he had descended the steps at the base of the Great Pyramid, been doing just that, clouding his mind, trying to reason logically with the illogical.

At his desk on November 8, he toyed with cylinder seal number five. He thought about the withered face of Malak and the subsequent inquiry. He remembered the surprised reaction of the police who were skeptical about the death, and although they could not explain the dusty, dry, cracked corpse, they did suspect him. The autopsy, however, blew their suspicions away. Malak was twenty-nine years old. The body that was dissected was that of an eighty-year-old man who had apparently died of old age, aggravated by fright, and unexplainably withered to dust.

To Cassim, the secret passage at the base of the pyramid seemed unimportant at the moment. So too did the piece of ancient, sparkling stone that he rolled back and forth across his desk. The simple truth, the simple question was...why? Why was all this happening?

Without enthusiasm, he made a copy of the cylinder. Afterward, he walked it to the basement of the museum, to the new acquisition room; a misnomer for many musty rooms varying in size and overflowing with research material together with an abundance of ancient artifacts.

Attending to the objects of human workmanship were a variety of able practitioners, labeling and sorting the wealth of Egyptian remains.

In the center of a wall in one of those rooms, a walk-in military-green safe had been encased in concrete. Inside were precious jewels that had escaped ancient tomb robbers. There also were the pre-Pharaonic cylinder seals, now numbering four. Cassim placed the last cylinder on the shelf next to the others. He closed the door and spun the dial.

As he left the room, Shawn barreled in from the stairs, anxious and out of breath.

"I'm glad I found you," he gasped. "Karl, I just came from the pyramid. The passage is closed."

"What?"

"It's sealed . . . as if it had never existed."

"What made you go there?"

"I don't know. I wanted to see. I wanted to go in. I brought flashlights and chalk, but I was too late. You're not angry are you?"

"No, of course not. I was going to go back with you as soon as I was finished here. Did you try to open it?"

"I tried. I tried to open it the same way we did yesterday. But no matter what I did or how I did it, nothing happened."

"Were you alone?"

"Yes."

Karl squinted, nodding. "My office," he said. "Let's translate the seal."

As they climbed the stairs, Shawn asked, "Why did you ask if I was alone?"

"For the same reason I closed the pyramid. I don't want anyone to know what we found. And evidently, we found nothing."

"But, Karl, we have the seal."

"Yes, that is the only proof we have, is it not?"

"What about Nancy and Julian?"

"You don't understand. If I acknowledge the fact that I have the seals now, what will be the consequences? First, where did they come from? You did not believe me at Abydos, did you? Second and most importantly, if I had seal number four, why did I not try to save all those people who drowned?"

"Yes, but you didn't know until it was too late."

"How do I prove that?"

"I see what you're saying. It's a mess, isn't it?"

"Please, close the door." Karl picked up the phone. "Sarah, no calls, no visitors."

He slid the copy to the center of the desk and adjusted the lamp. He pulled his yellow pad from the drawer. He thumbed through to a clean sheet.

Shawn leaned over his shoulder as he began to read the message.

"Please, don't do that."

"I was—"

"I know. But I'm not going to take any chances."

Shawn sat opposite across the desk.

Karl started again: "Beware! The eyes that fall upon this Providence . . ."

The curse shrieked from the page.

"Hail to you with your mouths equipped, the worthy of man. Make ready a strong place for yourself. For if you fail to make ready a strong place for yourself, you shall perish and the Earth will speak no more.

Thence, of thirteen moons take away seven. Of thirty days take away twelve, but place upon them the favored days of Great Well for the Great Year is at its zenith when the age of man will begin once more.

Sobmer m A San"

"All right," Karl said, "what do you make of that?"

Shawn leaned forward. "May I see it for a minute?"

Karl handed him the tablet.

He studied the page. "Okay. For starters, it sounds like some catastrophe is going to happen, something monstrous that will affect the whole world. It's saying that we should build something strong, probably like a bomb shelter. And it's giving a date."

Karl smiled, looking on, and encouraged him to proceed.

"Let's see," he thought aloud. "Thirteen moons was the Egyptian lunar year consisting of thirteen moons. Now, if we take away seven that would be June, no, July."

Karl nodded.

"The Egyptian months had thirty days and it says to take away twelve, but place upon them the favored days of Great Well. Karl, I don't remember what Great Well means."

"Very well," Karl said. He paused, thinking. "You know, this is quite remarkable."

"How do you mean?"

"I find it fascinating that they were so highly sophisticated and intellectually advanced in their observation of astronomy. To predict such an event proves that they were not only aware of precession, but also observed the zodiacal changes over thousands of years. You see, the Great Year occurs once every 25,920 years through the precession of the equinoxes. It is divided into twelve zodiac cycles of 2160 years. As you pointed out not too long ago, we are leaving the age of Pisces after 2160 years, and entering the Age of Aquarius in the year 2000."

"Karl, do you think it was possible for them to really have predicted such a thing so far into the future? I mean, according to mythology, to the Edfu Text, the Seven Sages advised Thoth in the epoch of the gods, when the gods ruled. How could they have known?"

A shrug. "My guess is that something happened. Evidently, some monumental event occurred that they observed. They are saying that it is going to happen again."

"Yes, but what?"

"For that, my friend, we will have to wait and see." His eyes settled on his desk, on the blue scarab taken from a tomb in the Valley of the Kings. "Where were we? Oh, yes, Great Well. You should know this. It comes from the *Pyramid Texts*. Great Well is her name. She is the goddess Nut, and her favored days are the last five days at the end of the Egyptian year. Remember, twelve months of thirty days is 360 days. They knew the year had 365 days and added five days. Anyway, these were the only days she could give birth by command of Ra. So, take away twelve and add the five days of Nut."

"That would be July 23," Shawn said.

Karl nodded. "Yes."

"In the year 2010."

"Yes."

"But what's going to happen?" Shawn asked.

"Maybe nothing. Maybe someone is playing some colossal game with us."

"Games don't part waters or blacken the sky. And games don't dry up rivers, do they, Karl?"

"Probably not."

Their eyes drifted in thought as the sun filled the room.

"Are you going to open the pyramid?" Shawn asked.

"Not until I have one more look."

"Can I go with you?"

"Yes, I want you to." Cassim picked up the phone. "Sarah, I want you to go home. I appreciate your coming in on a Saturday. Give your kids a hug for me."

Along the way to the Great Pyramid, Karl stopped at the Sphinx.

"What are you thinking, Karl? Is there something about the Sphinx that gives you a clue?"

"Not really. I want to check on the German team."

"I almost forgot," Shawn said.

"They say there are some anomalies in the Sphinx Temple. I would like them to explain. It will not take but a minute."

"What did they find?"

"Let us walk."

As they left their car, Karl explained. "Doctor Stiener presented a theory, a book and some interesting hypothesis regarding the temple to the Supreme Council for Antiquities. The book was written by Louis P. McCarty in 1907. McCarty wrote that there is a passage that leads from the northeast corner of the Great Pyramid to the Sphinx. I would not have given it much thought, but then, as you know, we found that passage. Stiener thinks the other end of the passage is at the Sphinx. They are trying to find it."

"Interesting theory," Shawn said. "What's the anomaly?"

"He claims to have found a 200 ton monolith that is receptive to sound."

"This I gotta see."

"Do not be so crass. How quickly you forget what happened in the pyramid. There he is."

"Doctor Stiener, how is it going?"

Disheveled gray hair stood on end. His small round glasses were covered with fingerprints. A black cigar was stuck in the corner of his mouth. "Hello, Karl, very well I think," he said in broken English.

"This is my assistant, Shawn O'Donnell."

They shook hands and Doctor Stiener pointed to

members of his team who were doing various tasks.

"We have found steps, Karl, similar to those at the pyramid. We are hopeful that they will lead to the opposite end of the passage, as McCarty had suggested."

"If it is true, it would save us the time of cutting up the plug," Karl said.

Shawn asked, "Doctor Stiener, I heard you found a huge stone that responds to sound. Is that true?"

"Yes, I will show you. This way."

Stiener led them through the temple to the farthest point away from the Sphinx. The gigantic stone block was twelve feet tall and nearly as wide. It was as smooth as glass, and he massaged it as if it were a pet. "This is it," he said proudly.

"Can you do it for us, Doctor Stiener?" Shawn prompted.

"Well, it doesn't work every time."

"Oh," Karl said, "what's the problem?"

"I'm not sure. Maybe the language, the inflection. It might be the harshness of the German language. In some respects, I think it is similar to ancient Egyptian, with its lack of vowels, you know. You see, we've only been able to move the stone twice."

"How did you discover it?" Karl asked.

"That was peculiar too, you know. Anger is what did it. Heinz, there, was working next to it, chipping off hardened sand, when he hit his thumb. Oh, he cursed very loud in German, and the stone moved! Karl, it swung 45 degrees!"

"What was on the other side?"

"A blank wall. But we didn't have time to examine it. The opening closed. Even the second time, none of us would venture inside for fear of being locked in."

"That is very interesting, doctor. When you discover the secret, please let me know. I would like to be a witness."

"Oh, yes, of course."

For several moments they stood and stared at the huge stone.

"By the way, Karl, I heard you closed the Great Pyramid," Stiener said. "May I ask why?"

"Bats. Lots of bats."

"Oh, my, frightful."

"Yes, well, we will be on our way. Good day, Doctor Stiener."

"Nice meeting you," Shawn said.

"Auf Wiedersehen," Stiener replied.

At the vehicle, Karl said, "Well, Shawn, what do you think?"

"I don't know. It would be something if it were the opening to the other end of the passage, wouldn't it?"

"Yes, it would be. It would prove what a lot of scholars have thought."

"Karl, do you really plan to remove the plug?"

"Yes, eventually." He started the car and drove to the pyramid.

To their disappointment, tourists were being turned away from the Great Pyramid by the guards. Cassim chatted with the guards for a moment, then he and Shawn climbed to the entrance.

Inside the King's Chamber, Karl felt along the wall behind the coffer, searching in vain for the door. "I do not understand this."

"I did the same thing, Karl. It was as if the passage was never there."

Karl thumped the coffer with his fist, then with one of his boots. The sound was different. The sound, it seemed, evaporated. "I have seen enough," he said.

"You think we should try forcing it?"

"That would require permission. It would be defacing the monument, and worse, I would have to give them a reason . . . to tell them everything. I . . ." Sweat suddenly poured from him.

"Karl? What's wrong? Karl?"

Karl grabbed his chest, leaning awkwardly against the coffer. Limply, he dropped to the floor.

"Karl!" Shawn lunged, catching him from hitting the floor. He laid him flat and unbuttoned his shirt. "Tell me what you feel, Karl. Karl?"

His eyes rolled as he moaned. "I can't breathe," he mouthed.

"Try, damn it. Try!" Shawn massaged his chest and tore off his own shirt to make a pillow.

Karl gasped.

"That's it, Karl, breathe. Take a deep breath, slow and easy. That's it, keep it coming."

A gray tinge blighted Karl's wet face as Shawn struggled to keep him breathing.

"Hang on, Karl."

His eyes seemed to focus. He seemed to stabilize.

"Karl, I'm going to get help. Don't try to move. Just breathe slowly, okay?"

He blinked his eyes.

Shawn ran through the Grand Gallery, stumbling with its angle, hollering for help. He shouted for the guards at the entrance. "Get an ambulance here now!" he screamed. "Doctor Cassim has had a heart attack!" He rushed back to the King's Chamber. "They're on their way. How are you doing, Karl?"

There was a nod, a lazy blink.

Because there was a health facility near the Mena House Hotel, an ambulance arrived quickly. Paramedics fought the incline of the Grand Gallery. In short order, oxygen was given. Tubes, looking like so much spaghetti, covered him. Injections were given. Monitors were hooked up and Cassim was placed on a stretcher and hurried to the hospital.

CHAPTER 20

"Oh God, Julian, I'm so glad you're here," she said as she opened the door.

"What's the matter?"

"Shawn phoned this morning. The passage is closed."

"You're kidding." He kicked the door closed. "How?"

"He said he went there early. He was going to check on it, maybe try to go in, but it was closed. He said you couldn't tell where it was. Julian, I'm afraid. This thing is getting too weird."

"There's nothing to be afraid of." He took her close and kissed her forehead. "No harm came to anyone. It was just a freak thing, that's all."

"I don't know how you can say that." She pulled away. "I love Karl dearly, but too many strange things are going on."

"Nancy—"

"Julian, I think we should leave."

"I can't leave. I'm hosting a convention. And besides, where would we go?"

"I don't know. The Riviera, Rome, Paris, anywhere."

"You're being—"

"Am I? Ever since that Tut exhibit—"

"A string of coincidences."

"Really? I don't believe in coincidences. How did an ancient Egyptian cylinder seal end up on your doorstep, halfway around the world?"

"Someone left it there."

"Yes, but why?"

"I don't know. What does it matter?"

"I don't know either, but I don't like it."

"Look," he said, trying to comfort her, "Thursday the convention is over. I have at least five days before Jennifer expects me back, although that doesn't matter anymore. We can go to the Riviera and spend some time basking in the sun. How does that sound?"

"I don't know, Julian."

"Now, now, just calm down. Everything will be fine." He kissed her.

"I suppose you're right."

"Of course I am."

They hugged, rocking just a little, nibbling an ear, a cheek.

"By the way," Julian thought aloud, "did Shawn happen to mention what was on the cylinder?"

"No. We didn't talk about that. Why?"

"Oh, nothing. I was wondering."

"When do you have to get back?"

"At three." He glanced at his wrist.

The phone rang. Their eyes locked.

"Something tells me all is not copacetic," Nancy said. She picked up on the third ring.

Shawn was in a panic.

"You're kidding!" she said.

"What's wrong?" Julian asked.

She held up her hand as she listened. "No, I don't know anything about Karl's daughter. Where did they take him? I'm on my way." She disconnected.

"What's wrong?"

"Karl." The words flew from her mouth. "In the hospital. Shawn thinks a heart attack." She began rushing about, grabbing her purse and keys.

"Oh, my God! How old is he?" Julian asked.

"I'd guess fifty-five, fifty-six. But Karl is healthy, he's not overweight, takes care of himself," she said, heading for the door.

Julian grabbed her in flight and wrapped his arms around her.

"I have to go to the hospital."

"Please," Julian said, "please, calm down. You're upset. I can't let you go like this."

For a moment, her eyes drifted then fell into his. "See what I mean? It's one thing after another."

"Things will work out, you'll see. We have to hope for the best."

"I'm a wreck," she said, looking drawn. "Poor Karl.

I feel so sorry for him. He's such a nice person."

"I couldn't agree with you more. Are you going to be okay?"

"I'm fine, really."

"Which hospital?"

"As-Salaam International, in Cairo."

"I'll find it. See you there about seven. Chin up, okay?"

As-Salaam International Hospital . . . 7:12 p.m.

The waiting area was quiet, disturbed only by the rustle of turning pages as anxious friends and relatives patiently awaited news.

Nancy sat in a corner unable to read in the large, tidy room with many chairs. A few plants were scattered here and there, and she mused at the flowing black robes and wrapped heads. The eyes behind the black cloth peered at her insensibly as she sat alone, unescorted, in her western attire. She shifted from her chair to the one next to Shawn.

A young man, apparently British, jostled the buttons on a television at the far end, bringing up the English language mode, and surfing the channels. Settling on CNN, he stood back and watched.

The lead story was the weather phenomenon known as El Niño. Around the world, freak storms, avalanches of rain, gyrating black tornadoes, and overwhelming tidal waves saturated previously sublime areas. Historically, dry places became inundated. Rain forests became dry. Global meteorological data processing centers in Melbourne, Moscow, and Washington reported rising temperature anomalies in excess of ten percent on all continents . . . except Egypt. The commentator noted that in her unique position of latitude—30 degrees north and one-third of the way between the equator and the North Pole—she, above all others, remained unscathed.

Rushing into the waiting area, Julian asked, "How is he?"

Shawn shook his head. "We don't know."

"We're still waiting for the doctor." Nancy covered her mouth. "Oh, Julian, I'm so worried."

"I wish I could get hold of his daughter," Shawn said, and made a gesture catching the attention of the young British man. "Would you please turn that down?"

"Sorry," he said, and lowered the volume.

"Do you know where she is?" Nancy asked.

"She's in Paris, but I haven't been able to reach her."

"She should be told. I know if it were my father I'd like to know," Nancy said.

With a practiced, unreadable face, a doctor pushed

through the double metal doors of the ICU. In an eye blink they were on their feet, surrounding him.

"Are you the Cassim party?" he asked, taking a step back.

"How is he?" Nancy burst.

"He is stable. Luckily, he was brought in quickly. It is still too early to make an assessment, but my best guess is that if he takes better care of himself he'll be fine."

"But he takes good care of himself," Shawn said.

"I can't debate—"

"Doctor," Julian interrupted, "what caused it?"

"It's called myocardial ischemia, a lack of oxygen to the heart. In other words, stress, hypertension. What was he doing when this episode occurred?"

Shawn said, "We were doing some research inside the Great Pyramid. But he didn't seem overly stressed. He's basically a calm person."

"It doesn't always show," the doctor said. "Sometimes people keep things bottled up and this is the result. If he doesn't slow down, it could lead to congestive heart failure." The doctor held their shocked eyes.

"When can we see him?" Nancy asked.

"In a few minutes. We are moving him to a private room, but don't stay long. He needs rest. A word of caution. Try not to talk about things that will excite him."

"Yes, doctor," Shawn said. "How long will you

keep him?"

"Three . . . four days. He is a relatively young man, and he is responding to treatment. The nurse will let you know when he's moved."

"Thank you, doctor," Nancy breathed.

He nodded and disappeared behind the double doors of ICU.

"He's going to make it," Shawn said.

Time dragged as they waited, as they watched another doctor come out of ICU to tell another family that they had lost their loved one. Moaning wails erupted, sending grief through the bones of those who still waited and wondered.

"I hate hospitals," Julian said.

Nancy held his hand. She made no comment, but the consensus was the same.

"By the way, Shawn," Julian said, "did Karl have a chance to look at the last seal?"

"Yes."

"Yes, what?"

"I wish to hell I knew what it was talking about."

"What did it say?"

"It says the Earth will speak no more, that some monstrous calamity is going to happen in the year 2010 on July the twenty-third."

"You mean it gave that date?"

"Well, not like that. It was mixed up with taking

away moons and adding days, but that's what it added up to."

"Did it say what kind of disaster?"

"No. I guess that's one of the things we're supposed to figure out. I don't know, Julian, maybe that's what set Karl off."

With authority, a nurse planted her feet, facing them. "Are you waiting to see Mr. Cassim?" she asked.

"Yes," Nancy said.

"This way," she directed, leading them through waiting and down the hall.

Coughs, groans, cries, and strange-sounding machinery stole their eyes as they followed the swaying skirt to a cul-de-sac with private rooms. Numbered 1 through 6, they were arranged in the semi-circle around a desk with three nurses.

"He's in four," the nurse said, "but only two can go in at a time, for no more than five minutes."

With that, Julian took the nurse by the arm a few paces from the others. "Look, we would like to go in together."

"That's against the rules," she said haughtily.

"Please," Julian said, "I promise we won't excite him. And besides," he put his hand on her shoulder with all the charm he could muster, "isn't it better if we only stay five minutes rather than ten?" He smiled with a full set of teeth.

She thought about that for a second as his smile defrosted her. "All right, but you didn't hear it from me." She gave him a little tilt and strode away.

"Let's go," he said.

"How did you do that?" Nancy asked.

"With charm," he said.

Karl was awake, in a gray room with a single small window. A weak light came from the bedside table and a tray, leaning over the bed, held a plastic pitcher of water and a paper cup. Oxygen tubes were in his nose. A heart monitor was pulsing on the wall.

"You look great," Shawn said.

"That, I would debate."

"How do you feel?"

"Very much better."

Nancy took his hand. "You gave us quite a scare, Karl."

"I did not do it intentionally, believe me."

"The doctor said you're going to be fine."

"Julian, one cannot trust doctors," Karl said. "Nonetheless, I am feeling myself at the moment."

"Karl, I tried to reach your daughter, but I didn't get an answer."

"Maybe it's just as well. I believe Nanette is on holiday. It would ruin her vacation. And what would she do but worry?"

"Shawn tells me that she lives in Paris," Nancy said.

"Yes, she is employed by the Egyptian consulate."

Another nurse came into the room. "Mr. Cassim needs to rest," she whispered.

"Do you need anything?" Shawn asked.

"I have all I need, thank you. So far, they have taken good care of me."

"We'll see you tomorrow," Nancy said. "Have a good sleep."

CHAPTER 21

It had been one week and a day, and Karl was back at work, armed with blood pressure medication and a new outlook on the frailty of life.

At his desk at the Egyptian Museum, he read a study Shawn had composed, concerning the King's Chamber, while Karl was recuperating in the hospital. Shawn had conducted an inch by inch survey of the stone wall behind the coffer, speculating on what might have triggered the door to open. However, after wrestling with every conceivable possibility, he concluded defeat.

Karl grinned. He appreciated the scholarly examination, the inventiveness of Shawn's work, but he had arrived at the same conclusion, albeit with much less effort. He set the folder aside.

"I'm sorry, Doctor Cassim." In tears, Sarah burst into his office. "He said I had to give it to you right away." Her hand trembled as she held out an envelope. "I didn't want to upset you. I am sorry, I'm so sorry."

"Calm down, Sarah. I'm not upset. What's wrong?"

"He didn't make any noise. I was at my desk

working. I looked up and he was standing there, staring at me. A big ugly man with scars on his face. He grabbed my hand and stuck that envelope in it. Then he crushed my fingers around it. He said I had to give it to you right now or he'd break my arm. I ran to your door and he left down the stairs."

Karl snatched the phone and dialed Security. "I want you to arrest a large man coming down the back stairs. Just a minute. Sarah, what was he wearing?"

"A black suit. A dirty black suit with a torn sleeve. His hair was parted in the middle."

"Did you hear that?" he yelled into the phone. After he hung up, he put his arm around Sarah. "You can go. I'll handle this."

He ripped open the envelope. The words screamed from the page.

Khan el Khalili eight o'clock tonight. Bring all cylinder seals or say goodbye to Nanette. No police. Release the messenger or she dies.

He knew Khan el Khalili bazaar, a maze of small stands, carts, and stores selling every kind of merchandise from carpets to gold.

His heart pounded as the sound at the other end of the phone was dull, repetitive, and without answer. He dialed another number.

"Egyptian Embassy, Paris office, how may I direct your call?"

"Nanette Cassim, please."

"Sorry, Miss Cassim is not at her desk."

"When will she return?"

"I don't have that information, sir."

"Please, this is her father. It's an emergency."

"One moment," she said, and put him on hold for what seemed like hours. "Sir, no one seems to know when she'll return. She didn't report for work yesterday, and no one has heard from her."

"Isn't that unusual?" he asked.

"Yes, sir. She is never late. Is there someone else you wish to speak to?"

"No. Thank you."

There was a knock on the door. Four men entered, one in handcuffs. He was a big, swarthy man wearing a dirty suit and a smirk.

"We caught him coming down the back stair, doctor, in no hurry at all," one of them said.

Karl glared at the scarred face. "Leave us," he said to the guards.

"But doctor—"

"Please, wait outside. There are some questions that must be answered."

"Yes, doctor."

The room was quiet. The smirk indelible. Defiantly, the man planted his feet and raised his hands. He wanted the cuffs off.

"Where is my daughter?"

"Safe . . . for now."

"If you hurt her, I'll kill you."

The man's dark brown, bloodshot eyes were cold and unimpressed. He shrugged.

Karl seethed. "Who wants the seals and why?"

Silence. He clanked the cuffs.

"I want to know who is doing this." Karl pushed him against the wall and grabbed his throat. "Did you hear me?"

Silence.

"Answer me or I'll tear your throat out!"

"Then she dies."

A pause. Karl let go. "Why are the seals so important?"

More silence.

Karl stepped back. He began to pace the floor and stopped, shaking his head. "The bazaar is a big place."

"You walk. They'll find you."

"And?"

"You give them the seals, all of them."

"And my daughter?"

"If you behave and the seals are turned over, she will be released."

"When?"

"When they are convinced they are safe."

"That's not good enough. When I turn over the

seals, I want my daughter. That is the only way."

"You are not in control here, Cassim. There will be an exchange, and it will be on our terms. That's the only way."

Moments passed. Karl walked to the door and turned. "Remember what I said. If you hurt her, there is no place in this world you can hide."

The man raised a brow and threw his eyes out the window, unconcerned.

Karl opened the door. "Release him. There's been a mistake."

Glances passed between the guards. Hesitantly, the cuffs were removed. The man in the dirty black suit walked casually away. Karl closed the door.

From behind glass, Nanette smiled perpetually on the desk. He took her picture into his hands, fingering her flawless skin, falling helplessly into her innocent eyes. "Nanette," he whispered, "I'm so sorry."

"Are you all right, Karl?"

He turned to face the voice. "Hassandi, what are you doing here?"

"Is that any way to greet an old friend? I heard you weren't well."

"I am fine."

"What's going on?"

"What do you mean?"

"Karl, your chief of security called the police."

"It was a mistake," Karl said, setting down the picture. "It was nothing."

"I understand that your secretary was assaulted and someone was put in handcuffs. And you say it was a mistake?"

Karl walked around his desk and sat. He fiddled with the turquoise scarab.

"What is going on?"

"I told you, it was all a mistake."

"You are not a very good liar, Karl."

The scarab turned in his hand.

"What is it, Karl?"

"If I tell . . ."

"Go on."

"I cannot. I just cannot."

"Karl?"

"If I tell you, you must promise you won't interfere."

"Why?"

"Because she will die. They'll kill my daughter."

"They're holding her hostage, aren't they?"

There was a nod.

"Lord knows you don't have any money; what do they want?"

"The cylinder seals."

"Why?"

"I don't know."

"There has to be something about them. What is it?"

"I wish I knew," Karl said.

But Hassandi Talib, the Minister of Police, wasn't buying it. This crusty, plump policeman with a lazy, twitchy eye couldn't be fooled. The food stains on his twisted red tie didn't say much for a law enforcement officer, but for all his shortcomings his mind was sharp to a fault. He tilted his fuzzy, graying head slightly. "One does not take a hostage to exchange for something worthless, does he, Karl?"

Karl didn't answer.

"So where do you keep them?"

A deep breath.

"Karl, I am your friend. These radicals need to be dealt with harshly."

"They are not radicals."

"What are they then?"

"Seekers of the truth."

"Karl, what are you talking about? They are criminals, kidnappers. They deserve to be put behind bars."

"They are not to be touched. Not until I have my daughter."

Hassandi rose, angry. On his knuckles, he leaned over the desk. "If you want to save your daughter, this is not the way. You must tell me everything."

Shawn walked in. "Oops. I'll come back later."

"Come in," Hassandi said. "Is this your new assistant, Karl?"

"Not so new," Shawn said.

Karl flipped a hand from one to the other. "Hassandi Talib, Minister of Police, meet Shawn O'Donnell."

They shook hands.

"Maybe you can talk some sense into him." Talib brushed his lip.

"What's going on?"

"His daughter has been kidnapped."

"What!"

"And your friend here refuses to cooperate with the police."

"Oh, my God. Why? What do they want?"

"They want the seals," Talib replied. "Now, why do they want them, Mr. O'Donnell?"

"Karl, please." Shawn pleaded.

Karl folded his hands and looked up.

"Karl, you've got to tell him for Nanette's sake...for yourself! You can't—"

"SHE WILL DIE!" Karl slammed the desk. "Don't you understand?" Karl leaped from his chair, sending it bouncing off the wall. "She will die!"

Coldly, Hassandi whispered, "She may die even if you give them the seals. Once they have what they want there are no guarantees, no rules, and no reason to release her. Do *you* understand? Your only hope is to cooperate with the police."

Shawn and Hassandi watched as Karl's mind

whirled and his face collapsed. Then, resigned, he shook his head and tossed the envelope across the desk.

"What is this?"

"Read it."

Talib's eyes swept the page. "So, the man you 'mistakenly' arrested was the messenger."

Karl walked to the window and looked down on the street. "What do I do now?"

"Do exactly as they say. I'll take care of the rest."

"You want me to give them the seals?"

"Yes. It's the only way."

"And when I do, what are you going to do?"

"Arrest them, take them into custody."

"And my daughter?"

"If she is not with them, we'll find her. We will find her, Karl."

Karl stared out the window not seeing the hustle of the street. He spoke to the glass. "My daughter comes first. You must promise me you will do everything you can to insure her safety."

"Of course."

Time slipped into the past.

"All right. If I have your word, I will do it."

"Very good, Karl. Now, tell me about the seals."

Karl's crimped breathing brought attention to the silence in the room. The humdrum of the city fell through the window. He sat and toyed with the scarab, fingering its intricately carved wings.

"You want me to tell him, Karl?" Shawn asked.

He slowly held up his hand. "They are ancient crystal cylinder seals," he began. "They are the prophesies of the Sages, the seven who at the beginning of our time recorded on stone a cycle of events that will affect all of mankind." He paused.

Hassandi looked on, more than curious. "Go on."

"As I said, there were seven Sages, and each one has left a message on a cylinder seal. By weird circumstances, even by very bizarre events, the seals have reached me. It is as if I have been singled out for some reason."

"And what do they say?" Hassandi unbuttoned his dark blue wrinkled jacket and leaned closer.

"They give predictions, but only in cryptic clues. They predicted what happened in Egypt a few months ago, when the Nile went dry and the sky turned black in the middle of the day."

"Incredible!"

"Yes, Hassandi, it is incredible. There is no mistake that these cylinders are foretelling some gigantic event. They also say that the seals must stand united. That's why these people want them all."

"But we don't have all of them," Shawn said. "One was stolen from the museum."

"And an attempt was made to steal another," Karl said.

"But what exactly is this big event?" Talib asked.

"I don't know."

Talib squinted. "Karl, why did you close the pyramid?"

"Because we found a secret passage and because that is where I got the last seal."

"So, now you have four?"

"Yes."

"And the passage, where does it lead?"

"Nowhere. It disappeared, sealed itself. All our attempts to re-open it have failed. So..."

"Still . . . it doesn't make sense. So what if they predict an event. Why would anyone go through all this for a stupid prediction?" Hassandi asked.

A shrug.

"The curse doesn't bother you?" Hassandi said.

"No. I don't believe in curses."

"Well, I have much to do before tonight," Hassandi said. "Do what the note instructs, exactly what it says. I'll be watching. Nice meeting you, Shawn O'Donnell." He nodded and closed the door.

CHAPTER 22

As planned, Karl entered the Khan el Khalili bazaar at eight o'clock. From Sharia el-Badistan, the main artery that runs with it, he walked among the tables, the shops, and the stands, which offered a myriad of goods. In the sea of bobbing heads speaking in many unfamiliar tongues, he meandered with the flowing masses, calculating and guarded, with a heavy paper bag under his arm, eyeing the crowd, searching for a face that would respond.

But without the sun deep shadows veiled age-old buildings that seemingly huddled closer together on the edge of night. Without the sun, the warmth slipped into bleak corners, fleeing from the hastily approaching chill. Without the sun, faces distorted, darkened, eyes hollowed and every movement became cause for concern. Lights and lanterns fought to force their rays through dingy glass and colors muted to the dark side. Like arthritic fingers, the bazaar wound its way down teeming crooked streets, narrow alleys, and any niche that would hold a table, a lamp, and a man ready to bargain.

Karl's eyes saw everything as he walked evenly, slowly, working the path through the market. Hassandi had told him that police officers would be everywhere, watching his every move. But he couldn't tell police officer from merchant, or merchant from shopper, and it didn't make him feel any safer.

Dressed in khaki slacks and a medium blue shirt, Karl looked like a tourist and blended with them as he walked among Egyptians clad in traditional garb. Merchants held up souvenirs and antiques as he strolled by, but a few words in their own language turned them away. A little further along, he saw two Egyptian women bargaining furiously for a gold bracelet, and wondered how long it would be before someone approached him. His nose picked up the scent of the spice market, and then the water pipes, but still there was no signal.

He turned an angled corner where Suleiman's Mosque came into view and a couple of vendors were having a shouting match. He walked on. His eyes gleaned the empty faces of the young and the old coming toward him, passing him by, as he searched for someone with an anxious glint.

For a moment, Karl stopped at a café window and scanned the reflection behind him. Someone could be following him to see if he were alone, waiting for the opportune moment. He saw nothing out of the ordinary. He put the bag under the other arm and turned away. He checked his watch. Twenty-five minutes had slipped by without a trace.

There was a scuffle just ahead; two young men were shoving each other. Fists began to fly. People were taking sides, shouting for a winner. Karl walked around the fray.

From behind, he was suddenly pushed with force and knocked down. Everything became blurred among the ankles and feet inches from his head. The bag he was so carefully guarding was yanked from his arm. A mass of heads and cloth swirled above him as he wrestled to his feet. Cursing under his breath as he thrust his body through the throng, he blamed himself for being diverted by such an ordinary prank.

On his toes, he saw the two who had set him up running through the crowd. He chased after them, screaming, "Where is my daughter?" But as they ran, they toppled stands and pulled merchandise from tables to block his path. They disappeared into an alley. So did Karl.

It was suddenly black. He had stumbled into a narrow strip that left little room to walk, let alone run. The alley corkscrewed up, down, and sideways. All he could think of was his daughter as he felt along the walls, the jagged bricks, determined to catch the thugs.

A split second of pain.

Karl woke up on his side with the worst headache he had ever known. Hassandi and Shawn were kneeling over him, saying something he couldn't make out. The light hurt his eyes. *Somebody must have pulled me from the alley*, he thought, because he could see people, see the bustle going on around him.

"Did you get them?" he asked, trying to move.

"Lie still," Shawn said.

Talib and Shawn looked at each other. Remorsefully, Talib answered, "They got away."

Karl squeezed his eyes shut.

"I'm sorry, Karl," Talib said.

"Sorry doesn't help my daughter," he said, struggling to get up. "Where were your policemen?"

"Don't move, Karl," Shawn said. "The ambulance will be here any minute."

"I do not need an ambulance. I need to get out of here."

"Did you see them, Karl?" Talib asked. "Could you identify them?"

"No. I had other things on my mind. But let me tell you . . . it is not over yet."

"What do you mean?"

Karl glared at him. "I will be hearing from them again . . . soon."

"Why? What did you do?"

"It's what I did not do, Hassandi."

Shawn's eyes focused on Karl. "You didn't."

"You are absolutely right, Shawn, I did not."

"Will somebody tell me what is going on?" Talib was becoming agitated.

Shawn said, "They didn't get the seals."

Talib looked astonished. "None of them?"

Karl swayed his head back and forth.

"What then?"

"Rocks. Nothing but rocks."

Talib's eyes became angry. "That's very dangerous, Karl. You don't know what you've done. When they—"

"Hassandi, if you had caught them, it would not have made any difference would it? Someone had to insure my daughter's safety."

Hassandi gnashed his teeth, saying, "You're going to get her killed."

"Think about it, Mr. Policeman. Now they know they will never get the seals if something happens to Nanette. Next time there will be an exchange, and it will be on my terms."

"You are a fool, Karl Cassim. You ruined everything. You could have had your daughter tomorrow. But no, you have to play games."

"You do not know that."

"They made a deal, Cassim."

"And you believe them?"

"We will never know now, will we?"

The cool kiss of an Egyptian winter crept through Cairo, caressing stone and brick, nibbling cheek and lip, laying a blanket of crisp air that will surely be tempered by the breath of a new day.

Karl refused to grace the hospital with his presence early that Friday morning, the ides of November, the Muslim Sabbath. Beneath a lump, his headache waned.

Hassandi arranged for two armed police officers to escort them to Karl's home in Zamalek, on Gezira Island's northern tip.

Karl mumbled sarcastically, "He should have been this efficient before."

Shawn agreed.

The police officers overheard. One made a face, but said nothing.

After they had checked Karl's flat, the taller of the two officers posted himself outside the door on the second floor, while the other, the burly one, took a position in the car and watched.

Shawn and Karl moved to the large homey kitchen. Karl held an ice pack on his head and they sat at the table.

As if it were a thought not meant to be heard aloud, Shawn said, "I wonder why Mr. Talib got so excited when he found out you switched the seals."

"I do not know and do not care. Shawn, I thought about it for a long time. And the more I did, I decided that I was not going to give up the seals. Not without absolute assurance that Nanette would be set free. As it was, I had nothing. I was simply supposed to give them what they wanted and wait and hope my daughter would be allowed . . . allowed to come home."

"Well, I suppose you're right," Shawn replied.

"Of course I'm right. Anyway, it's done."

Shawn smiled admiration of Karl's self-confidence. "Karl, how long have you known Mr. Talib?" he asked.

"It has been some time. Let me see, we first met when Sadat was assassinated. Yes, I believe that was it. Why do you ask?"

"Oh, nothing, I was just curious."

"I could use some coffee. How about you?"

"I'll get it, Karl. Just tell me where everything is."

As Shawn went about the yellow kitchen putting the makings of coffee together, Karl's mind wandered. Aside from an occasional housekeeper, no one had been in his kitchen in years. He pictured his wife Sinta, cooking breakfast, fussing with dinner, so many years ago. With his work taking so much of his time, he hadn't realized how lonely he really was.

Shawn filled two mugs with coffee as the aroma

sweetened the room.

"Shawn, you are welcome to spend the night. It's half past two and there's plenty of room."

"If you're sure it's all right. I don't want to impose."

"No trouble. I would like the company," he said, looking off into empty rooms.

"What is it, Karl?"

"Oh, I was just thinking. It has been years since I have had guests in my home, not since Nanette left for France. These walls have been dull with silence."

Shawn toyed with his cup and his sandy hair fell forward as he said, "How long do you think it will be before they do something?"

"I have no idea. I guess it depends on how badly and how quickly they want the seals." A bitter smile as he went on. "One thing is for sure. They are going to be damn mad when they open that bag."

For a measure of time, they sipped and thought, reliving the night and the day past, wandering even to the discovery of the first cylinder seal.

"I have so many questions about those seals," Karl mused.

"I wish I could help."

"If you could it would be damn convenient, would it not?"

"I suppose so. Give it a try. Nothing ventured, nothing gained," Shawn said. "I might surprise you."

"Very well. I will ask one that will drive right to the heart of it."

Shawn nodded pleasantly although skeptical of his ability to answer, knowing the far reaches of Karl's expertise.

"Why would they go to such extreme lengths to possess them?"

"I don't know for sure, but it seems to me that somewhere there was a mention of treasure. That I think would give someone the reason to kill."

"You're right. But the treasure of Thoth could mean something other than treasure of the normal variety." He sipped his coffee. "You make a good cup of coffee."

"My mother taught me," Shawn said, grinning.

Karl leaned back and nodded, rolling his eyes. "Thank your mother for me."

A moment later, Shawn said, "Is there nothing in the texts about the seals?"

"I have read and reread everything I know of. They are not mentioned anywhere. And there is damn little about the Sages. Why don't you turn in? I'm going to thump my mind for a while and see who answers."

"I am kinda tired, but you're the one who needs rest."

"I won't be long. Yours is the second door on the right."

"Good night, Karl."

CHAPTER 23

"Julian, you can't do this!" she said, her eyes round and accusing. "You promised."

"Please, Nancy, try to understand."

"I am trying, but you said we'd go to the Riviera. You said we'd have five days before Jennifer expected you back. You said—"

"I know, I know, but now Karl needs me more than ever. I feel compelled to stay and help him."

"Help him? Help him with what?"

"Listen, Nancy, I was with Karl for a half a day, yesterday. We talked at great length about his daughter. It was inevitable that the seals came into the conversation. Nancy, he believes there is a connection between the Belt of Osiris mentioned in the third seal and the nebula I've been tracking in Orion. To make a long story short, I agreed to stay on and do some research for him. The clincher was . . . the deal with the kidnappers went sour."

"Yes, I know. Why do you think I'm so upset? My stomach has been in knots ever since I heard. Julian, I feel for him, my heart goes out to him. That is one more reason why I was looking forward to leaving. I can't just stand by and watch him being torn to pieces."

"You could help him, you know."

"No. I can't. I'm scared, Julian. I'm really scared."

He pulled her inside his arms and held her close and tight, kissing her forehead, her cheek, her moist lips. "Nancy, you know he's in desperate trouble. He may never get his daughter back. I can't turn my back on him now. Don't you see, it seemed like such a small thing to do? I just couldn't say no."

She whimpered softly, "I know, I know. I'm just being selfish. I want you all to myself. I can't help it. I'm sorry."

"You have me, love. After all, I'll have my nights free."

"Julian, I'm sorry, but I can't stay here."

"Why?"

"I told you before. I'm afraid. This is all too weird, like some horror novel written by Stephen King. You're brave, Julian. I'm not. I can't take it."

"But you don't have to have anything to do with this business. You can stay in the hotel, lounge by the pool, and go shopping at the bazaars. We can have late dinners together and walk along the Nile. Honey—"

"Oh, no, not after what happened to Karl at the market."

"That was different. It's very safe and you know it.

These Egyptians are fine, caring people."

"Let's not argue any more."

"We're not arguing," Julian said. "I'm just trying to keep you here with me, trying to convince you you're not in any danger."

Quiet tears dotted her flushed face. She had so looked forward to this rendezvous with the simplest intentions, a simple untangled affair. It was to be a sexual outlet with someone new, different. She wanted the intimacy with a stranger, an encounter that would once again dazzle her senses much like the very first time.

But now, with doors opening in stone walls, bats as thick as mud blackening the light of day, someone snatching her purse and all the convoluted misadventures blighting Karl, the affair had lost all its attraction for romance.

She loosened herself from him and took a small step back. "I'm sorry, Julian, I can't stay."

"Just like that?"

"Yes, just like that."

"Isn't there anything I can say to change your mind?"

"Julian, I shudder to think about it. I can't explain it. Something inside tells me to run, to leave this place now, as quickly as I can."

"I'm so sorry."

"Don't be. We had a good time. We had something

that I had dreamed about and it came true. And I'm not ashamed to tell you that I wouldn't have missed it for the world."

"What will you do?"

"It depends on how soon I can change my reservations. I'm going to try for Rome, I think, or Paris. Then I'll go home. I'll tell David what happened, not about us, of course, but the other things."

"Will I see you afterward?"

"Certainly, if you visit the museum. But there can't be anything else. You understand, don't you?"

"I—"

"Of course you do. I'm not sure about my feelings for David, but I'm going to try to make it work. I think you'll do the same with your wife. We had a wonderful time, a wonderful affair, and I'll keep it tucked away in my mind forever."

"I wish I could change your mind."

"Julian, look. Karl needs you and I can't stay here. It's as simple as that."

For the last time, he took her into his arms and kissed her, a lingering kiss that said goodbye.

"Goodbye, Mrs. Gottlieb. I'm going to miss you very much," he whispered.

"Goodbye, Doctor Rutledge. You'll be in my dreams."

CHAPTER 24

Weeks went by without a word from those who held Nanette, slowly stripping Karl of his self-assurance.

Nancy, he heard, had left for Rome, while Julian, commingling the crafts of ancient mythology and modern science, was investigating his ideas about the constellation of Orion, the Belt of Osiris, and the Winding Waterway — home of the gods.

Re-reading the *Mythical Origins of the Ancient Egyptian Temple*, a translation by E. A. Reymond, Karl reviewed the only surviving texts mentioning the Venerables, the Sages. Though he had read it a dozen times since the first cylinder seal, he reviewed it again, hoping to find some tiny clue previously overlooked.

He noticed a note in the margin, a faded scribble he had made some time ago. He stared at it. It was a name, a name that had long ago disappeared from the roster of well-known Egyptologists.

Karl gazed at it, recalling the man. His name was Sir E. Osborne Hunsdon, a man known for his strong convictions, his dogged pursuit of the facts; a man whose voice had shaken the archeological world to its very foundation by proclaiming the age of recorded history to be in error by twelve thousand years.

Karl smiled as he remembered Hunsdon's explosive paper. He had pointed a finger at past popular historians, accusing them of altering facts with artificial truths. He had exampled ancient Egyptian religious and other supporting texts, selecting passages from its bowels whereby such things as iron, hollow drills, and, most importantly, precession were commonly mentioned and understood. Precession, he pointed out, is the wobble of the earth's rotating axis through the constellations. This is noted by an imaginary circle in the heavens above the North Pole. These things, these ideas, he went on, were said not to exist in that epoch.

Furthermore, Hunsdon cited the construction of the Sphinx and the Great Pyramids as proof of the technical wizardry conceived over a great length of time. Over many thousands of years, Egypt developed into a sophisticated civilization recording its history. That by and of itself testified to its rightful age.

However, the league of learned men denounced the facts, calling them mythological.

But Sir Hunsdon fired back, revealing their religious roots which caused them to base their professional opinions solely on biblical chronology.

Sir Hunsdon's work was, therefore, publicly and privately deemed positively apocryphal.

Karl's memory of the melee was clear as he ruefully smiled to himself. "One religion denouncing another on religious grounds. What an idiotic world," he muttered.

Thumbing his chin, Karl thought about Hunsdon.

For years, Sir Hunsdon had been the foremost authority on ancient Egypt. He was widely published and respected. Then, following the highly publicized "difference of opinion" he disappeared from public view. However, this loudly thundered disagreement, it was rumored, was not the cause of his withdrawal because Hunsdon was a fighter, famous for his flamboyant and crusty style. Even now whispers concerning the actual reasons still persisted.

Suddenly, Karl's enthusiasm swelled. If he had any hope of solving the mystery of the seals and answer the many questions that robbed his sleep and intellect, this was the man.

In a lengthy letter, Karl outlined his entire adventure with the cylinder seals, describing the events surrounding each one. He concluded by introducing the foreign element that had taken his daughter hostage. While posting his letter to England, he hoped that Sir Hunsdon could bring out the sun on an otherwise very dreary day.

"Oh, Karl, I was just going to come looking for you," Shawn said.

Karl replied, smiling. "I came looking for my yellow pad, and I see you have it."

"You don't mind, do you?"

"Not really."

"You weren't here when I came in and Sarah thought you wouldn't mind . . ."

"So, why do you have it?"

"I had this idea about the seals. It occurred to me that every time one showed up, it was the beginning of the month. I checked your famous yellow pad and look what I found." Shawn handed him his pad.

"This is . . . Every time a seal appeared, it was on the seventh day of the month. What made you think of this?"

"Well, I'm not exactly sure," Shawn replied. "But yesterday I was at the University with Julian. Maybe that's what got me thinking. He was trying some new astronomical software on their new computers. He took the information you had given him from the seals. You know, the length of the Great Year, the Belt of Osiris in Orion, and the Sphinx. He kind of worked backward with the constellations, entering their duration of 2160 years for each cycle. He used the Age of

Leo for the Sphinx, as you suggested, and he input all the information about the Egyptian zodiac. Julian explained the procession of the equinoxes and how many years it takes for all the signs to pass through one complete cycle.

"With this new software, he can position the stars, the constellations backward and forword for thousands of years. And here's the best part. Based on ancient Egyptian records and using the zodiac of Dendera, he estimates the Sphinx to be 11,000 years old, and built during the Age of Leo."

Karl smiled. He handed a magazine to Shawn. "Turn to page four," he said.

"What is it?"

"Read. It will only take a minute."

Shawn opened to the page and read:

"Rain Determines Age of Sphinx. John Anthony West and Robert Schock of Boston, respected authorities of geology and paleontology have estimated the age of the Sphinx to be between 11,000 and 15,000 thousand years, based on the weathering patterns of the limestone, and their study of erosion from rain. These conclusions have inflamed the status quo."

Shawn looked up. "Well, Karl, it looks like you were right."

"Yes, but I couldn't prove it. Shawn, let me see my

pad for a moment. I have an idea."

Karl flipped the pages to his notes on the second seal. He read aloud, *"Be fleet of foot for time has spent and the heavens hold no mercy. Seek the Watcher of the Horizon for in his recline lies the secrets of the universe. To know him look to the heavens."*

"There are several clues here that I didn't get before. We know the Watcher of the Horizon is the Sphinx. But it says, 'For in his recline lie the secrets of the universe.' In his recline . . . that I take to mean under him. I wonder if the seal wasn't referring to the Hall of Records."

"Do you really think it exists?"

"It is possible. But finding it is another story."

"Julian thinks that if he goes back far enough in time, the stars can solve some of the problems we're having," Shawn said.

"In a way, it all seems to be coming together. I must admit, Shawn, that I find this both exciting and depressing. Sort of a bittersweet journey to . . . to . . ."

". . . some kind of catastrophe?"

"Not very encouraging, is it?"

Shawn shook his head. "Karl, still nothing from the captors or Talib?"

"Nothing." Karl seemed to drift. A pained expression darkened his virile face.

Shawn quickly changed the subject. "Have you

read the papers lately?"

"Not really. I always say I'm going to, but I gather them up and end up throwing them in the trash. What have I missed?"

"The weather."

"There's nothing unusual going on."

"Not in Egypt, but every place else has been going bonkers. Back in the U.S., in the south and the midwest where I come from, tornadoes and floods have been wreaking havoc. It's happening all over the States: heat waves, fires, storms, and wind gusts of a hundred miles an hour. The same in Europe. China, India, and Japan have had earthquakes, volcanic eruptions, and more floods."

"Don't get too excited about it. There are logical reasons. El Niño for one."

"You think El Niño is responsible for earthquakes?"

"Maybe not directly. But if memory serves, every five hundred years weather patterns change. It's historical record. Places that were once lush become deserts. Temperatures change. Now, if you are finished with my pad, I have work to do."

"Oh, sure."

"And by the way, thank you for the research. The seventh of the month; I'll have to remember that. I'll be in my office."

As Karl topped the stairs to the second floor, Hassandi Talib was talking with Sarah. She was saying, "My hand is just fine," as Karl approached her desk.

In a greeting in Arabic Karl said, "Sabaah el-kheer," good morning.

In response, Talib said, "Sabaah en-nur."

"I hope you bring me news."

"Let's talk in your office."

"Of course." Karl led the way and offered a chair. "Why so mysterious?"

Hassandi's voice became formal and authoritative. He buttoned his wrinkled jacket and sat straight. "Karl, are you sure you didn't recognize any of the men who took your package?"

"As I told you, Hassandi, I was knocked down from behind. I could not see who it was. Why do you ask?"

"In the past few weeks, we questioned the vendors in the vicinity of the incident. One of them said he saw one of the three involved. A light-complexioned young man with sandy hair."

Karl leaned into his desk. "I only saw two men."

"And," Hassandi added, "the man the vendor described is . . . Shawn."

Karl shook his head. "That's totally ridiculous. Shawn is not the only fair-complexioned, sandy-haired man in Cairo."

"We know that, Karl. But—"

"It makes no sense at all," Karl interrupted.

"Shawn has access to the seals any time he wants them. And to my translations. There would be no godly reason for him to—"

"We have concluded that he has accomplices. Shawn may have staged the theft at the bazaar to remain incognito. After all, you said there will be seven seals. I think he wants them all, and the best way to do that is to remain anonymous, as well as your friend."

"Absolutely preposterous!"

"Karl, I mean to question him."

"You are wasting your time."

"Where can I find him?"

"If you insist on making a fool out of yourself, I demand to speak to him first."

"Where is he?"

"I have no idea."

The two men glared.

"I mean to question him at my headquarters."

"If I find him, I'll bring him to you."

"Karl, this is not your affair. Don't interfere."

"Damn it, Talib, this is my affair! He is my friend, my associate, whom I trust!"

With a deep breath and a brush of the lip, Hassandi said, "When will you bring him in?"

"If I can find him, I will bring him in tomorrow morning at ten o'clock. And I will remain with him."

"Karl, please."

"You should be out there, Hassandi," he said, pointing to the window, "searching for the real culprits and my daughter."

Brashly, Talib stood and stormed to the doorway. "Ten o'clock," he said, and slammed the door.

Karl went to the door, hesitating for a moment, thankful that Shawn had not come up from the basement and walked in without knocking as usual.

Giving Talib a few minutes to leave the museum, Karl hurried to Sarah's desk. "Sarah, I have a favor to ask. From now on, I don't want you to tell Talib anything about Shawn, or me, or any excavations we might be doing. Would you do that for me?"

"Doctor Cassim, of course. My lips are sealed. He's being nasty, is he?"

"Something like that. Thank you, Sarah."

On his way to the basement, Karl scanned the museum as far as he could see. Passing one of the guards, he said, "Have you seen the Minister of Police?"

"He just left the building, sir."

"How about Shawn? Have you seen him?"

"No, not yet. I think he's late today, doctor."

"Very well."

Shawn was at his desk where Karl had left him a short while before. He sat on the other side of the desk. "How is it going?"

"Fine."

Nervously, Karl's eyes darted around the room.

"What's wrong, Karl?"

"I have some disturbing news."

"Not about Nanette?"

"No, no." Karl took a deep breath. "It concerns you."

Shawn's eyes grew round. His brow wrinkled. "Disturbing? About me?"

"Talib thinks you were one of the attackers at the bazaar."

Shawn blinked. "You don't believe that, do you, Karl?"

"Of course not. He's a fool."

"Karl, I was with one of his men during the whole thing!"

"He says a vendor described you. I know it's stupid. But he wants to talk to you. I told him that if I found you, I would bring you to headquarters at ten o'clock tomorrow morning."

"Karl, I would never do such a thing," he whispered.

"I know. It will all be straightened out."

The interview with the Minister of Police was lengthy and heated. The questions were repetitious and demeaning. Most disturbing was the fact that Shawn's witness, the officer who had been at his side at the bazaar, was on a leave of absence.

Hassandi assured them the officer would be questioned and things would be resolved.

During the month of December, Karl had dashed off three more letters to Sir Hunsdon. Allowing for the slow post and the time of year, he did not think it extraordinary that there was no reply.

Near the end of the month, he decided that in early January he would fly to England.

CHAPTER 25

Karl decided to check into the hotel and proceed immediately to meet with Sir Hunsdon.

Knives of snow fiercely stabbed the windshield in well-below-freezing temperatures. A vast chiseled blanket lay tightly against the ground, where brittle flakes crunched beneath the taxi's weight as the vehicle slowly, perilously searched for a horseshoe drive 500 meters off the road. Wet depressions warned of a creek bed off to the left, while a stand of pines howled eerily in the wind. Shapeless boulders, here and there, suggested an untraveled way which spread in untouched white against the black of night. As if a curtain were suddenly drawn at the hairpin curve of the shoe, a Tudor mansion stretched across the landscape. A considerable stoop jutted out beneath the main door like a pompous chin, and the taxi slowed to a stop.

The passenger said, "You're sure this is Hunsdon House?"

Warily, the driver nodded.

"Well, what's wrong?"

"Nothing . . . sir."

"What's wrong, damn it?"

The driver scooted down in his seat. "There are rumors about this place, sir."

"Rubbish. Wait for me," Cassim said.

Nervously, the cabby bit his lip as his eyes flashed from the house to his rearview mirror.

Karl stepped into the wind. It whipped his heavy coat like a flogging as he gathered his collar, in ankle-deep snow, bowing toward the front door. Bootless, he struggled with balance while climbing the vague outline of stairs as the gale nipped his sun-drenched skin. At the large seven-panel portal, ice splintered as he freed the knocker and struck the door.

Shivering uncontrollably, he squinted at his watch. "Useless," he muttered. Stepping back, he shielded his eyes with his briefcase, leaning to the left and then to the right. The house remained lifeless. Again, he struck the door meaningfully and wondered if the wind hadn't carried away the sound. Minutes passed. Doubt crossed his mind.

Finally, there came a glow in the arc window above the door. Bitterly creaking, the door opened. A tall, sizable, goateed, black-suited man filled the entrance. A practiced smirk reeked with imposition.

"What is it?" he said briskly.

Cold and put out, Karl said, "That isn't exactly the greeting I expected."

"I beg your pardon, sir, but at half past two in the morning, you could expect little else."

Karl scoped the man from head to toe. "This is Sir E. Osborne Hunsdon's house, is it not?"

"It is."

"Well, I'm Doctor Karl Cassim."

With indignant arched brows the man stared.

"Sir Hunsdon is expecting me."

"I'm afraid not, sir."

"But I sent a telegram announcing the day and time of my arrival. Of course he's expecting me. He did receive my wire, didn't he?"

"Yes, sir. I mean, no, sir."

"Good God, man, what is your name?"

"I am Otto, sir."

"What is your position here, Otto?"

"Sir, I am steward to the House of Hunsdon."

"Well, then, as steward I demand that you present me to your employer."

"That is not possible, sir."

"Why not?"

"Sir—"

"Look, Otto. I am growing numb. May we discuss this matter indoors?"

"Do come in, sir," he said without hesitation.

Otto closed the door and turned on more lights in the massive hall.

"All right, Otto, why not?"

"Oh, very well. Sir, Doctor Hunsdon does not receive, nor has he received, guests in years. I can make no exceptions. My apologies, sir."

"But my letters, my telegram?"

Otto pointed to a long table next to a door some twenty feet down the hall. Mail had been neatly piled in stacks, filling it completely. It was not possible to tell how many months' worth of mail was there.

"Your entire correspondence rests there," he said.

"You mean to tell me that Sir Hunsdon hasn't opened any of it?"

"Regretfully, no, sir."

"But . . . but why?"

"Doctor Cassim, Sir Hunsdon works very long hours for days on end. He considers mail to be an intrusion, an invasion of privacy, a disturbance, if you will."

Karl looked befuddled, distraught.

"May I be permitted a question, sir?"

"Yes, Otto."

"Didn't you think it curious, unusual that Doctor Hunsdon hadn't responded to your letters?"

"Well, not really. They did not require an answer. I simply detailed information that I had gathered. I only made vague suggestions about discussing my findings with him some time in the future. But, lately, a number of things have happened. I felt desperately in need of his considerable talents. I explained all this in my telegram. Otto, it is urgent that I speak to him."

"I take it then that you have never met Doctor Hunsdon directly, sir?"

"No, I'm afraid not."

"Well, sir, there is very little I can do. Perhaps another time, Doctor Cassim?"

"Look, Otto, I have happened on certain discoveries said not to exist. Because of these discoveries, my daughter has been taken hostage. Don't you understand, I must see him?"

"Doctor Cassim, I do extend my sympathy, however, I will enlighten you the best I can. First, Doctor Hunsdon receives no one. Those are my instructions. Secondly, Doctor Hunsdon does not speak, nor has he spoken for over ten years. He has had no contact with the outside world whatsoever. Thirdly, it is half past two in the morning and hardly a proper time to visit, important or no."

"That's impossible. I have every tape he made. I've collected his books, his translations of ancient Egyptian Texts. That's why I'm here. I've come thousands of miles to see him and I'm not leaving until I do."

Otto took a deep, tired breath. "Doctor Cassim, I do understand your dilemma. I cannot promise you anything, but the best I can do is speak to him in the morning. Perhaps—"

"You tell him this. Tell him there are seven cylinder seals written by the Seven Sages, and I have five. Do you understand?"

"Yes, sir. I will do my best, sir."

Karl bolted to the door and flung it open. He stepped over the threshold and peered into the thicket of darting snow. His taxi was gone. He turned back into the house. Disgruntled he said, "Otto, would you be so kind as to call me another cab? It seems that my driver has gone."

"I'm terribly sorry, sir, but we have no telephone."

Karl gave a woeful turn of the head, sighing audibly.

"A moment, please, sir." Otto strode to the long table near the door down the hall. He glanced over the stacks of mail, waving a hand as if he were certain of every piece. He pulled out Karl's telegram from the last stack near the edge and opened it. Reading it with moving lips, Otto's eyes flipped from the page to Karl and back again, much like an inspector at Immigration, verifying all that he had said was true. Briskly, he then returned it to its exact spot on the table. Walking back, he said, "Doctor Cassim, I may be reprimanded for doing so, but I will take it upon myself and permit you to spend the night here."

"Thank you," breathed Karl.

"This way, sir."

Filling his eyes with trappings of elegance, Karl

followed. Lavish Persian carpets snaked down halls decorated with gilded portraits of relatives, flowers, and hunting scenes. He was ushered to the second floor of the east wing where marble pedestals mounted with bronze busts littered the way. At the end of the hall, Otto stopped at the last door. In spite of the apparent cleanliness, the surroundings reeked of must and age.

Otto opened the door. "I hope you find these accommodations suitable, Doctor Cassim."

"Thank you again, Otto. I appreciate what you've done."

"Not at all, sir. You'll find suitable clothing in the wardrobe. I believe they will fit modestly, sir. Breakfast will be served at eight o'clock in the main dining room. Good night, sir." He closed the door.

Karl meandered to the four-poster bed some distance across the room where he flung his coat. He looked around the massive chamber. A fire was blazing in the walk-in fireplace as if it had just now been tended. The bed had been turned down and the pillows fluffed. Off to the side, lights were lighted in the sitting room and down the hall the lavatory was open and lit. "Strange for not being expected," he mumbled, "damn strange, indeed."

At six twenty-nine the next morning, his eyes burst open. Perhaps it was the strangeness of the surroundings or some foreign, distant sound; and maybe it was the chill that had seeped in as the fire dwindled to soft white ash. Sitting up, he swung his stockinged feet to the cold parquet floor and felt his body complain from the ironstone mattress. His joints ached as he stood and ravenous sounds moaned from his stomach. He hurried to the fireplace and stacked wood on the smoldering ash. With several longwinded breaths, he kindled a flame and the warmth returned.

He checked the time . . . a quarter of seven. Anxious to meet his host, he went to the wardrobe and tried on a suit. He found that they fit him as well as his own. After bathing and grooming, he donned the fresh clothing and hurried down the halls and stairs. The beamed ceilings caught his eye, as did the great throne-like chairs set here and there between tapestries.

Suddenly, he realized that these areas were all lit, more than lit. For a moment, he thought about standing on the stoop outside looking into a lifeless house and wondered who or how many tended to Hunsdon House. "Strange," he mumbled. He hadn't seen a soul other than Otto.

With a few more steps and through an archway, he found the immense dining room. Twenty-four burgundy velvet chairs pressed against a shiny cherry table. On the sideboard, ornate candelabra grasped tall candles that never felt a flame, while a massive crystal chandelier gleamed gracefully from above. Sconces like turned up fingers sprayed haloes on the walls. Leaded windows opposed him from across the room, catching his reflection as snow speckled the glass.

From a distance, heel and toe clacked against the wooden floor, growing louder. A door pushed into the room and Otto entered, carrying a large tray. He set it on the sideboard. "Good morning, sir."

"Good morning, Otto."

"Coffee will be a moment. How would you like your eggs, sir?"

"Scrambled, please."

Otto arranged plates and silver next to the tray. "Do you wish to be served, sir?"

"I'll help myself, thank you."

"As you wish." Otto approached the door.

"Will Sir Hunsdon be joining me for breakfast?"

"I rather doubt it, sir. He was up most of the night, working."

"But you said it was late when I arrived, and you couldn't disturb him."

"I beg your pardon, sir. But I distinctly remember saying that he did not receive guests."

"Whatever! Does he know that I am here? Waiting?"

"No, sir."

"Why not?"

"Because he sleeps, sir."

"When will he not be asleep?"

"This evening, sir."

"This is very disconcerting, Otto."

"Yes, sir."

"I repeat . . . I have vital business to discuss with Sir Hunsdon. Do you understand?"

"Coffee is ready, sir."

"Coffee? Didn't you hear me?"

"Sir. May I remind you that this is Sir Hunsdon's house, that this is Sir Hunsdon's schedule, that I am Sir Hunsdon's steward, and, pardon me, sir, but there isn't a damn thing I can do about it. Do you wish to leave, sir?"

"No, I do not wish to leave."

"Coffee, sir?"

"When?"

"When what, sir?"

"When will you see him?"

"As I have said, this evening."

"You're impossible."

"Yes, sir. Coffee, sir?"

"Yes."

"Breakfast?"

"Yes."

"Will that be all, sir?"

"Yes."

After breakfast, Karl spent the day in Hunsdon's

enormous library. Lunch was brought in on a tray with Otto's usual arid pomp. But Karl hardly touched the tray. His interest was consumed by Hunsdon's handwritten, in hieroglyphics, collection of the ancient Egyptian funerary texts, known as the *Book of the Dead.*

In great detail, Hunsdon had organized the rituals, the sacred Words of Power, the gates to the netherworld with all their pageantry. Under glass were numerous papyri unknown to others in the academic world.

The library was a treasure trove. It contained original work from nearly every historian, archeologist, philosopher, or mystic who had ever been to or lived in Egypt. But the most remarkable surprise was Manetho's Kings List.

Karl knew that during the reign of Ptolemy I, a high priest named Manetho had compiled a list of kings dating far beyond what is accepted as the First Dynasty under Menes, the first king. Karl had seen the remains of the Kings List, fragments of god-kings and the dynastic period, in Turin, Italy.

But now, he stared at the entire papyrus of Manetho—some fifteen feet long—under glass, in absolutely pristine condition, on a shelf in Sir Hunsdon's library.

As an Egyptologist, as a member of the Supreme Council for Antiquities, as curator of the world famous

Egyptian Museum, Karl Cassim gaped in awe at a priceless collection of work, undoubtedly the finest in the world. So lost had he become in the depths of discovery that when Otto appeared, he was shocked that the day had slipped by. It was eight-fifteen.

Otto said, "Doctor Cassim, Sir Hunsdon will see you now. However, I must first explain the rules."

"Rules? What rules?"

"I am obliged to say there are rules for your meeting, Doctor Cassim."

"You're joking?" Karl said, standing.

"Not in the least. May I remind you, sir, you asked for this meeting and a rare occasion it is. After I told Sir Hunsdon what you instructed, he agreed. But, there are rules."

"All right, Otto. What are the rules?"

Patiently, Otto said, "One, you are to address Sir Hunsdon only as Sir Hunsdon. Two, you will speak only when spoken to. Three, you will not engage in unimportant conversation. Four, do not speak loudly. He cannot speak, but his hearing is exceptional. Five—"

"Otto," Karl interrupted, "how am I supposed to speak only when spoken to if he cannot speak?"

"You will see. Five, you are not to touch anything. He is in the depths of some tedious research and does not want anything disturbed. Six, and most important of all, do not challenge his opinions. I do hope you know what you are doing, Doctor Cassim. He has a ferocious temper. Please, don't waste his time."

"You make him sound like some kind of monster."

Otto did not reply. "Are you ready, doctor?"

"Yes. I'm very ready."

"Your briefcase, sir."

"Oh, thank you."

"This way, sir."

As they walked, Karl paused to ask a question. "Is it just you and Sir Hunsdon in this huge house?"

Otto replied. "There are six domestics, a complete kitchen staff, and a chauffeur. Now, sir?"

There was a nod.

Otto led the way to the hall of the previous night and to the door near the long table stacked with mail. He approached the mammoth oak door and rapped quietly. He waited several seconds, turned the knob, and opened it. He stood to the side inclining his head slightly. Karl hesitated for a moment and stepped in.

CHAPTER 26

The room was mostly dark with patches of light descending like rays from the sun, a cavernous room filled with wondrous things. Magnificently carved beams defined the ceiling and black velvet cradled the windows. Bookcases lined the walls and tables huddled at their feet, covered with open books.

In the distance, two overstuffed chairs faced a gigantic fireplace where gargoyles held the mantel. At opposite sides of the fireplace, in the corners, two highly decorated coffins, one of gold the other of silver, stood on end. Maps, round and flat, were everywhere. Maps of the earth and the sky. Maps of the zodiac and the constellations. Especially maps of Egypt from predynastic eras, showing a much wider Nile, to the present. Ten-foot golden statues of Ra, Osiris, and Isis reigned between the black velvet folds of the draperies.

Entranced by this extraordinary collection, captivated by the glint, the dazzle of everything that screamed Egypt, Karl, moored in place, raw with thrill, visually devoured more than he could comprehend.

Screeching pierced his brain like nails across a blackboard. Chalk exploding, shattering from pounding, jerked him from his splendid distraction. Karl spun toward the fireplace. A school-size blackboard read, "WHAT DO YOU WANT???"

Standing to the side stood the menacingly tall figure of E. Osborne Hunsdon, with a candle-size chalk stick protruding from his hand like a weapon. *He must be in his sixties*, Karl thought, but Hunsdon's bearing spoke of much younger years. Powerful black eyes glared through round wire glasses, thick brows shading them like tattered awnings. Askew, his dense, heavily salted black hair had the remains of a part to the side. Karl stared at the sallow, deeply checked skin that draped afore and beneath woolly mutton chops, barely disguising the large pointed ears of a wizard. A well-set jaw, coupled with a demeanor of importance, was exactly what Karl had expected. But a rounded paunch parting a royal blue, floor-length robe, embroidered with five-pointed stars, was not. It was the robe of a kher heb, an Egyptian high priest. Sir Hunsdon, great in every detail, straight as a girder, frowned with curiosity at the disturbance before him.

"Sir Hunsdon," Karl said, "I'm Doctor Karl Cassim and . . ." He winced as chalk raked the board. Hunsdon circled the question.

Quickly, Karl set his briefcase on a nearby table

and sprung the latch. A pointer lashed a desk, fracturing in two.

"Excuse me, I'm sorry," Karl said, setting his briefcase on the floor. He didn't mean to disturb the papers. He removed one of the cylinder seals wrapped in cloth and haltingly walked it to Hunsdon. Hunsdon looked at the package. His brows nearly obscured his eyes as he frowned and unwrapped the seal.

"I must warn you, Sir Hunsdon. The last man to read from the seal withered and died."

A defiant lip raised. Hunsdon threw the burlap cloth on the desk and examined the crystal seal under a high powered light with a glass. Stooping over, he set the seal on its cloth and rolled it slowly as he read.

Expectantly, Karl searched Hunsdon's face, looking for signs of doom, recalling the dusty face of his deceased assistant, Malak. But as Sir Hunsdon read the seal, it became apparent that he was immune.

Hunsdon straightened, bringing his hands together as if in prayer, squinting and nodding.

"I have three more," Karl said, "all different in content."

Hunsdon moved to the board. "You said five," he wrote.

"Yes, I did. But the first one was stolen from the museum."

"So," Hunsdon wrote, "there is another player."

"Yes, I suppose so."

He scribbled, "What are you?"

"I don't understand the question."

He erased the board. "You look Egyptian, but you speak like an American. What are you?"

Karl shrugged. "Is that important?"

"YES!" he wrote in capital letters.

"Why?"

Twice, he underlined the question.

"I am an Egyptian schooled in Boston, California, England, and Egypt. I am . . ."

The board screeched. "I know."

Karl shook his head and took a deep breath. "This is not at all what I expected, Sir Hunsdon," he said.

Hunsdon wrote, "Why have you come to me above all others???"

"I thought that was obvious."

White flakes spit from the board as Hunsdon slashed X's under the question, turned, and stared.

"It's really quite simple, Sir Hunsdon. Because you are the foremost authority on ancient Egypt. Because I have been made privy to these cylinder seals not known to exist. And because they seem to have a certain power about them, and messages that I do not completely understand."

The board became a flurry of white lines. "What power?"

"Of prophecy, of death. My assistant and friend died hideously after reading the seal. I've been the only one able to read them till now. But you . . . you are without . . ."

In capital letters Hunsdon wrote, "AAKHU!"

"Protective spell?"

There was a nod.

"I thought that only the high priests knew how to use such things."

Hunsdon stared through him. His all-consuming eyes said what Cassim had suspected. The star-studded robe was not for comfort. Neither was the Aakhu-t, the eye of Horus strung around his neck. They were the symbols of the Ur-ma Ur-hekau, a high priest great with magic, power.

Hunsdon pointed to one of the chairs in front of the fire. Karl picked up his case and moved to his appointed seat.

Hunsdon wrote, "Show me the others."

Karl reached inside his case and took out his yellow pad. He flipped to his translations and handed them to Hunsdon.

Hunsdon glared. His lips puckered, smothering his generous nose. He spun to the board and the chalk sparked as he scribbled, "What the hell is this?"

"My . . . my translations."

"I want to see the seals!!!" he disdainfully wrote.

Karl's face collapsed as Hunsdon tossed back the pad. Watching him clear the board, Karl held up the next seal. Hunsdon set down the eraser, took the crystal and examined it.

Hunsdon read, his well-formed lips moving slightly. He picked up chalk and wrote, "Tell me how you came by it."

The fire danced and crackled while Karl explained how Julian Rutledge found a seal on his doorstep.

Chalk screeched again. "And the next?"

Uneasy with the tale of the desert temple, for fear of being ridiculed, Karl skipped over dramatic details and shortened the story considerably.

"STOP!" was pounded in huge letters. Beneath it, he wrote, "I want the whole story, every detail, whether or not it suits your fancy."

With a deep breath, Karl began again. This time he did not fudge the colorful eccentricities of his account. Without prompting, he went on to the next and the next, while Sir Hunsdon parted his robe, eased into the matching chair, folded his hands thoughtfully across his stomach, and settled his gaze among the coals.

Outside, beyond the leaded windows, the wind faintly grieved as it whipped flakes into spools.

Telling Sir Hunsdon about the last seal, Karl actually spoke of the first, repeating that it had been stolen. Rising to speak, he referred to his pad. "This seal was found at the entrance of a passage below the northeast corner of the Great Pyramid . . ." Graphically, he described how and what he had found, mimicking the curled, skeletal fist with his own, remembering aloud every minor and major facet, including the seal's short exhibit at the museum. He concluded with the theft, and finally the murder.

Sir Hunsdon continued staring into the flames.

For a moment, Karl looked at him, at his flat, black, liquid eyes when a question uncontrollably leaped from his mouth. "Why can't you speak?" he whispered, the crackle of fire nearly drowning out his words.

Hunsdon's eyes grew thin and hard as he turned his head toward his insolent guest. Agilely, his arms boosted his hulking frame from the chair. He stalked to the board. "CONTINUE!!!!"

Karl's eyes followed the royal blue, star-studded robe swaying back to the chair, not sorry for the attempt. "I was just curious," he whispered.

Karl went on with his chronicle of the seals. When he finished, he hesitated. He expected a comment, an opinion.

But Hunsdon sat mute, pensively staring into the fire.

Karl cleared his throat and ventured his own opinion. He estimated the age of the seals to be 24,000 years old.

Not an eyelash flickered.

Karl ventured further. He said he believed the Sages to be immortal, to be the essence of all knowledge given to man by way of Thoth, who recorded and understood all. Stepping further into the historical abyss, Karl suggested, in the most casual way, that the Sages and the gods of which the sacred manuscripts speak may have been extraterrestrial.

Still Hunsdon stared in silence.

Karl went on as if possessed, giving voice to a belief he had sworn in his heart never to say aloud to a living person. "The possibility exists, sir, that one or more of these beings **is** with us still."

Hunsdon rose slowly from his seat, passing Karl with a stream of flowing robes. He raised his splintered chalk to the board and wrote one single word. "Why?" And he turned, facing him squarely, gathering skin around his eyes into a squint.

"Because," Karl said, "I do not believe it a coincidence that the happenings involving the seals have occurred by chance. Someone is trying to tell us something."

Hunsdon spun to the board, shredding chalk, underlining the question. He folded his arms in a challenge.

"Because I think that something catastrophic is about to happen."

Again, Hunsdon struck more lines under the question.

With shallow breathing, Karl picked up his pad and began to read. "Beware! Death comes on wings to he who violates the word. Beware! The eyes that fall upon this Providence must be pure. Beware! It is—"

"Meaning?" filled the board.

"Meaning, this warns of impending death!"

"NO, NO, NO, NO," Hunsdon wrote, running off the blackboard. Furiously, he began to sign.

Karl stood back. "I don't understand sign language."

Hunsdon threw up his arms. He turned, erased the letters. "It warns stupidity to stay away. It encourages intelligence to step forward and learn what the gods are about to teach!!!"

"What are they trying to teach us, and why?" Karl asked.

He wrote, "The what is written on the seals. The why you'll know when you discover the what."

Karl took a deep breath. "Why has this fallen to me?" he whispered.

Hunsdon shook his head, blinking heavily. Once more, he erased the board. He quickly scribbled, "Is it a further coincidence then that wherever you travel one of these seals happens to appear?"

Karl did not respond.

"Why was a seal delivered to Rutledge?"

"I don't know."

Hunsdon wrote, "I thought you were an Egyptologist."

"I am. I have studied in the finest universities in the world. I am—"

Screeching, chalk flew in bits with Hunsdon's impatient anger. "More the contempt. You are deaf and blind, Karl Cassim. You've been schooled by idiots who take this and throw out that, because it doesn't fit into their neat little rows. Demagogues!!!" he pounded.

Karl stepped back.

Hunsdon glared.

Slowly, Karl let out a long breath. Slowly, he smiled as he said, "That is why I am here!"

For a moment, Hunsdon curiously looked at him. His black eyes shed their anger as he too began to smile and nod. Not looking at the board he wrote, "Good!" Facing it he scribbled, "Why to Rutledge?"

"He is an astronomer."

The board filled with words. "Exactly. The Egyptians were masters of the stars. They knew precession. They invented the zodiac. They named the constellations thousands of years before anyone!"

Karl looked puzzled. "I don't remember anything about stars on his seal."

Hunsdon motioned for the yellow pad.

Karl obliged.

He pointed to the last two lines of the Rutledge seal.

Karl read, "Seek the watcher of the horizon for in

his recline lies the secrets of the universe. To know him look to the heavens."

Hunsdon, squinting and nodding, wrote, "There's your answer." He cleared the board and began again. "Now explain your assumptions about extraterrestrials."

"Very well." Karl took a thick binder out of his briefcase and thumbed the pages. "This is from the *Book of the Dead.* It reads, 'Homage to thee, Osiris, Lord of Eternity, King of the Gods, whose names are manifold, whose forms are Holy'. In chapter 42 it says, 'I am among you, I am alive. Eternity is my home'."

Karl flipped more pages. "Heliopolis Theology is emphatic in its description of the gods of the first time. It clearly states that in the beginning, Ra rode his golden bark through the black firmament, that he made the sun shine, the flood flee. From his golden bark, his boat of millions of years, his space ship, if you will, he called forth his company . . .

"In the *Pyramid Texts*, Utterance 214 is entitled, 'The King goes to the Sky'. There are so many references to the Winding Waterway that we call the Milky Way. In Utterance 509, it is stated that the sky thunders, the earth quakes, the clouds roar as Ra ascends to the sky. Surely, this is no ordinary boat floating on the Nile. And the many references to iron are uncanny: iron throne, iron bracelets, iron ships. Iron wasn't discovered till thousands of years later. There is so much veiled in these pages!"

Hunsdon wrote, "So, you have taken literally all these wonderful morsels?"

"Yes."

"Our learned colleagues," he scratched, "will think you insane."

"I don't discuss these morsels with our learned colleagues. Doctor Hunsdon, no one has ever looked at these documents with a dissecting eye. Strip away the metaphors, the flowery anecdotes, and what remains is the legacy of immortal beings who brought us out of the darkness. Literally, the missing link."

With a glint in the eye, Hunsdon's chin went down. He turned and slowly wrote, "And?"

"I believe that somehow the texts and the seals are intermingled. And unless you know the meaning of one, you will not know the meaning of the other."

"Fine," he wrote. "Why do you need me?"

Karl looked deep into the black recesses of Hunsdon's eyes. "Because I am not prepared to deal with . . . I don't know how to . . . I've never studied . . ."

The board spit words like bullets. "Magic. That's it, isn't it?"

Karl stumbled into a chair. "Yes," he whispered, his fingers digging into the armrests.

With his back turned toward Karl, he wrote, "I will not."

"But, I haven't asked."

"Yes, you have."

"All right. Why? Why won't you help me?"

In large letters he said, "You don't know what you're dealing with."

"That's why I came to you."

Hunsdon stared at him, forgetting himself, and his hands flew. "God damn it," he mouthed. In long strokes he wrote, "Egypt is the mother of magic."

"I know."

"I can't help you."

"But why?"

He scribbled, "I thought it obvious."

"Not to me."

He wrote, "HEKAU!!"

The bricks fell. "You can't speak!"

Hunsdon stared.

"Is that so important?"

He wiped the board clean. "You know the story of Moses."

"Yes. What about Moses?"

"THINK!!!" he pounded.

"Moses was a Jew?"

Hunsdon rolled his hands, encouraging him to continue.

"Moses was a Jew who was raised as an Egyptian Prince."

Hunsdon pointed a finger.

"I'm not good at charades," he said wearily.

Hunsdon threw him a scowl and wrote, "Go on!"

"Well, as a prince, he was taught by the priests. He parted the sea . . . he changed his staff into a serpent . . . he . . ."

The board sparked, "How? Wallis Budge — *Magic* — 1899. Did you read it?"

"Yes."

"Well???"

Karl turned the pages in his mind while Hunsdon stared, waiting. Then he quoted verbatim, "Mighty in Words . . . like Isis, Moses was Strong of Tongue and uttered the words of power which he knew with correct pronunciation, and halted not in his speech, and was perfect both in giving the command and saying the word."

He went on, "Moses knew how to control the power with the word. He knew the spells. He inherited his skill from the great priest/magicians of ancient Egypt like Aba-aner, Nectanebus, Teta, Zaclas and Tchatcha-em-ankh. The art was passed from one generation to another and with it came the knowledge for using a talisman. With this combination, a priest/magician could turn the waters of the sea into blood, raise the dead, level armies, bring on a plague, repel evil, or kill the first born of Pharaoh."

In script as large as the board Hunsdon scrawled, "EXACTLY!"

For a long time their eyes locked. Karl asked, "Do you think I'll find the rest of the seals?"

Hunsdon shook his head. "They will find you," he wrote. "Give them what they want."

Startled, Karl searched his face. "You know?"

Hunsdon's expression was blank. He scrawled, "Take care that your daughter is not sacrificed in vain. Give them what they want."

"But . . . but the seals?"

"They will come back to you . . . mark my words," he scratched. He turned toward the fire, looking into the flames, his hands clasped.

Karl watched him as the fire hissed and crackled. Outside, the wind raged. "Why can't you speak?" he whispered.

Ignoring him, Hunsdon walked to a far corner of the room and surveyed a bookcase that rose to the ceiling. He removed a dark wooden box strapped with brass. Like a platter, he carried the box to Karl. Towering over him, Hunsdon hesitated for a few seconds. Then, in a sweeping gesture, he gave the box to Karl. Swiftly, he walked to the blackboard. He scratched, "Good bye."

Shocked, Karl gawked.

Expressionless, Hunsdon looked down on him.

"But . . . but there is so much . . ."

Twice more he underlined the dismissal, set his splintered chalk on the ledge and glided to his chair. Pulling his robe tightly, he sat. His eyes rested in the fire, moving only to capture a spark, a fizzle.

Karl gathered his paper, his briefcase, and the box. He took one last look at Hunsdon who raised a hand and snapped his fingers.

The huge oak door opened.

CHAPTER 27

Once more, Karl stood in the grand hall of Hunsdon House, stunned by the sudden dismissal.

"Sir," startled him, as Otto stood near the front door, holding Karl's coat. "The car awaits."

"But, but . . ." he stammered, "I have so much to ask him . . ."

"Yes, sir," Otto said.

"This is all very strange, Otto."

"Yes, sir," he said, helping him on with his coat.

"How will I . . . Where did the . . ."

"Doctor Cassim, it has been a pleasure, sir." He opened the door.

Karl buttoned his coat and stepped into the wind.

A chauffeur held open the door to Hunsdon's limousine. "Heathrow. Correct, sir?"

"Yes, please."

In a little while, Karl collapsed in seat 5B of the first-class section of the plane. Once airborne, he picked up the telephone mounted to the seat and called his London hotel. They were very obliging. He instructed them to charge his credit card for the one night he hadn't slept there and forward his one small unopened suitcase to Cairo.

He checked the time and wondered why Sir Hunsdon had given him a gift. From under the seat forward, he picked up the box and opened it. Dazed, he stared. The sixth crystal cylinder seal sparkled in its velvet nest. He slowly blotted his brow.

"Are you all right, doctor?" the stewardess asked.

"I could use a drink. Something potent," he replied.

He took a mouth full of hundred-proof vodka and let the essence of refined potatoes rest on his tongue, tingling, burning with sedation. Out the small oval window, his mind swirled among the stars.

The overhead light refracting from the crystal pulled him back to the box. He noticed some papers held to the lid by a leather strap. They appeared to be written in Hunsdon's own hand. There was a title: "Tep Ret," meaning instruction, prescription. A dozen pages covered amulets to wear, Words of Power to recite, the tone in which they were to be spoken. It was a guide to the use of magic.

Hunsdon defined magic. White magic, he wrote, protected the true of heart, the worthy, protecting the user against evil. Black magic incited calamity of every kind.

From ancient Egyptian priests, Hunsdon quoted the spells to walk on water; from Zaclas, the great magician, the Words of Power to raise the dead, incantations to level armies and cause lightning to do one's bidding.

Verse after spell after incantation supplied every sort of information to defend one's self. From stelae, texts and tomb walls came utterances for transformation into another creature, into any other creature. From Thoth and Anubis came the roots of this power, Hunsdon wrote. In bold letters he added, "Learn them, guard them well."

"What in hell am I guarding against?" Karl muttered. He sipped his drink and stuffed the papers under the strap.

He wiped his hands on a napkin and lifted the seal from its place. The message read:

"As for him who knows the word, it is the promise of Thoth that he shall go forth by day everlasting. Armed with the knowledge of Thoth as given to Zaclas and Teta, he shall climb the ladder to the sky where eternity rests.

Sobmer m A Neferpehui . . . Companion of Thoth."

Karl returned the seal to its nest and closed the lid. In a muddle of thoughts, sleep overtook him and the stewardess caught his glass as it tumbled to the floor.

CHAPTER 28

With a shudder, Egyptair's 747 from London hit the runway at Cairo's International Airport. Karl's first thought was for the box, but it was on the empty seat next to him. Evidently, the stewardess had put it there. The plane taxied to the terminal as the radiant sun poured into the cabin chasing away the dank, dreary, frigid breath that had smothered the British Isles.

Nearly two days had flipped by in a moment, it seemed, so quickly in fact that Karl had not had the opportunity to evaluate the bizarre encounter with E. Osborne Hunsdon.

As he entered the arrival area at Terminal Two, agents stood waiting. With his impressive credentials, he passed quickly through customs. He saw Shawn waiting on the other side.

"How was your trip?"

"Unbelievable."

"Is that good or bad?"

"Let's just say we have a lot to talk about," Karl said, at the entrance.

"Your bags, Karl?"

"I only took one and the hotel is shipping it. This is all I have," he said, raising his briefcase and the little box.

"Home, Maestro?"

"Yes, please." Stepping into the car, he asked, "Any word about my daughter?"

"I'm sorry, Karl. Nothing."

"What are those bastards waiting for?" he said out the window. "Did Hassandi talk to that officer about you?"

The smells of Cairo invaded the car. Karl looked at Shawn. "What's wrong?"

"Oh, probably nothing."

"Very well. Tell me about nothing."

Traffic was thick and slow, and Karl welcomed the heat.

"A vendor was murdered at the bazaar," Shawn said. "It happened where you were assaulted."

"That's awful. But what does that have to do with us?"

"Well, he was selling replicas."

"That is not so unusual."

"No, Karl, he was selling replicas of the seal. He displayed enlarged photos of the one stolen from the museum. And, Karl, whoever murdered him took all his merchandise."

"Oh, my God!"

"There's more. Hooded men beat his wife and ransacked his home. My guess is they thought he had more seals stashed away."

Karl gripped Hunsdon's wooden box close to his chest.

"What's in the box?"

"Take me to the museum."

"Karl, what's the matter?"

"Hunsdon had a seal, and he gave it to me. It's in this box. The others are in my briefcase."

"Jesus Christ!" Shawn slammed on the brakes just before the bridge to Gezira Island. He made a U-turn on 26th July Street and aimed for the museum.

"Go to the back entrance," Karl said anxiously.

"Wouldn't it be better if we went in the front door where there are lots of people?"

"There were a lot of people at the bazaar."

"I see what you mean."

"When we get there, keep your eyes open. If anything looks suspicious, just keep going."

Shawn glanced in the mirror. "Karl, I hate to say this, but I think we're being followed."

Karl glanced over his shoulder.

"Do you know anybody in a dark blue Mercedes?"

"No. Can you go faster?"

"Too much traffic. Hang on."

Shawn suddenly turned halfway through an intersection and scraped a light pole. The Mercedes tried to follow, but an on-coming car smashed into it, forcing the blue car into another car.

Shawn exhaled and made a right. "Is this what we have to look forward to?" he breathed.

"I hope not. I'm getting too old for this," Karl said, locking his jaw, staring out the windshield.

Shawn slowed near the back door. "What do you think?"

"It appears safe. I'll just be a minute." Karl jumped from the car and ran up the steps.

Shawn nervously looked around, eyeing people walking by and cars slowing down. He watched Karl talking to security guards through the thick glass door. After a moment, he faded inside the building. When Karl re-appeared, the guards escorted him to the car.

"Who do you think it was, Shawn?"

"The same people who have Nanette. I'm sure of it."

"Where is Hassandi when you need him?" Karl said.

"I was thinking the same thing. Karl . . . how did they know you had the seals?"

"I don't know. I can't think. I'm exhausted and very hungry."

"Let's grab something at the Ibis," Shawn suggested. "It's probably safer than going home."

A small smile. A nod.

The Nile Hilton was on the square a street away from the Egyptian museum. It had the reputation for excellent dining, attracting natives and travelers alike.

Seated at a table with a panoramic view of the Nile and the island, they ordered English tea and an appetizer of mazzah followed by kushari.

"I read you had some exceptional weather in London," Shawn said.

"Yes, if you like cold, wind, and snow. It went right through my bones."

"The paper said eighty degrees."

"Well, the paper is wrong. I was there. It was dreadfully cold."

"That's weird." Shawn spotted a copy of USA today left by a patron at the next table and gave it Karl.

"This is crazy. This is today's paper. Last night, when I left England, it was well below freezing."

"That's a hell of a swing. Why do you think it's happening?"

"For lack of reasons, the experts blame El Niňo. I think it very possible that we are experiencing the semi-millennial weather shift."

With that said, the many small plates of the mazzah appetizer were set on the table. The Ibis' selection began with various salads, followed by sausages, meatballs, eggplant, pickles, onions, nuts, green olives, and white beans, accompanied by white and brown flat bread.

Shawn picked and Karl gorged.

The plates were cleared and crumbs swept from the table. The fragrant kushari was served, with its layers of rice, macaroni, and dark lentils embellished with rich tomato sauce and garnished with sautéed onions.

The tea steeped as Karl inhaled its delicate scent.

Shawn said, "Feel better?"

"Wonderfully full."

"Karl, I have an idea."

"I'm listening."

"Why don't we get out of town for a while? Somewhere where we can be safe, and have time to figure this thing out. We can assemble a team and go back to Abydos. Maybe we can excavate the boat pits. We'd have plenty of security there, and—"

"I have a better idea. I think it's time to unlock the passage where all this began."

Shawn couldn't believe his ears. "You're not kidding, are you?"

"I've put it off long enough."

Two policemen entered the restaurant. They were escorted to a table next to them.

Frowning, Shawn turned his back toward the officers.

"What's bothering you? I thought you would be pleased."

"I am, Karl," Shawn whispered. "It's just that the police have been showing my picture around the bazaar."

"I thought we cleared that situation."

"The officer I was with that night can't be found. If they find me . . ."

Karl motioned for the check. "On the way to my place," he said, "we are going to get your things. You're staying with me until this damn affair is settled."

CHAPTER 29

Over the several days that followed, Karl made plans to gather a team and reopen the passage. Shawn's curiosity about Hunsdon had filled lengthy conversations, and the seals even more. It was a great circle that always led to Nanette.

In the early hours before dawn, Wednesday, Karl struggled with sleep. The telephone invaded. He pushed back the covers and stared at the clock. It was four-oh-five. Irritably, he grabbed the wire. "What?"

"And hello to you too, Karl."

"Hassandi? My daughter?"

"I'm afraid not."

Karl sighed deeply. "What then at this hour?"

"Shawn O'Donnell. He is missing."

"You are joking? Because if you're not, I'm hanging up."

"Karl, we have to talk."

"What do you want?"

"Shawn O'Donnell."

Karl listened.

"Karl, this is important. O'Donnell is missing."

"I hadn't noticed. Why are you looking for him?"

"Do you know where he is?" Talib asked.

"No," Karl said.

Talib hesitated. "He has been identified as one of your assailants."

"That's ridiculous and you know it."

Dead air hovered at the other end of the line.

"Did you talk to the officer?" Karl asked stiffly.

"He's been on a leave of absence. We haven't been able to reach him."

"That is convenient, isn't it? It would make more sense if you spent your time trying to find him. He was with Shawn all that night."

"Has he been to work?" Talib persisted.

"Frankly, I don't know. I was in England over the weekend."

"Why are you being evasive, Karl?"

"Look, Talib, I don't micro-manage his affairs. Why don't you spend your precious time trying to find my daughter?"

"That's what we're doing. O'Donnell was picked out of a half a dozen photographs. The vendor is positive he saw your friend."

"I'll say it again. He was not involved; I don't care what the vendor says. Find the officer. Good night!"

"Karl, wait, don't hang up. Karl?"

Karl swung to the edge of his bed.

"Karl, are you there?"

"You are wasting my time, Talib."

"One more thing."

"What?" Karl asked, more irritated than ever.

"Where do you keep the seals?"

"Safe, why?"

"I'm going to ask that you turn over the cylinder seals and the translations to me—"

"What?" shouted Karl.

"—for your own protection."

"Out of the question!"

"Karl, they are evidence."

"If you want evidence, find the stolen seal. The others have nothing to do with you."

"Fine. I'll go over your head. I'll send a demand order to the Supreme Council for Antiquities."

"I've already spoken to the chairman and he agrees with me," Karl lied. "The seals stay under the protection of the department."

"They could lead us to you daughter."

"I don't know how you think that, and I don't believe you," Karl shot back.

"Damn it, Karl, I'm tired of playing games. You are going to—"

Slam!

He sat in the dark, staring at the clock. The second hand ticked away time, and his anger grew. Sleep was no longer a consideration. He pulled on a robe and walked to the door. The light in the kitchen was on. Shawn was sitting at the table nursing a cup of coffee.

"Morning," Karl said, filling a mug. "You're up early."

"I couldn't sleep," Shawn said. "He's looking for me, isn't he?" he asked despondently.

"You heard?"

"Yeah. Your door was open."

Karl sat down across the table.

"Karl, there's a cop in a car watching the house."

Karl took a deep breath.

"Maybe I should give myself up."

"No. That's not an option," Karl protested. "Do you know what Egyptian jails are like?"

"Karl, what if he comes here with a squad of goons and searches your flat?"

"He wouldn't dare. He knows all I have to do is pick up the phone."

"Karl, your friends in the department can't stop the police."

"Shawn, President Mubarak and I go back a long way."

"I didn't know you had such a high reach."

"I've never abused that privilege. But for a friend, I would."

The sky lightened far in the distance at the cusp of the earth. The two men sipped and thought.

Breathing the words, Shawn said, "Why do you think he suspects me?"

"I've asked myself that question a thousand times."

"Did you tell him about the Mercedes?"

"No," Karl replied.

"Why?"

When no answer came, he added, "Why would he want the seals?"

Karl looked at Shawn.

"Karl, do you really trust Talib?"

Their eyes fastened in silence.

CHAPTER 30

Clothed in black like ants in the night, scurrying to and fro, a dot on the Giza plateau hummed with a melody inspired by discovery.

Indistinguishable in the time between dusk and dawn, the horizon of the Egyptian scope melded land and sky into one; elaborate jewels hung in the heavens while their mirror image, reflected in the Nile, revealed no line to the eye.

Thirty-two members of Cassim's team labored, unearthing the steps at the northeast corner of the Great Pyramid. To discourage tourists later in the day, stakes had been sunk and strung with yellow tape. Moreover, Karl had tripled the number of guards assigned to the area, a third of them on horseback. The extra guards were a gift from President Mubarak himself.

Strong native arms lugged buckets of sand and stone away from the site, and while dawn peeped over the land, the stars still sparkled. With the light came the poetic chanting of the workers.

With anticipation, Karl watched as the steps took

form. A turbaned man stood alongside. Bedouin robes covered him. Deep blue eyes saw the stairs swept clean, and he softly hummed in tune with the rest.

Before the sun was bright in the sky, the passage was clear. All work stopped. Fattah, Karl's headman, went down the steps and into the passage, setting gas lamps along the way. Karl was with him, checking the ceiling and the walls for weakness. All was secure.

The room-sized granite plug stood as it had, solid and defiant. Karl, the turbaned man, and Fattah examined the edges. The fit was extremely tight. No more than a fingernail would fit between the plug and the smooth limestone surface of the slot where it rested. Karl called for more light, and the man in the turban covered his face. Measurements were taken. Sketches were drawn and possibilities discussed. Fattah offered suggestions.

Fattah was no ordinary laborer. He was practically an engineer, with considerable hands-on experience. When the Aswan dam was built, he had worked with the Russian engineers. When the temple of Rameses the Great was moved, he had measured the giant blocks to be cut, working for UNESCO. At Abu Simbel, the temple had been moved 680 feet from where it stood and now overlooks Lake Nasser.

A wiry man in his late fifties with deep folds around the eyes, Fattah drew lines on the block from top to bottom, a foot apart. Along the lines, diamond drills bored holes into the plug. The men used wedges, and wooden beams were hammered in place to keep the stone from sliding. Small charges were fitted deep inside the drilled holes and fuses were lit. The chamber was emptied, and section by section the plug would be pealed like the thick skin of an orange.

Scratching his gray beard, Fattah explained that the plug could be a foot, or as much as four feet wider than the passage it concealed.

"Very well," Karl said, "it might take a little longer than we expected."

"But," Fattah went on, "there could also be another plug behind it."

Karl would not be swayed. "That, we will find out soon enough."

After each explosion on each line, time was spent waiting for the air to clear. Then, men rushed in and the wedges were adjusted. Chunks of rock were carried away as the day faded.

As the last blast shattered the plug, expectation loomed high. Karl and Fattah examined what remained of the monolith, and the order was given to free the restraints. The block slammed into the wall. There was only one plug, leaving more than a yard's width in which to pass. The passage was open.

Joyous songs carried success into the night, while

Karl and the turbaned man inspected the opening. They did not venture one inch beyond. Karl called the day, praising Fattah and his team.

At dinner that evening, Karl and the turbaned man, Shawn, reread the translation of the first seal. Karl closed the cover on his yellow pad and glanced up. "When we go into the passage, we don't want to make any mistakes. I don't relish the thought of ending up like Mr. Farley, and having my innards splattered to pieces. If the ancients went to all the trouble of installing that plug, you can rest assured that there are more traps inside."

"Karl, what do you think they were hiding?"

Karl sipped his coffee and said, "Maybe they were not hiding. Maybe they were trying to protect the outside world."

Shawn looked on, astounded.

"Or maybe it's just another plundered tomb."

"What about the treasure of Thoth?" Shawn said.

"Evidently, Farley thought it meant gold and jewels, and he risked his life for it." Karl went on, "The treasure of Thoth could mean many things. If you think about Thoth, what do you see? The texts say he was an astronomer, a scientist, a healer, a magician, and a recorder of history. He must have been a very smart and able man. Not anywhere does it say he was a rich man."

Shawn looked disappointed. "I see what you mean."

"On the other hand, we may find the famed Hall of Records. Or, maybe just catacombs and tunnels. The only thing we can be sure of is that we will be the first to enter that passage in one very long time."

"I have the feeling that something extremely important is in there," Shawn said, his eyes bright. "And somebody went through a lot of trouble to conceal it."

"Well, I wouldn't be all that surprised if we find nothing," Karl said half-heartedly.

Shawn looked at Karl. It wasn't like him to downplay something that could be bigger than finding Tut's tomb.

Karl's eyes slowly fell to the table, his cup, and he brushed unseen dust from his yellow pad.

"Karl, you're acting funny. What is it?"

"Nothing, nothing, really."

"You can talk to me, you know? Whatever you think, I'll go along with."

"Very well, Shawn. You are right." Karl leaned into the table and played with the pad. "I don't want you to go into the passage."

"But why? It's Talib, isn't it? You think somehow I'm involved in that mess. That's it, isn't it?" he said nervously.

"You could not be farther from the truth. I would trust you with my life, please believe me, Shawn. It's just that . . . Well, if you could have seen Malak's face . . . a young man, your age . . . withered and dried like a mummy . . . his veins concave as if they had been sucked dry . . . I can't get it out of my mind. Please understand. I may have lost my daughter. I can't lose you, too."

Pain etched Karl's face.

"I understand." Shawn went for more coffee and refreshed their cups. He squeezed Karl's shoulder. "It'll be okay, you'll see."

Standing at the top of the steps early the next morning, Karl frowned toward the road feeding the Great Pyramid. With blue lights flashing, a line of police cars slowly drove up the road, passed the ticket booth and stopped a hundred feet from the dig.

"Cover your face and mingle with the team," Karl said to Shawn. "Go! Hurry!"

Men on horseback moved quickly, setting themselves between Karl and the cars. Other guards followed suit. Early tourists, camel drivers, vendors, and cabbies looked on.

For a time, Hassandi Talib leaned against his car smiling, chatting with an officer and a well-dressed man Karl didn't recognize. No doubt the soldiers, the cavalcade, and the string of jeeps came as a surprise.

Karl glanced for Shawn among his team. He was lost from view.

With confidence, Karl strode between the horses and walked to the road with another man, his epaulets indicating that he was a major in Mubarak's army.

Distant but cordial, Karl said, "You must have important news to be traveling with such an elaborate escort, Mr. Talib."

Talib's smile was set, practiced and annoyed. "Soldiers, huh?" he said snidely.

"Well, I did not wish to bother you," Karl said. "I know you are a very busy man."

Talib sneered, nodding.

"What do you do with all your money?" Karl said insolently, looking at his clothes.

Talib looked down. His tie was as it always was, off to the side and dotted with his breakfast. His wrinkled, mismatched suit and scuffed shoes were the same that Karl remembered from the last time they had met.

Talib's eyes thinned as he pursed his lips. He exchanged glances with his officer and the well-dressed man he failed to introduce. He turned full face to Karl. "All work stops now!" he spat. "Immediately!"

"By what authority?"

Talib reached into his breast pocket and withdrew

an envelope. "Read," he said smugly.

Karl tore open the letter. He recognized the stationery and the signature of its president and chair, a man with whom Karl had had a frosty but respectful relationship. The letter simply stated that his permission to excavate at the base of the Great Pyramid had been withdrawn pending further investigation. It instructed him to seal the opening and dispose of his team.

Talib posted that same irritating smile.

Karl was stunned. Abruptly, he walked away. A slight breeze lifted the sand from his feet in puffs. He looked at Fattah. "Close the dig. Seal the opening. Send the men home till further notice."

In shock, Fattah said, "Yes, sir."

Karl turned and faced Talib all those feet away as he got into his car and pulled away, trailed by his retinue.

Shawn sprinted to the steps where Karl was standing. "What's going on?"

Bitterly, Karl said, "I've been ordered to close the dig."

"But why?"

"I'm not sure."

"But, Karl, you have all these soldiers. You could have told Talib to kiss your ass."

Karl looked at him. "The order came from the Supreme Council for Antiquities. You know that was not an option."

"I know, but, damn it, we're so close."

Karl shook his head. "There's more here than meets the eye," he said.

CHAPTER 31

Two weeks had passed since the abrupt closing of the dig and still Cassim waited for a special meeting of the EAO. Despite the closing, Karl had assigned more guards than normal to secure the area, because the possibility existed that this passage could prove true all the legends of labyrinths, kingdoms, and underground vaults beneath the Great Pyramids. From Herodotus to Ahmed Fakhry, the legacy of ancient Egypt had been written, rumored, and theorized.

Thursday had begun as usual. At his desk, Karl was reviewing findings of the German team at the Sphinx temple. Sarah was at her desk, reviewing her calendar for future Tut exhibits, and Shawn had been squirreled away in the basement, reviewing his notes of the passage excavation as far as it had gone.

For a moment, Karl had set aside his notes. The smile inside the brass frame filled him with memories, anxiety, and emotion. "I am so sorry, Nanette," he breathed.

There was a knock on the office door. Karl cleared

his throat and said, "Come in."

With arms balancing books and maps, Julian rushed in, excited and out of breath.

"Sit down and relax," Karl said, smiling. "You're winded."

"Karl, you won't believe—"

"Try me. Right now, I'm very vulnerable."

Julian leaned against the desk. "Karl, what I found is . . . I don't believe it myself."

"Here," Karl said, clearing the corner of his desk, "set those things down. You're going to give yourself a hernia."

"Oh, thanks." He fanned himself with a folder.

"Would you like something cold to drink?"

"Oh, no, I'm fine."

"Shawn told me you were working with some new software at the university. It sounds like you might have found something interesting."

"And how," Julian said. "Karl, I've been doing a lot of reading . . . one thing leading to another. References and that. Some of them I had a hell of a time tracking down because they're out of print. But it all came together, boy, did it come together!"

"Take it easy. I have no place to go."

"I will, I will. But Karl, it's so fascinating. First," Julian began, "I read *Budge's Osiris* to familiarize myself with the legend. Then I read Herodotus, Diodorus, and a couple of other ancient historians which led me to Manetho's Kings List that speaks of the time of the gods. Some of this I'm sure is very familiar to you, but to me it was all new and terribly exciting."

Karl smiled and nodded.

"What I found most striking was that the Egyptians claim a history of nearly forty thousand years, being ruled first by the gods, then the followers of Horus, and then man. I think that's the right order. Well now, this is particularly interesting because it fits with anthropology like a tooth in the rim of a gear."

"How so?" Karl asked, leaning forward in his seat.

"Well, Neanderthal man dominated the Earth for about a hundred, a hundred and fifty thousand years. Then suddenly around forty thousand years BC, Neanderthals died out completely. Moreover, just as suddenly we have Homo sapiens, or modern man. How this happened so rapidly, no one knows. As you can see, this corroborates perfectly with Manetho's Kings List and Egyptian mythology."

Karl's demeanor sharpened as he considered this and the opinions he had expressed to Sir Hunsdon. "Please, go on."

"This coincidence, if you want to call it that, leaves a wide gap begging for answers. Why did the Neanderthal die out? Why do we suddenly have Homo Sapiens? Where is the missing link? What was the impetus? Why do the Egyptians claim that gods descended from the sky at the same time Homo Sapiens appear? Other cultures have similar mythologies, but the Egyptians have left a preponderance of architectural, cultural, and religious information, which calls into question the validity of history. And, Karl, although, as you have pointed out, the mainstream archeologists debunk such vast age to Egypt's history, I believe you're right." Julian's eyes sparkled with discovery.

"So," Karl said, "you equate the arrival of the gods with the arrival of modern man?"

"Yes. But that isn't the only anomaly I've uncovered."

Amused by Julian's enthusiasm, Karl found it hard not to smile. "Proceed."

"Remember the conference where I spoke of the unusual nebula occurring in the constellation of Orion, particularly around the belt stars?"

"Yes, very well."

"There is something more," Julian went on. "Sirius, which was known to the Egyptians as Sothis, rose in the twilight before dawn once a year. This was important because it marked the annual flooding of the Nile.

"Sirius is also known as the Dog Star, the brightest star of the constellation of Canis Major as well as the heavens. Now, this star travels a wavy course, or a spiral course. Until the mid-eighteen hundreds, it was not known that Sirius has a traveling companion, half its size, which appears once every fifty years."

"I'm not sure where you're going with—"

"Karl, Canis Major is southeast of Orion near the Milky Way . . . the Winding Waterway. It is situated on a straight line across from the belt of Osiris. Now, I discovered an invisible planet that reveals itself only once every forty thousand years. It circles the companion star to Sirius, and, when it can be seen, it is as close as it can get to our solar system, to Earth. It is visible at the same time the nebula is expanding in Orion and will be at its peak in July, in the year 2010. The planet becomes optical three years before, and remains visible for three years after."

"Are you saying that the appearance of this invisible planet, the appearance of the gods and Homo sapiens are—"

"Yes, Karl."

"You think, you believe that the gods came from this invisible planet?"

"Obviously, I can't prove it, but it certainly explains an awful lot of coincidences, doesn't it? This presumption adds more fuel to the fire. Look, our life cycle is based on the rotation of the Earth. It takes one year to circle the sun. Manetho says the gods ruled for nearly 14,000 years, followed by the demigods, their offspring, for another 11,000 years. This would explain the sudden appearance of Homo sapiens, wouldn't it?

Now, the companion star circles every fifty years, and I have calculated that the invisible planet, even though we can't see it, circles that sun once every one-hundred years. The life cycle of the gods would be one hundred to one. If, say, Osiris reigned for 1,500 of our years, to him it would be only 15 years."

"They would have two suns, one circling the other," Karl said in amazement.

"Yes."

"Fifteen-hundred years to him would be a drop in the bucket."

"You could say that."

"Julian, I must say this all sounds very far-fetched."

"It depends on your perspective. To Manetho, forty-thousand years was a reality. To most people today, it sounds far-fetched. I grant you that I have made certain assumptions here, but the further I go the more sense it makes. Trying to back up my findings with some fragment, some evidence that the Egyptians might have made some record, some testimony, that would complete my theory, I came across some very provocative statements in the *Pyramid Texts*. In considering a certain passage, I read that the double, or Ka, was also the soul, the spiritual essence. As I read this, I considered my theories in relationship to the two stars. In other words, I listened between the lines."

Julian fumbled in his papers and found a folder.

He opened it and read: "In Line 2059 it says, 'The king is one of *them*, even those who are *favored* by the Bull of the sky. The king lifts his double aloft, the king *turns* about the king. Oh, you good *companion*, lift thy double aloft, turn about on the underside of the sky with the beautiful *stars* upon the bends of the Winding Waterway'."

"You think somehow they knew," Karl asked, "or were told about the invisible planet?"

"That's my guess. Here's the connection I made. The gods, which include Thoth, recorded, the ancient books say, recorded and understood all. He and Osiris taught the Egyptians, and they were meticulous in writing things down, albeit flowered with mysticism."

"Julian, this is mind boggling."

"It is, isn't it?" he said proudly.

For a long time, the air was quiet and their voices still as they considered the possibilities, the far-flung implications of this work.

Finally, Karl said, "You're a heretic, Julian Rutledge."

"I know. I've been called worse."

"If you were born in another time, you'd be put to the stake."

"I'd be in good company, wouldn't I?"

"Yes, I suppose so."

"Karl, I brought the star charts and photographs of what I saw. Maybe they will be of some help in unraveling the seals."

"They're spectacular, Julian."

"I knew you'd like them."

Engrossed, Karl nodded.

"Karl, I brought you a book called the *Message of the Sphinx* that I thought you should read. It's written by Hancock and Bauval. Have you read it?"

"I've heard of it, but so much has happened, I haven't had the luxury of reading anything. I do remember that their theories caused quite a ruckus among my colleagues."

"Make room for it, because they have some pretty convincing evidence that the Sphinx is thousands of years older than is commonly thought."

"Need I say a word?" Karl said, marveling at the photos, the star charts, and Julian's notes.

As he rose, Julian said, "I hate to . . . I think about it all the time . . . we all do . . . I . . . any news about your daughter, Karl?"

Karl shook his head. "Nothing. I'm beginning to fear—"

"Hope, Karl, you've got to keep hoping for the best."

His eyes wandered about Julian's work stacked on his desk.

"I'll leave all this information with you. I made copies for myself so I can chase one more idea I've been thinking about."

"Thanks, Julian."

"A pleasure. I've got to get back."

"Heard anything from Nancy?" Karl asked.

"I got a note yesterday. She's in Rome doing what Romans do. She sends her love."

"When you write, send her my regards."

"I will."

"And thanks again. I appreciate the tremendous amount of work you've done, really."

"You can thank me by being a guest speaker at the convention next year."

"I accept."

Julian gathered his belongings and hustled off as excited as he had come.

Karl flipped through Julian's folders, neatly labeled and divided by topic, skimming their extraordinary contents. Believing more than ever in his convictions, Karl headed for the stairs to the basement, to the museum inside the museum.

Traveling the maze, he glanced at the people lost in their work, paying no attention to his goings and comings. He pointed himself toward a room in a remote corner, secreted by boxes stacked to the low ceiling. He opened the door. Shawn sat at a used school desk, a small fan trying desperately to move the air, its buzzing hum drowning out sound.

Karl cleared his throat. Shawn jerked.

"I'm sorry, I should have knocked."

"I thought it was—"

"God forbid," Karl said. "Shawn, I have wonderful news."

His eyes lit up. "Nanette?"

"Not that wonderful."

Karl sat on the corner of Shawn's desk and dropped a dozen manila folders.

"What's this?"

"Julian's work. Fabulous work."

Shawn took the pile and leaned back, his chair groaning. Slowly, he opened the first folder and began. He rocked while his eyes zipped down the pages, visiting planets, Homo sapiens, and the glaring possibility that Manetho's Kings List was all it purported to be. "Fascinating," he whispered. "Absolutely fascinating."

"Yes, isn't it?"

"Karl, have you read *Chariots of the Gods*?"

"That is the second time in less than an hour that my reading material has been questioned. It's a conspiracy. No, I haven't. I've heard of it, but—"

"The author, Erich von Daniken, made certain assumptions similar to Julian's, only he used earthly evidence, such as the pyramids in Egypt and Mexico and the statues on Easter Island. It's an interesting read."

"I'll get caught up with all my reading on my next vacation. Meanwhile, I'll be in my office."

CHAPTER 32

Sarah was on the phone when Karl walked by her desk. He took note that her work was always neatly stacked. She gave him a glance and a small smile that formed a dimple. There was a petite vase on her desk with a pink flower, and, off to the side, the computer waited for her attention.

Sarah was slender with chestnut eyes and dark, flowing hair. She had the longest eyelashes Karl had ever seen. Her bronze-toned skin reminded him of his daughter's, with its impeccable clarity. High on her cheek, just below the corner of her eye, a tiny sensual birthmark had been placed by nature. Her lips were rich and full, and when she spoke her voice carried a distinct but melodious Arabic intonation. She was intelligent, but a little quirky.

Sarah's husband was a liberal-minded Egyptian, greatly influenced by the West. As a result, he encouraged her to be less conservative. She never wore black or covered her face and easily bubbled with laughter. And that day, she modeled a white print dress with pale yellow flowers.

Karl smiled as he closed his door and glanced at *Message of the Sphinx* that Julian had left him. A few minutes later, a brief knock brought Sarah into the office.

"The mail just came," she said. "I know you've been waiting for this one." She pointed to a letter on top of the stack.

"You're right, thank you. But I expected a call, not a letter." he said.

Karl tore open the missive. As he read it, his heart pounded and his face reddened. Lengthy and wandering, the letter gave vague reasons about disturbing the integrity of the Giza Plateau and interference with tourist activity. Escalated armed security was the last motive and the weakest, since security was always present anyway. As yet, the letter went on, no conclusion had been made concerning his excavation at the pyramid, but he would be informed when a decision was reached.

He tossed the letter and picked up the phone. When it was answered, he choked back his anger. "Mr. Al Dakkha." His words were short and punchy.

A pleasant voice said, "May I ask who is calling?"

"Doctor Cassim," he growled.

"I'm sorry, doctor, but Mr. Dakkha left last Sunday on holiday."

"But I just received this letter, and it is dated two days ago."

"Yes?"

"Well, when was the meeting?"

"Last week."

"Why wasn't I informed?"

"I can't answer that, doctor, I'm sorry."

"Of course you can't." He slammed the phone. He leaned back, his chair squawked, and he squinted out the window, mumbling under his breath.

The office door opened and Shawn slipped in quietly. Absorbed, Karl didn't notice. His eyes were shackled to a cloud, with his mind racing for reason.

"Karl, are you okay?" Shawn asked.

Cartilage caught in his neck and snapped when he turned. He pushed the letter across the desk.

Shawn's eyes fell on it. "I thought there was supposed to be a meeting."

Karl pushed it a little further and Shawn picked it up and read.

"How can they do that?"

"Very easily, I'm afraid."

"But you're on the Supreme Council."

"It's politics. Obviously, someone is applying pressure. Rather than face a confrontation, they chose to step around it . . . at least for now."

Shawn said, "Now what?"

"We wait. We petition the council for a positive decision and hope for the best."

"Isn't this a little unusual?"

"Unfortunately, no. Usually when I make a request, a positive decision is rendered. Either someone on the council or someone with a great deal of influence has raised objections. Rather than create enemies, they chose not to make a decision at all. And to avoid pressure, the chairman went on holiday. Very convenient."

"Damn, we're so close."

Karl breathed agreement. "Was there something you wanted?"

"It wasn't important. I just wanted to return the folders."

Later that evening over dinner, Karl and Shawn were mulling over Julian's work and the SCA's fickleness.

Shawn asked, "Did you bring home the folders?"

"As a matter of fact, I did."

"Do you mind if I have another look at them?"

"They're on the table near the door," Karl said.

"I have an idea. What do you think—"

A hard rapid knock.

Karl motioned Shawn to a back bedroom. "Take your plate," he whispered.

The knock was more persistent, louder.

Karl stood by the door, his heart pounding, suspecting the police, and waited for Shawn to clear out. He opened the door a crack. He threw it open.

"Doctor, there are people at the dig with papers demanding we let them in the passage," Fattah blurted.

"Whatever you do, don't let them in! I'll be right there. Go!" Karl whipped the door closed and ran through the house. "Shawn!"

Shawn bolted from the back room with a putter ready to swing. "What's the matter?"

"Somebody is trying to take over the dig. Put on the disguise."

Moments later, they flew out of the flat, and Shawn drove wildly through the streets. As they approached the pyramid, the lights of the monument sent the long shadows of the intruders across the sand. A half-dozen cars and trucks loaded with equipment were strung along the Pyramid Road. They could see angry forms waving arms, and his guards resisting and poised.

Shawn stopped the car and covered his face. They walked not so quickly to the scene. Things were under control. Karl looked at the group of men he estimated to be about twenty. His men were more than equal in number and well armed.

Several of the guards fell in behind Karl. The captain, who was on horseback, leaned and whispered in his ear. Karl nodded. "Who is in charge here?" he whispered back. The captain pointed to a man wearing a suit.

The man pressed forward. "That would be me," he said, in a nasal voice.

Karl's eyes fell on him with a scowl. Addressing the captain, Karl inclined his head and said, "What do you suppose he wants?"

Shawn smiled behind his bit of cloth. Karl was playing games.

The captain shrugged. "Maybe they're lost."

Karl nodded sympathetically.

"Listen here," the man said, "we mean to open this excavation."

Karl covered his mouth with the back of his hand. "Did you hear something?"

The captain said, "I'm not sure. Maybe."

"I have the authority to take over this site. If you know what's good for you, you won't interfere."

"My, my, we are testy. What do you think, Captain? Do you think he's testy?"

"Oh, yes, very testy."

"Hum," Karl said, "I am inclined to agree with you."

"Enough of this," the suit said. "Do you know who I am?"

Karl recognized him, all right. He had been with Talib when he closed the dig. He was the same arrogant man in the same white suit who smirked even then. Karl leaned closer to the captain. "Who do you think he is?"

A shrug. "Doctor, I don't know."

"The name is Krubrick," he said with emphasis, scattering presumed dust from his shoulder. "This site is now under my sponsorship. Doctor Reisner here will head the team. For your information, he is the grandson of the esteemed Egyptologist, George Andrew Reisner."

Sheepishly, Reisner took a step and mumbled, "I'm so sorry Doctor Cassim. I—"

Krubrick pushed him back in line. "This is my letter of authority." He whipped out a letter and held it at arm's length.

Karl's face grew hard and dark in the shadows of the pyramid. He stared at the tall pale man in a suit who looked like he needed a hot meal and a transfusion. Karl wondered where this emaciated wraith got his energy. His extra long nails dug into the letter he held, and his eyes were nearly colorless, more the faded look of an albino.

Karl reached for the letter and let it drop. His stare didn't flinch as Krubrick's eyes followed the letter to the ground. "Get off this site," Karl ordered. "Now!"

"You can't do this," Krubrick whined, his stringy, nasal voice leaping an octave. "I have offical permission to complete this work."

Rifles clicked. Standing astride, Karl folded his arms. Krubrick stepped back. Karl quietly said, "What is your name?"

"I told you. Krubrick, Floughs Krubrick."

"Noted. Now, get out! My men have a propensity to shoot trespassers."

For a moment, Krubrick stared at the rifles, at the soldiers staring back. "You haven't heard the last of this, Doctor Cassim."

"See to it that they leave the plateau," Karl said to the captain.

Shawn moved to Karl's side. "I liked the way you handled that. Real cool."

"Well," Karl said lightly, "my mother always told me to keep a cool head."

"You told me you were raised by your uncle."

Karl hunched his shoulders indifferently. "Same, same," he said.

Shawn laughed. "Karl, how do you feel?"

Karl frowned. "I feel fine, why?"

"Oh, I have an idea."

Karl looked at him more intently.

"Well, we're here now," Shawn said, a touch of conspiracy in his voice.

"Shawn, what are you saying?"

"Who would know?"

"Shawn?"

"The men would help. We have lanterns and flashlights in the trunk."

Karl raised his chin as his eyes widened. "Do you know what you're proposing?"

"Sure."

"Now? At night?"

"Karl, it's dark in the passage. What difference does it make if it's day or night? And besides, who would know?"

For a long moment, Karl looked at Shawn. He glanced at the soldiers. He saw men willing to do almost anything he asked. Men dedicated to the President of Egypt, and at this moment supporting him in whatever decision he made.

He turned back to Shawn. The shadows seemed to make Karl's eyes even larger than they were, more intense, almost deviant with the prospect. As his heart pounded against his shirt, he said, "Get the lamps."

"Yes!" Shawn burst, and sprinted to the car.

The escort returned. Karl told the captain of the guard that he and Shawn were going to make a routine inspection of the passage. "Keep a keen eye out," he said. "We shouldn't be too long."

The Pyramid road was deserted. The temperature was a cool 64 degrees and the first Wonder of the World looked ominous against a sky so black and yet lighted with billions of tinseled stars.

In less than fifteen minutes, soldiers set aside the barricade and Shawn was counting the steps down to the passage. Karl checked his watch. It was 9:46. The small relief of Osiris stared dully into space as they passed.

They entered the passage; Shawn placed lamps at intervals as they walked. What was left of the granite plug gave off sparks from the flashlight's glare as they approached the black hole. For the first time, Karl sent his light beyond the threshold, deep into the unknown.

Shawn removed his Bedouin cover and said, "Well?"

Karl looked very serious.

"What is it, Karl?"

"Shawn, if anything happens, I want you to leave, run. You understand?"

"What do you think is going to happen?"

"I don't know, maybe nothing. Promise me."

"Sure. Okay. Whatever you say."

Karl stepped into the space previously occupied by the plug, a space he estimated to be six by twelve feet. He threw his light around the cavity. Whatever had released the plug couldn't be seen, but somehow, something had.

They entered the next section. The light beam hit a wall in the distance.

"Oh, no. Don't tell me there is another plug."

"No, Karl, look off to the right, the shadow."

"I see it. A quick turn."

As they carefully inched through the passage, Karl said, "Remember what the seal said. 'Enter skillfully, for his eyes judge'."

"You don't really think someone is watching us, do you?"

"It wasn't meant literally. It means watch your step. Look for traps."

"Karl? What are those spout-like things near the ceiling?"

"My guess is that they are spouts."

"Thanks."

"You are welcome."

"No, really. What are they for?"

"Sand. Maybe even for arrows. That's what I mean. Watch your step and don't lean on or touch anything. You might set something off."

"Boy, they didn't fool around, did they?"

The walls, the ceiling were as smooth as glass, not a blemish anywhere. *The corridor was completely empty of decoration*, Karl thought, as they neared the elbow and shined the light into the next section.

"What are those things on the floor?"

"Don't step on them."

"They're all over the place."

"Yes, and some have been broken. If I were a betting man, I would say that is what got Farley. Just don't step on them," Karl said.

"They look like pie-plates turned upside down."

"Yes. Go around them."

"Yes, sir."

Very carefully, they walked around the small humps. This section of the passage was perhaps seventy feet long. Another elbow turned to the left, and everything changed. The walls were knife-sharp, with pointed edges, and sand crunched beneath their feet. It was a short section half as long as the one they had left.

"My God," Shawn said. What is that?"

Karl shined his light.

"Holy shit!" Shawn exclaimed. "You don't think—"

"It looks like Farley's friend, or what's left of him."

The outline of what remained of a body had been smashed against the wall with such force that it had been reduced to mush. It seemed as though a bucket of reddish-black paint had been thrown and spun, leaving long spiked fingers jutting out in all directions.

Karl said, "Look over there." He turned his light to the opposite wall. "It's another plug with the exact same impression. What I don't understand is how the plug got back into place, into the wall. What's that smell?"

"I don't want to know," Shawn said.

"Don't move."

Shawn froze as sand trickled slowly from the

ceiling and stopped. "I don't like this," he whispered.

"It's okay, it quit," Karl whispered back and bounced his light along the floor away from where they stood. "He must have triggered the plug down there. See the broken crockery? He ran this way and it smashed him here as he was trying to get out the way we came."

"Yes, but how did it get back in the wall?"

"I cannot answer that."

Frozen in place, they sent light traveling down the corridor. Small mounds covered the floor.

"More pie-plates," Shawn said.

"Tread carefully."

"Maybe this wasn't such a good idea."

"Too late for second guessing."

Their lights flitted from one mound to the next. It seemed to take forever to reach the next turn, which veered to the right. Karl fixed his light on a rough-honed tunnel, where they had to bend to go through. Again, the change was dramatic.

Red granite was everywhere, with smooth walls and a spotless floor. It was a descending passageway whose length couldn't be determined because the light stopped before reaching the end. As in the Great Pyramid, a corbel ceiling rose massively above them. Crisp, clean-cornered blocks gave the feeling of freshness as if this hall had recently been built. The gigantic blocks weighing hundreds of tons were laid with such precision the natural design embedded in the granite matched precisely. The air too seemed spring-like in its fragrance.

"This is incredible!" Shawn gushed. "I wish I had my camera." He stood there, chin raised, eyes taking in every feat of engineering.

Karl smiled. "Very intimidating, much like being in a huge mosque." His quiet words carried, echoing in the huge chamber.

"How far do you think we've come?"

"Not sure. But when we reach the end of this vault we had better consider our options. There is no way of knowing how far this passage travels. It could go on for many kilometers."

Their flashlights reflected off the floor, sending a misty light glowing all around them. Carefully, they descended the ramp.

"Extraordinary," Karl said. "It is immaculate, not a speck of dust or a grain of sand anywhere. After all these many years . . . unimaginable!"

"It would have to be air tight," Shawn quietly said. "But if it were, we couldn't breathe."

Karl nodded. "Yes."

The end of the chamber came into view. A dead end, they thought, until they saw a deep recess, a deep recess that dropped their mouths wide open.

A set of gold and inlaid doors forty feet high stopped them cold.

"Similar to those I saw at Abydos," Karl breathed, his light combing the exquisite detail, the ringed handles knotted with rope.

"The royal insignia is still intact, Karl."

"Yes, I noticed. A djed pillar embedded in the wax. Is your pocket knife handy?"

"Oh, yeah. Whose seal is it?"

"It appears to be one of the seven symbols of Osiris. See the arms with the crook and flail?"

Shawn held his light close as Karl held the seal and started to cut through the rope.

"Damn it!" Karl jerked back.

"Did you cut yourself?"

"No, a charge of electricity as if I stuck my finger in an electric socket." Karl stared at his hand. An impression of the seal was burned into his palm. "Damn," he said, and sliced through the rope. "What gave it energy?"

Shawn shook his head.

Karl shined his light on the door making sure there were no more surprises.

"Should we open it?"

"Carefully." Karl took a step back. "Open it."

Shawn grabbed hold of the rings and pulled. Hinges moaned a horrific groan that echoed a thousand times throughout the granite chamber. It was dead black beyond the threshold. Side by side they crossed over, with their lights straight ahead.

Beams of light shot back at them, blinding them.

"What the hell?" Shawn gasped.

"A mirror, Shawn! A reflection of ourselves!"

From everywhere it seemed as though eyes were staring. A greenish glow began to grow as if the Northern Lights were somehow captured in this room; in a matter of seconds, the light was as bright as sunshine. But it came from everywhere and from nowhere.

They gawked at their own reflections, doubling, tripling, quadrupling around them. A veritable hall of mirrors in an octagonal room, mirrors which shot their images too many times to count.

High up on the ceiling, a zodiac encircled the entire room, with stars and symbols and figures etched between them, in color so intense as to seem freshly painted. Karl stared in amazement. "It is nearly a duplicate of Dendera," he breathed.

The zodiac circled the ceiling, with figures facing counterclockwise like the stars. There were 36 decans representing ten-day weeks of the Egyptian year. Twelve figures with raised arms symbolized the twelve months of the year, and intersecting circles depicted the equinoxes. It was a calendar going back to remote antiquity.

Karl took his eyes off the ceiling. "I do not believe

what I am seeing," he said. "You do see the same thing, don't you?"

"Oh, yeah. I see it. Why?"

"Because I wanted to make sure I was not dreaming again . . . that when this is over I am not the only one who saw it."

"You're not dreaming, Karl. And if you are, so am I. Karl, look!"

Another set of large doors with a lintel above did not reflect in the mirrors. They were solid gold, with seven panels each, decorated with reliefs. An inscription in red hieroglyphs ran across the lintel.

Slowly, Karl read the ancient words, breathing life into them:

"In the hall of mirrors, you have seen the many faces of his soul. You have looked to the heavens and seen the Mansion of Osiris. Henceforth, enter if you are equipped. Enter if you are worthy, for the Seven Masters await united."

"What does it mean, Karl?"

Karl read and reread the inscription.

"Karl, are we in trouble?"

"Not exactly. But we cannot open these doors."

"Sure we can." Shawn grabbed the handles and pulled. The heavy doors yawned. "See, they're not locked."

"Stop! Don't!" Karl screamed.

Shocked, Shawn instantly released the handles. "I'm sorry. What did I do?"

"You nearly opened the door. My God, don't ever do that again, please."

"Why?"

"Because we could be struck dead! Shawn, listen carefully to what it says. 'Enter if you are equipped'. We are far from being equipped. The *Book of the Dead* says you become equipped to enter the Mansion of Osiris if you pass through the Arits, the Seven Gates to the Kingdom of Osiris. To pass through these gates *unharmed* you must know the names of the doorkeepers and the watchers. The last thing the lintel says is 'the Seven Masters await united'. The cylinders also say that they must stand united. It all fits, don't you see? And we don't have all the seals.

"Shawn, take this literally. I've seen too much to test the powers that I know nothing about."

"I didn't realize—"

"I know you are anxious. So am I. But let us not get killed trying."

There was a nod.

"One last thing," Karl said. "The *Book of the Dead* instructs that besides knowing the names, you must also know the secret Words of Power."

"I guess that's what they mean by 'worthy'," Shawn quietly said.

"Shawn, we have seen what happened to Farley and his friend back there. And I saw what happened to Malak. No, my friend, this is as far as we go until we are damn worthy."

CHAPTER 33

They backed away from the solid gold door. Their reflections caught in the Hall of Mirrors followed their every move thousands of times. They reached the massive doors leading to the red granite hall and pushed; as they did, the light of day dimmed as quickly as it had brightened into a dull glow, green as the moss on a tree. Then suddenly, all was black. The doors screeched shut. The echo sang its repetitious song and they began to retrace their steps.

As they walked, a hard, stiff silence followed, broken only by the shuffle of their shoes on the glossy floor. The red corbel ceiling seemed to press down on them while the ramp rose, and exertion brought deeper, labored breaths.

Once again, Karl and Shawn tip-toed through the sand around the small, dangerous mounds and turned the corner where the remains were pressed forever upon the granite plug. Oddly catching the light, the spouts looked like noses, faceless noses ready to sneeze. And nearing the end, they hurried through the last section of the passage where the steps came into view. Much relieved, they took them two at a time and inhaled the cool fresh air as the stars winked overhead.

"Everything is fine," Karl said to the captain. "Close her up."

Without a word, he and Shawn drove down the Pyramid Road and through Giza, mulling over the excitement and the danger, wondering what mysteries were yet to be learned.

As they crossed the bridge to the island, Saint Joseph's Catholic Church struck its bells to herald the new day. They passed the Opera House and the Cairo Tower on Shari Umm Kalthom along the Nile, where trees sheltered lovers romancing on its banks.

"I'll be glad to crawl into bed," Shawn said as he turned the corner.

"And not too soon," Karl agreed.

Shawn parked in front of the flat. As they took the stairs to the second floor, Shawn was a single pace behind. Karl turned the key and flipped on the light.

"Good evening, Karl."

Karl stared. Shawn bolted. Talib sat in the center of the room, facing the door.

"Get him," Talib ordered, and black-uniformed police pushed Karl aside in pursuit of Shawn.

Scuffling noises came from the hall as Shawn fled down the stairs and across the street.

"That was not a wise move," Talib said, blowing

smoke.

"What are you doing here?" Karl said angrily.

"Finding criminals. What were you doing at the pyramids, Karl?" he said acidly.

"That's none of your business."

"The council ordered your little excavation closed. You were—"

"What do you want?"

"What I want, Karl, is running down the street." Ashes fell on his belly.

"You'll never catch him."

"We'll see."

More police came from the kitchen and the bedrooms.

"What are they looking for?"

"Evidence, Karl. After all, you are harboring a criminal."

"He's not a criminal."

"A criminal wanted for questioning, a criminal I believe is holding your daughter hostage, a criminal identified by a witness."

"That's ridiculous and you know it."

"You are obstructing justice, Cassim, and I'm placing you under arrest." He blew smoke in rings into the air.

"You wouldn't dare."

Talib snapped his fingers. Karl dashed for the

phone. He was wrestled to the floor and handcuffed.

"You cannot be that stupid," Karl said.

"You two," Talib said to his officers, "take him to police headquarters. The rest of you finish searching." He stood and ground out his cigarette on the carpet.

Karl was hauled away, driven to police headquarters and put in a cell in the basement surrounded by hardened criminals. Across the aisle, a huge bearded felon in ragged clothes argued loudly with someone in the next cell. Before long, fists were flying through the bars. Karl turned away. He sat on the edge of a cot that reeked of urine and sweat, wondering if Shawn had been caught. The shouting subsided when the jailer rattled bars with his iron stick and unlocked the cell. A young man was thrown into the cell with the huge bearded man who smiled as the lad cowered in a corner. Karl could imagine what was about to happen. The jailer grinned and walked away.

Feeling utterly helpless and strung out, Karl leaned his aching head against the stone wall, covered his ears, and closed his eyes.

Suddenly, he was alert and gazing into the sky. The bars, the foul smells, the criminals were gone. All around him were stars twinkling, comets soaring, galaxies glowing, planets circling suns, all with a clarity he had never known. He could touch them, if he wanted, his reach was that sure. A vitality felt only in his youth, accompanied by inner peace, filled him.

And then, a voice . . . a voice in mid-sentence. A rich, deep, comforting voice, familiar yet unidentifiable, drawing him into a conversation.

". . . a great emptiness."

"What?" Karl said.

"In loneliness, in boredom and in solitude, I became enraged. Devoured with such anger, I wildly threw my fists where lightning flashed like javelins, illuminating boundless depths, and darkness was no more. At my own power I was astonished; the limits of which I did not know, having never used or employed such mightiness. With immense fascination, I rolled open my hands, emitting leviathan rays of light, and, like a child with wet hands, I flung droplets into the extent of space, where they glowed and collided, bursting into millions and millions of sparks. Thusly, I created what you see, a vast and wonderful novelty. And with my new-found power, I began to experiment, creating many things near and far."

After a long pause, Karl found himself asking a question, a question that felt as though it was being drawn from him unwillingly. "Am I, then, one of your experiments?"

A swath of heaven glowed as the voice breathed, "Yes."

"And the Earth?"

"Yes."

"Is there only one Earth?"

Amusement. "No. There are many, for the universe is beyond imagination, even beyond your heightened awareness."

"Are they all like us? I mean, are we all the same . . . humans?"

"There are no two the same in all my creations."

Time passed as Karl thought. For all the questions, for all the years he had pondered these questions, he now found himself overwhelmed by the lack of them.

Finally, he said, "Why did you create us?"

"As I have said, out of loneliness and boredom."

"Then, why have you forgotten us?"

"I forget nothing. It is what you might call benign neglect."

"Neglect?"

"Yes. Don't you see that the pleasure of observation comes from the potential, the unexpected that can only be accomplished with free will."

"What of your will?"

"What about it?"

"People say that when things happen, especially tragic things, it is your will, your great design. Are you saying that you have no design?"

"Yes."

"What do you . . . how do you view this concept

perpetuated by various religions?"

"I don't."

"Why not?"

The stars, the suns suddenly grew brighter. Comets crashed, and the voice became impatient and angry. "Because by any standard, those who lead these religions are thieves, feeding on innocent, empty minds, minds that are and have been plied with unguents and ceremony. If my creations truly wish to know me, the worthy will look to the heavens. They will learn what is to be learned."

"And the rest?"

No answer came.

"But some of these people, these religions, have done many good things."

Stars burst. Lightning filled the vastness of space and mist swirled violently. "Name one," he shouted.

Karl grew uneasy. "Well," he stammered, "they provide aid and comfort to . . ."

Planets wobbled, galaxies tumbled, the universe was filled with chaos as his anger thundered, "For every drop of comfort, they have given a thousand drops of pain! In my name they have murdered, pillaged, raped, enslaved, destroyed, and created evil where none existed! Throughout time, they have blamed the devil when the devil is within!"

In the pause that followed, peace returned to the

universe. The glowing swath returned as he spoke once more.

"You profess no faith, Karl Cassim. Why do you ponder such things?"

"I . . . it is curiosity. I have read and wondered about what they say, what they teach."

Moments dwindled in silence as jewels glittered, softening the dark.

Humbly, Karl asked, "Why do we die?"

"So that you may live."

"But . . . but why? Why, then, are we put through the aimless agony of life?"

"So the worthy will live forever in my company, with all the joys and pleasures...if they choose wisely."

"I don't understand. There are no rules. There is no path. How would we know—?"

"I will put it to you this way. You are all accidents. You have been created through random selection. Some grow. Some prosper. Some do not. I do not interfere. You are an amusement. Of billions, some will be worth keeping, most will not. The worthy will live forever."

"What do you mean by worthy?"

"Ah, the questions. It is a very simple guide. The worthy will realize, learn, and remember one simple, single sentence which should be clearly obvious. *Do to others as you will have done to you.* You have been given a world of plenty; make the most of it. You have been given a mind; use it."

"What of the ten commandments?" Karl said.

"They are not of my making. Consider deeply what I have said with all its implication. It is simple. Remember it."

"May I ask—"

". . . you . . . up! Somebody wants to talk to you."

"What?" Karl said, dumbfounded.

"On your feet!"

Karl was prodded, handcuffed, and pushed into the aisle separating the cells. He looked in the cell across the way. The lad was on the cot, naked and crying. Bitterly, Karl squeezed his eyes shut as he was shoved down the corridor to a flight of stairs. At the top, a hall led to another hall and, finally, to a door with no name. His custodian drove him in and shoved him into a chair.

It was a dark, musty, windowless room. A single bulb glared in his face. There was a small table and another chair against a moldy green wall. Two black-uniformed policemen stood quietly behind him. While he waited, Karl's mind wandered for a moment. *It was a dream, wasn't it*, he thought.

Briskly, the door opened. Karl couldn't see the face of the man who walked in and sat at the table.

"Could you turn that light away?" Karl asked.

The man lit a cigarette and Karl knew who it was, the one whom he expected. "You didn't catch him, did you?"

Smoke blew in his direction. "Where are they?" Talib demanded.

"What are you talking about?"

"You know what I'm talking about. The seals, the cylinders, where are they?" He flicked ashes on a floor soiled with mahogany blotches and crushed cigarettes.

"Why?"

A fist hit his face. Blood ran.

"Where?"

Karl took a breath. "Why?"

Another knuckled fist struck him, blinding him as more blood oozed.

"I have all the time in the world," Talib sang cynically.

"So do I, it seems."

"Look, Karl, make it easy on yourself and cooperate with the police."

"If it were the police asking questions, I would be more than willing to cooperate."

Karl vomited from the blows to his stomach. His eye swelled shut. When he hit the floor, pain shot up his spine as stiff leather shoes kicked him. He heard himself groan uncontrollably as he was lifted back into the hard wooden chair. He could barely keep his head up.

"Let's try this again," Talib said acidly. "Where are the seals?"

"It seems to me, Hassandi," Karl said, taking a moment to breathe, "that you are asking these questions on behalf of someone else. Who is it?"

A guard poised for a blow. Talib raised a hand. "Whatever gave you that absurd idea?"

Karl droned, "It seems to me that on the one hand you know more and care more about the seals than you should. On the other hand, you don't know what they say, what they mean. So, to you they are worthless which means someone else is involved. You are exposed, Hassandi."

Karl could feel belligerent eyes on his skin. He could see smoke being forced from Talib's lungs and hear the gush of air that propelled it. Finally, Talib said, "That does not concern you."

"How much are they paying you?"

"Where are they?"

"Safe."

More blows to the stomach and to the face.

Talib said, "We searched the vault at the museum, but they were not there. Sarah was very cooperative."

"Sarah is a fine woman."

"They are not in your flat, or in your car. So, where did you put them?"

Karl said, "Beyond your reach."

Talib stood. He ground out his cigarette on the floor and looked down at Karl. "One last time," he said. "Where are the seals?"

Karl looked up, but he couldn't see Talib's face. He blinked blood. "Gone," he said.

The blows came quickly, persistently, intolerably as Talib stormed out of the suffocating room.

When Karl awoke, he was on the floor, on his back, in his cell. He realized only one eye could open and the other was blurred. Close to the ceiling ran a long range of squalid windows that strained the light of day. In every joint, pain gnawed. He tried to raise himself from the filth, from the putrid odor. Even breathing hurt. He moaned. He moved his hand. It seemed to be the only thing he could move without stabbing pain.

Hard, knocking footsteps woke him. Still he lay on the floor. Mumbling, someone was mumbling close by. He heard the footsteps creep away. He had to move. He managed to get on all fours and in one horrendous burst of pain lunged for the cot. Through slits, he looked at the ceiling, at the paint peeling like scales. The window was black. *It must be night,* he thought.

What he wouldn't give for a mouthful of water. His tongue was swollen and his throat arid as the desert. Beyond the smell, the coolness of the night ebbing from the weathered seams of the window bathed his pain.

He lost all track of time. He had seen light and darkness, but the order confused him as he lay there. Flashes of his daughter's face came and went as he considered what might be happening to her if she were still alive. "Oh, my God," he whispered, "my little girl."

He thought about Talib and about the Great Pyramid. The emaciated image of Krubrick came to mind. "Where have I heard that name?" he mouthed. "Why was he at the pyramid so late in the night? How was he able to persuade the council to . . ."

The desperately thin, pale face appeared again in snapshots, a memory that had aged some twenty years. Now it came back with the speed of light with all its glaring perversities.

Krubrick—expelled from Iraq.

Krubrick—barred from excavating in India, Mexico, Peru, and the Himalayas.

Krubrick—first to inquire about the disappearance of James Farley.

Floughs Krubrick—billionaire, authority on the occult.

Floughs Krubrick—proprietor of the largest pharmaceutical company in the world.

Floughs Krubrick—suspected in the disappearance of four archeologists and numerous ancient artifacts.

Floughs Krubrick—asked questions about the Sages at the astronomical symposium.

"I see you're awake."

Karl looked toward the cell door. He tried to speak but the dust scratched his throat.

"Give him some water," Talib ordered.

Iron bars creaked. Water drenched him.

"You fool. I said give him the water."

The fool hustled away.

Slowly and with care, Karl sat up. A ladle was pressed to his lips.

"Clean him up. Get him some clothes." Talib marched away without another word.

Someone who looked like a doctor came in with a black bag and began to sponge his wounds and cover his cuts with bandages. When he was finished, someone else trotted in with pressed, mismatched clothes and helped him dress.

"What is going on?" Karl said softly.

The man looked at him, but did not reply.

He was paraded to the large entry hall with the help of two policemen. A dignified-looking, well-dressed man paced impatiently. Karl's escorts left him, barely able to stand, and hurried away. Quickly, the man came forward to help him.

"Do I know you?" Karl asked.

"I've not had the pleasure," he said. "My name is Jerrod Akmed. I'm from President Mubarak's office. I've come to get you out of here. Are you in much pain?"

"I'll manage. But how did you—"

"You'll see in a moment. Can you walk?"

"I think so."

A black Mercedes with presidential seals idled in front of the building. Akmed opened the rear door. Sarah burst into tears as Karl was helped in the back seat.

"Take him to the hospital," Akmed said to the driver.

"Please, take me home." Karl turned to Sarah. "How did you know?"

"Shawn came to my house and told me what happened. I called President Mubarak."

"So, he got away. Good."

"He's waiting at your place."

"How long have I been here, Sarah?"

"Three days. Are you going to be all right?"

"I'll be fine, Sarah, just fine. I can't thank you enough," he said as she tried to hold back the tears.

The driver and Sarah helped Karl up the stairs. She knocked and Shawn threw open the door.

"Those bastards!" Shawn muttered.

They put him into bed, and fed him some broth and soft fruit. He asked for some brandy. It hardly had touched his lips when he fell asleep.

CHAPTER 34

Sun filled his room. The sweet smell of fresh air flowed from the window. The body of inflamed tissue survived beneath clean sheets, throbbing from head to thigh. Groaning, he rolled out of bed.

Listening, patiently waiting for him to stir, Shawn opened the door. "Good morning," he said softly. "How do you feel?"

Karl shook his head.

"Would you like a pain pill?"

"I don't think so...maybe some aspirin."

"Coming right up."

While Karl sat on the edge of the bed, Shawn obliged.

"Do you think you can eat something.?"

"Oh, you bet. I'm starved. But first I've got to take a hot shower. I can't get the smell of that place out of my system."

"Let me help you into the bath. I'll fix breakfast."

"What time is it?"

"Almost eleven-thirty."

Ravenous, Karl ate everything put in front of him.

Eggs, minced meat, peppers, cheese, and rolled phyllo topped with honey and chocolate, all drowned with strong black coffee.

"What do you think will happen to Talib?" Shawn inquired.

"That depends. I hope he gets thrown into one of his own cells with one very large, sex-starved Bedouin. I was thinking," he went on, "how we take freedom for granted until something happens."

Shawn said, "We take a lot of things for granted, Karl."

"That's true in more ways than you think. Too young too soon, too smart too late, and don't ask me where I heard that."

They smiled.

"You are feeling better."

"Much. You know, Shawn, when I was in that cell, I remembered where I heard Krubrick's name. He is a U.S. citizen, a billionaire, and mixed up in all sorts of scandals. All dealing with archeology."

Shawn leaned into the table.

"I believe he is very generously spreading his money around. That's how he was able to get that letter of authorization to close us down." Karl sipped his coffee. "Did Sarah tell you that Talib went to the museum to search for the seals?"

"Yes, she told me. I understand he got a little

rough with her."

"I was sorry to hear that," Karl replied. "Shawn, I would like you to do me a favor. Would you ask Julian to go to the U.S. Consulate and use his influence? I need a profile on Floughs Krubrick. I strongly believe he is behind Talib."

"Why would Krubrick go through all this trouble?"

Karl took Shawn into his eyes. He whispered, "The treasure of Thoth."

Shawn whistled. "Then you must think he took the cylinder from the museum. And if he did take it, then he has Nanette."

Karl closed his eyes. "Oh, Shawn, what if . . . what if they . . . ?" His lip quivered.

"Don't even think it, Karl. If she weren't alive, there would be nothing for him to bargain with."

"I suppose that makes sense." Karl squeezed his cup. As Shawn cleared the table, he said, "Talib didn't find the seals, did he?"

"No, and he'll never find them. I hid them where they'd never look."

"I don't want to know. If Talib ever catches up with me, I want nothing to give him."

"At this moment, I believe his mind is occupied with more urgent matters. With Mubarak's people breathing down his neck, he has a lot of explaining to do." Karl glanced at the clock. "Shawn, what day is it?"

"Saturday."

"No, I mean the date."

"February first. Why?"

"Six days. We have six days."

"For what?"

"For the seventh."

"You mean the seventh seal? But it could come the seventh of any month," Shawn said.

"Yes, it could. But I have this feeling that it is coming sooner than later."

"But Karl, even if we get the seventh seal, we're still missing the stolen one."

"I know. But there might be a way around that."

"What are you thinking?"

"I have to go back to London."

"Karl, you're in no condition to go chasing around London."

"I have to go, Shawn. Hunsdon is the only hope we have. He knows much more than I previously thought. He gave me a folder with spells, with Words of Power that with all my years of study I've never seen. He numbered them one through seven. I believe they are for the seven gates of Osiris."

"They're in the *Book of the Dead*, Karl. The formula, the words and all spelled out," Shawn said.

"They're not the same. Hunsdon wrote that these

were secret, used only by Pharaoh and the high priests. He said these came from the gods themselves."

"How would he know about the gates, when we just discovered the Hall of Mirrors?"

"Good question. But as I said, he knows much more than he told me. Shawn, I saw things in his library said to be lost or non-existent. For example, he had Manetho's Kings List complete and in pristine condition. There are only fragments in Turin! There were books on Egyptian magic and prophesies. I can't begin to tell you the extent of what he has at his fingertips. Oh, he knows, all right!"

For a moment, their minds strayed.

"I've got to see him," Karl whispered.

"Karl, please, for your own sake, take a few days to rest."

"Time. There isn't time."

"Very well, when will you leave?"

"As soon as I can get a flight to London."

CHAPTER 35

Karl arrived in London at twelve forty a.m. with an estimated hour's drive to Hunsdon house. Musing about a telegram he had sent, Karl wondered if he wouldn't arrive before it.

This taxi driver was far more amiable and chatty. While he went on about the Irish, about the Lutherans and the Catholics, about five-hundred years of war, Karl was elsewhere. His mind was on the passage, on Krubrick and Talib, but mostly on Nanette. In this swirl of reflections, Hunsdon's image invaded with his silent tongue and loud thoughts struck vividly in chalk.

In the light of a full moon, Hunsdon House appeared more baneful, more threatening in the stillness of aged timber, than it had in the moan of a shiftless wind.

Even from the road in the dead of night, Hunsdon House spread its wings between the pines, the giant oaks, squatting its massive girth on the landscape like a windowed caldron on hollow's eve.

Struck with this portrait painted in shadows, the

driver fell silent entering the grounds, allowing the car to slow to a crawl.

"Why are you slowing? What's wrong?" Karl asked.

"No reason," the driver said, speeding up. "It's this place. I've never seen it before." He wiped his face and mumbled, "Haunted, I'll bet."

The cabby stopped at the stoop. Karl paid him thirty-five pounds plus ten for a tip and asked him to return in twenty-four hours. He gathered his lone suitcase and stood on the porch as the driver hastily made his escape.

Karl lifted the knocker and struck the door three times. Expectantly, he waited and looked about. For February, the air was modest; not cold, not warm, just staid, aloof, and indifferent in the shrill light of the moon. Without the wind and the snow, dark smudges lurked beneath the spreading trees, deceiving the eye and tweaking the brain with ghostly images.

Otto appeared as indignant, as pompous as ever. Seeing Karl, Otto breathed deeply, burying his upper lids in his lower, grimacing with the words that followed. "Do you ever venture out-of-doors during the light of day, Doctor Cassim?" he asked. "Do come in."

"And how are you, Otto?"

"He will not see you, you know, doctor!"

"Of course, he will."

"May I remind you, doctor—"

"No, you may not." Karl stole the liberty of turning on more lights in the large entry hall, and noticed the mail table near the door had not been touched. He strutted to the large oak door, presuming that Sir Hunsdon was behind it and knocked loudly.

Otto galloped over and stood in front of the door, edging Karl away. "How dare you, sir . . . such impertinence!"

"Stand aside, Otto. I will not be kept waiting a night and a day. Not this time."

"But, sir . . . this is . . ."

The door flew open. Scowling between muttonchops, Hunsdon glared over his glasses.

Karl said, "We have to talk."

Despite his annoyance, Hunsdon's face did not reflect surprise. Karl saw something else in those dark eyes.

Hunsdon slammed the door and marched to his board. He scrawled, "What took you so long?"

"You knew I'd return? How?"

The board screeched, "Why are you here?"

"To find out what you haven't told me."

Priestly robes following his every move, he turned back to the board. "So ask."

"Fine," Karl said. "How did you know about the Arits?"

Sparks burst from the fire behind Hunsdon's strident figure. Droopy jowls buried in his massive neck, arms folded, legs apart beneath his robe, he waited. He wanted to hear it all.

Karl went on. "When did you get the seal you gave me? How do you know the secret Words of Power?"

Hunsdon turned his back as Karl continued question after question. He wiped the board clean and wrote, "Have you been in a street brawl?"

"What?" Karl said, beside himself.

Hunsdon underlined the question.

"Very well," Karl replied, taking his prescribed chair near the fire. "I was arrested and beaten," he began, as Hunsdon flowed to the next chair. He told him about Krubrick, the passage, the Hall of Mirrors and his rescue at the hands of President Mubarak. Hunsdon nodded solemnly, his eyes fixed on the dancing flames.

Karl studied him. Hunsdon's curled knuckle slowly brushed his lower lip as his eyes squinted and opened. His lips began to move as if he could speak. Then with a jerk, he boosted himself from the chair and stalked impressively to a far corner of the cavernous room. He fumbled for keys, unlocked a door and stepped inside.

Moments later, he sluggishly ambulated back to the fire. In his hands was what appeared to be a dark blue, veined book. Not until he set it on the blackboard's ledge did Karl realize that it was not a book at all, but a square of lapis lazuli filled with hieroglyphs.

Hunsdon shot a look straight into his eyes. Behind the glasses, he beamed as if he had raised Lazarus from the dead. He snatched his candle-stick chalk and scribbled, "Read!"

Karl stood and walked to the board. He slid his finger gently about the inch-thick slab, appraising its gold veins and . . . sparks jumped to his touch. He pulled back, eyeing Hunsdon.

"It's energized," Karl said.

Hunsdon nodded. His eyes smiled as if he'd revealed a magician's secret.

"I can't make it out. It's very..."

Chalk spit flakes as he wrote, "Try!"

Staring intently, he began to piece the unusually graceful symbols together. In his mind he read, his lips moving slowly. Karl jumped.

Hunsdon's pointer lashed the board. "Read aloud!" he scratched.

"All right. Must you be so . . . so unreserved?"

Pontifically, he lifted a brow and underlined.

Twenty inches high and fourteen inches wide, the Lapis tablet was not like any other. Karl had to ask, "Where did it come from?"

"Read!" was his answer.

Karl grew impatient and prickly. "I am not a student or an idiot. I have come—"

The pointer split into pieces. Hunsdon's anger

couldn't be contained. His cloak cleared tables as he spun, fisting the board, writing over what was there, piercing the ear, the teeth, and the brain with the horrible etching sound only chalk on board could make. "None of your business!" he scribbled. "Read!!!" He faced him.

Karl staggered back. Hunsdon's impressive hulk set for a skirmish . . . of words, he hoped. "Why must it always be like this? Can't we talk to each other civilly?"

For a moment, Sir Hunsdon was undisturbed.

Karl was prepared for another outburst.

Hunsdon's face dropped its expression. His eyes met the floor. He nodded, clearing his throat, and erased the board. In small letters, he wrote, "I am sorry. It's been so long since . . ." He rubbed out the sentence. He started again. "This Lapis tablet came from the seat of Osiris near Abydos, beyond the Mother of Pots, the field of shards. It was found about the time as the Rosetta Stone and shipped to France by a man named Jomard in 1802. There, it was lost for over a hundred years.

"With the fall of Czar Nicholas II in 1917, royalty fled Russia. In 1966, I purchased this tablet from her Imperial Highness, the granddaughter of Grand Duke Cyril, the last head of the Romanov dynasty." He scrubbed the board and started again.

"She shared this sketchy story, adding that she was

forced to sell many of her treasures, because her assets had been taken by the Soviets."

"Fascinating," Karl mumbled. "What causes the electrical charge?"

"When I received it, it was in a decomposing leather pouch. The Grand Duchess never mentioned its unusual properties; probably she was unaware of them. I nearly dropped it, having received several shocks. I proceeded to have it analyzed. The report said, 'It is impossible for lapis to store energy. The source in this stone cannot be scientifically explained'."

"Thank you," Karl said.

Hunsdon cleared the board, took up his chalk and wrote, "Please read, aloud."

He leaned closer to the tablet and began slowly, fumbling on words he wasn't sure of.

"High priest, Chief Royal Seal-Bearer, Beloved Companion to Surid, King of Upper and Lower Egypt, Son of Ra, follower of Horus, descendant of Osiris, foremost of the westerners; Overseer of horn, hoof, feather, scale, and pleasure ponds; Keeper of silver and gold, Master of Secrets, whose coming is awaited, in year 81, third month of winter, day 12 of the Divine King Surid, Nophi Ur Ma, Nophi the Great seer sayith these words." Karl stopped and asked, "How am I doing?"

Hunsdon smiled, nodding. He wrote, "I thought you couldn't read it?"

"After a while, it comes to you. I must confess some of the symbols I'm guessing at. A question."

There was a nod.

"I don't remember much about Surid. Could you refresh my memory?"

Another nod.

"Surid was thought to be an antediluvian king," Hunsdon wrote, "who built the pyramids around 15,000 BC to preserve all knowledge, all secrets, all magic worth saving."

"I see. But how does this shed any light on the cylinder seals?"

He scribbled, "Read on."

Karl scanned the tablet and found where he had left off. He read:

"I have seen the seven knots of hair. I have gazed upon the seven pots of sheep's blood. I have read the seven secrets of Osiris on seven seals scribed upon turning stones of crystal. I have measured the water of the Great Sea. I have studied the imperishable stars and seen the face of Ra.

"Oh, my Divine King Surid, who lives forever, the stars have foretold a great devastation. Prepare yourself. Gather all which is sacred to you in a strong place. For when the heart of the Lion rests on the head of Cancer, the Four Pillars of the world shall vanish beneath the Great Water, an inundation shall wash the

Earth clean. Prepare! Prepare! Prepare! So sayith Nophi Ur Ma High Priest to Surid."

"Amazing!" Karl said. "Why haven't you made public this marvelous piece of history?"

Hunsdon's eyes thinned as he poured disgust over his glasses. He wrote, "Why should I???"

"It's . . . it's important. This tablet could very well force them to rewrite history."

Chalk screeched. "Let the arrogant bastards moor themselves in quicksand. After I'm dead, I'll have the last laugh." He stared into the fire, nodding, grinning with the confidence of the proverbial cat.

Karl could appreciate his sentiment because of the badgering he had endured when he had made his own assumptions known many years ago. Somehow, Hunsdon's feelings were justifiable.

"Well," Karl said, "now we know that the seals are at the very least 15,000 years old."

Hunsdon swung that grinning confidence out from the fire and leveled it at him. The chalk screeched on the board. "Turn it over."

Karl swept his eyes from Hunsdon to the lapis tablet. He turned it over as sparks tingled his fingers. His jaw went limp. He glared.

There was a map of the pyramids and the passage he had uncovered. Beneath the causeway of the Great Pyramid, the passage led to the Sphinx. The tablet described in every detail what an initiated man, a worthy man, must know to circumvent the dangerous traps set by Surid. It described the Hall of Mirrors and the Arits, the seven gates to Osiris. But most important of all, it contained the seven secrets, the Words of Power to pass safely through the gates. Moreover, Nophi praised Surid and the Venerables for protecting the Kingdom of Osiris.

"So, this is how you knew about the Arits."

He smiled.

"Do you think this will lead to the legendary Hall of Records?"

Hunsdon's brow gave a twitter. He wrote, "Possibly something more enigmatic."

"Sir Hunsdon, you must come with me to Egypt. You have to. I believe that the seventh seal will reveal itself on the seventh of February. Be with me then."

He flowed to his chair and sat spreading his robe over the arms. Settling his eyes in the flames, he stared. Sparks spit. Flames danced. E. Osborne Hunsdon stared.

"Please, Sir Hunsdon," Karl urged. "If anyone deserves the credit for what we'll find, you most certainly do. You must return to Egypt with me."

Slowly, Hunsdon rose. He delicately embraced the candle-stick chalk and wrote, "That's why you have been chosen."

"I don't understand."

Hunsdon wrote, "You will."

"I'm not sure I understand, but will you come with me?"

Hunsdon shrugged. He scratched, "Leave me. Let me think. Otto will look after you."

"Sir Hunsdon, I told my cab to return in twenty-four hours."

"Go!" He set the chalk on the ledge. He ambled to his chair. His eyes were lost, consumed by the steady, nearly silent, always comforting fire.

Karl left him peering into the eternal flame and headed quietly toward the door. By itself, it opened. He threw a look over his shoulder one last time.

Otto was dutifully perched yards down the hall. "Would you care for some refreshment, sir, or would you care to retire?"

"Both," Karl said. "A question, Otto."

"Certainly, sir."

"How does he open and close that door?"

"When I figure that out, sir, you'll be the first to know. This way, sir," he said, and led him to the dining room. "Be seated, sir," Otto said. "I've prepared a tray which I'm sure you will enjoy."

A moment later, he brought in a large silver tray. Karl salivated at the sight of it. Arranged like a deck of cards were three denominations of cocktail breads, shrimp, salmon and pickled herring, steak tartar, sweet meats, an array of stuffed and unstuffed vegetables, shelled nuts, sliced fruit, and a peach flan immersed in caramel.

After coffee, Karl was led to a suite on the main floor. "Otto, I'm going to nap for a little while. Please wake me when Sir Hunsdon has made his decision. Oh, one more thing, my cab. It will arrive at 1:30."

Otto didn't reply. Instead, he tilted his head and dropped his lids in agreement.

Four hours later, Otto rapped on the door and strode in. "Doctor Cassim, sorry to disturb you," he droned. "Sir Hunsdon has made his decision."

"I'd like to see him," Karl said, awake in an instant.

"That's not possible, sir."

"Otto . . ."

"Sir, he is making arrangements to accompany you to Cairo . . . on one condition."

"Which is?"

"You must agree that there is to be no press, no announcement of any kind."

"That would be the farthest thing from my mind. Agreed."

"Very well, sir. I will alert Sir Hunsdon."

"Thank you, Otto"

An incline of his head.

"Don't forget my cab."

"I shall send it away."

"You can't do that. We'll have—"

"Sir Hunsdon doesn't take taxis, doctor. They are too cafeteria and very confining. His driver will be ready."

"Oh."

Another incline with heavy lids.

CHAPTER 36

An Egyptair transport glided over the southwestern tip of Europe above the clouds, heading for the African continent. Surely, somewhere beneath the boiling gray-to-black cloud cover, rain was raging. Bolts of lightning perforated the bleak popcorn shawl like snaps from the paparazzi. On occasion, the plane jarred, most likely reminding its occupants of the turbulent weather not only here, but around the world. Fires brought on by drought, flash floods, temperatures in the triple digits, earthquakes, erupting volcanoes, seasons out of whack, all causing unspeakable tragedies.

But here and there the sun shone, the seas calmed and the multitude attributed the naughty rumblings of Mother Nature to PMS, or ozone depletion, or global warming, or whatever cantankerous remedy that fit.

However, Egypt remained untouched from the tantrums of an uncontrollable, misbehaving mater, and as the puffy blanket lifted over the Mediterranean, the coast of Alexandria came into view sharp and clear.

Sir Hunsdon slept.

Because Sir E. Osborne Hunsdon had special needs, Otto was a necessity. He could sign, took care of his personal business, and traveled with Hunsdon with a pride of baggage. As his station required, Sir Hunsdon checked into the Nile Hilton, into a suite of rooms befitting his dignity, his wallet and rank, declining to stay at Karl's modest flat.

Under the assumption that the seventh cylinder seal would appear in three days' time, an agenda was set. Whether or not the crystal appeared, the passage would be explored on the seventh.

After depositing Sir Hunsdon at the Nile Hilton, Karl dropped by the museum for a catch-up with Sarah. Except for the German team seeking permission to drill into the bedrock of the Sphinx, everything was normal. He boarded his official vehicle and hurried home. Shawn would be ecstatic to learn that Hunsdon was in Cairo.

Karl opened the door. An envelope lay on the floor. He set his bag on a chair, picked up the plain envelope and called out, "Shawn. Shawn, I'm back with great news."

The feel of the house told him it was empty. It was late in the afternoon and he guessed that Shawn had stepped out, perhaps to do some shopping.

He opened the envelope. And gasped. "Your last chance," the note said. "All the seals at midnight or she dies."

"Thank God," Karl muttered. "She's alive."

"Stay by your phone," the note went on. "You will be called and given instructions. This is your last chance."

"My God, how long has this letter been here?" Karl paced the floor, his mind racing in all directions. Pain shot through his chest. "Not now," he growled, and grabbed the phone. "Julian?" he said, his voice taut with worry and anger, "is Shawn with you?"

"No, Karl, I thought he was at your place."

"Please, can you come over right now?"

"What's wrong?"

"Please, I'll explain when you get here."

"I'm on my way."

In less than ten minutes, there was a knock on the door and Karl rushed to open it. "Nancy!" Julian was tucked close behind her. "I thought you were in Rome."

"It's a long story. Karl, you darling, what happened to your face?"

"Julian didn't tell you? Where are my manners, come in."

"She was at my door right before you called," Julian explained. "I didn't have a chance—"

"Please, in the kitchen." Karl led them to the letter.

"What is it, Karl?"

With a trembling hand, Karl handed the letter to Julian.

"My God! When did you get this?"

"Just now. I just got back from London. I opened the door, and there it was on the floor."

"Calm down, Karl, your heart," Nancy said.

"To hell with my heart. Nanette could be dead, don't you understand? I've been gone for two days. I don't know how long this sat on the floor, and I can't find Shawn."

"Did you try calling his place?" Julian said.

"How stupid! I didn't think of it. He could have gone to get clothes or something." Karl got up and started for the phone.

"Let me," Julian said. He dialed the number and waited facing the wall. He sighed. "No answer."

"Damn . . ." Karl's fists clinched.

"Take it easy, Karl, please?"

"Oh, Nancy, how can I take it easy?"

"She's right, Karl, you've got to calm down. Did you check his room? Maybe he left something behind."

"Julian, I haven't checked anything."

Nancy held Karl's hand while Julian went to Shawn's room.

"Nothing," Julian said. "His shower and sink are bone dry. There's no telling how long he's been gone."

"Now what?" Karl asked.

"All right. Let's try to figure this thing out," Julian said. "When did you leave for London?"

"I got a flight late Saturday night."

"Okay. Did Shawn take you to the airport?"

"Yes."

"Did he say he was coming back here?"

"No, I just assumed . . ."

"That's okay. What time did you leave here?"

"About ten. I wanted to make sure I was on that plane."

Nancy said, "That means the letter could have been here all that time."

Karl's eyes dropped. "That's what I'm afraid of."

She regretted having mentioned it.

"All this for some old pieces of glass," Karl whispered. With rancor, his stomach boiled. "Well, they can have the damn things. All I want is my daughter. I didn't ask for this. I was just doing my job, what I was trained to do, what I love to do and where did it get me? Now, it's too late."

Leaning across the table, Julian said, "Not necessarily."

Karl looked up. "What do you mean?"

"I'd give these guys a little more credit than that."

"I don't understand."

"Well, look, I think they would have made sure you were going to be home. The bottom line is . . . they want the seals."

Karl nodded. "But I don't have them all, Julian.

With the one I got from Hunsdon, I have five. I am assuming the seventh seal will appear on the seventh of this month."

"Shawn told me. He also said you were going to try to bring Hunsdon back with you."

"I did."

Nancy was amazed. "You must have been very convincing."

"I told him the truth. And what I didn't tell him, he already knew. He knew about the Hall of Mirrors and the gates. Most importantly, he knows how to get through the gates. He thinks there might be a way to do it without having all seven! But now, all the effort was for nothing. It's either my daughter or the seals. It's all been a waste of time."

"Maybe not," Julian said with a small grin.

"You're losing me, Julian."

"I think you rattled their cage. You went into the passage that night, the same night you were arrested. But you didn't tell them anything, and they didn't dream you'd be released.

"It would not be hard for them to find out that you went to London, would it? They're not stupid," Julian went on. "I'll bet they've been watching your every move. They know there is only one reason you'd go to London, and that is to talk to Hunsdon. What's more, Shawn told me you remembered that Krubrick is an

Egyptologist. It all fits! Krubrick is getting nervous. Don't you see that's why you got the letter now?"

"I think you're right. It does make sense."

Nancy put her hands together forming a T. "All right, you two," she said, "I think we all deserve a break. How about some coffee?"

"You're right, dear, as usual." Julian brushed her arm. "I could use some coffee. What do you say, Karl?"

"Sounds good. We're going to need it."

While Nancy busied herself with water and grounds, Karl said, "I'm glad you came back, Nancy."

"Well, there wasn't any point in going home."

"You can say that again," Julian breathed.

"What's the mystery?"

"While I was in Rome, I was served with divorce papers."

"How terrible! Did you know it was coming?"

"Not really. I suspected David was fooling around, but I wasn't sure. I didn't expect this."

"Yes," Julian said, "and I wondered how Jennifer knew so much about David Gottlieb. It seems, Karl, that my wife and Nancy's husband have been having an affair for quite some time."

"Sorry to hear that."

"Oh, don't be. Living with Jennifer was getting to be . . ." His voice trailed off.

Nancy filled their cups.

Julian said quietly, "I hate to ask this, Karl, but you don't think Talib found Shawn, do you?"

"No, I don't think so. Not with Mubarak's people keeping busy."

Nancy said softly, "I guess all we can do for now is wait."

"What time is it?" Julian asked.

Karl looked at the clock on the wall. "Nearly eight. This waiting is driving me crazy."

"I know," she said, and took his hand. "They marked you up something awful, didn't they?"

Karl nodded.

"Animals," she muttered. "They're nothing but animals."

"This isn't the States, Nancy. The police here can be your worst enemy."

"So, you think that Talib and Krubrick are partners?" Julian asked.

"I don't think there is any doubt about it."

"Shawn told me Krubrick tried to take over your excavation. I thought that was a bold move, exposing his hand like that. It shows he's getting desperate."

Under his breath, Karl said, "If I knew where he lived, I'd—"

"Karl, don't think about it. Your health is more important," she said.

"I know." He thought out loud, "I guess I won't

need that report on Krubrick after all, Julian. It seems we have pieced it all together without it."

"It can't hurt. I should have it by tomorrow. Maybe we'll find something we don't know."

Karl nodded and sipped his coffee.

"Karl, tell me about Hunsdon." Nancy said. "He is quite an enigma. Never gives interviews, lives reclusively . . ."

"Oh, there is much more than that."

Her eyes begged for explanation.

"He can't speak, you know."

"Since when?"

"I don't exactly know. I'd guess ten, twelve years from the way his steward talked."

"How did that happen?"

"He wouldn't say."

"Well," Nancy asked, "how did he talk to you?"

"He uses a blackboard."

"I should have thought of that."

"The man is a fountain of knowledge. He's forgotten more about Egypt than most people will ever know. You wouldn't believe the collection of artifacts he has, things I never knew existed."

"Will we have a chance to meet him?" she asked.

"That, I think, would be a very delicate situation. He is an impatient man with an extraordinary temper. I had to promise not to tell anyone he is in Cairo."

"You know, Karl, in his heyday he used to get a lot of press. It seemed that every time he made the slightest discovery, it was highly publicized," she recalled.

Karl glanced at the clock. "It's 8:35," he said. "Isn't there something we can do?"

"Yes, Karl," she said, "we can patiently wait."

He shook his head.

Julian looked at Nancy and then at Karl. "Are you really going to give them the seals?"

Karl leveled his eyes without blinking. "Absolutely." He wasn't ready to reveal Hunsdon's prediction that the seals would return to him.

Nancy sipped her coffee and tried to change the subject. "What do you think is at the end of the passage?"

Karl fingered the rim of his cup. It was a simple enough question, but his reply was not. "Answers," he whispered. "The ancient Egyptians, men or gods, hoarded, secreted their knowledge for thousands of years. For whatever reason, they have waited until now to reveal it. Those crystal cylinders have given us hints, and they have given us potent curses. All I can say is that whatever there is at the end of that passage, it must be earth-shaking."

"Do you think it's the Hall of Records?" Nancy asked.

"It could be, but I think it's more than that."

Julian set his cup down. "Karl, what about the

curses? Do you really think they pose a threat?"

His face tightened. His eyes darkened. "I've seen with my own eyes what those curses can do. What awaits in that passage . . ." He trailed off. He slid back in his chair and steepled his fingers. "It's five of nine and this waiting is unbearable."

The kitchen was quiet. Nancy moved closer to Julian. His arm wrapped her closer as he pressed his lips to her cheek. "I'm glad you're here," he whispered.

Karl paced; the silence grew louder.

Like smashing glass, ringing broke the quiet. Eyes froze. Heartbeats thundered. Karl dashed for the telephone.

"Insist on talking to her," Julian blurted, as he said, "This is Karl."

A voice began to give instructions.

Karl interrupted. "I want to talk to my daughter," he said harshly.

The voice was taken back by the sudden insolence and for a second didn't reply.

"Did you hear me? I talk to her, or you can forget the seals."

Karl heard a hand cover the mouthpiece. His heartbeat shook him as time ticked away.

"Daddy, they told me—"

"Nanette, are you all right?"

Her phone hit the floor. The voice said, "Now—"

"Put her back on."

"You listen and follow directions, Cassim, or that's the last time you hear her voice."

Karl listened.

"Leave the seals at the stela between the paws of the Sphinx."

"Oh, no. Not this time. I'm not playing that game. We exchange seals for my daughter. That's how it's going to be. Period!"

He vaguely heard mumbling, arguing in the background.

"All right. Seals for your daughter. Midnight at the Sphinx. You come alone. If we suspect anything, she's dead." The line went dead.

The phone fell from his hand as he staggered backward. Julian and Nancy rushed to catch him and eased him into a chair.

"Karl, you've got to see a doctor," she said.

"No, I'll be all right. Just some water."

"He's sweating and cold," Julian murmured.

She wrung out a cloth and pressed it to his forehead. "Hold this, Julian." She filled a glass and held it to his lips.

He swallowed a little and leaned back, his arms dangling at his sides. Limp and wet, he closed his eyes. "I'll be fine," he managed.

Julian's gaze clamped on hers. "Let's get him to bed."

They carried him into his room and stuffed pillows under his head.

"What are we going to do now?" Julian breathed.

"My pills," Karl mouthed, "in the cabinet."

Nancy ran to the bathroom and flung open the medicine chest. Behind antacids, she found the bottle and read the dosage. One under the tongue, it said.

"Open your mouth, Karl." She slid a small pill under his tongue.

She and Julian waited, holding hands. When Karl fell asleep, they tip-toed back to the kitchen.

CHAPTER 37

"He'll be in no condition to handle this," Julian said softly.

Agreeing, she nodded. "If only Shawn were here."

"Nancy, what do you suppose happened to him?"

"I don't know. It isn't like him to disappear like this, is it?"

"Not that I know of. Right now he could be a very large help to Karl."

Time passed as their thoughts wandered.

"I thought all this intrigue was getting to you. What happened to change your mind?"

"It was getting to me something awful. But when I was in Rome thinking about you and Karl and Shawn . . . I don't know. Then I got the papers. Suddenly, I had nothing but my job. I thought about my life and David." She looked into his eyes. "I realized how much in love with you I am. And everything that I was afraid of wasn't so frightening any more."

He took her hand. "Do you think we can make it work?"

"Do you love me?"

"With all my heart."

"It'll work. I just know it will. My God! Karl, what are you doing out of bed?"

"I feel much better. I'm glad you lovebirds have settled things."

"Just how long have you been standing there, Doctor Cassim?" Julian said.

"Long enough," he quipped.

"You're a devil," Nancy teased.

"I've been called worse and it is all true."

"You look much better. How do you feel?"

"A little weak, but a lot stronger."

"Do you think you are well enough to go through with—"

"I would go through hell for my daughter."

Nancy said, "We still have a couple of hours. Why don't you lie down and rest?"

"I can't. Hear anything from Shawn?"

Heads shook.

"I do worry about that boy."

"Karl, what about the seals? Do you have them here?"

"No. I have to go to the museum."

"Can I drive you?" Julian offered.

"I think you had better."

"Good," she said, "I'll grab my purse."

"Maybe you'd better stay here," Julian said, "just in case Shawn shows up."

"You're right. Someone has to tell him," she said.

"You want to leave now, Karl?"

"Yes, I think so. I want to have plenty of time."

As they crossed the bridge into Cairo, Julian asked, "Nervous, Karl?"

"No, I'm scared to death."

Preoccupied, few words were exchanged while Julian drove. At the rear of the museum, he stopped.

"Want me to come with you?"

"I'll just be a few minutes. I have to pay my respects to Rameses the Great."

"I thought you were getting the seals."

"I am." He closed the door.

Julian waited. The car idled. People walked by and cars passed. Until then, he had not been so intimately involved. But now, shadows seemed villainous, and faces became impostors and every foreign noise a calamity. "Nervous is not the word," he mumbled, "but it will do."

Abruptly, the door flung open. Startled, Julian hit the horn. Karl slipped in.

"Sorry. I've got the jitters."

"It's okay. We have one more stop to make."

"Karl, you shouldn't be pushing it."

"I'm fine, really."

"Where to?"

"Right over there." He pointed to the Nile Hilton.

"What's over there?"

"Not a what, a who. Sir Hunsdon. I've got to ask him something."

"This time, do you mind if I wait in the lobby?"

Karl smiled. "Of course not."

He parked and they entered. Karl headed for the bank of elevators, and Julian made himself comfortable, watching carefree tourists come and go.

After several knocks, Otto answered the door. "Enter," he said flatly.

"Is Sir Hunsdon in?"

"Naturally. One moment." Otto carried himself through an elaborate archway and down a hall and disappeared from view.

Karl heard a knock, a door open and close. Several moments later, Sir Hunsdon strode in. He nodded a greeting and began to sign. Otto, his interpreter, put voice to his graceful motion as if his hands spoke.

"Have you news?" he asked.

"May I sit?"

A nod.

"I had a little bout with my heart, I'm sorry."

"Nonsense," came back loudly. "Are you all right?"

"Yes, thank you. Just weak, but it will pass. Sir Hunsdon, this evening I received a call from my daughter's abductors. They want the seals for my daughter's life. I'm going to do it."

A cynical smile came to his face. "By all means," he signed. "Let them have the seals. But get your daughter first."

"Why are you smiling?"

"You forget."

"I do?"

His hands flew. "Death comes on wings to he who violates the word".

"I used to think so."

"What do you mean?"

"The person who stole the first seal is evidently still quite healthy. If something was going to happen, it would have happened by now."

"Don't be naïve," Hunsdon replied. "He, too, can take precaution. But he will be judged. He is not the chosen one."

"And you think I am?"

There was a full nod.

"Whatever. At this point, all I want is my daughter."

"And you shall have her." His hands clipped along. "Let me send Otto with you."

"I don't think so," Karl said skeptically.

"Don't be deceived. He is much more than he appears."

"Sir Hunsdon . . ."

"Listen to me," he signed, banging a chair. "I do not send an amateur. I am giving you a warrior. Beneath that austere pomposity is a man schooled in the occult, in martial arts, in weaponry, in mythology. He is quite capable of taking care of both you and himself. I do not give him lightly. These leeches might just as easily kill you and take the seals. And furthermore, what makes you think your daughter is still alive?"

Shocked, Karl stared. "I spoke to her."

"Do you know that it was not a recording?"

Karl's jaw dropped.

"I thought not."

Karl gazed out the large partially draped window as beads of sweat grew on his face.

"Are you all right, doctor?"

"I hadn't thought of that."

"Otto will escort you. He will make sure you get your daughter . . . if she is still alive."

Karl whispered, "Thank you."

"Thank me when it's over. Remember, in a little while it will be the seventh. Are you prepared to enter the Arits?"

"How can we attempt the Arits without the seals?"

"Mark my words, Karl Cassim. Beyond your wildest dreams, they will return to you."

Not sure of what he meant, Karl searched his face.

Hunsdon signed on. "When you get your daughter,

bring her here. I will see to it that she is cared for. One last thing. I will go into the passage with you. Are you well enough to face this task?"

"Do you think it wise?" Karl asked.

"It is mandatory." Hunsdon turned to Otto and signed. Otto left the room.

Karl held his head and closed his eyes. He felt the presence of Sir Hunsdon inches from him and looked up as a strong hand patted his shoulder. Hunsdon's eyes said, "Everything will be all right." He nodded.

Not many minutes passed before Otto returned unrecognizable. The emulsion that kept his hair brittle and parted chameleonized into soft fluff, flattering him youthfully. The beard was gone; his skin was wrinkle-free. His height had not diminished, but the black sweatshirt seemed to add miles to his shoulders, a physique that had been hidden in the regalia of steward. Karl had not placed an age on Otto, but what he saw now was a bullnecked man in his middle forties, built like a diesel engine.

"Astounding!" he whispered.

Hunsdon threw a brow.

"Had I not seen you before..."

Hunsdon signed, "If danger lurks, do not be surprised."

"I don't know what to say," Karl breathed.

"My friend, bring back your daughter."

CHAPTER 38

Introductions were made in the Hilton lobby, and again Otto was full of surprises. No trace of the British butler-steward remained. His pronunciation, inflection, phraseology became as American as apple pie.

Karl gawked.

"What are you looking at?"

"What happened to the man we all knew and loved?" Karl asked.

Otto smiled for real. "He's got the day off. I think he's catching some *zzz's*," he said as they pushed through the glass doors to the parking lot.

As Julian turned on Corniche Street, toward the bridge, Otto said, "Would you fill me in on the details of the exchange, Doctor Cassim?"

"Karl."

Otto looked at him. "Okay, Karl, spill the beans."

Julian didn't quite know what was going on. Karl shook his head and smiled. "I needed that. Well, Otto, at midnight, I'm supposed to stand between the paws of the Sphinx at the dream stela of Tuthmosis IV.

There, I am to wait. Then there is to be an exchange of the cylinder seals for my daughter."

"I see. Do these people know what you look like?"

"I think . . . I'm sure they—he—does."

"You know who he is?"

"We're pretty damn sure," Julian said. "The guy's name is Krubrick."

"And I take it that you have the seals with you?"

"Yes," Karl replied. "They are in that black bag."

"I'd advise, Karl, that Julian not come along. It will be difficult enough for me to keep track of you and slither around in the glare of the lights."

"I understand," Julian said. "I could wait in the car?"

"It's too dangerous. We want the girl and we don't want any problems."

"I can see that. All right, I'll drive to your place, Karl, and wait with Nancy."

"Good," Otto said.

"What time do you have?"

Julian glanced at his watch. "Eleven ten, Karl." He turned left on 26th July Street toward the island, to Zamalek, to Karl's flat. In front, he said, "If Nancy has heard from Shawn, I'll open and close the shade. If not, I'll blink the lights."

They watched the second floor. The light blinked.

"Damn it!" Karl said.

"What's the matter?"

"My assistant and friend, Shawn, has been missing since I left for London. It's not like him."

"I take it that he knows the situation?"

"Yes, all of it except what we're doing now."

Otto took the wheel.

"You know the way?" Karl asked, surprised.

"I've been here before. Tell me about Shawn."

"What do you want to know?"

"What does he look like?"

"Well, he's about my height, six feet, sandy hair and blue eyes. A pleasant person to be around."

Otto drove along the road that paralleled the Nile to the third bridge to Giza.

"He's thin but muscular, he's energetic and smart. I hired him last spring after Malak, my previous assistant, died."

"What happened to Malak?"

"He read the cylinder."

"And Shawn didn't?"

"No. I made copies. I didn't want to lose—"

"Wise move. Potent stuff, that. Does Shawn know about Krubrick?"

"Yes, we talked about him."

Otto glanced at Karl for a split second, then found the road again. "I don't mean to be morbid, but did you check the morgue?"

"Oh, my God, no!"

"There could have been an accident--intentional or otherwise."

"You think something tragic has happened to him, don't you?"

"It's a possibility. Tell me, Karl, does Shawn have any enemies?"

"Not really . . . well, maybe the police . . ."

"Explain."

The road was smooth, dark, and windless. Karl thought a moment. He began with the trouble at the bazaar. "Talib, the Minister of Police, accused Shawn of being involved with the kidnappers. At that point, Shawn became suspicious of Talib's involvement. But I had known Talib for years," Karl said, "and at first I dismissed the idea. But then, it all became very clear when I was arrested and beaten. Thank God for friends in high places."

"The promise of wealth speaks loudly, does it not?" Otto said, with a brief return to British highbrow.

"I suppose it does."

"Shawn may simply have taken a few days off."

"Not likely. He knew when I'd be back. He had promised to pick me up at the airport."

"How close was he with your daughter?" Otto asked.

"What are you implying?"

"Nothing. I just asked a question."

Karl thought about that. "To my knowledge, he

has never met Nanette."

"Pretty name."

"Otto, you'd better slow down. We don't want to get there too early."

"Yes, we do."

"We do?"

"You're going to drop me off as soon as we see . . . there it is. Now you drive and then park until just before midnight. Do you have a watch?"

Karl shook his head.

"Take mine."

"What are you going to do?"

"Scout around. I want to see what we are getting ourselves into. We have about thirty minutes."

"Otto?"

"Sir?"

"I hope you have a weapon."

Otto patted his side and smiled as he stopped the car in sight of the Sphinx. "Do exactly as you were told," he said. Then he was gone.

The engine idled while Karl slid behind the wheel. At a snail's pace, Karl approached the Sphinx enclosure. The monument's majestic form, brilliantly lighted against the black, speckled sky, gazed to the east. Far beyond, the mystical pyramids, engulfed in a raven's shawl, pointed to the heavens. Karl's skin puckered with gooseflesh, with trepidation of the unexpected. He stopped at the low end of the enclosure near the paws. He checked the time. Eighteen minutes. Painfully, slowly, the seconds jerked by, flipping on the face of the digital timepiece.

He looked up from his window to the face towering above. Following the body to the tail, he looked around the enclosure and saw nothing out of the ordinary, no cars, no people, nothing. He wondered about Otto.

Nervously, he lifted the black bag from the floor to the seat next to him. He glanced at the time again. He thought of a nursery rhyme. "I'm losing my mind," he muttered. "Fourteen minutes."

He leaned back on the headrest and stared at the ceiling. He closed his eyes. He opened them. He counted back from a hundred and closed his eyes again.

Ratcheting! His door yanked open. His neck snapped as he jerked upright.

Into his face stared the scar-faced man in black, wearing the same torn sleeve and smelling of urine. It was the same man who had almost crushed Sarah's hand. "Where's the seals?" he grunted.

Karl moved away. "Where is my daughter?"

"Safe. Give 'em to me."

"Not on your life. Where is your boss?"

"Get out of the car."

Karl slammed the door. Scarface pulled it open.

He stuck a gun in Karl's face.

"Next time, you're dead. Get out!"

Hesitantly, Karl slid off the seat. He was pushed to the side of the car. "Where is my daughter? Where is my daughter?" he screamed.

"Shut up. That bag . . . is that the seals?"

"That is for your boss! Where is he?"

"You ask a lot of questions."

"Is it a secret?"

"It's no secret, Karl. Here I am." Hassandi Talib stepped out of the shadows.

In shock, Karl's eyes measured the bulbous Minister of Police as sarcasm dripped from his every word. "It is hard to believe that you are boss of anything. Where is your leader?"

"Thank you for the compliments, Karl, but you're mistaken. I am in charge here."

Despite the coolness of the evening, moisture shimmered beneath Hassandi's thin mustache, leading Karl to believe that all was not well within the brotherhood. "Well, Hassandi, how did you manage a night off? I thought you were preoccupied with other important matters," Karl said caustically.

"One day very soon," Hassandi warned, "your wagging tongue will beat you to death." With his eyes on Karl, he spoke to his man. "Junker, get me the seals and take him to the passage."

Junker reached in and grabbed the bag. He handed it to Talib.

"Did you check it?"

Scarface shook his head.

"Check it!"

The bag was swung to the fender. The latch was sprung and the bag spread apart. The man counted five bundles. "They're all here," he said.

"Unwrap them, stupid!"

One by one, each bundle was unwrapped and the cylinders examined. "They're all here," he said again.

Talib swiped the bag and quickly walked off, disappearing into the shadows that had released him.

Junker forced Karl behind the wheel with a pistol to his head. "Drive."

The Pyramid Road was deserted. The monuments of eternity clad in light stood defiantly on the sandscape, seemingly not of this Earth. Driving slowly to the Great Pyramid, Karl edged his nose toward the window, trying to lose the stink of Scarface whose eyes were sewn to the road.

As he applied the brake, Karl's secret hope vanished. Mubarak's Special Forces were gone. He thought about asking the obvious, but held his tongue.

"Get out!"

With the pistol imprinted on his neck, he was shoved from the car. Behind them, Talib, with three black-uniformed policemen, rolled to a stop in his official police car. Behind them came another car, carrying three more policemen.

Self-importantly, Talib strode up to Karl. Sneering, he said, "Surprised?"

Standing mute, Karl stared contemptuously.

"I know you are wondering, so, I'll tell you," Talib said with a zip to his voice. "Mubarak's people were very understanding. Especially when I went out of my way to bring in the witness and explain my case. It was all documented, you know. Your assistant, Shawn O'Donnell, was identified as a thief and possible murderer. As for you, I made them see that your participation in hiding a crook made you a co-conspirator in the commission of a crime." He wiped his mouth.

"You're a liar!" Karl flared.

A fist came from nowhere, knocking Karl to the ground.

"Naughty, naughty. Such a temper," Talib chided. "Pick him up."

Two men in black raised Karl from the sand.

"What have you done with Shawn?" Karl demanded.

"Unfortunately, I don't have him . . . yet. But it's just a question of time."

Karl felt relieved. "Where is your boss? I had an arrangement with Krubrick, not you."

Talib flipped a hand. "That is a problem, isn't it?"

"I should have known better," Karl said.

"Oh?"

"I trusted Krubrick. We made a deal."

"Yes, I suppose you did. But, Karl, you should have trusted me, you should be thanking me. Krubrick wanted to snuff your lovely little daughter a long time ago. She has been quite a lot of trouble, you know."

"Where is she?"

"Soon enough."

"This was supposed to be a simple transaction. I would have been long gone with my daughter, minding my own business." Karl lied and Talib knew it, but it was worth a try. Anything was worth a try.

Talib gave a bitter smile. "Ah, well, best laid plans and all that."

"You couldn't have done all this on your own. You're not that smart. Where is your boss?"

Talib's lip raised. His eyes turned to slits. "I told you, I'm in charge here." He looked to his man and brought down his chin.

They pushed Karl to the stairs where he squeezed out another question. "What happened to the soldiers?"

Talib stood on a flat stone at the top of the steps. His hands shot up. "Gone," he said, his eyes round and stupid.

Karl glanced at the terrain while Talib mumbled to his friends. Hard looks came his way as they talked.

Suddenly, they held him, twisting his arms and binding his hands.

"You don't need to do this." Karl struggled.

"Relax, Karl, it won't be long."

"Be long for what?" His question was ignored.

No sign of Otto. Just six men standing around with guns strapped to their waist. Karl surmised that Mubarak's men must have been gone for a while, because his host had had time to string lanterns down the steps and into the passage. It was aglow.

"How far are we going?"

"I'm going as far as it takes me," Talib snarled.

"You do just that and I"

Blackness. The blow was too sudden for Karl to feel any pain.

"Gag him and drag him out of the way. I don't want him seen, you understand?"

"Yes, Minister."

Karl was dragged to the base of the pyramid and left unconscious.

Talib began taking the steps, carrying the bag of cylinder seals with him. "Are you coming?" he said to Junker.

The mass wobbled over and followed down the stairs, through the passage where the granite plug had been removed. Junker stopped. Talib carefully went on ahead, minding the small flags Krubrick had placed neatly on the mounds that spelled death. After reaching the end, he waved to Junker, and he, too, tip-toed through the mine field.

At the next elbow, Talib turned and raised a finger. "Not a word, you hear?" he warned. Junker nodded as he stared at Nanette. Drugged, her delicate body lay in a fetal position next to the wall, bound with black tape. A tiny moan escaped her as they hurried by and on to the corbel hall. At the next turn, the smooth polished granite cast back their elongated images and extended before them where Krubrick had placed more lanterns illuminating the high ceiling above. With quicker steps they crossed the expanse and approached the last turn. The mammoth ornate doors stood closed. Junker gawked and Talib burst through.

Krubrick threw them a look, having been disturbed in conversation.

As was his custom, Krubrick wore a shocking white suit meticulously pressed, shiny white shoes, and a white tie. His attire, pale skin, and frail build created a death-like aura. He spoke in a whisper with his friend and confidant, the Egyptologist Reisner.

Reisner, too, was dressed as he had been the last time he was seen in public; he wore Khaki trousers and an open shirt.

Junker looked at his image reflected many times in the mirrors.

Talib stared indignantly as he waited for the supercilious Krubrick's attention.

"How did it go?" Krubrick finally said.

"As planned." Talib held up the bag.

"Good. You checked the contents?"

"Yes. I'm not an idiot."

"Touchy, aren't we?" Krubrick's nostrils flared. "And the girl?" he asked.

"She is in the arms of her father safe and sound." The mirrors reflected the tilt of his head.

"All right," Krubrick said, "we'll have to hurry before Cassim gathers his people and causes problems."

Reisner extended a hand. "May I see the crystal seals?"

Talib walked them over and withdrew. Reisner set the bag on the floor, knelt down and sprang the latch. One by one he unwrapped the sparkling crystal cylinders, turned them round and lined them up. Wide-eyed, he said, "Incredible! I've never seen anything like them."

"They are beautiful, aren't they?" Krubrick smiled.

"Oh, yes, very beautiful."

"See?" Krubrick said. "I told you, Cassim is a trustworthy fellow." He turned back to Reisner.

Talib sneered at his back.

"All right, Mr. Reisner, read the lintel over the door for us."

Reisner left the seals and moved slowly to the gold door, gazing admiringly at the lintel. He frowned as he read, "You have seen the many faces of his soul . . . What the hell?"

Splattering bits of skull and fluids splashed his face. Blood bubbled from what remained of a shattered head. Chunks of brain oozed down from a gaping hole as Krubrick dropped to his knees, twitching, drooling red, violating his white impeccable suit. Nearly faceless, he lurched to the floor, jerking, snapping in uncontrollable spasm.

"God damn, God damn!" Reisner shrieked. "What the hell did you do?"

Junker's smoking pistol was now pointed at him.

Talib smiled acidly. "I saw what I needed to see. He lied. All this time he made me believe he could read hieroglyphs, that he knew exactly what they said."

"That's no reason to kill him, Jesus Christ!"

"Of course it is. If he couldn't read the cylinder, he was useless, a pompous ass. Why should I share the treasure of Thoth with him?"

"My God," Reisner said, "this was his project. He put his—"

"Keep reading," Talib growled.

As if in a trance, Reisner stared.

"Read!" Talib shouted.

Shaking, Reisner eyed the gun and turned to the

door. In a quivering voice he went on: "You have l-looked to the heavens and s-seen the M-Mansion of Osiris. Henceforth, enter if you are e-equipped. Enter if you are w-worthy, for the Seven Masters await united."

"It doesn't say anything about treasure?"

"No."

"You're lying!" Talib screamed.

"Why would I lie?"

Talib examined Reisner's face, his earnestness. "All right. Maybe it doesn't have to. Take the seal out of Krubrick's pocket and put it with the rest."

"Are you going to kill me?"

"Do it!"

Reisner recoiled in revulsion. "No. I can't. I can't do it."

"What the hell's wrong with you? You look at death all the time."

Trembling, he muttered, "Not like this."

Talib motioned to Scarface. "Get it. Put it with the others."

Without a thought, Junker yanked the cylinder out of Krubrick's blood-soaked pocket, rolled it over to the others and frisked him. He found and took his wallet, thumbed his credit cards and smelled a quarter-inch wad of his money. A grin lifted his scar. "Lots of money," he said, showing fractured teeth, and slid the wallet into his own torn jacket.

"Thief," Talib sneered.

Junker shrugged.

"I don't believe you people," Reisner said, horrified.

With hard eyes, Talib ordered, "Read me the seals, all of them. I want to hear exactly what they say."

"I thought Mr. Krubrick told you what they said."

"Only bits and pieces, what he wanted me to know."

Reisner looked at the pistol and knelt. He picked up the first in line. "Why did he need all the cylinder seals anyway?" he asked.

"That's what I want you to tell me."

"Mr. Krubrick told me they held clues to treasure, like a pirate's map."

"Read," Talib shouted again.

"Okay." Both ends were between his palms as he gazed into the glass. "I never saw the actual seal," he said. "Mr. Krubrick only showed me a printed page."

Talib asked, "You didn't translate for him?"

"I told you. I never saw them."

"Who did?"

"I don't know."

Talib stared and growled, "Read."

"All right, okay." He took a breath. "It says, '*Beware! The eyes that fall upon this Providence must be pure*'." He felt odd, a little strange. He went on. "'*Beware! Death comes on wings, on wings to he who, uh, who violates the . . . the word'."* He wiped his face.

"Keep going."

"I feel sick."

"I said keep reading."

Reisner blotted his head with a sleeve. "I'm going to throw up. I'm sick."

"You want to end up like your friend there? Read!"

Junker smirked.

Reisner looked sick and struggled to go on. *"'Beware! It is Amemait, eater of souls, who . . . who destroys the . . . the . . .'"*

Before their eyes, Reisner's face began to collapse, shrivel. He clutched his throat, vomiting, falling to the floor. His eyes were blinded with a thick white membrane, erasing his pupils, while his skin blotched with sanguine dust.

Talib peered, gasping. Junker stepped back, gaping.

Reisner's moan rose to an agonizing scream as he gagged and wretched, thrashing about helplessly on the floor. Deep wrinkles creased his flesh as he dehydrated. Gnarled hands reached out. Nubby limbs quaked beneath khaki cloth as his body caved in upon itself, as life was being sucked from his very soul. Withered lips cracked. A final gasp escaped as eyelids fell into empty holes and his skull rapped the floor like a dropped boot.

With his eyelids blinking and fluttering, Junker

backed away, all the way to the outer door.

Panting, Talib stared. Long moments passed while he studied the hideous, shriveled corpse, trying to fathom what he saw. The mirrors watched, reflecting again and again the horror.

The crush of silence was broken with Junker's shout. "It's a curse! This place is cursed! We're going to die!"

"Shut up."

"I tell you, it's a curse!"

"And I tell you he was a sick fool. The plague, you hear, the plague, that's what it is!"

Junker whispered, "Curse, plague, same, same."

"He was sick! Now, put the seals in the bag."

Junker filled the bag methodically. "Why do we need them?" he muttered innocently.

The question confused Talib. He thought about it. "Reisner said they were a map . . . to find our way here. We are here. We don't need a map. We only need to go through that door to the treasure." Talib looked on Junker more differently than he ever had. *For once, he was right*, he thought. He had heard Krubrick say the very same thing. He nodded slowly. "For once, you are right," he said softly.

Scarface smiled, a self-confident smile.

Talib gestured. "Go on, open the door."

The huge hulk of a man moved his head to the left

and to the right, looking about suspiciously.

"Sissy," Talib spat. "Give me the damn gun." He twisted it from Junker's hand, throwing him a smirk.

Huffing like a spoiled child, Talib walked around the corpses, sizing up the solid gold, elaborately decorated door. Without a second thought, he slid aside the shiny bolt and pulled the doors wide open.

With curious eyes, Junker watched Talib's every move, pushing up his tattered sleeves, getting ready for a fight.

Talib raised his pistol and pointed it into the black. Slowly, he placed one foot in front of the other and gingerly crossed the threshold as if stepping on eggs. Flapping the air with the pistol, he said to Junker, "Come on."

Scarface fiddled in his pocket and withdrew a flashlight. He focused the beam, letting it fall beyond the doorway to Talib's back, sending his shadow deep inside. He did not answer, and did not follow.

What Junker could see from his moored post was total absence of light, color, image . . . a tarred blackness that doubled onto itself. For some uncanny reason, he felt that the space where Talib now stood exhaling mist was exceedingly large and terribly cold.

Throwing his voice over his shoulder, Talib said, "Bring me your light, I can't see." And he cautiously ventured a few more steps.

Refusing to cross the threshold, Junker leaned forward, avoiding touching the door, and rolled his flashlight along the floor.

"Bring me the light!" Talib shouted. But his voice was absorbed by the dark, returning to the door in a whisper.

"It's by your feet. Look down," Junker said, and stepped back.

Talib picked it up. "You sissy shit," he grumbled, fooling with the switch. "It doesn't . . ." He looked up.

Glowing, white, wispy tendrils floated gently from above, descending, circling, seemingly aimless in its course.

Mesmerized, Junker observed the thin cottony strands, twisting and turning like silk worms in a nest. Of little notice, aromatic myrrh wafted delicately, bringing unguarded smiles to their faces. Taking several more slow steps, Talib gazed in awe, rotating, flagging his gun-held-hand through the wispy tendrils. "Can you see this?" he asked with amazement. "It's supremely beautiful!"

Without voice, Scarface nodded. He would not move one inch closer as he skeptically eyed the supernatural attraction. "It's the devil!" he breathed.

In the distance, too far to fathom, a tiny, tiny disc flickered, but went unseen while Talib toyed with the phosphorescent fingers that brushed his ear and whisked a lock of greasy hair. Disarming, the sweet aroma comforted as the match-sized disc wavered in flame.

With another step, the floor under Talib was no more. He became weightless, lighter than air, moving without effort, free of gravity. And concern eluded him, because a swooning song whispered somewhere, soothing him, captivating him, occupying his senses. Like a floating doll, he dangled, stringless.

Snaking up to and around the pyramids, the Pyramid Road slices the plateau seventy, a hundred feet from the base of the Great Pyramid. Three cars were parked on the road. Along the east side of the Great Pyramid, three much smaller pyramids rest. From these, spreading to the city, countless mastaba tombs rise from the desert floor, casting their shadows one on top of the other, folding darkness on top of darkness.

Two black-uniformed men leaned on Talib's vehicle, chatting softly, smoking, wondering how much of their night would be wasted.

At a small hill, next to the steps leading to the passage, the third policeman stood listening, talking to the fourth, who squatted on the first step. His wife was in labor with their fourth child; he wanted to be home.

Next to the Great Pyramid, Karl groaned, coming

to consciousness. His two guards, shifting from one foot to the other, remained alert as they were told. They were not friends, but tolerated each other because they had to. It was their job.

All six policemen were within earshot and eyeshot of one another, but paid little or no attention to each other's small groups. They were confident and self-assured. They were policemen.

Otto surveyed the placement of the guards from the mastabas, from where he could easily move in the long shadows. He had seen Karl knocked out and tied. As Talib and Scarface entered the passage, he moved closer . . . but he was not alone. He sensed someone there, just ahead of him. He heard the quiet shift of sand under shoes.

Glued to the mud-brick wall of a tomb, he froze. *Perhaps Talib has another one of his goons hiding out here, maybe a sniper posted deceptively*, he thought. Then the soft grinding sound retreated . . . toward him . . . and stopped. One tomb away, a profile jutted out. It crept around a corner, ducking low, looking toward the steps. Otto poised and leapt, bringing him down to the ground, straddling him, pressing firmly on his mouth, staring pensively into light blue eyes below a fringe of sandy hair.

Otto leaned closer. Whispering, he said, "Who are you? What the hell are you doing here?"

The man on the ground shook his head, nostrils flaring, his mouth blocked.

"I'm going to lift my hand," Otto said. "But if you make a sound . . ."

The head shook.

Otto released the pressure slightly.

"I'm Karl's friend."

The hand clamped down. "Are you Shawn?" he asked, searching the youthful face.

"Yes."

Otto let him up. "What the hell do you think you're doing? You could get yourself killed!"

"I've been watching them for days," he said softly. "They have Nanette."

"Yes, I know. And now they have Karl."

Shawn nodded. "Who are you?"

"Otto; I'm also a friend of Karl's."

"They took Nanette into the passage," Shawn said, "but I couldn't do anything about it."

"She's alive, then."

"I saw her move. They carried her inside. We've got to get her out of there."

"Not so fast. You stay here out of sight."

"What are you going to do?"

"Even the odds."

Otto left Shawn sitting on the ground. Before he could stand, Otto had drifted among the tombs, the shadows, out of sight.

On his stomach, Otto crawled to the road behind the cars. The two policemen were talking low. One flipped his cigarette and said, "I hope he's not going to be all night. I'm supposed to meet a friend at a café."

A creaking sound behind the last car.

"What was that?"

"I didn't hear anything."

"I'm going to check it out." He walked along the road to the end car. He looked behind it. He surveyed the road and the sand alongside. He bent and peered under the car. "I could swear I heard something," he mumbled, retracing his steps. "I guess I was—"

A mouthful of fist knocked him down. Dazed, he scrambled to his knees wildly grabbing for his pistol. His partner was on his back, out cold. He did not see what hit him again.

Quickly now, Otto tied one man to the steering wheel through the window and propped the other against the first, leaning on the door.

Fading in the sand, Otto slithered back into the friendly community of the dead who readily offered quietude, solace, and cover.

At the foot of a twenty-ton block, Karl blinked blood from his eye, trying to speak through black tape.

"Shut up," a guard said, kicking sand in his face.

"Leave him alone," his partner said. "Who's going

to hear him?"

"Mind your own business."

The cops at the steps heard and looked on as the two squabbled. They knew these two didn't get along and hoped Talib would come out of the passage to catch them in the act. "Shit would hit the fan if Talib caught them arguing," one said.

Facing the mastabas away from the pyramid, Karl thought he saw something. He blinked. It moved. Cops faced him muttering insults and threats at one another.

It came closer in the shadows. He knew who it was and smiled behind the tape as he beat his feet on the sand. With a garbled voice, he shook his head, twisting, trying to free his bonds, while the shut-up guard strode over and kicked him.

Karl would not be stilled. Bending over, the cop back-handed him. Wondering why his partner was so quiet, he turned. Wide-eyed, he stared into the smiling face of a large man who whipped his jaw with a brick-like fist.

From the steps, the standing guard heard the ruckus, spun, and bounded for Otto. An eight-inch knife caught the light as the man in black wildly swung, swooping and bending like a cock in a fight. Seemingly amused, Karl watched.

A shadow moved from the mastabas. The sitting guard shot up, grabbing for his sidearm. A rock took him down. Shawn struck him again.

Otto saw the knife coming when the guard lunged. He caught him by the wrist, stepped aside and wrenched it around into his gut. Staggering, the guard stared at Otto. For a second, he teetered, clenching his stomach and dropped to his knees while blood covered his hands. Swearing in Arabic, he sprawled, burying his face in the sand.

Shawn peeled back the tape from Karl's mouth. "Are you okay, Maestro?"

"Shawn, thank God! My daughter . . . ?"

"They took her into the passage, Karl."

"Untie me, we've got to get her out."

"Take it easy, Karl," Otto said. "You've got a two-inch cut on your head. Stay put. I'll get your daughter."

"You don't understand. The passage is riddled with traps."

"I'll take him," Shawn said.

"I'm going," Karl said firmly.

"You've got guts for somebody with a bad heart, I'll give you that," Otto said. "Are you sure you're well enough?"

"Otto, my daughter is in there."

"Very well."

Whirling, the disc spun throwing flames. It gathered sound, whooshing, spitting sparks, inciting the air violently.

Talib slowly moved his head, catching something out of the corner of his eye, growing larger. The smile, the delight withered, while the soft wispy tendrils slithered tightly about him, becoming mass, becoming tentacles, lashing him to the air like the Jew upon the cross. The subtle infectious siren's song grew steadily louder, coarser, roaring evilly, cracking with thunder that resonated the foundation which held it.

Before his eyes, the fired disc churned in a blaze equal to the sun, larger than the sky with a glaring face painted in flames. And Talib bellowed, whooping in horror.

Gyrating on the cusp, flames, a thousand arms of flame, zapped Hassandi Talib with bolts of fire, exploding him into a million bits of smoking flesh, missiling in a million directions.

A rolling mass billowed into the Hall of Mirrors, throwing heat and threads of a disintegrated carcass while Junker backed to the door, the cold mirrors capturing his terror, defining it over and over. Blocking the sight from view, he covered his face with the torn sleeve, shuddering against the door.

As quickly as it had advanced, the flaming disc retreated, shrinking smaller as though sucked by a vacuum, seeking the darkness from which it had come. And suddenly, the tumultuous roaring ceased. The tiny disc, far in the distance, wavered and, with a breath, vanished. The massive solid gold doors slammed shut with a staggering clap.

Cringing, trembling, Junker lowered his arm. A few paces away lay Talib's gun, splattered with his remains. Hurriedly, Junker grabbed the gun, wiped it on his coat and bolted over the polished floor as if chased by the hounds of hell. Leaving the grand corbel gallery, he ducked into the sandy passage. Stumbling along, he came upon the plug imprinted with burgundy entrails. He turned at the elbow.

Suddenly Junker and Otto stood face to face. Junker began firing at Otto. Bullets ricocheted off stone walls as he kept firing, backing away to the elbow. Otto went down and the pistol clicked away on empty chambers. Junker stood at the elbow, eyed the body on the floor and the broken pieces of pottery he had crushed. The ground shook under him. The ferocious grinding of stone against stone echoed as the granite plug shot from its place, spreading him over the remains of Farley's friend.

While echoes faded, Otto groaned, his shadow moving on the wall from Krubrick's lamps. He felt his head. His hand sparkled with blood.

Shawn rushed to his side. "Otto, you're bleeding."

"I'm okay. He was a lousy shot. The damn fool just grazed me. How's the girl?"

"She can't talk, Otto. Her eyes . . ." Tears welled. "She just moans."

"Let's go."

Shawn helped him up.

"I can make it."

They heard Karl crying as they tip-toed to the end of the passage.

"Karl, we've got to go now. She needs a doctor."

"I'm so glad she's alive."

"Hurry, let's keep her that way."

Shawn carried Nanette to the steps.

Karl looked over his shoulder. "Talib and Kru-brick, where are they?"

Otto said, "I don't know, but the way that fellow came flying around the corner, I'd say they had a bad night."

In the night air, they felt the ground quake. Otto frowned and looked down the steps. "Now what?" he said.

Karl wiped his face. "It's the plug. It's reloading," he said. Pale and sweating, he staggered and collapsed.

CHAPTER 39

February 4, Tuesday 4:33 a.m.

A mature doctor in wrinkled green scrubs pushed through the double doors.

Shawn and Otto quickly stood, trying to interpret the blank look of a rehearsed face.

The doctor strode into the waiting area, identifying himself as Doctor Frank and quizzed them as to their relationship to Karl Cassim.

"I see," the doctor said. "Very well then. Doctor Cassim is extremely dehydrated and he has a possible concussion. His heart has stabilized but, when he is released, I must insist that he refrain from any activity other than what is absolutely necessary. He has been warned before. He needs bed rest for an extended period of time."

Otto said, "Will he be all right, doctor?"

"If he takes care."

Shawn took a step. "Nanette? How is she?"

"Would you care to sit down?"

"What is it?" Otto intervened.

The doctor shook his head. "I really can't—"

"Doctor, I have to know. Will she make it?" Shawn's face was torn with anguish.

"Look," the doctor said, "I know how you feel. All I can say is that her condition is extremely critical. Drugs have been administered over a long period of time. An overdose can go either way."

"She can't die, you understand? She can't die!"

"Mr. O'Donnell, please control yourself. I promise you we will do all we can."

"That's not good enough. You've got to save her, do you hear? You've got to."

Otto took his arm. "Thank you doctor. Is it possible to see her?"

"It's not a good idea."

"Please," Shawn implored, "just for a moment."

The doctor took a deep breath and looked off at a dreary plant that needed care. "All right, but two minutes . . . that's all I can give."

He led them through the double doors into the intensive care unit. "That room there," he pointed. "Two minutes, no more."

"Doctor?" Otto said. "Karl Cassim?"

"Oh, room 421. He's under mild sedation, but lucid. Don't stay long."

"Thank you, doctor."

Shawn was already in the room when Otto walked

in. The sight took him back. Tubes were everywhere. A respirator sucked air. IV drips in both arms hung on both sides of her bed.

Shawn stood paralyzed. "Oh, my God," he whispered.

"Take it easy," Otto said. "It looks worse than it is."

Shawn stared at the lovely, fragile face bibbed with an oxygen tube as quiet tears streamed. He reached for her small, delicate hand, kissed it, caressed it, and softly called her name. He bowed onto the bed near her side. His muffled sobs didn't wake the form sleeping near death's door.

Otto pressed a shoulder. "I didn't realize that you knew her," he whispered.

Wiping back the tears, Shawn said, "We're engaged to be married."

"I see. And her father doesn't know, does he?"

Shawn shook his head.

"Come along, Shawn, we don't want to disturb her. A new day always brings hope." Otto helped him from the room. "Do you want to come with me?"

A nod. "Yes."

They waited for the elevator. Otto looked down on the handsome, stricken youth, wondering what Karl's reaction would be to the lovers' secret.

Doors parted and they stepped inside.

Otto said, "Are you going to tell him?"

"I had planned to tell him when all this trouble was behind us. I thought this would have been over a long time ago, and it would have been had Karl given them the seals at the bazaar. I mean, if it hadn't gone sour. But things kept going on and on and now this. Now I have to tell him at the worst possible time. Otto, how am I going to tell him?"

The bell rang when they reached the fourth floor. As they stepped from the steel box, they were reminded of what time it was. The overhead lights down the hall were off and scant rays from the rooms fell into the corridor. There was hardly a soul in sight.

Otto said quietly, "Just let it happen. Don't make it an edict or he'll balk."

"Otto, we were engaged even before I came to work for him. That's how I found out he was looking for a new assistant. He's going to think—"

"Just let it happen. Be truthful and honest. Give Karl the benefit of the doubt. Keep it straightforward without *mea culpas*."

"I'll try."

"Do it."

"Otto, what room?"

"421, right over there."

A subdued light came from a table near the bed. A curtain, partially drawn, separated Karl from his roommate in the semi-private accommodation, and tumbling shadows darkened the corners. IV bags hung from above. Monitors pulsed with red numbers, and squiggly lines indicated the status quo.

Karl was asleep. The sallow tone of his skin gave them pause. Thin strips of tape covered several stitches on the right side of his forehead. Dark circles aged an otherwise younger man and subtle creases had become apparent where none had been before. His arms were crossed over his stomach, and his head was deep into the pillow.

Shawn and Otto exchanged glances, but did not speak. Minutes passed as they wondered if they should leave and come back at a better time. Otto quietly cleared his throat and nodded toward the door. They backed out of the room.

"Just as well," Otto said. "He needs the rest."

"How are you holding up, Otto?" Shawn asked.

"A little headache, more from the stitches than the wound. In the emergency room, they numbed it, but it's wearing off. I'm not too bad, really." Otto replied. "Are you going home or to Karl's place?"

"I think I'll go to Karl's. I desperately need a drink and I don't have anything potent." Shawn replied.

"I know the feeling."

"By the way, Otto, I don't know who you are."

"Of course you do. I'm Karl's friend."

"I know that."

"In truth, I'm Sir Hunsdon's steward and companion."

"You mean the E. Osborne Hunsdon?"

"The one and only. He's here in Cairo, you know."

"I'll be damned!"

"We all might be."

"Oh?"

"We are here because of Karl and the cylinder seals."

"I see. Now I understand."

"There's one more thing I forgot to mention. Julian and Nancy are at Karl's flat."

"Nancy?"

"Yes. Is that a surprise?"

"It certainly is. But that's another story."

Otto found this humorous and smiled. "I'd like to hear it sometime," he said. "Fact is always more intriguing than fiction."

Lightened somewhat by Otto's interest, Shawn said, "Over martinis?"

"Of course," Otto said. "Not to change the subject, but since Karl is incapacitated, you should do something about protecting the passage."

"Yes, I'd better. I hadn't thought about it."

"Well, think about it. We really don't know what happened to Krubrick or his associates."

They came into the lobby.

"Drop me at the Hilton, will you?"

"Sure, Otto. What time are you coming by

tomorrow?"

"Around noon I think."

"Good. I'll meet you here."

"You know," Otto said, "I wonder if someone should stay with him. We really don't know what happened to Krubrick or Talib."

"They have the seals. Why would they hurt him now?"

"I guess you're right. But in this business you can't be too careful, can you?"

They left the hospital, taking Karl's car. Little or no conversation was exchanged during the short ride as exhaustion took its toll.

"About noon, then?" Otto said.

There was a nod. "Good night, Otto, and thanks, thanks for everything."

His Britishness poked through as he said, "Not at all, dear fellow, not at all."

Shawn turned the key in the lock and opened the door. In the living room, Nancy was asleep on the couch. Julian was snoring in an overstuffed chair with a meager light throwing shadows at his side. Exhausted, Shawn chose not to wake them and tip-toed to the kitchen. He filled a large tumbler with spirits, took a gulp, and left a note on the table. In his room, he took one more sip and laid back fully clothed, losing his mind to dreams.

CHAPTER 40

February 5, Tuesday, 5:31 a.m.

The attaché case was sprung wide. Helter-skelter, papers reposed upon the table. A single desk lamp lighted the near and darkened the far, where penumbrae, still and fragile, watched. Bags and suitcases were strewn within arm's reach, and lurking behind glasses, eyes scanned books, notes, and papyri. A cigarette smoldered in an overflowing ashtray, while wide-open windows allowed a soft, salty breeze to clear the air. Cloaked in a star-spangled robe, he hunched over his desk, giving an occasional rake to the hair, a brush to his prim whiskers. Sir E. Osborne Hunsdon was at work.

Liturgy, heka, recitation, Words of Power are the tools against the unknown, the armament of priests. Should it become necessary, he would be equipped, he would be True of Voice, judged worthy and vindicated by the tribunal of gods, where all power stems from Osiris, he who lives.

Soundlessly, Hunsdon reviewed, memorized his

own hand-written notes, handling them like a newborn infant, like the holiest of books.

At half past five in the morning, in the quiet, a tumbler clicked. His ear tuned in. A knob creaked. The door opened and Otto walked into the suite. Hunsdon leaned back, rubbing his eyes.

"Am I disturbing you, Edward?" Otto inquired softly.

Gracefully, Hunsdon's hands began to sign. Questions rolled one after the other.

"Yes," Otto said, "everything went as well as could be expected."

More signing.

"I was shot by an extremely poor marksman. It's nothing. Well," he sighed heavily, "the girl is alive . . . for the time being. I can't say that I think she is going to make it. And Karl...Karl has a nest of stitches on the forehead as well as another bout with the heart. He's very weak."

This news visibly affected Hunsdon and he shook his head and signed slowly. "Look at us, Otto," he said, "one mute, another badly weakened, attempting to face a power the world has never seen or known. I don't believe in miracles, but that's what we most desperately need right now." A deep breath.

"Is there nothing I can do?"

A sway of the head. He signed, "Unfortunately,

you have not been chosen."

The sky lightened far, far in the distance. Shades of crimson and powder-blue ebbed away the deep royal, preceding the morning sun in a cloudless firmament, as the two men sat quietly.

Otto asked, "Care for a brandy?"

A nod.

Otto slid the amber liquid into Hunsdon's hand which closed around it. Hunsdon's thoughts raced over the events to come. He sipped and set down the glass, careful of the papers. With a sudden spark in his eyes he signed, "Tell me about the passage."

With infinite detail, Otto drew a portrait of the passage and added the brutal demise of Junker. The whereabouts of Krubrick, Talib, and the archeologist were left to speculation, but Sir Hunsdon's concerns were centered on the course itself. The initial trial, as it were, of the justified, the worthy.

When Otto finished, Sir Hunsdon reached across the desk for a leather case. He withdrew the lapis tablet, comparing its description with Otto's; without flaw, they were identical. If there had been any doubt about the passage being the true way to the treasure of Thoth, it was summarily dispensed.

Hunsdon firmly took Otto into his eyes and signed, "We are about to embark on an adventure where the slightest infraction could imperil our lives.

Do you wish to continue?"

Gravely, Otto nodded.

"Then rest, my friend," his hands said. "We have a mammoth undertaking at hand."

While their minds wrestled with problems, the tip of the sun peeked over the horizon. Otto drew the shades.

"Were the seals retrieved?"

"No, Edward, lives were at stake."

"You know what must be done."

Silently, they sipped, content in each other's company. Hunsdon lit a cigarette, inhaling deeply, enjoying one of his few vices.

Otto watched him carefully.

They sipped sparingly, deep in thought while an empty sky slowly filled with the light of day.

"Good night, Edward," Otto said.

A nod followed.

CHAPTER 41

The first one up, Nancy headed straight for the kitchen. She made a pot of coffee, noting that Karl's groceries needed replenishing. Opening the cupboard she took down two mugs and set them on the . . . "Oh, my God, Shawn's back!"

"He is?" came from the doorway as Julian wandered in.

"He left this note on the table. Julian, they are both in the hospital, Karl and his daughter."

"What happened?"

"It doesn't say. Here, you read it."

Julian glanced at the note. "I see what you mean. I wonder what happened?"

"God knows. Maybe it's Karl's heart, poor dear. But his daughter, they had her for so long . . . Oh, Julian, this is terrible."

Julian embraced her. "It's going to be all right," he said. "It has to be."

For a little while they hugged, standing in the kitchen.

"Holding on to someone somehow makes it feel

better, doesn't it?" she asked softly.

"It works for me." He smiled.

"I love you, you know, Mr. Rutledge."

"I love you back, Mrs. Gottlieb."

"And I love you both," Shawn said, leaning against the door jamb. "A regular love fest." He yawned.

"Are you making fun of us?" Nancy squinted playfully.

"Never! Would I do a thing like that?"

Julian rubbed his chin. "I'll have to think about that one. What in the world is going on?"

"First, I need—I really—need some of that brew."

"Have a seat," Nancy said. "I'll get it."

Julian sat at his elbow. "Okay, let's have it, the good, the bad, and the ugly."

Shawn gulped coffee and reviewed the evening with all the particulars. It wasn't until he reached the part about Nanette in the hospital that his emotions came crashing down. With a quivering lip, he described her appearance, trying to dam the tears.

"What did the doctors say?" Nancy firmly held his hand.

"It wasn't good. She'd been drugged for so long."

"Oh, my. And Karl? How is Karl?"

"I don't know. They said he needed rest, that his heart had stabilized, but…but he looked so old, so old . . . and tired . . ."

Nancy squeezed his hand. "Does Karl know about you and Nanette?"

Shawn shook his head. "I'm scared to tell him."

"Don't be silly," she said. "If I were Karl, I'd be proud to have you as my son-in-law."

"You're not Karl," Julian said. "And I'm glad you're not. People would talk."

A small light shown in Shawn's sad eyes.

"When can we visit?" she asked.

"I'm not sure. After I take a shower, I'm going to see them, rules or not."

"We'll go with you," Julian said.

Shawn smiled. "I'm glad you're both here. I don't know what I'd do without you."

Julian patted his shoulder. "You don't have to think about that. We are here and we're going to stay to see this through to the end."

The drive was quiet in the light of day, and the bustle of Cairo occupied their thoughts, even if only for a few moments.

Julian parked near the emergency entrance. Shawn noted the difference from the night before. The halls were crowded, all the elevators were in use, and the nurses hurried by. Shawn hoped that the activity of the living would carry over into the rooms of Nanette and Karl.

On the second floor, they entered the ICU waiting

area. Shawn attempted to push through the double doors. A doctor was attempting the same from the other side.

"You can't come in here," the doctor said sternly, "this is ICU. Do you know what that means?"

Shawn raged, "You go to hell. Where is Doctor Frank?"

Julian and Nancy stood solidly behind him.

Stunned by the impertinence, the doctor stared. "Listen, you. I'm not accustomed—"

"I don't give a damn. My fiancée is in there, and I want to know how she is without your mouth. Where is Doctor Frank?"

"In surgery."

"In that case, get me someone who knows what's going on, or step aside." Shawn glared.

For a cold second, the doctor also glared. He abruptly spun into the doors and disappeared. A few moments later, a nurse came out. Cordially, she asked, "May I help you?"

Softening, Shawn asked, "How is Nanette Cassim?"

"Let's sit down over here," she said, walking to a row of chairs.

They followed. Shawn sat. "Please, don't treat me like a child. Is she worse?" he asked.

"I'm only trying to make you comfortable," the nurse said, touching his arm.

"There has been no change in her condition, but that's not bad. The body needs time to heal, and we are doing everything to help that happen, I assure you."

His eyes fell into his hands. He said nothing.

"What's your name?" she asked quietly.

Without looking up, he replied, "Shawn O'Donnell."

"Mr. O'Donnell, I'll be perfectly honest with you. You know the circumstances of her condition, and I'm not a doctor. But I've nursed here for fifteen years, most of which has been spent in ICU. I've seen devastating illnesses, and I've seen miraculous recoveries. What I'm trying to say is that she has a good chance. That's the best hope I can give you right now. Someone is with her round the clock. I promise you, we will do everything possible."

Shawn looked into honest eyes, eyes that reminded him of his mother's. Even her inflection, and the way she wore her hair brought back images of his mother.

"If you like," she said endearingly, "you can look through her window."

Without hesitation, he said, "I'd like that."

"Come this way."

The three looked through the window without comment. Nanette's frail form was as it was the night before, surrounded by tubes, IV bags, monitors. Two nurses were with her, checking the drip, turning her on her side, adjusting her pillow, her blanket.

"They're taking good care of her," Nancy whispered.

"If only I could do something," Shawn breathed.

"You can," Julian said. "Love her, pray for her."

"I don't know that I believe in any of that," he answered woefully.

"Do it anyway. It can't hurt."

They moped along to Karl's room on the fourth floor. Not knowing what to expect, they approached his room cautiously.

Nancy peeked in. "Oh, Karl! I'm so happy you're awake. How are you feeling?"

"A headache, but much better. My God, Shawn! I was so worried about you!"

"I'm sorry, Karl. I should have left a note or something, but I found out where Krubrick lived, and I couldn't let him out of my sight."

"I'm glad you're all right. I had visions of you being arrested, or hurt in an accident. How is Nanette? Have you seen her?"

A wedge welled in Shawn's throat as he grasped for words he couldn't speak. With blurred eyes he merely shook his head. Nancy took his hand, speaking for him, soothing Karl's noticeable concern with his daughter's fate.

"She's resting comfortably," she said. "She's in ICU, and she is making slow progress."

"Am I missing something here?" Karl said,

alarmed with Shawn's empathy, his eyes not quite believing Nancy's interpretation. "She *is* alive, isn't she?" Karl demanded.

Shawn turned toward the door.

"Tell me the truth, damn it!" he shouted.

"Karl," Julian said, "she most certainly is alive, but she is not out of the woods. Nancy was not lying to you. Nanette is gaining strength."

Confused, Karl said, "Shawn? What's wrong?"

"Maybe I better answer that," Nancy said.

"I can handle it," Shawn said. "I love your daughter very much."

"That's the fastest romance I've ever heard of," Karl said.

"It isn't like that, Karl. I didn't exactly tell you everything."

Wary, Karl took a deep breath, folded his hands, and waited.

"I'm sorry. Please don't be angry."

"Shawn . . ."

"All right. Nanette and I are engaged. We were engaged before I came to work for you."

"I see." A rise in his voice.

"That's how I knew you were looking for an assistant. She told me about Malak, and I needed a job. I was going to tell you, but things kept happening. It never seemed like the right time."

Karl took a sip of water. His dark eyes settled on Shawn. He did not reveal what he thought.

"I was in Paris when I heard that a French team was about to come to Egypt. At that time, restoration work on the tomb of Nefertari was a priority. But I was too late. The team had already been chosen. Then I went to the Egyptian Consulate and made inquiries about other expeditions. And that's where I met Nanette. I fell in love with her the moment I set eyes on her."

"Was she equally inspired?" Karl asked softly.

"At the time I didn't know. But later, she confessed it was mutual. As time went on, we grew closer, and she told me about you."

"Why didn't you tell me these things at the interview?"

"Well, sir, if you remember, it didn't go smoothly. I thought that if I told you, you'd think I was trying to take advantage of my relationship with Nanette. I had to do it on my own, on my own merit. You might not have hired me just because I knew your daughter. Fathers are tough."

Julian smiled. Nancy looked on with sympathetic eyes. Karl's face revealed nothing. He sipped and swallowed and said, "Where have you been?"

"That's another story."

"I'd like to hear it since I have no place to go. I

was worried sick at your disappearance."

"I'm sorry—"

"Stop apologizing."

"Yes, sir." Shawn replied.

"Yes, Karl."

Shawn nodded. He gathered what was left of his confidence and cleared his throat. "After I took you to the airport, I went to see Julian like you asked. We talked about the seals and Krubrick and Talib. On my way back to your place, I figured that those two had to be working together. So, I turned around and went to the police station and waited for Talib to come out. Sooner or later, I thought, he had to lead me to Krubrick.

"Well, it happened. I followed him, and sure enough he drove right to Krubrick's estate, right on Gezira Island, very near where you live. I couldn't get close to the house, so I waited. The place was so big I didn't know where to start looking for Nanette. I was alone. What could I do but wait and watch for a chance that she could be alone?

"Then Monday night, around nine, there was a lot of activity, people coming and going, carrying equipment. A short time later, I saw them carry Nanette to a car. Krubrick left the compound with the archeologist, and I followed them to the pyramids. I parked my car at the Mena House Hotel and went the distance on foot. Then I ran into Otto. The rest you know."

Karl nodded while considering all the details. At last, he said, "Shawn, we'll have to do something about guarding it...the passage, I mean. They could—"

"I've already taken care of it, Karl."

Julian said, "Karl, why do you think Krubrick wanted the seals?"

"Money, treasure. If you remember, he stole the first seal, which specifically says treasure of Thoth. So I can only guess that he took it literally. Speaking of Krubrick, what happened to him?"

"We don't know," Shawn said.

"You haven't been back to the passage?"

"No."

"How long have I been here?" Karl asked.

"Nearly two days."

"Then tomorrow is the seventh isn't it?"

Shawn nodded.

"Has anyone spoken to Hunsdon?"

"No," Shawn said.

"I've got to be out of here by tomorrow," Karl said flatly. "There are things to be done."

Nancy said, "Your first priority is to take care of yourself. Second, you'll leave when the doctor says so."

"You don't understand. I—"

"Karl," Julian interrupted, "Nancy is right. Your health comes first."

"I know you mean well, but tomorrow is—"

"We know," Julian said. "Let's just play it by ear, okay, Karl? Now, get some rest. We'll be by later."

"Karl, I'll talk to Hunsdon," Shawn offered.

"Good, let me know what he says."

There was a nod. "Of course."

There were words of encouragement and departure as they left. In the car, Shawn said, "I guess he wasn't too happy about me."

"He wasn't unhappy," Nancy whispered.

Julian glanced at them both. "Look. Karl has been through a lot. He's worried about his daughter and he's worried about the cylinders that nearly consumed his life. Give him a chance."

Sadly, Shawn stared ahead and breathed, "I guess you're right."

"What happened to the seals?" Julian asked.

Their eyes exchanged concern.

"Maybe Otto knows," Shawn said. "I think we should pay a visit to Sir Hunsdon."

CHAPTER 42

"Julian, what time do you have?"

"About two-thirty. Is there a problem?"

"Well," Shawn said, "Karl told me that Hunsdon works at night, all night. Do you think it's a good idea to disturb him now?"

"I don't see where we have a choice. We don't want to upset Karl any more than we have to. He is convinced that the seventh seal will somehow appear tomorrow."

Nancy pushed back her hair. "Why is Sir Hunsdon so important in all this?" she asked.

"Karl believes that he is the key to the seven gates of Osiris," Shawn went on. "But frankly, I don't understand it. He can't speak. To pass through the gates, you must say the Words of Power and the names of the Keepers. And, there are the secrets. Hunsdon knows the sacred words."

"I'm sure Karl knows what he's doing," she said.

"I hope you're right," Julian mumbled.

"There's a parking spot." Shawn pointed.

Standing at Hunsdon's double doors inside the Nile Hilton, they looked at each other. No one, it seemed, wanted to knock.

"Karl said he has an awful temper," Shawn whispered.

"Oh, you men!" Nancy said, and knocked loudly.

It was more than a few minutes and several knocks before Otto opened the door. He was somewhat surprised to see the cadre at the threshold. "Do come in," he said, in a low throaty voice. "I was about to order coffee. Make yourselves comfortable."

Otto was dressed in the same black clothes as the night before, and, except for a tired voice, he looked none the worse for wear. He pointed them to a group of chairs near an open door to the balcony, and ordered coffee with an assortment of pastries. "Karl and Nanette, how are they doing?" he asked.

"Karl looks better today, but Nanette is still . . ." Shawn's voice dropped off.

"Otto, I apologize," Julian said. "This is Nancy Gottlieb..." He hesitated. "My fiancée."

Nancy shot him a look and smiled to herself.

Otto nodded. "A pleasure, madam," he said. "What can I do for you?"

"We hoped we could speak with Sir Hunsdon," Shawn said.

"I'm afraid that is not possible at this time. Is there something I might do for you?"

"Karl," Shawn went on, "is worried about tomorrow

and the seventh seal. But I'm worried about something else."

"Go on."

"Well, none of us went back inside the passage. We don't know what happened to Krubrick and we don't know what happened to the seals. I know Karl is worried about the seventh cylinder seal, but without the others—"

Otto put up his hand.

"We've got to get them back! We've got to search the passage! We've got to find out what happened to—"

"Shawn, please!" Otto said. "Not to worry. I can answer all your questions."

The trio exchanged glances as Otto rose to answer the knock at the door. A waiter rolled in a cart and extended the leaves. Several pots of coffee steamed amid trays of pastries. Otto signed the tab and closed the door.

"Coffee?"

Nods all around.

Coffee was served.

Otto lit a cigarette and tasted his coffee while they looked on anxiously.

"Rest assured," he said, inhaling, "I have the seals. I went back to the passage early this morning. And I must admit your man Fattah gave me some problems. I didn't expect anyone to be there."

"I phoned Fattah from the hospital," Shawn said. "The passage had to be guarded."

"I agree," Otto said. "Nonetheless, after I explained who I was and told him about you and Karl, he reluctantly let me into the passage. And by the way, Karl was right. The plug at the elbow reloaded itself. I found Junker spread all over it. A gruesome sight. If I hadn't recognized his clothing, I wouldn't have known it was him. Anyway, I also found the Hall of Mirrors and the remains of Mr. Krubrick. He had had a rather amateurish lobotomy."

"A what?" Nancy asked.

"Half his skull was missing."

"Oh, my God!" she gasped.

"Yes, well, it gets worse, I'm afraid," Otto said, enjoying their reaction. "There seems to have been some sort of power play. That's the best twist I can give it. I did not find Mr. Talib, but I did find the archeologist Reisner. Also a gruesome sight. He looked like . . . like a withered mummy, all dusty and dehydrated. No doubt he had attempted to read the seal."

"Oh, my God!" Nancy clutched her mouth.

"I wonder what happened to Talib," Shawn said.

"I could guess."

"Guess," Julian said.

"It appeared to me that the Hall of Mirrors had been immaculate. There were no streaks on the mirrors; the place was dust free as if someone had taken great care to keep it clean. But everywhere I looked, small bits of toasted flesh had been freshly splattered about the place. My opinion is that they emanated from beyond the great door."

"You think it was Talib?" Shawn asked.

"That's my guess."

"Oh, my God!" Nancy said. "What on earth could have done such a thing?"

"A force not of this Earth," Otto replied eerily.

"He attempted the gates, then?" Julian asked.

"That's my supposition."

"And to think I almost opened that door! I could have been toast," Shawn breathed.

"Very likely," Otto agreed. "If you know how to read it, the mantel above the door is very specific. But as we all know at this point, Talib either couldn't read it, or was blinded by his own greed."

Julian said, "You know an awful lot about these things, Otto. I venture to say you are much more than you seem."

"I'll take that as a compliment."

"Please do."

"I was an archeologist," Otto explained, "with deep interest in Egypt before I came to work for Sir Hunsdon. As you know, he is the foremost authority on ancient Egypt. An education in that realm is woefully incomplete without his tutor."

"I see."

"More coffee?"

"Please," Nancy said.

Otto filled their cups and offered pastries. He lit another cigarette.

"What do you think about tomorrow?" Shawn asked.

"As I understand it," Otto thought aloud, "the seals have presented themselves on the seventh day of the month. Is that correct?"

"Yes," Shawn said, "but they have not always been consecutive."

"I see. Well, Sir Hunsdon is determined to wait the day," Otto went on. "He has confided that he also believes a seal will appear. At any rate, he has set aside midnight of the seventh to enter the passage. However, he will not enter the Great Door without the seventh cylinder seal. And most importantly, he will not enter without Doctor Cassim."

"In other words," Shawn said, "he's going to case the joint?"

"Exactly. Now, if you will excuse me, I plan to get some rest."

"You must be exhausted," Nancy said.

"A little."

Julian said, "We'll tell Karl the seals are safe and

in your hands."

"It was a pleasure meeting you, Otto," Nancy said.

"The pleasure was mine, madam."

CHAPTER 43

Doctor Cassim, are you through with your tray?" a nurse asked.

"Did I ever tell you that I hate hospital food?"

"You must be feeling better," she quipped.

"Because I'm cranky, I'm feeling better?"

"In your case . . . yes."

"Thank you, nurse." He made a face.

"How about the dessert? Do you want it?"

"No. I've had enough sweetness for today. Thank you very much."

"Snip, snip, snip. Don't get too comfortable. I'll be right back with your medication."

A grimace as he lowered the bed and turned the volume up on the television. "The news always seems the same. Only the pictures change," he muttered.

CNN aired catastrophe after catastrophe. Floods in China, Bangladesh, and Italy. Hurricanes flying off the coast of Africa, heading for the Virgin Islands, Haiti, and Aruba. Storms smashing through the Gulf of Mexico, leveling parts of Texas, Louisiana, and points northeast. Tragedy followed by horror, disaster, and calamity.

There was one saving grace, however, and it amused Karl something like a cartoon following a dreadful drama. A salacious affair had been exposed in the White House of the United States. A chippy, some called her, had volunteered her services to the President. "Nothing but muckraking," he mumbled cynically, "followed by crass commercial messages." He flipped the channel to Superman, the movie, dubbed in Arabic.

His nurse floated into the room, carrying a tray with two small paper cups. "You shouldn't be watching TV," she lectured. "It's too stimulating."

"Well, in that case, you shouldn't be my nurse." He threw her a look. "What is that?"

She breathed deeply. "One is to give you some rest, and the other is for your blood pressure."

"You take them," Karl said, "so I can get some sleep."

Grimacing, she handed him the little cups with a glass of water. "Drink," she ordered.

"Just this once," he said. "And do not touch the television."

Leaving, she tossed a snarl over her shoulder.

Karl resumed watching the epic adventure, thoughts drifting to Nanette, Shawn, and the passage, while Superman rescued a busload of children dangling on the edge of a cliff.

"I love your daughter very much," Shawn had said.

"That's the fastest romance I've ever seen," he had replied. He blinked recalling the unsettling revelation, not sure how he felt.

"I like Shawn more than I care to admit, but . . . but a son-in-law? All that's happened . . . my fault . . . my poor Nanette."

All at once, Sir Hunsdon flowed into the room, passing through the doorway that barely allowed him entrance. He was regal, swathed in his Egyptian robe spangled with stars, carrying a leather-bound book he could barely manage.

Karl glimpsed the book's spine. *Book of the Dead*, a very old manuscript.

"How are you feeling, Karl?" Hunsdon said.

"Much better. How did you get past the nurse?"

"Influence," he roared, his brows brushing his hairline. "Now then, Karl, we have work to do. Are you up to it?"

"Yes, I think so. What do you have in mind?"

"Are you sure? I don't want to be responsible for a relapse."

"I'm fine, really. The nurse gave me a sedative, but it doesn't seem to be working. As a matter of fact, I feel quite good."

"Good enough to enter the passage?"

"Certainly."

"Where are your clothes?"

"In the closet."

Hunsdon gathered his clothes and helped him dress. "Wait a minute," he said, grabbing pillows from the top shelf, "this is just in case they snoop in on you," he snickered, stuffing them under the blanket and turning out the light. "The TV will do the rest— see the shadows?"

He took Karl by the arm, cracked open the door and peered down the hall. "It's clear," he said, quickly leading Karl to the elevators.

Sir Hunsdon's limousine purred under the canopy at the hospital's front entrance. Karl did not recognize the driver, but Hunsdon spoke to him as if they were friends. "All right, Felix," he said, "take us to the Great Pyramid."

"On my way, Osborne," the driver replied.

The limo accelerated as Hunsdon opened his great book and thumbed the pages. "Ah, here we are. The gates to the Mansion of Osiris," he said. "Do you remember them?"

"Yes," Karl said, "but not verbatim."

Hunsdon looked disappointed. "Doesn't matter; I know them by heart." He mumbled to himself as he read, quickly scanning the pages.

When they reached the pyramid in the dead of night, not a star shown in the cloudless sky. Only the moon lighted the giant triangles overshadowing the limp floodlights which appeared as though the power was being drained.

Hunsdon asked, "What time do you have?"

Karl looked at his wrist. "I don't have a watch."

"Felix, the time."

"Two minutes past midnight," Felix answered.

"Oh my, we've got to hurry!"

"Why?" Karl asked. "Are we missing something?"

"You'll see, you'll see," he said, rolling out the door. "Come along, come along."

They hurried for the steps, sand crunching under their feet.

"What happened to the guards?" Karl asked.

"I sent them away. No need, no need," Hunsdon said, flowing down the stairs in billows of cloth.

How odd, Karl thought, following. *Torches are lit along the walls, but there's no heat or smoke.*

Hunsdon rushed down the passage, turning the corner at the plug, mumbling as he went.

Karl could hardly keep up. "Sir Hunsdon, wait!"

Ignoring Karl's plea, Hunsdon tip-toed around the small domes on the floor, seeming to know his way. At another corner, he slipped out of sight.

Trudging along, Karl entered the corbel hall and glimpsed Hunsdon's robe flowing around the corner at the Hall of Mirrors. Out of breath, Karl clutched the handles of the door. With effort, he staggered into the reflecting room, gawking at Hunsdon's undivided attention on the ceiling of the universe.

"What is the hurry?" Karl asked.

"Just a minute, just a minute," Hunsdon said, turning about, eyes glued to the relief of the heavens.

"Sir Hunsdon—"

"There!" Hunsdon shouted, pointing to a marble square at the threshold of the great door.

"There what?" Karl asked, confused.

Hunsdon strode to the square. In his hand he held a brilliantly colored staff taller than himself, topped with a golden curve, and struck the floor with it three times. He loudly said, "The seventh seal is where you find it." His voice filled the chamber, resonating in echoes.

Fearful, Karl's eyes were pulled to where the staff had struck the floor.

"Lift it!" Hunsdon roared. "Pry it open, quickly, before it disappears! Only you can pull the stone! Only you!" he shouted.

"Doctor Cassim, Doctor Cassim wake up. Are you okay?"

Karl blinked heavily.

The nurse was shaking him, staring down at him. "I told you to turn off the television," she carped.

"Go away and leave the TV alone." He rolled over.

"You were moaning so loudly I could hear you

down the hall. I had to . . ."

"How am I supposed to sleep if you keep waking me up to tell me to sleep?"

"Fine. Have your nightmare." She stalked out in a huff.

Karl raised his head and looked around the room. He took a deep breath. "What a weird dream!" He stuffed the pillow under his head, staring at the television. Superman was over. Lucille Ball was gyrating in a large tub, stomping grapes and chirping with another soul . . . in Arabic.

CHAPTER 44

Seven February.

It was one of the few days in Egypt when the lady of the sky wept and her dank breath chilled the very marrow of one's bones. Her smooth gray essence lay across the country in a dreamy haze, inviting sleep.

They had all slept late. Pressure, strain, and tension, the three sisters of stress, had been shackled in slumber. Nancy was the first to rise and hummed while she flitted about the kitchen, making coffee, fixing breakfast. At twenty past ten, she sipped, looking out the window, welcoming the change.

"That smells so good!" Shawn said.

"It does, doesn't it? The only thing better is bacon sizzling in a pan."

A smile. "Have a good sleep?" he asked, pouring himself a cup of coffee.

"Did I? I didn't realize I was that tired."

"Is Julian still sleeping?"

Nancy nodded. "I hated to wake him. He looked so peaceful."

"It's that kind of day," Shawn said, and sat across from her.

For a moment their eyes hung out the window in the haze of the day.

"Shawn, what do you think is going to happen?"

"God, Nancy, I don't know. Nanette has taken up so much of my mind, all the rest seems . . ."

"She'll come out of it," Nancy replied.

"I hope you're right."

"Good morning!" Julian yawned. "The aroma of coffee woke me up." He shuffled to the counter and helped himself.

"You could have put on some clothes," Nancy chided, eyeing his boxers.

"I did," he laughed. "You know I sleep naked."

She shook her head. "Yes, but Shawn didn't."

"Are you offended, Shawn?"

With a grin, he said, "Not in the least."

"See." He tweaked her cheek. "You two look like you've been conspiring."

"We were just taking about Nanette," she said.

Julian nodded and joined them at the table. "When are you going to the hospital?"

Nancy looked at Shawn.

"As soon as I finish my coffee and take a shower," he replied.

"I'll go with you," Nancy said.

"Would you mind dropping me off at the university?" Julian asked. "There are some things I need to check on."

Shawn nodded. "No problem."

Nancy looked at him. "What is it, Julian?"

"Oh, nothing important. Just an idea."

On their way, Shawn dropped Julian at the American University and picked up a newspaper at the corner. As they pulled into the parking area of the hospital, Nancy cried out. "My God, the police are searching for Talib! The paper says they want to question him. They suspect him of trafficking in black market antiquities."

"So, there's another side to the Minister of Police," Shawn remarked. "And to think, he had Karl fooled all this time. Anything in there about his buddy Krubrick?"

"Yes, he's missing too. Oh, and listen to this. Officers found a horde of Egyptian artifacts in a storeroom on his estate, including jewels from a Nubian queen."

"They don't know the half of it!"

She tossed the paper in the back seat. "I'm glad I never met either one of them."

The sky began to clear. Arm in arm, they made their way to ICU as Doctor Frank came down the hall.

"Doctor Frank?"

"Mr. O'Donnell, isn't it?"

"Yes. Nanette Cassim, how is she?"

He exhaled and looked him straight in the eye. "The same, I'm afraid. The only encouragement I can give you is that her blood work has improved. Other than that, her condition remains the same."

"I was hoping . . ."

Doctor Frank put his hand on Shawn's shoulder. "Look, son, these cases are very difficult. She is young and strong. We'll know more tomorrow." He turned and walked away.

Nancy tugged at his sleeve. "You want to get a cup of coffee?"

"I want a cigarette."

"You don't smoke."

"I want to start."

"No, you don't," Nancy said. "Let's go see Karl."

"What am I going to tell him?" His lip quivered.

"The truth. That her blood has improved. That she has a good chance and we'll know more tomorrow. That's what you say." She squeezed his arm. "Now, let's go." She took his hand and led him to the elevator.

When the doors opened on the fourth floor, a crowd had gathered at the door of Karl's room.

"Oh, Jesus," Shawn said. "Now what?"

They ran to the room and pushed through. A doctor and several nurses were huddled at the bedside exchanging loud, angry words with Karl.

"Oh, Shawn, Nancy! Will you please tell these

idiots," Karl groaned, "that I'm leaving this place?"

"Doctor Cassim," the doctor lectured, "you are in no condition to go anywhere. Don't you understand? You are a sick man!"

Nancy threw up her hands.

Shawn tapped the doctor on the shoulder. "Let me talk to him."

"Talk?" Karl interrupted. "There is nothing to talk about."

"Karl, please. Doctor, give us a minute alone with him," Shawn said.

"Talk some sense into him." The doctor stalked out, motioning the nurses to follow.

Nancy closed the door. "All right, Karl, what are you doing?"

"I have to leave. It's as simple as that."

"Karl—"

"It's the seventh. I can't stay here."

Nancy said, "Listen, Karl, we talked to Otto."

"It's Hunsdon you have to talk to."

"Please, Karl, give me a chance."

"We've got to find the seals," Karl insisted.

"Otto has the seals," Shawn said, slowly and deliberately.

Karl stared and leaned back on his pillow.

"So . . . take it easy before you give yourself a heart attack." Nancy rubbed his shoulder.

"Very well. Talk to me."

Nancy sat on the other side of the bed as Shawn explained what Otto had found in the Hall of Mirrors. "Otto recovered the seals," he said. "And tonight, Hunsdon is going into the passage. Everything is okay, Karl."

Karl's face relaxed as he absorbed the information. But still, something bothered him.

"What's eating you, Karl?" Nancy took his hand.

His eyes closed. He turned his head. He whispered, "I saw her . . . my doll. She looked so . . ." He pressed his face into the pillow.

Shawn faced the wall, trying to swallow his feelings.

Nancy held him firmly. "Karl, we talked to the doctor. He says her blood has improved. That's a good sign." She hesitated a moment and went on, "Be brave and thank your lucky stars that she doesn't look like that Russian nurse of yours."

A burst of air, a small laugh as he put his hand on hers. "Thank you," he said. "I'll bet she lifts weights too."

Tension eased with smiles. Nancy blotted his tears.

Karl took a breath. "When did you say Hunsdon is going into the passage?"

"At midnight, and I know what you're thinking."

"Yes, Shawn, I have every intention of going with him."

"Karl, you can't," Nancy insisted.

"Yes, I know, my heart. But I simply must go."

"Where are you going?" Julian asked, casually breezing into the room.

"I think you know," Karl said. "And don't we look awfully fit today."

"I am fit. I feel fit."

"Save it," Nancy piped in. "You're going to need it."

Julian looked at her and then at Karl.

"I am dead serious," she said. "If Karl insists on going into that passage tonight, you and Shawn are going with him."

"I'm not sure that's a good idea."

"Julian, I have no choice. I must go."

"The doctor is not going to release you," Shawn said.

Softly, Karl said, "There are ways around that."

"What about the last seal, Karl?"

"I'm not sure, Nancy. But...don't think me foolish, but I had a dream." He felt their eyes.

Shawn said, "Are you going to share it with us?"

Karl hesitated. "Let's wait and see."

The television muttered in the background as they wondered about the dream.

Knowing Karl's determination, Shawn said, "What time, Karl?"

CHAPTER 45

A turbaned man in Bedouin robes casually took the elevator to the fourth floor at six minutes after eleven. He held the door, checking the hall for life. Several doors down, he caught sight of a nurse going into a patient's room. He breathed, pulled a cloth over his face and walked to room 421. Inside, he closed the door.

"Karl?" He moved to the bed and shook the covers. "Karl, are you awake?"

"I'm over here."

Shawn spun. Karl was standing in the closet fully dressed. "Holy shit, Karl!"

"How are your nerves," he asked teasing.

"Okay, till now. I brought you these robes."

"Good, very good."

Karl slipped into black Bedouin robes. "How do I look?"

"Like the real thing. How do you feel?"

"Not bad. Here, hang on to this."

"What is it?"

"My sleeping pill."

"Thanks."

"Stuff these pillows under my blanket, and turn up the TV."

Karl opened the door an inch. "It's clear."

The elevator doors stood wide open as they quickly stepped inside.

"How did you manage this?" Karl asked.

Shawn reached up and pulled a small wedge from the top of the door. It closed. "Going down." He smiled.

Except for a cleaning crew, the lobby was deserted. Their robes swayed as they edged to the glass doors unnoticed.

Outside, Shawn said, "Now don't get upset, but Nancy insisted on coming along."

Karl took the steps slowly, his eyes on the ground. He stopped on the last step. "I don't like it."

Shawn mumbled, "I warned her it could get dangerous. There's Julian."

"We'll see. Let Hunsdon decide."

Julian stopped at the entrance with Nancy at his side. Shawn jumped in the back seat and Karl slid in front.

"Have any trouble?" Nancy asked.

"No. It went very smoothly," Karl said. "I won't be missed."

Anxiety permeated the vehicle as Julian guided it over the bridge to Giza. In the dark, the stars shown so bright, so close, they seemed just above the street lights. The cool air, now cleansed from the day's rain, carried with it the distinct scent of desert sand, a scent captured in the dunes, the cliffs, and released in miserly fashion into winter's wetness.

"There they are," Shawn said, as the spectacle of the first wonder of the world towered in the distance, guarded by the watchful Sphinx who gazed into the eastern sky.

Julian slowed to a stop. "That must be Hunsdon's car. He's early."

Karl was silent, his heart beating rapidly as he looked to the steps.

"Are you okay?" Nancy asked.

"Yes, fine."

They trudged from the road to the side of the Great Pyramid. Four men greeted them, with Fattah in the lead, grinning at Karl's apparent recovery.

"I am so delighted you are well," Fattah said.

"Thank you, Fattah. I see my friends have arrived ahead of us."

"Oh, yes. As you can see, they brought their own equipment."

The stairwell to the passage was brightly lit. Karl nodded. "Allow no one entrance."

"You can count on me, Doctor Cassim. No one gets in."

"Karl, look." Julian pointed to the sky. "Look at

the belt of Osiris."

"Incredible."

"Yes, it is. It's more than that. It's a phenomenon not seen on earth in nearly forty thousand years."

"What are you looking at?" Nancy asked.

"Look, right there."

As though a portion of the Milky Way had been scissored and pasted in the wrong place, a gigantic glowing, cottony cloud surrounded the belt stars and reached out with feathery limbs. The uneven stars twinkled like loose diamonds on a powdery cloth.

"It's beautiful!" she breathed.

"Yes, indeed," Julian said. "The Hubbell telescope is taking pictures of it as we speak."

All eyes were raised to the heavens.

"That's what you can get me for Christmas," Nancy whispered.

Julian looked at her and said, "A star?"

"No, silly, a diamond."

Julian rolled his eyes. "Listen, I'm a scholar not a jeweler."

Karl interrupted. "We have work to do. I think this can wait?"

"Sorry." Julian nudged her.

"Shawn, you keep Nancy close. Guide her through the passage behind us. Julian, follow me and watch every step."

Karl led the way into the passage. Lanterns were strategically placed along the corridors that ran straight as a rail, elbowed, and ran straight again. They approached the first plug.

"Wow!" Julian exclaimed. "Will you look at the size of that stone?"

Karl raised a brow. "The question is . . . how did they get it in here?" He walked through the space behind the stone and said, "This next area is treacherous. Be careful not to step on those small mounds. They are triggers."

They inched around the domes into the next section. An unearthly stench came from the end of the corridor.

"That must be Mr. Talib's friend," Karl said. "Or what remains of him. I recognize the torn sleeve."

Eyes widened as they scampered by, covering their noses, gaping at the paper-thin remains of Junker. With another turn and a bow through a tunnel, the immense corbel hall loomed. Suddenly, they were stone still silent in awe with the beauty of granite, of skill, of the hall's enormous size.

"Just a little further now," Karl said as they gawked, moving over the floor that seemed to be covered with glass.

At the end of the hall the double doors stood open to the Hall of Mirrors. Sir Hunsdon's eyes were locked on the mantel over the Great Door while Otto peered at the celestial ceiling.

Karl abruptly stopped and stared. As in his dream, Hunsdon stood before the door in his priestly robes, a large leather-bound *Book of the Dead* held firmly in his arm. He turned to face them and waved Otto to his side. He handed over the book and began to sign.

"How is your health, Karl?" Otto asked for Hunsdon.

"Good," Karl said.

Hunsdon nodded, looking concerned with furrowed brow and pursed lips. He pointed to the bag on the floor that Talib had taken from Karl. He signed, "I have read all the seals. Do we still lack the seventh?"

Karl nodded.

"Then we cannot go further," Hunsdon warned.

Again, Karl nodded.

Nancy tugged at Shawn's sleeve. She whispered, "What's that on the floor over there?" She pointed.

Suspecting what it was, Shawn shrugged.

Otto smiled. "Would you like to take a closer look?"

Nancy swayed her head.

"Wise choice," he said. "Those are the remains of Mr. Krubrick and Mr. Reisner. I thought it fitting to cover them."

Gasping, Nancy covered her mouth.

Hunsdon moved to Karl's side. His hands flew

while Otto translated.

"The mirrors are made of highly polished silver. I find it impossible to date them. Suffice to say, they are many thousands . . ." Otto stopped.

They both faced the Great Door. The granite beneath their feet trembled. Before the Great Door, a square seam etched itself on the floor as if made by a finger. Thick blue smoke seeped slowly upward, engulfing the square. Odorless and dense, it rose to the celestial ceiling, swirling in clouds. Terrified eyes followed its winding trail across the expanse, spiraling, puffing as if it breathed.

From the center of this rolling vapor, a slender coiling growth emerged, pointing, slithering like a snake, descending jerkily, then poised. With the crack of a whip, with the flash of lightning, with the speed of a cobra, the snake-like growth lashed around Hunsdon's neck with the surety of a rope. He gasped, heaved, and clutched his throat, laboriously sucking air.

Suddenly, the vaporous blue cloud was gone, vanished, disappeared. The deeply etched granite was as smooth as it was before. And upon that very spot, the seventh crystal cylinder seal lay on end before six pairs of unbelieving eyes.

Hunsdon took a great, loud breath and released his neck. In shock, he stared at his hands and then at his friends. He cleared his throat and shuddered as if iced to the bone. Staring into a mirror, he turned in a circle and examined himself. He signed, "I don't understand. I'm all right. What happened?"

Round, wide eyes met his question with shrugs.

"More than strange," Otto said. "Are you sure you're all right, Edward?"

Hunsdon felt himself and stood at the mirror again, bending close, looking at his throat, his face. His reflection mutated hundreds of times in all directions. "I am perfectly fine," he signed. "Just fine." With a measure of confidence and flowing robes, Hunsdon walked to the Great Door and hesitated. He looked at Karl and pointed to the floor. Karl stared.

Hunsdon pointed again, more forcefully, but Karl was deliberately bound where he stood. A tinge of fear was caught by the mirrors. His dream had come alive.

Impatiently, Hunsdon bent and picked up the seal. He glared at Karl. "What's wrong with you?" he roared in a loud, deep voice. "I can speak," he whispered, then thundered, "Do you hear, I can speak!"

In amazement, mumbles echoed through the hall as faces searched faces and eyes exchanged glances.

"My God!" Hunsdon said softly, "I can really speak."

The glint of tears sparkled in Hunsdon's eyes. Twelve years of silence vanished in an instant. With a wavering voice, he said, "I have you to thank for this, Karl."

Karl slowly shook his head. "No, oh no. I cannot claim credit . . . It was the mist, the seal, this room . . . something much more powerful than I."

"Very well," Hunsdon said, his eyes resting on the floor. "But still," he looked at him squarely, "still, you were instrumental." He brought his chin down and raised it again. "Now, please read the seal," he said, extending the cylinder.

Involuntarily, Shawn took a step forward. Karl's weakened condition seemed to encourage his assistance.

With dark circles skirting his eyes, and bent frame, Karl claimed the seal. Sir Hunsdon stood at his side.

Holding the cylinder between his palms, Karl saw that this, this seventh seal, was different from all the rest. There was no curse, no foreboding threat. In a less than normal voice he began to read the message.

"Hail! Hail to you the worthy. You have traversed the pitfalls of the netherworld. You have waged the war of righteousness. You have sought the council of wise men."

Karl looked to Hunsdon whose eyes remained on the crystal. He went on,

"Gather unto yourself the wisdom as set forth, for the final judgment is before you. Anpu watches.

Sobmer m A . . . (Companion of Thoth)

Ka"

Shawn took a step forward. "I'm not sure I understand it," he said.

Hunsdon and Karl exchanged glances. Hunsdon picked up the question.

"It's very simple, my boy." He smiled at the sound of his own voice. "The pitfalls are those traps, those plugs back there in the passage that have taken the unworthy. If one has made it this far, one had been successful. One has avoided the netherworld, the world of the dead. As for war of righteousness, the losers are there under that cloth."

"And the wisdom?" Julian asked.

"Well, sir, first address the council of wise men. All but one of whom has given freely of his knowledge to Karl. The German chose not to get involved. But you and I, Mr. Rutledge, and all the people in this room have chosen to participate. And for the wisdom set forth, it is in that book Otto is holding. It is the *Book of the Dead*. In it are the names and the secrets of the seven gates, the Arits, to the Kingdom of Osiris which are no doubt beyond the door."

For a moment they absorbed the explanation and then Karl added, "This is the final judgment, the last trial to test the worthy. As for Anpu . . . Anpu is the Egyptian name for the Greek equivalent of Anubis. Anubis watches. If you will recall the most famous Egyptian drawing in the world, Anubis stands before the scale of justice, weighing a person's heart against a feather. If one has been truthful, honest, led a good life, the heart and the feather will be of equal weight. If not, if the heart outweighs the feather, the person is doomed and his soul is destroyed forever by Amemait, eater of souls."

Nancy whispered to Julian, "I don't think I want to go through that door. If you don't mind, I'll just wait here."

"You'll be alone," Julian said quietly. "Because if they let me, I'm going with them."

For a second she looked at him. "Forget I said that."

"All right," Hunsdon said, "I think we are ready." He waved Otto over. "Open the book to the gates." He turned to Karl. "You know what we have to do."

"Yes, I know."

"Shawn," Hunsdon said, "you carry the seals. Make sure the bag is ready at all times. What part the seals play in all this, I don't know. But I'm sure it will be made clear.

"Julian, Nancy," he went on, "follow close behind us. Listen carefully. You must also recite aloud the names Karl will speak. It must be exact. There will be three gods for each gate. The Gatekeeper, the Watcher, and the Herald, and Karl will say their names first. Then, together, we will follow. You must say these names loudly, with authority. Do you understand?"

Heads nodded.

"Good. A word of caution. These gods are capable

of transformation. That means that they can and will take on the likeness, the talents, of other creatures. Some will remain in their true form, in human form, but they will show no mercy, so expect none.

"Now, now is the time to choose. If you do not wish to enter the trial of the Arits, now is the time to withdraw." Hunsdon looked into each and every face. With a sure and steady voice, he continued. "This is no game. There can be no mistakes. Errors will most certainly be paid with death. We have just seen an example of the power that lies beyond that door. If you choose not to enter, no one will judge you unfairly. It is your life. Choose!"

Apprehensive looks passed between them as each in his own mind reached a decision. In short order, it was clear. There would be no withdrawal.

Meaningfully, Hunsdon said, "You must be absolutely sure."

Confident, silent nods were his reply.

CHAPTER 46

"All right then, I will begin," Hunsdon said.

Otto held open the oversized *Book of the Dead*. Hunsdon turned to the Great Door and bowed deeply, meditating for a length of time. Rising slowly, he extended his arms, hands outstretched, palms forward. In his generous high priest's robe of sapphire spangled with golden stars, he called out in a rich baritone, "A Asr-Neb-heh, a Tchatcha-t Asar auah Tchatcha-t-urt Neb-maat-heri-tep-retui-f . . ."

Nancy nudged Shawn and whispered, "What is he saying?"

Shawn leaned close and replied softly, "He said, 'Hail Osiris, Lord of Eternity. Hail the court of judges of Osiris and the Great Council.' He's addressing the ancient gods, those on the left and on the right."

When he had finished, the Great Door swung open by itself. They looked into a blackness such as no one had seen before.

Slowly, from all sides, the blackness inside lost its cut, withering to the misty light of a gray day. From the threshold inward, a knee-high cottony vapor hid the floor.

Sir Hunsdon stepped aside, inclining slightly, allowing Karl to pass into the unknown. Warily, Karl led the way over the mark and all trailed closely in order.

As the last in line entered, the Great Door closed behind them. Karl walked on into the haze, which greeted them with sultry air that made them most uncomfortable. In all directions as far as the eye could see, the vastness of space was incomprehensible. No odor, no sound, no movement of any kind came from the dense cloud which rested on the floor. For several long moments they silently searched their surroundings.

Breaking their solitude and coming on quickly, the knee-high vapor swirled ahead of them. Piercing the lowly fog, an island rose from the depths, parting the cretaceous substance. Like a mirage, it wavered as cloth in the wind while it rose. Suddenly, an immense gate, supported by huge blocks of dripping green granite, clearly materialized in the distance.

The change in the environment, the hasty appearance of the first gate, took them all by surprise.

Occupied with the unfolding drama of bright sun and cold, still air, everyone's head and eyes darted about as the sound of enraged water elevated beneath their feet. A sizable boat wrapped around them, keeping them dry. To the left and to the right, thick trees and tall grass formed as if painted by a gigantic brush.

A stiff breeze rose, enhanced with the scent of freshly mown grass, contradicting the sight of tall grass.

Not to be swayed in the confusion of sight and sound Karl paid no mind, but kept his eyes riveted to the gate, its massive keyhole and the human form seated bent-kneed before it. Wearing the mask of a timid white hare, the god held a whisk made from an animal's tail. Above the gate, a substantial, brilliantly colored cornice prominently displayed the ankh, the sign of life, the djed, pillar of stability, and the staff, signifying power.

The hare's large blue eyes peered innocently, attempting to hide his evil with frailty, but Karl returned the gaze and said strongly, "Sekhet-her-ashtaru," calling the name of the Gatekeeper. Five perfect echoes followed.

Stricken by his name, the Gatekeeper rose. He grasped the key dangling at his side, walked to the bronze gate, and twisted it in the lock. The massive gate instantly flung open, bringing into sight the Watcher. Standing in human form, the brown serpent-headed Watcher skillfully brandished a gleaming curved knife.

Karl stared into the glowing eyes of the hooded serpent, remembering that these gods took on forms to frighten, to alter concentration, to overcome intruders.

Sir Hunsdon took this hesitation anxiously. Too

long a time would set things in motion that could not be reversed. He poked Karl in the back.

Karl drew a weak breath and said, "Smetti, Smetti is thy name. Take thy venom and flee from us."

A chant by five strong voices followed, arousing the Watcher who sped away.

Minutes passed as the water around them rolled in fury. They expected the Herald, but he did not appear. Karl turned to Hunsdon.

"Be patient," Hunsdon said. "Remember, they are crafty creatures."

Time passed as their eyes searched every hiding place around the huge blocks and in the shrubbery. Finally, from beyond the gate, the tall grass rustled with movement. Slithering slowly into the mouth of the gate in the form of a dragon, the Herald dragged a blade of enormous size strapped to his waist. His human form gave way to a reptilian head, and a tail that lashed the hazy floor and the tall grass into a frenzy. His teeth chomped and gleamed as an unearthly guttural dirge welled from his throat.

Taken back, Karl faltered. Hunsdon prodded him, knowing that this creature intentionally meant to horrify and subdue. He prodded him again.

Squeezing his eyes shut, Karl uttered, "Thy name is Hakheru."

"Again," Hunsdon said, "louder!"

"Hakheru, still thy fire and bid us passage!" Karl shouted.

In sequence, all repeated the Herald's name, spurring him to the other side where the Gatekeeper and the Watcher waited.

Hunsdon whispered, "The secret formula, speak the formula now!"

Karl's strength had noticeably drained.

"Now, Karl, now!" Hunsdon urged.

Slowly, forcefully, Karl uttered the sacred words from the great book. "I am the mighty one who createth his own light. I have come unto thee, O Osiris, and purified from that which defileth thee. Hail, Ra, thy father, who goest round about in the sky, I say, O Osiris in truth, that I am Sahu. I beseech thee, let the way be opened in Rastau. Open the way to Rastau!"

On those words, the gate and all its surroundings disassembled before them, falling to dust. Unmasked, the three gods bowed, becoming transparent, evaporating into thin air. The gray light of day, the dense fog, the boat that carried them and the sound of rushing water were all that remained.

Hunsdon put a hand on Karl's shoulder and nodded. "Very good, Karl," he said.

Karl smiled weakly.

"How do you feel?" Shawn asked.

The dark circles beneath his eyes and bent posture

were evident. "I'm okay, just tired, a little tired."

Hunsdon said, "Review the book, refresh your memory, Karl, especially the sacred words."

"I've studied them. I know them as I know my own name."

"Otto will hold the page just in case. Sometimes, the shock of seeing these gods in all their finery can chase thoughts from your mind," Hunsdon said.

"Don't worry, Karl," Otto softly said, "I'll be right next to you all the way."

They all held on as the boat bucked on the waves and Nancy struggled to Julian's side. "I'm scared," she said.

"It'll be all right," Julian said. "Just hang on to Shawn like he said. Be strong." He pecked her cheek.

Hunsdon hung on to the sailless mast searching the distance.

Nancy tapped his arm. "Sir Hunsdon, will they all be as hectic as this one was?"

Hunsdon looked at her calmly and said, "Mrs. Gottlieb, that first gate was a treat, a test. As we speak, that Herald is spreading the word that the gate has been opened. They know now that we are equipped and they are going to make it harder, more horrifying and more bizarre than you can imagine. Be prepared for anything, and above all, please don't be frightened. That is exactly what these gods want."

"I understand," she said bravely. "But can they really hurt us?"

His eyes narrowed as he took her into them. "More than that," he said. "Death is the payment for failure."

She looked into the fog circling the boat, the tips of the waves poking through. "How long before the next one do you think?" she asked.

He shook his head. "It could be a minute, an hour, a day. I don't know."

She moved back to Julian's side as the waves seemed to settle.

Not hearing the conversation, Julian said, "That wasn't so bad now, was it?"

Nancy looked at him and then at Hunsdon who overheard and stepped close. He did not repeat himself. He leveled his eyes sternly and simply said, "You were warned in the beginning. Like all things, there are no two the same. You'll see for yourself." He turned and leaned over the rail, scanning for what he could see.

More time elapsed on the calm waters as the boat moved along, propelled, it seemed, by an unseen hand. Karl nodded into a light sleep, but Shawn tried to stay awake. Otto squatted against the side, holding firmly onto the book; Hunsdon stood, continuing to scan the distance.

Suddenly, their vessel rolled, struggling against a violent, boundless sea while the fog was swept away by gale-force winds, and the sky became a pot of boiling pitch.

"Hang on for dear life!" Hunsdon shouted. "There is no recovery here."

Thrashing about for what seemed like hours, they clung to ropes and wooden beams, trying desperately to keep the salt water from burning their eyes.

Seeing Nancy's grip weakening, Julian threw his body on top of her, pressing her against the mast while she latched onto him with all her strength, weeping gratefully.

At the bow, Karl was nearly flung overboard as the boat slapped the churning sea and twisted on the crest of a rising wave. Shawn reached out, grabbing Karl's shirt, and yanked him back at the same time a swell poured over the deck. In full control, Otto had lashed himself to the stern holding the great book firmly to his chest when, as quickly as it had begun, the gale abruptly quit.

The sea was glass. A giant sun sat on the horizon like a crimson ball in a cloudless, radiant sky. And to their amazement, the vessel had changed. The boat was now longer, wider, and with oars, fourteen to a side, paddling great gulps of water; deep circling dips in rhythm to the beat of a drum.

Confused, anxious glances passed between all those on board while their mumbling tongues were brought to a halt.

"Stop it!" Hunsdon shouted. "That's exactly what they want. Confusion! Pay attention! Focus your minds or we are lost!"

With all eyes on Hunsdon, they saw behind him, into the distance, and pointed to a slip of land. He turned. For a minute or two, it appeared as a lump of green on a sparkling blue sea. But as they watched, it grew larger, quicker than the boat could possibly travel. And in moments they were grounded on shore, staring at the second gate.

Set back from the shoreline, the second gate was made of gray mud-brick, twice as high and twice as wide as the first, and then the island was suddenly larger than the sea that lapped its shore! All around were trees whose limbs and leaves had been reduced to stubble, burnt and still smoldering with the smell of sulfur. The sun had set and the moon was rich and full.

Before a single brown door, three platforms of different hues rose high above, where three deities sat, legs crossed beneath them. Clearly, they were all of human form, all with glowing white eyes, glaring at the boat's occupants. The first deity wore the mask of a lion, the second wore a nemes headdress, and the last wore the head of a dog.

Hunsdon helped Karl to his feet. Karl raised his head and pointed to the first. "I fear you not," he said loudly, "for I know thy name. Thou art Unhat, Keeper of the Gate."

Unhat stood, arms straight and stiff at his sides. His head rolled back in a roar to shatter glass. His head, teeth, and mane melted like wax upon the shoulders a young, handsome man whose naked, athletic body bore no blemish or shame, but stood upright and glided to the gate.

They all recited his name.

Karl gazed at the next, in the likeness of a pharaoh. The nemes crown gleamed in gold and royal blue. His beard was braided. His arms were folded on his knees, and Karl bowed in reverence. "My lord," he chanted, "wisdom precedes thy holy form. I call thee with thy name of Seqt-her, Watcher of the Gate."

Five times more, Seqt-her's name was carried over the quiet sea.

The Watcher rose. He glanced to the left and then to the right, settling his eyes squarely on Karl. His white linen robe transformed to brilliant red and, in a blink, he joined the naked one at the gate.

The hound-headed deity lowered his lids, half covering his eyes, and began snarling. In a flash, he flew from his pinnacle, landing at Karl's feet, snapping, chomping at his leg while black clouds blotted out the moon.

"The name," Hunsdon shouted, "say his name!"

Stunned by the creature's swiftness, Karl fumbled for the name. On the ground, backing away he blurted, "Ust! Ust, be gone, be gone!"

He vanished at the sound of his name, like so much dust, and Karl felt the blood run, his pant-leg dangling in shreds.

"My God!" Nancy shrieked.

"Say the sacred words, Karl! Say them now," Hunsdon loudly prompted.

Shawn helped Karl stand. "Can you do it?" he asked.

Karl nodded. "Osiris," he mumbled, perspiration beading.

"Louder!" Hunsdon ordered.

Taking a breath, Karl enunciated clearly and loudly, "Osiris, whose word is truth, protect us on our journey. We advance on the path. O grant thou that we may continue and attain the sight of Ra."

Blackness, total and complete, swallowed them.

"What happened?" Julian whispered.

"Quiet!" Hunsdon shouted.

As a door opened, the black sooty clouds parted ever so slowly, revealing a full moon, setting alight the barren waste of a desert.

"Jesus, where the hell are we now?" Shawn gasped.

Otto replied, "I thought it obvious."

Hunsdon patted Otto's shoulder. "Take care of Karl's leg, will you?"

"Of course." Otto helped Karl to a small, flat row of stones. With only pieces of the shredded clothing, he bandaged the leg as best he could.

"Sir Hunsdon," Julian said quietly, "are we hallucinating all this?"

Hunsdon brushed his lip and pointed to Karl. "Does that look like a hallucination to you? No, my friend, this is real as real as it gets."

"Dreams can seem just as real, sir."

"All right, Mr. Rutledge, have it your way. But I warn you, death comes but once, dream or no."

Nancy put her hand in Julian's, pulling him away. "Let it be," she whispered.

A moment later, Shawn asked, "What happened back there, Sir Hunsdon? Why did that hound go after Karl?"

Hunsdon hugged his arms. "Karl waited too long," he said. "There can be no hesitation, no breach in time. That staggering moment signals the deity that you are not equipped, that you do not know his name. If Karl hadn't uttered his name when he did, he would have been killed."

"I had no idea!" Shawn said.

Hunsdon removed his glasses and rubbed his eyes. "Get some rest, lad," he said, "you're going to need it."

He strolled over to Karl. "How are you, Karl?"

Karl looked up with glazed eyes. "Frightened."

"As are we all," Hunsdon said. He leaned close. "Karl, can you make it?"

"I don't have a choice," he breathed.

Hunsdon nodded, frowning. "Rest. Lean back and rest."

The air was cool, crisp, and dry. Powerfully, the moon shined, lighting the dunes, outcrops, and fingers of stone that scraped the sky.

"There's not a single star in all the heavens," Julian said. "How strange."

"Don't for a moment compare these things to reality," Hunsdon said. "Everything we see is meant to deceive, to instill fear. Pay it no mind."

"Easier said than done," Nancy whispered.

"Look, over there." Shawn pointed.

Eyes followed his finger.

Into the darkness beyond a rise, what appeared as the walls of an ancient temple loomed in splashes of silver light. Deep shadows revealed many doors, many entryways into the temple. Before the walled fortress, lion sphinxes stood watch. Not a breeze, not a sign of life, not a sound or scent gave a hint as to its purpose.

"Come on, Karl, I'll help you. I think it's show time," Otto said, wrapping Karl's arm around his neck. "I rather preferred the boat." He smiled.

"I agree," Karl said.

They trudged through the sand in deathly silence, taking comfort in hearing their own shoes crunch. As they approached the wall, they were in awe at its unscaleable height. The sphinxes, too, dwarfed them. They seemed like ants in a jungle of giant demons.

"If we are to go inside, how do we know which door is the right one?" Julian asked.

"I don't know," Hunsdon barked. "Maybe it's a ploy. The ancients always made false doors to confuse. Typical of what we're dealing with here."

They walked perhaps six hundred yards to a corner, passing many faux doors.

"This is very strange, Edward," Otto said.

Hunsdon glowered. "Yes, it is," he puffed. He stopped and turned and for a moment stared at Otto. "It's a trick," he breathed. "Reverse the order."

"I don't understand," Karl said.

"We have to return to where we started. I'll explain."

Julian took one of Karl's arms and Otto the other. The long walk on the malleable field of sand had taken its toll on Karl's stamina.

"This is it!" Shawn said. "There's our path from the hill."

"All right, Karl, are you ready?" Hunsdon asked.

"What are we doing?"

"We have to reverse the order. You must say the

sacred words first. I do believe, Karl, that the gods are here, right in front of that false door. They're invisible. It's all a trick, don't you see? By saying the sacred words first, you are commanding their presence. This gate is the opposite of the others. Before, when you recited the sacred words, they disappeared."

"I understand," Karl said. "They are a devious bunch, aren't they?"

"Intentionally so."

Karl began. "I am he who calls forth the hidden in the great deep. I am the judge of judges. I have come and I demand your presence. I have made a path, you cannot deny me, for Osiris watches. Open the way!"

In anxious quietude, they searched the unchanged surroundings. Shawn looked at Hunsdon who was fixed on the false door.

Slowly, a wind began to whistle and whirl in front of the wall. Small tornadoes grew from the sandy plane and twisted upward to the sky. Lightning flashed. Thunder shook the ground as they leaned close and shielded their eyes from the blizzard of sand.

Suddenly, wavy images flickered before them like a loose bulb; the howling wind tired and the whirling sand settled. All became calm as three deities appeared and gazed upon the party quizzically, as if surprised by their cunning.

With the head of a jackal, the Gatekeeper held

out his hands, then dropped them to his sides. The Watcher wore the headdress of a baboon, and the Herald, the mask of a black serpent.

"I knew it," Hunsdon breathed. "Now, Karl, continue."

Flanked by Otto and Julian, Karl stood on his own. "I know your name," he said clearly. "Your name is Unem-hauatu-ent-pehui. Lord, let us pass."

The jackal raised his arms, imploring the moon. He said something indistinguishable and began to fade, melt into the air.

Karl took a step to the Watcher. The baboon growled, showing his teeth as a single eye glowed red. He pointed a crooked finger and began to utter a curse.

"Karl!" Hunsdon called out.

"Seres-her! Seres-her, begone in all haste!"

The baboon bent as if stricken and whined. He circled, chasing his tail. Like the whirling wind, he rose above them, spinning, whining, and yapping madly. High over the wall, he faded into the moon.

The serpent-headed Herald widened his neck like a cobra, spread his legs apart to stand firm. Moaning enchanted words, he sliced the air with a gleaming dagger, raising his pitch in eerie tones.

"He's a spell caster!" Hunsdon shouted. The serpent's bewitching utterance forced Karl to his knees, groveling in pain.

"Say it, Karl! Hurry!"

"You are . . . you are . . ."

"Do it!"

"You are Aa, Herald to the Gate of Mischief. Speed from me! Let me pass!"

Quaking, the ground beneath their feet became violent. The great wall cracked like dried mud. As it did, the serpent-headed Herald sprayed a rancid liquid of rotting fish, then faltered and crumbled to dust. A tumultuous violent roar arose, carrying the sound of destruction. The earth opened and swallowed temple, wall, and sphinxes.

In total darkness, without moratorium, they were viciously flung onto a flat barge, a rudderless boat that rode a lake of fire where white caps leaped in flames. Boiling eruptions burst on all sides as they were heaved about, to the edge of the barge, tumbling about the deck like loose stones.

"We're going to die!" Nancy shrieked, as glowing embers fell from above. "We're going to die!"

"Not if I can help it!" Hunsdon snarled, scrambling to his feet.

As all aboard were rolling frantically, reaching for something, anything, to hang on to, Hunsdon stood astride. Raising his spangled robe as a shield, he held out a talisman at arm's length. Propelling his voice above the roar of flames, he bellowed, "Ra-Horakhty, Ra Atum, deliver us from this evil!"

Four times more, he implored the god of gods and called on Osiris, Isis, Thoth, and Ra to enforce the laws of the Arits.

A streak of lightning, a thunderclap boomed. The lake became smooth and the flames cooled. Wailing screams of pain, cries for mercy, arose in the veil of darkness as the evil spirits responsible received punishment.

At the same moment, the barge transformed into a rock ledge, a generous plateau slapped on the side of a mountain so high its peak was lost in the clouds. A breeze raised their hair and pulled at their clothing.

"Don't look over the edge!" Julian screamed. "You can't see the bottom!"

"Stay focused!" Hunsdon shot back. "Don't stray. Don't let danger take over your mind!"

Shawn breathed, "This is a nightmare."

"Sir Hunsdon," Nancy said faintly, "what was that, what happened back there?"

He took her hand, patting it, and said, "Lost souls, my dear, the failed ones. They are the jealous ones who lost their way, and they are bent on destroying all those who succeed where they have failed. You see, my dear, even here there are laws, rules to obey."

Otto nudged Hunsdon's arm and whispered behind his hand, "I don't think Karl is going to make it,

Edward."

Hunsdon's thick brow fell over his eyes. "Do what you can and hope for the best."

"And for the worst...?" Otto said softly.

"I don't know. I don't know what happens when the chosen one . . ." His voice faded into breath.

The overcast became dense and heavy, and the air bitter to the tongue. Dark clouds rolled in tufted wafers as they sat on the ledge, considering the remaining gates. A light drizzle began to fall, dampening their spirits, dousing them to the bone. Time passed.

Julian tapped his watch. "Otto, what time do you have?"

"I'm afraid I can't tell you. It quit." Otto's eyes jumped to Karl.

In the black and gray scheme of things, Karl's face was deathly white, marked only by the deep, dark circles of his eyes.

"He looks very bad," Hunsdon whispered.

There was a nod.

Julian grasped Otto's arm. "Am I seeing things?"

The mountain was melting. Every single drop of moisture absorbed its equal weight in stone, turning it to liquid, like wax on a candle, dripping down, bringing everything to one and the same level.

"I don't believe what I'm seeing," Nancy said tensely.

No one responded. No one moved. Eyes scanned

the leveling as their bodies took on shadows that lengthened in front of them.

The mountain had spread to the horizon, where a line divided sky and ground. All around them, in every direction, flatness fell into the sky. As they staggered, turning, marveling at these effects . . .

"What the hell!" Shawn gasped.

Julian asked, "What's the matter?"

"Find your shadow!"

All eyes fell to the ground.

Shawn said, "Now turn."

As they turned in their own circles, their shadows turned with them, stretching out in front of them no matter how they moved; each shadow turning in sync with its own body.

Shawn and Julian faced each other, and their shadows touched on the ground as if each body had its own sun.

But . . . there was no sun.

Weakly, Karl began to laugh.

"Get hold of yourself, Karl!" Hunsdon said sharply.

Hysterical, knee-slapping whelps of laughter came from Karl as he hugged his stomach and bellowed.

With hard eyes, Hunsdon walked straight to Karl. His towering presence did not curb the joviality. He slapped Karl hard, his robe swaying with the strength of it.

"I'm sorry," Karl said. "I'm so sorry."

Hunsdon wrapped his arms around him. "So am I. Just a few more gates, Karl, just a few more."

A few moments later, Julian tapped Hunsdon's shoulder. "Is there no way out of this?" he said brashly.

"You were warned at the start."

"But we're going to die!"

Hunsdon faced him straight on. "You listen to me. There is no turning back. This is no fickle woman who changes her mind and allows you leave. You must settle your wits and realize that what you see is not real."

"What about Karl's leg? Is that my imagination?"

"Julian, keep it down," Hunsdon warned. "You will frighten the others."

"I don't give a damn. They have every right to be frightened."

Hunsdon glared.

"What are you going to do?" Julian huffed.

"I have things to discuss with Karl. You go back with the others."

"I said, what are you going to do?" Julian demanded.

Hunsdon turned his back.

Otto forcefully took Julian's arm. "Let it be. He knows what he's doing."

Hunsdon huddled with Karl. Subdued conversation went back and forth. Karl shook his head matter of factly. Hunsdon's voice grew louder, argumentative.

Karl refused. Hunsdon insisted on something and walked away.

As far as the eye could see in all directions, the grayness of the stagnant sky and the grayness of the flat stone beneath their feet melded one to the other. They whispered.

At first, the far-off sound was hardly audible, a slow, back and forth graveling sound of fine sandpaper like someone filing his nails. Everyone noticed it vaguely, but it was lost in the exchange of ideas. But it persisted, demanding attention.

Slowly, the volume grew to hellish levels, vibrating their feet with an electrical charge. The thunderous rasping caused the smooth, flat stone upon which they stood to violently tremble, fracture, and liquefy into a moving swell.

The party found themselves clinging together, riding a massive, rolling wave. In a gust of wind, the mass hardened instantly into a huge and solid wall. They tumbled from the force of the sudden stop.

Gathering their wits, they looked about. What appeared to be a distant moon sped toward them, morphing into the wretched face of a hag.

Twisting as she came, her sagging, deformed, green eyes spun inside her head, while her zero mouth gushed the sickening stench of decayed meat.

As quickly as she had flown, she stopped. Her

bilious green eyes examined the creatures below. Her grotesque head swayed to and fro as a kite in the wind; her ghostly body trailed downward into a tail. She hovered before them, mesmerizing them with slitted orbs.

They stood speechless. The pace and temerity of the thing's happening shocked them. Buffering himself from the salivating hag, Hunsdon raised his cloaked arm, growling, chanting a spell. "Ink Sbk-hry-ib-nrw, f. Ink dt-hfly-hr-sdt." He shouted, "Karl, the Gatekeeper! Now! Say it now!"

From the emotional impact of this dreadful apparition, Karl had slumped. Otto shook him in vain.

"Can you do it?" Shawn yelled to Hunsdon.

"I must try!" Hunsdon blared. He pointed his finger and loudly gave voice. "Khesef-her-asht-kheru is thy name. Plague us no more."

With boldness, the name was recited five times.

Spiraling aloft like a giant corkscrew, the hag spun, fraying at the edges, diminishing to nothingness as she chased after the moon.

Karl moaned.

Otto softly reassured him. "Relax, my friend. Edward made it work."

"Thank him for me," Karl whispered.

"Where are the others?" Shawn asked. "There should be two more gods."

Hunsdon held up his hand, quieting everyone.

"Be still."

As he said this, a cold, dense essence emanated from the wall. As it became clear, a child, dressed only in a short linen kilt and a gold collar, sat cross-legged on a white stone bench. He held the feather of power, and from a shaven head hung the sere, a braid, the lock of youth wound with golden thread. Despite his adolescent freshness, his eyes were set with maturity.

As the youth preened his feather, the child-like god moved to Hunsdon and raised himself by will, floating up to eye level. "What is it you seek?" the Watcher asked softly.

"Seres-tepu, we seek the Mansion of Osiris," Hunsdon said politely.

"You have answered wisely," the youth said. "You may pass." The Watcher lowered himself to the ground. He rose, turned and walked through the stone wall.

While they waited for the next happening, Otto breathed, "This is nothing like I expected."

Hunsdon nodded. "Nor I. How is Karl?"

"Not good. He'll have to be carried, I'm afraid."

"Will he survive, Otto?"

"I don't know," he said gravely. "I have my doubts."

"This has gone far enough!" Julian said.

"Not now," Hunsdon said forcefully.

"Yes, now."

"Otto, take care of this." Hunsdon turned in anger.

"Julian, stop it!" Otto said, grabbing his arm. "You'll be our ruin."

"Please, Julian," Nancy said, tugging at him.

Hunsdon held out his arms, mumbling in the ancient tongue, trying to force the Herald to appear. "Khesef-at, great of voice, Herald of the fourth Arit, make your presence known. Hail, Khesef-at".

Everyone stared at the wall.

Whizzing from the sky, a sword plunged into the ground, missing Hunsdon by merely a hand's width.

Gasping, Nancy began to cry as Julian held her to him.

"Silence!" Hunsdon barked. "Recite his name!"

The Herald's name was mimicked.

Immediately, Hunsdon followed with the sacred words. With a loud voice he chanted, "I am the Bull of the sky, the son of Osiris. I have breathed life eternal unto my father, his grace is upon me. Bear witness, ye gods, and make safe a path for me to the Mansion of Osiris." He bowed.

The high impregnable wall became as glass, cracking into small circles, rounding into a billion agate marbles precariously stacked one atop the other, rolling, bouncing from top to bottom like hordes of locusts, spinning in all directions with the spine of water. Endlessly, they rolled wave after wave and the thundering water crashed the shore, until the wall was leveled.

With scarcely time to notice, at their backs, the fifth Arit rose in the warmth of the rising sun. Dotted with puffy gold-streaked clouds, the blue sky beckoned and the spice of ginger filled the air. In amazement, they turned to the welcomed dawn of a new day.

Tightly, Shawn held onto Karl as he smiled, scarcely keeping his eyes open. "Is it another trick, Karl?" he asked.

"Oh, I hope not."

Julian and Nancy looked into the dawn. Otto diligently kept the *Book of the Dead* open and close. Hunsdon suspiciously narrowed his eyes.

Two huge pylons, decorated with hieroglyphics, supported a spiked gate of many rods. In the shadows of the sun, two gods sat on thrones while the last stood.

The first, the Gatekeeper, wore the colorful head of a hawk and was clothed from shoulder to foot in a white pleated garment.

The sun rose higher. A soft breeze came and went.

Quickly, Sir Hunsdon turned in a circle, flaring his robe, and threw a finger at the Gatekeeper. "Thy name is Ankhf-em-fent! I pray thee, let us pass!"

In succession, his name was repeated.

With folded arms, in submission, the god bowed his head.

"Watcher," Hunsdon said, wasting not a second, "thou art Shabu! I fear thee not for I know thy name!"

His name echoed.

The god rose in his pleated robes and, with a sweeping gesture, plunged his lance into the ground, his Egyptian eyes unblinking.

Otto made an attempt to whisper, but Hunsdon waved him away.

The third deity stood naked as the fertility god, Min, with plumed headdress and erect phallus. He stared at Hunsdon, daring him, defying him.

Hunsdon removed his glasses. With straight arms tight to his sides, he raised his chin. In a full voice, he called, "Thou art not Teb-her-k ha-kheft, the Herald! Thou art the deceptive one, the demigod impersonating Min! Be gone! Be gone!"

Following suit, the group said the name. Their recitation forced the gate wide open.

But the gods remained. Their power grew as spikes of energy formed a pointed aura about them.

Moving quickly, Hunsdon took out a fetish from inside his robe. Making circles with his fist raised to the sky, he blustered the sacred words. "I have brought unto thee the jawbone in Rastau." He held up the fetish. "I have driven back Aapep for thee. I have spit upon the wounds of his body. I have made a path among you. I am the Aged One among the gods. I have defended Osiris with the word of truth. Pray, I beseech thee, let me pass." Hunsdon brought down his fist with a jerk as if to smash.

The gods became still as death. Slowly, they began to crack, as though all their bodily veins had been forced to the surface. Then, disjointing like so much confetti, the pieces floated down in small drifts. And upon a gentle breeze they were swept away.

Absolute blackness.

CHAPTER 47

Then came the light. They found themselves in the noonday sun in a lush savanna, an easy moving river at their feet. The air was calm and sweet, and the leaves were still.

Sitting on a fallen tree, his feet in ankle-high grass, Hunsdon wiped his forehead, rubbed his eyes, and breathed deeply. "How is Karl doing?"

Shawn said, "He's awake."

"You can talk directly to me," Karl weakly said. "I'm not dead yet."

"I'm sorry, Karl. I didn't mean to . . ."

"That's okay. I know what you meant."

Otto asked, "Karl, did you expect these tricksters and impostors? Is this what you imagined it to be?" Otto went on, "Edward, did you expect this?"

"Nothing like this, no," Hunsdon replied. "I visualized a much simpler ordeal. You can see now that without the knowledge of the ancients, we would have been dead long ago. At this point I'm sure you can appreciate what the seals meant by 'worthy and equipped'. This is no game for amateurs."

"What do you really think we'll find at the end?" Julian asked. "If we make it, that is."

"At this moment, I would not venture a guess. With all that we have seen . . ." A sigh. "Get some rest. We still have two to go."

Nancy washed Karl's wound and changed his bandage. Shawn and Otto meandered to the crystal clear stream where the steward of Hunsdon house bent down and splashed his face with cool water, tasting its sweetness.

"This is quite good, you know," Otto said.

Shawn did the same. "You're right. It's good. It tastes like spring water with fizz."

Sir Hunsdon sat with his eyes closed, his chin resting on his closed hand. His lips were puckered in thought, and his bushy brows formed a nearly straight line across his forehead. Like The Thinker he sat, frame bent, elbow to the knee, swathed in an Egyptian robe, meditating.

Julian wandered a short way into a litter of trees, marveling at the abundant growth and the sugary smell of the wild flowers. He touched the dewy leaves of a hip-high plant. Its long slender fronds were speckled with pink dots. He shook his head. "Where the hell are we?" he thought aloud. "We started in a passage, in a room full of mirrors below the desert floor, and now . . . This can't be real."

Nancy said, "We're dreaming. It's all a big, ugly, nightmarish dream."

"I don't ever remember touching a dream," he said. "And, how do six people have the same dream?"

Overhearing, Hunsdon stirred. "They don't," he said. "Look across the stream."

Their eyes scanned the thick foliage.

The sixth gate stood amid the undergrowth, sitting back from the stream. Two gods sat motionless atop brown rectangular platforms, peering through heavily painted eyes. Giant ferns bowed fluidly in a gentle breeze. Palm, oak, and cedar nearly hid the gate that rose to the tree tops.

Julian whispered, "Why are there only two?"

Hunsdon stood, his eyes reaching into the bush and skeptically moved toward the water.

From behind the gate, a drum began to beat, deep and low sounds spaced far apart, resonating so as to tingle ear, skin, and heel. Suddenly, a hard wind picked up debris and filled the air with missiles, bending trees, ripping leaves, rolling in gusty waves.

Something moved at light speed, thrashing water. A mammoth crocodile snapped huge jaws. Otto fell back from the stream, scrambling away. A lethal tail spurred the creature onto land.

Holding up his hand flat toward the beast, Hunsdon brought down his chin and shouted, "Atektau-kehaq-kheru, Gatekeeper, Guardian of the Gate, evil predator, be gone! Be gone!"

The others stumbled over the name.

"Say again and do it right! Hurry!" Hunsdon bellowed.

The second time was perfect.

A low growling escaped the beast as it hesitated, turned, and slithered back into the stream, its great bulk viciously parting the water.

"Jesus Christ!" Shawn said to Otto, "are you okay?"

Otto breathed, "Just barely."

Ignoring them, Hunsdon strode to the very edge of the stream. With outstretched arms raised above his head, he said, "I call upon thee, Watcher of the Gate to Osiris! I know thy name for I am equipped! Thou art called An-her! An-her, let us pass!"

The name was recited.

The Watcher inclined and folded his arms. He remained seated and visible.

Sir Hunsdon sidestepped toward the Herald and grasped the ankh he wore. He held it up, saying, "Thy name is Ates-ari-she, Sharp of Face, Herald of the sixth Arit! Let us pass, let us pass in peace!"

They said his name.

The Herald, like a statue, did not move or blink.

Hunsdon stepped into the water. In a booming voice, he issued the sacred words. "I have come as Anpu watches. I am Lord of the Urrt Crown. I am the possessor of the knowledge of the words of great magic, according to the law. I have defended Osiris. Therefore, I call upon the powers of Ra, and he shall open the holy paths. In truth, let me pass in peace, in peace!"

The sharpness of the noonday sun began to dim, changing into a silver moon, lengthening shadows in the outgoing light. As surely as the moon had appeared, it speedily strayed to the horizon. The robust growth of plants, trees, grasses, and flowers withered comically in the deepening darkness and, one by one, they were sucked into the earth. The river dried. The grandness of the sixth gate rusted to powder, and six people huddled together in the pitch of night.

Above the line where earth and sky parted, the moon rose, brightening, demanding their attention. Around them, in the well of a cul-de-sac, a wall of coal grew ten stories high, consuming the light. Pocketed as they were, the way toward the moon was the only way out.

Hunsdon called, "Move toward the light! Keep away from the wall! Now, do it now!"

Together, they moved up the incline out of the pocket. Shawn carried Karl and the seals.

"I've got him," Otto said.

Julian clutched Nancy while Hunsdon led the way.

At the top of the incline, something drew Hunsdon's

attention. He looked over his shoulder and gasped.

"What's wrong?" Otto said.

Hunsdon pointed with his head.

The entire party turned and gaped.

Before the light-consuming wall, three gods stood, arms crossed, clothed in liquid gold finery. Behind them, a set of gigantic, elaborately decorated golden doors gleamed half as tall as the black wall it had parted.

"The seventh Arit!" Hunsdon breathed. "The most dangerous of all."

All of the party's eyes were glued to the shimmer, the glint, the majesty of the last gate. All that they had seen, all that they had endured, was suddenly dwarfed by the presence, the splendid spectacle before them. Here and now, in the midst of this raven-black hole, the final challenge would be faced.

For many moments, the small group felt no fear. Without movement, the deities stood upon a polished golden altar. At their feet, clouds of incense rose. To the left and to the right, huge feathered fans disturbed the air. Below and all around the altar, vessels of every description held astounding quantities of gold and jewels. Glittering rings, collars, bracelets and chains, statues, plates, and amulets dripped from their containers, washing down onto the coal black ground.

"The treasure of Thoth," Shawn whispered.

So serene, so pharaonic, so magnificent were these

gods, and their surroundings, that the idea of mortal danger completely escaped them.

Slowly, the gods came to life. Their eyes, that had been stationary on perhaps some distant speck, now scrutinized the group one by one. A chin lowered. A head bent. The liquid cloth the deities wore raised and lowered from breathing, an incidental action suddenly noted. With their movement came music, as if their stirring brought it forth, a gentle sound which caught in the mind. These subtle happenings were indeed disarming.

Nearly without notice, the first deity to the left began to ascend, floating cautiously upward, his lined eyes rising to the moon. His arms unfolded and stretched out as he hovered above the group. Large, black eyes slowly fell from the moon and focused on Otto. While the party was intrigued by the god's graceful levitation, his eyes grew larger. A thin round beam of white light shot from his sudden glare, zapping Otto with charged current.

"No!" Hunsdon roared. "Sekhmet-em-tesu-sen! Gatekeeper, I cast thee out from the House of Osiris! Be gone, and with thee take thy magic!"

Quickly, all repeated his name.

In an instant, the Gatekeeper became limp above them, fracturing into flakes, and disassembled into gold dust, fluttering to the black ground in a sparkling heap.

Taking no chance with the Watcher, Hunsdon raised an arm, pointing his fore and little fingers. "Aa-maa-kheru! Thou art the Watcher of the seventh Arit and I know thy name!"

Unaffected, Aa-maa-kheru stared grotesquely at Hunsdon, his mouth drawn back from his teeth in contempt.

"Say the damn name," Hunsdon screamed, spinning round, glaring at them.

But Karl and Otto both were on the ground, delirious.

"My God!" Hunsdon said. "Shawn, say it for them quickly. Say it now or we are finished."

The god's eyes widened while he gathered his power.

Sweat beaded on Shawn's forehead and he spit out the name like a curse. He said it three times, each time quicker and louder. Nancy and Julian instantly followed.

The Watcher shut his eyes, raising his chin parallel to the sky, humming in disconnected sounds. Arms shot straight out from his shoulders as he began to spin, becoming a smear. With his spinning, wind surged with tremendous force, blowing them all to the ground. Aa-maa-kheru blasted toward the moon, bursting into stars, exploding into a million flares.

As they struggled to stand, dodging the rain of sparks, the party's attention was suddenly snatched by the Herald who now stood taller than the gate. Rays of sunbeams rolled from his extended hands, flooding them in whimsical light.

In a state of madness to pass through the final gate, Hunsdon lifted himself on tip-toes, yelling as if making up for his years of enforced silence. "Khesef-khemi! Khesef-khemi! Herald of the final trial, the final Arit, hear thy name! Thou art One who repels demolishers. Do thy duty and grant us passage into the Kingdom of Osiris!"

In response, Shawn recited three times and the others followed in all the voice they could muster.

Hunsdon set his legs astride solid on the black ground and raised his fists to the sky. With his cloak draped about him, the deep blue fabric of his robe began to glow, the five pointed stars to shine brilliantly as he loudly called out the sacred words. "I have come unto thee with a pure heart! I have been beckoned to the presence of Ra, thou One! I am delivered from destruction by him that cometh! Prepare thou for me all the ways which lead to Osiris, God of the heavens, the netherworld, Lord of the two lands, Keeper of just souls!"

He bowed and let out a deep breath.

The whimsical light dancing at their feet multiplied again and again, climbing the coal wall. And suddenly, a bolt of lightning burst open the mammoth gold doors.

With one tick of a clock, the gold doors were behind them. To their left, they could see the Hall of Mirrors. Around them were the walls of the passage they had entered what seemed like months, years ago.

They stared at their surroundings, at each other.

Nancy sobbed into her hands.

Julian took her into his arms with his eyes on Hunsdon. "We're right back where we started!" he yelled accusingly. "You made us go through all this shit for nothing?"

"Listen to me, all of you," Hunsdon commanded. "Keep your heads! This is not over! Look there, ahead of you!"

Before them, a long narrow hall lit by no obvious means, stretched into the distance.

Hunsdon turned and thudded down the long corridor, his robe swaying with his determined steps.

Shawn carried Karl, and Julian dragged Otto who was still delirious and covered with burns.

The corridor shifted to the right and came to a dead end at a wall where a shenu, a cartouche, circled hieroglyphs twice with oblong rings. Hunsdon examined the ancient writing.

"What does it say?" Shawn asked.

"Asar-ankhti," Hunsdon said. "Osiris, the Living One."

"Is that all?" Julian asked.

"I'm afraid so."

Shawn felt the corners of the huge block. "Sir Hunsdon, it's sealed with pitch."

"Hum, watertight," Hunsdon said under his breath.

Despondently, Julian leaned against stone and folded his arms.

Nancy shook her head.

Propped against the wall on the floor with the seals at his side, Karl looked up. Weakly, he said, "Shawn, press the cartouche. Press it hard."

With both hands pressed against the cartouche, Shawn braced and pushed with all his strength.

"It can't be that easy," Julian whispered.

But the rasping of stone shook the passage while the huge block inched into the floor, smearing the pitch as it cleared the way.

They stared.

They stared in utter, complete, total amazement.

They stared in utter amazement at a city alive with people, with Egyptian people adorned as they had been five thousand years before.

"It's another hallucination!" Julian said. "This can't be real!"

Paying him no mind, one by one, they stepped into the light of day, into the city, into the waiting arms of royal soldiers amassed on either side. Drums beat. Trumpets blared.

Startled, they hesitated when the commander of the guard walked toward them, followed by a long column of spear-carrying soldiers.

Their small group gathered closer with Hunsdon at their head. The commander stopped and addressed them in a language not heard in thousands of years.

"What is he saying?" Shawn asked.

Hunsdon turned his head just a little. "He wants us to follow him."

With a clap of the hands, silken litters were brought forward. Karl and Otto were placed on them and carried by soldiers. The commander turned and their escort marched them down a wide thoroughfare lined with lion-headed sphinxes.

Roads worn by time and use led off the thoroughfare in all directions. Houses had been slapped one to the other as cadence to a drill. Smoke rose from ovens carrying the aroma of fresh bread, of fish roasted with rosemary, meat spiced with garlic. High above them, a massive dome ceiling, plastered white, fingered out like the tines of a huge umbrella, lifted as it were by lotus-topped columns a hundred feet up, as far as they could see.

They passed through open squares where stenciled eyes watched the new arrivals with curiosity. Hundreds of people collected along the way cheering, waving, calling out in unknown words.

The legends of vast catacombs, chambers, galleries, and cities beneath the Giza plateau were no longer myths. With uncanny brightness, smokeless torches filled the streets, the alleyways where shadows, even in the light of day, should have lurked. Garlands were strung from rooftop to window and flowered wreaths hung on doors all over the city. All the accoutrements of a lavish festival were everywhere.

Shawn eyed the soldiers from golden anklet to polished armor, wondering if this too wasn't some absurd joke, but realizing deep inside that this was all, indeed, real.

Coming into view, six colossal statues and two obelisks stood before a pylon where huge doors opened into a colonnade. Far more than the width of the thoroughfare, the pylon had been embossed with brilliantly painted images of Osiris, Isis, Thoth, and Anubis.

Taking in the splendor of ancient Egypt, they fell speechless.

Through the entrance, they walked into a pillared hall that dwarfed them. Their escort marched through a second door where the commander ushered them into a cavernous room. Wearing splendid garments, dignitaries parted before them. Men in white priestly robes and clean-shaven heads posed before a throne many risers above the floor. The litter-bearers left their charges at the foot of the steps, bowed toward the priests, and departed.

Contrasting to the white in his royal blue robe, Sir Hunsdon gazed about the palatial room, enthralled with the grandeur of it all.

Interrupting his distraction, a priest thrice gaveled his staff against the glassy granite floor and announced an arrival in a thunderous voice that reverberated from block, pillar, and wall.

"Down on your faces!" the high priest began in English. "Hail, Ombus."

Drums beat. Trumpets blared. The court fell on their faces like scythed wheat. Gowned in orange tunics, novice priests fanning incense urns, flanked a pillared archway.

"Hail Ombus," the priest went on, "the living Horus; King of Upper and Lower Egypt; Son of Ra; Beloved of Osiris the truly risen, Whose place is among the Gods forever and ever."

Through the archway behind the priests appeared the blackest of Nubians. As they marched in step, their muscles bulged and glistened with fragrant oils. Wrapped with radiant golden armbands, collars, anklets, and kilts, they bore upon their shoulders . . . Pharaoh.

One by one, the small party rose from the floor enchanted, captivated. Their eyes were on the king, on the blond hair beneath the atef crown, on his emerald green eyes which the black kohl outlined so well.

Effortlessly, slowly, the Nubian bearers lowered the qenu, the royal chair of state, and Ombus stood before his throne, looked down at his court, at his weary, trial worn visitors. As he descended the many stairs, torchlight danced in the folds of his glittering robes.

Intimidated by his height, his translucent, penetrating eyes, his striking regal features and bearing, the small party inched back. Pharaoh took each one of them into his eyes. He rolled open a hand, palm up, his long delicate fingers straight, and said, "You have fulfilled what no man has or ever shall again. I extend welcome."

Sir Hunsdon took a step forward. "My lord, we have . . ."

Ombus raised a hand. He walked to the litter that held Karl and, bending, whispering softly, smoothed his hair like a parent would a child. Instantly, Karl was revived and healed. Pharaoh turned to Otto and repeated the ritual. The effect was sudden, breathtaking.

"My God!" Nancy whispered, awestruck by the rapidity of healing.

Karl's color, eyes, energy reflected in a youthful smile as he breathed, "Thank you."

Feeling the absence of his burns, seeing their total and compete disappearance, Otto looked spellbound into the captivating green eyes of Ombus, thankful beyond words.

Pharaoh turned toward the steps. "Follow me," he instructed.

Up the steps they walked past the priests, the guards, past the huge Nubian bearers, through the great archway and into a wide corridor. Gleaming metal doors opened soundlessly, of themselves, at the wave of Pharaoh's hand. They entered a sanctum of startling elegance and beauty. In proportion to everything Egyptian, the room was vast, the ceiling high and ornamentation elaborate. Pharaoh motioned them to salmon-colored hassocks, evenly spaced around a large sunken bowl with a wide ledge where blue flame flickered knee high.

"I am Ombus. I am called Sire, Lord, King, God," he began, seating himself high on a mother-of-pearl throne. "Your time here is limited, but I shall endeavor to answer your questions."

Hunsdon, with nervous apprehension, said, "You, my Lord, and your people are the Keepers of the Way, are you not?"

"We are the descendants of the gods, the living representatives of Horus. We are the guardians of tradition. We shall survive when all else fails."

Puzzled by the last sentence, Hunsdon said, "Sire, I don't understand."

"It will become clear," he replied with a wave of his hand.

Karl asked, "My lord, how were you able to heal us?"

Ombus brought him into his eyes. "You are a scholar of my people, are you not?"

"Yes. But—"

"Then, you know."

"Sire, there are many legends of healing and resurrection by ancient priests such as Teta, Zaclas, and Tchatcha-em-ankh. But are they true?"

"Have you not seen?" Ombus said, dismissing the question.

Hunsdon mouthed, "Hekau, magic," which received a passing glance.

Otto said, "Lord, why were the pyramids built?"

"To show the way, to initiate the worthy, and to receive Osiris."

Pharaoh's answers only led to more questions. Ombus regally looked on.

"Osiris lives, Sire?" Shawn asked.

"He does."

"How is this possible?" Julian said.

"He is a God descended of Gods from the world beyond," Ombus answered.

"Sire," Julian continued, "do you mean that Osiris comes from another place, another planet?"

"As is written, Osiris dwells near the Winding Waterway on Nekht-ti."

"The constellation of Orion," Julian whispered.

Karl asked, "Sire, why have we been chosen? And what will happen in the age of Aquarius?"

"As in the beginning," Pharaoh replied, "only a few, only the worthy were chosen from the inhabitants of this world. The nature of that choice was His."

"You mean Osiris?" Hunsdon asked.

"Osiris has chosen," Ombus replied.

Nancy said, "My lord, your city appears to be in the midst of a celebration."

"We celebrate the arrival of Osiris. We celebrate the arrival of the chosen."

Julian tried to narrow a previous point. "Sire, when was the beginning?"

"In your custom, forty millenniums past."

Julian turned to Karl. "Just as I thought. That's when the Neanderthal disappeared. The third age of man."

Hunsdon said, "Do all the original nine gods still live?"

At the same time Julian asked, "How do they travel to our earth?"

"You have read the ancient texts. Therefore, you know."

Nancy asked, "Sire, how long has this city been here?"

"The Venerables instructed its building in the beginning."

"Will we meet Osiris?" Shawn asked.

Ombus gestured to his guards. "I can no longer answer your questions. Your time is completed. The Great Portal beckons."

Anxiously, Hunsdon stood. "But . . . but there is so much . . ."

Soldiers flanked Ombus. The Nubians entered. Pharaoh rose up in his gilded chair on their shoulders and was carried from the room. The commander of the guard pointed to a draped wall. "There," he said. "There is what you seek."

Karl and Shawn went to the wall and together pulled open the drape.

"A blank wall!" Shawn said.

Karl turned to the commander. He was gone. Except for their small party, the vast room was empty.

Hunsdon muttered aloud, "This is very strange."

"Everything is very strange," Julian said.

Otto examined the smooth limestone wall, feeling it, pushing it, sniffing it. "I don't understand," he said. "What are we supposed to do now?"

At that moment, tremors vibrated through the room.

"Oh, Jesus!" Shawn said. "An earthquake!"

"No, look!" Karl shouted. "The wall!"

Fragments, pieces of stone, particles of dust, and sand shed from the wall. From top to bottom, one after the other, hieroglyphs formed row upon row of ancient symbols, carved, it seemed, by an invisible hand. The tremor ceased.

Hunsdon stepped back from the wall, wiping his glasses free of debris.

"What does it say?" Julian asked.

"Shawn," Hunsdon said, "bring me the seals."

Hunsdon made a tight circle of the seven seals, setting them on end, one touching the other, in a circle on a circle embossed on the floor. "We must form a circle around the circle," he said, "and hold hands."

When the human circle was complete, Hunsdon called upon the Sages, the Aakhut, the Venerables as the hieroglyphs on the wall commanded. "Neferhat, Neferpehui, Nebtesheru, Ka, Bak, Kheph, San."

As if heated from within, the seals began to glow with eerie luminescence. Colored spheres rose from each cylinder's hollow end in a wedge of light. A series of balls scattered toward the ceiling, spinning, turning, revolving in what seemed to be senseless order.

"It's a hologram." Karl breathed as the blurry manifestation sharpened to clarity.

Suddenly, Karl's memory was sprung. The temple in the desert loomed in his mind. The vision of the hypostyle hall, the grand chamber, shook his sensibilities as the solar system balanced itself in the foreground. And there was music, a soft, exotic tune from the strings of a far off harp, flute, and tambourine.

In three dimensional color, miniature planets

rotated in their proper orbits around the sun with precision. On the periphery were the constellations of Orion, Sagittarius, Leo, Aquarius, and all the rest.

"I don't understand," Shawn whispered, as they marveled at this grand scheme . . .

Tremors!

Trembling with static electricity, the engraved wall began to smoke. The ancient symbols melted, corroded as if bathed in acid, leaving the wall blank, clean. Then it started carving out hieroglyphs. With great speed, the unseen scribe filled the surface. All the messages written on the seals shot across the stone. In hardly enough time to scan the words, as if merely a review, the wall began to smoke, liquefy, and shudder. As before, the slate was wiped clean. Then, silence.

Looks passed between them. They wondered, watching the wall, glancing about the room and the planets circling undisturbed.

Karl stood at the wall, staring at it. He turned to Hunsdon and shrugged in frustration.

Nancy was about to speak when a date inside a large circle was slashed on the stone by an invisible, magical blade. It was a date all too familiar to Karl. "The twenty-third day of the third division of the second season of the Great Year. July 23, 2010 . . ." he whispered.

Moments of absolute quiet.

A blue white beam descended from the ceiling. Dots, millions of tiny dots scurried about within the light, swirling, sparking like so many minute stars. Suddenly, they came together in vibrant unity and then there was form, a glowing form that took the shape of man.

He stepped from the light.

CHAPTER 48

Numbed by the succession of numerous indescribable anomalies, they stared at the manifestation standing before them, not wary, not with fright, but rather with curiosity.

As if he wore liquid shimmering without seam, his generous silver garment moved effortlessly with him. About the neck was a raised collar which opened in a V to the middle of his chest, where a medallion of the djed pillar hung from a knuckle-link chain. His forefinger was adorned with a large ring strung with a similar, smaller chain to a wide gold bracelet embedded with glowing stones. Silver sandals were strapped to his feet. His sandy, shoulder-length hair was swept back from his face, and his chiseled, Caucasian features bore a striking resemblance to Shawn, except for the eyes; they were brown. With well-developed shoulders and a height of at least six-foot-four, he was exceedingly handsome in every detail.

Slowly and one by one, he brought them into his consuming eyes, as if scrutinizing the choices he had made. In a soothing voice, he said, "I bid you welcome."

Hunsdon was neither shocked nor surprised. Hunsdon bowed and said, "You are Osiris, the Great Teacher, are you not, my lord?"

"I am." His very presence, his demeanor, his attitude, his voice projected calm and invited trust.

"But . . ." Nancy gasped, "that would make you ten, fifteen thousand years old!"

"I am that and more, madam" he said. He looked at Karl and held his return.

Karl said, with all humility, "Your holiness, for some reason you chose me to find these cylinder seals. May I ask why?"

Still, Osiris held his eyes. "The choice was an easy one. Yours is an old soul, Karl Cassim, one that is righteous and worthy. You have suffered greatly on my account, for which you shall be recompensed with enormous power." For a moment, he gazed over them and went on.

"Of mankind, I have favored seven to bridge the fourth age of man. Shawn, Edward, and you, Karl, have chosen as your life's work to learn the birth of your kind, the discipline of my people, the legacy I have bequeathed and, as far as you were able, the origin of my family."

Osiris looked at Julian. "Yes, Julian. I know your mind, and the answer is yes. Yes to the creation of man through our intervention. Yes to the extinction of what you call Neanderthal. Yes to your recent discovery of my planet, and yes to my age."

Julian's wide-eyed expression revealed that Osiris had indeed read his thoughts.

Osiris turned his attention to Hunsdon. "Yours is a complex mind, Sir Hunsdon. I will get to your question in a moment, as well as that of Otto Hummer, since they are the same.

"As for you, Shawn O'Donnell, it is not only your mind that I have harvested, but your seed. It shall be carried into the next millennia."

Osiris held out his hand, and Nancy took it. "My beautiful one," he said, "your gifts are many. Your doubt, your questioning, your meticulous scrutiny in the face of controversy, is your gift. Above all, you will be looked upon as the mother of a new age. You also will be endowed with certain powers. My brother Thoth will teach you the way, as he taught my beloved Isis."

He pointed to the revolving solar system. His face became somber, expressing sadness. "This, I cannot alter," he said. "This is why you have been chosen and why you must seek sanctuary in a strong place, perhaps in that which was built for me, for my return, the Great Pyramid."

He pressed a blue stone on his bracelet.

The planets began an eerie glide in their orbit about the sun. One by one on the cusp of Pisces and the advent of Aquarius, an alignment of celestial bodies formed. Behind the Earth, Venus, Mercury, Mars, Neptune, and Uranus formed a straight line with the sun. The Earth wobbled in its orbit as volcanic eruptions blackened the seas, and white clouds turned to raisin brown, veiling the planet.

"My God!" Julian exclaimed.

"What does it mean?" Nancy burst out.

Osiris raised a finger, answering, "Once every forty thousand years, this alignment occurs, wiping the slate clean to begin again. Once every forty thousand years, the face of your planet changes, caused by the continental shelves drifting to new locations, changing weather patterns, raising many mountains and lowering others, taking centuries to stabilize."

Sir Hunsdon shook his head and muttered, "Gravity, the awesome power of gravity from all these planets. They will have enormous impact upon the Earth."

"Why?" Nancy persisted.

"Example," Hunsdon said. "The moon, our moon causes the tides, pulls at the seas, causing shifts in the water levels of the earth, all over the earth. The moon is a minor satellite, hung about the Earth at a distance of 221,600 miles. It is one-eighth the size of our planet, and yet it has tremendous power over our seas. Now, multiply this gravity again and again, adding gravity of the sun, which holds all the planets in our solar system, in their orbits. The alignment will be devastating!" he breathed.

"Is that what happened to the dinosaurs?" Shawn asked.

"Yes, and to the Neanderthal," Osiris responded.

"But you said you intervened," Julian said.

"Yes. We bred those few remaining, to increase their intelligence. They are your ancestors."

Despondent, exhausted, Nancy's frustration caused her to desert caution, as well as any vestige of respect in addressing Osiris. "Why did you put us through all this if you knew about us before? Why couldn't you just gather us together and tell us what you wanted us to know?"

The answer came back in an emphatic tone. "To prove that you were truly worthy. To show you the power of intelligence. To teach you what lies ahead. Had you failed before any of the seven gates, you would have been destroyed. There would have been no transition to the next age. There would have been no knowledge carried into the next millennium. If any of your species survive, they will be newborns, ignorant of their past and troubled with an indecisive future without promise."

"My lord, pardon my skepticism, but why?" asked Otto. "Why do you care what happens to us, to the next age?"

Osiris sighed. Benevolently, he looked upon those whom he had chosen. "Because my blood flows through your veins. Because you, and all those who have come before, are my children. I have spent thousands of your years traveling about the Earth teaching them the Ma'at, the laws by which they should live, the idiosyncrasies of nature, of farming, of breeding animals, of building, thus ending the cycle of ignorance."

For a moment, silence.

Then, Hunsdon said, "But, my lord, with such power, such knowledge, can't you stop the tragedy, this catastrophic alignment of planets?"

"I am not the creator of the universe. I cannot change it."

This answer prompted the next question which Hunsdon could not help but ask.

"Who, then, did create the universe?"

"A force you can only imagine."

"A god? A god greater than you?" Hunsdon pushed.

"I am revered as a god because of an attribute called knowledge. However, it is true that I possess enormous powers, as you have seen. But I am not a god in the truest sense of the word."

"And this force, this god, he can't change things?"

"He will not."

"Why?"

"Because he enjoys the folly of men. He has created

free spirits. He allows them to choose their own destiny and does not interfere." Momentarily, Osiris looked at Karl and then continued. "His care is only for the worthy. What happens, happens not only to your Earth, but to thousands of other Earths over the expanse of the universe."

"Why do we die?" Nancy said.

"So that some may live."

"But not everyone?" she asked.

"As with the seven gates that you have accomplished, only the worthy will find eternity."

Shawn said, "My lord, is the legend true? I mean, were you really mutilated, and then resurrected?"

"Yes."

"But how?"

"If you know the legend, then you know."

"But that would take the intervention of a God of the force you speak of," Shawn said.

"Yes."

Julian seemed disturbed with his answer. "What of the prophets, of the others who claim to know God, to be God, whom people worship?"

Osiris shook his head, refusing to answer.

Hunsdon asked, "Religions are of man's making?"

Dismissing the question, Osiris said, "Now, your journey begins. As the seals have foretold, prepare. You have earned the rite of passage. Therefore, each one of you will be endowed with certain powers which shall become clear."

"My lord, you are leaving us?" Hunsdon asked.

"Yes."

"Will we meet again?" Otto asked.

"In time."

"May I ask one last question?" Shawn said.

There was a nod.

"We are only six. Who is the seventh?"

"In time." He stepped back into the light, into the blue-white light beaming from the ceiling. As he had come, he departed.

CHAPTER 49

The hologram snapped off. The crystal cylinder seals fragmented into billions of bits, decomposing to sparkly sand. The blank wall shuddered and became engulfed in flames, trembling to cinders, collapsing into the open air of a new day.

The first rays of the sun bled from the horizon, folding into the gaping hole that invited the chosen out onto the sand, onto the plain of Giza. The skyline of Giza, of Cairo, lay in the distance. The powdery blue sky arose with the sun, pushing the black of night off the edge of the Earth.

Nancy whispered, "It's over. It's finally over."

Hunsdon grinned wryly. "You're wrong," he said. "It's just begun."

While spreading his arms and lifting his face to the sun, Shawn said, "All this is real. The sun is real. I can feel it."

Hunsdon bent down, swiped up a handful of sand and smelled it. He looked into the sun. "It's real all right," he said, tossing away the sand. "Look there, the pyramids in all their glory, and there right next to us, the Watcher of the Horizon, and over there, the camel drivers are coming for the tourists."

Karl said, "I should have asked him about the Hall of Records."

"There are a million questions I, too, wanted to ask," Hunsdon said. " But time, time is always our enemy."

"It seems we have much to discuss. We should get together very soon," Nancy said to Hunsdon.

Hunsdon patted her shoulder. "Always down to business," he said fondly. "If there are no objections, in a few days. I am sure we can all use the rest and time to think. Say, day after tomorrow at my hotel. How does that sit with you?"

In agreement they nodded, and meandered toward their cars in the light of the rising sun.

From his car, Hunsdon curiously looked back, one more time, toward the gaping hole from where they had just come. To no surprise, it was completely gone.

Shawn took the wheel of Karl's official vehicle. Overwhelmed, stunned and tired, both men sat in silence while the vehicle ate up the road.

Shawn drove directly to the hospital. Oddly, it seemed like months since they had visited. The spectacular journey, with all its gods and phantoms, had dragged time out of sync.

He turned off the engine and they walked inside.

They entered ICU. They walked to Nanette's

room. The bed . . .

"Nooo!" Karl moaned.

Shawn grabbed the arm of a passing nurse.

Karl, filled with emotion, stared at the empty bed, at the sheets and blankets neatly folded to one side. His heart thudded from all the signs of death. He touched the mattress, feeling it cold as tears . . .

"Karl! She's all right! She's okay! She's in her own room upstairs!"

Karl latched onto Shawn's shoulders.

"It's true, Karl! She's fine! The nurse said Nanette came out of the coma this morning. She called it an amazing recovery, a miracle." Their eyes locked.

"What room," Karl blurted.

"420, right next to your old room."

They rushed to the elevator. It rose painfully slowly as Karl kept pushing buttons. When the doors opened, they ran to the room.

Nanette was eating breakfast, looking as beautiful as ever. From both sides of the bed, Karl and Shawn fawned over her, kissed her, hugged her, laughed, and cried.

The seventh was somehow miraculously cured.

CHAPTER 50

Installed comfortably on a Queen Ann chair next to a tall, potted plant on the verandah of his penthouse suite, Sir E. Osborne Hunsdon sat smoking, gazing at the pyramids across the Nile.

It was the evening of the second full day following their extraordinary journey. Otto had resumed his profile as the Steward of Hunsdon House, suitably garbed in a tuxedo and bristling with British flair.

They had gathered. With drinks in hand, they were sorting out the details of their incredible trials. After an hour of revisiting their experiences, Julian had the floor.

"I can easily see how he-they were thought of as gods," he said.

Hunsdon lowered his chin and peered over his glasses. "By my estimation," he said, "Osiris is a god."

Nancy ventured, "Sir Hunsdon, do you believe?"

"In what?"

"In a god, or in God."

"First, let me say that I believe in Osiris. I believe that there is a power, a force throughout the universe.

That aside, my investigation into the subject has convinced me that from the beginning, what humankind could not understand, it made supernatural. Fascination with longevity, with legends of resurrection and everlasting life, inspired the creation of many gods. No, I don't know if I believe in man's god."

Julian said, "I wish we had more time with Osiris."

With Nanette's hand firmly lodged in Shawn's, she said, "Now that we have this knowledge, what are we going to do with it?"

"My advice," Hunsdon said, "would be to find reasonably high ground perhaps in the center of the largest continent, build ourselves a concrete bunker and stock it with provisions, books, generators, anything that will sustain us for many years."

Karl said, "How do we explain our behavior?"

"May I interrupt for a moment?" Otto asked smugly.

"By all means," Hunsdon said.

"We should not explain. They won't believe us," Otto said. "They'll think we are crackpots."

"I think you're right," Nancy breathed. "All we can do is warn them."

"Indeed," Hunsdon said. "However, they'll debate it, trash it, and mull it over on talk shows. As we have seen in the past, the powers that be will interview scientists, astrophysicists and the like, who will express opinions pro and con . . . if we are taken seriously. Others will merely contemplate their navels until it is too late."

Shawn asked, "Julian, what will it be like when it happens?"

"Mind you, I can only guess. But if we look back on legend and what we believe happened, it will go something like this. Weather will be catastrophic, with tornadoes, monsoons, and hurricanes. The gravity from the planets, from the sun, will pull the molten lava through weak fissures in the Earth's crust, and many volcanoes will erupt causing massive cloud-cover. The sun will be blocked out for years. The Earth will cool, and possibly cause another Ice Age. The continents, as we know them, will shift, break apart. A few may jam together, forming new continents. Food will be scarce. Many animals will die. Many people will die."

"I'm not sure I want to live through that chaos," Karl commented.

Nanette smiled at Shawn and hugged her father. She said, "Don't you want to see your grandchildren?"

AUTHOR'S NOTE

Egyptology with all its myths and legends has been of particular interest since I first saw the film *The Mummy* with Boris Karloff. If memory serves, the first book I read about Egypt was the 1960 edition of *The Book of the Dead*, by E. A. Wallis Budge. Budge's version included hieroglyphics, translations, and pictures. The more I read the more fascinated I became with the land of the pharaohs. That single volume led to a collection of more than fifty Egyptian literary works.

There were several controversies that influenced the creation of *Rite of Passage.* The most significant question was the age of the Egyptian civilization. Much has been written about its longevity. During my research I found conflicting arguments based in flawed and contrived data. I am by no means an authority on Egypt, but in my attempt to find an answer I could find only one, *The Message of the Sphinx* written by Graham Hancock and Robert Bauval. These gentlemen were thorough, substantiated their findings with sound facts, and contradicted long accepted conclusions.

THE DREAM THIEF

HELEN A. ROSBURG

Someone is murdering young, beautiful women in mid-sixteenth century Venice. Even the most formidable walls of the grandest villas cannot keep him out, for he steals into his victims' dreams. Holding his chosen prey captive in the night, he seduces them . . . to death.

Now Pina's cousin, Valeria, is found dead, her lovely body ravished. It is the final straw for Pina's overbearing fiance', Antonio, and he orders her confined within the walls of her mother's opulent villa on Venice's Grand Canal. It is a blow not only to Pina, but to the poor and downtrodden in the city's ghettos, to whom Pina has been an angel of charity and mercy. But Pina does not chafe long in her lavish prison, for soon she too begins to show symptoms of the midnight visitations; a waxen pallor and overwhelming lethargy.

Fearing for her daughter's life, Pina's mother removes her from the city to their estate in the country. Still, Pina is not safe. For Antonio's wealth and his family's power enable him to hide a deadly secret. And the murderer manages to find his intended victim. Not to steal into her dreams and steal away her life, however, but to save her. And to find his own salvation in the arms of the only woman who has ever shown him love.

ISBN#1932815201
$6.99
Fiction
December 2005
www.helenrosburg.com